All Because of the Cat & Other Tales

Jennifer Word

All Because of the Cat & Other Tales

Jennifer Word

EMP PUBLISHING

EMP PUBLISHING
Atchison, Kansas

All Because of the Cat & Other Tales
Copyright © Jennifer Word
All Rights Reserved

ISBN: 978-0-6924382-6-8

EMP Publishing
Find us online at www.emppublishing.com

Cover design by Fatlind Colaku © Jennifer Word by Licensing Agreement c/o 99designs.com

Printed in the United States of America

In loving memory of Kay Withers, Courtney Tomlinson, and Jim Tomlinson–three beautiful souls who never got to see my stories or books. I know they would have been proud. I miss you guys.

Contents

"There is nothin' fair in this world…
There is nothin' safe in this world…
And there's nothin' sure in this world…
And there's nothin' pure in this world…
Look for something left in this world…

Start again."

–Billy Idol

Tales and Tails: The Beginning of a Writer's Life

When I was a kid, I was asked on a semi-regular basis the proverbial question we all get asked when we are young: "What do you want to be when you grow up?"

Even as a kid, I abhorred that question. I hated it, because I simply didn't know the answer. Other girls my age would say they wanted to be a model or an actress, a teacher *–princess*. The boys would give cookie-cutter answers like astronaut, fireman, police officer *–superhero*. Where we all got these ideas from, take your pick: television, children's books, movies *–our parents*. Seriously though, I never said any of those things named above. I would always just shrug and say, "I don't know." Even at age five. And age six. And seven, eight, nine…

When I was ten-years-old and in fourth grade, my answer finally changed. It changed because I discovered I could do something that not necessarily everyone else could do, and because the thing I found out I could do, I did *well*. As far as I can remember, I'd never actually been *good* at anything before that time in my life.

In fourth grade, my class was assigned to write a story. That's really all I remember. We just had to write a story, about anything, I guess. So, I just wrote a story. I didn't put much thought into it, not that I can recall now. I wrote a story about a shopping trip I'd taken with my grandmother and the stuffed animal unicorn she'd bought me. I turned it in to my teacher along with the rest of my class on the morning it was due, then we all went out to morning recess. The rest of the day was uneventful. The next day in class, as everyone was rushing out the door for morning recess again, my teacher, Mrs. Bernard, called me over to her desk. I couldn't understand why I'd been kept in for recess; I figured I must be in trouble for something, although I didn't know what I could have done wrong. I walked tentatively up to Mrs. Bernard at her desk. I remember that she looked troubled. *Man, I must have really messed up somehow*, I figured. Then she held up my story and asked, "Did you really write this?" *Huh*? I didn't understand what she meant by that. Of course I wrote it. Who else would have?

I was scared, so I just nodded that, yes, I wrote the story. Then she asked, "And no one else helped you?" Again, *Huh*? I shook my head. She didn't seem to believe me, so she asked again, "No one helped you write this? Not your mom or dad, or anyone?" I said, "No. I wrote it all by myself."

Next thing I knew, she was asking me where I learned some of the words I used in my story, words that were long and complicated, words we hadn't ever gone over in vocabulary or spelling lessons in class. I just shrugged my shoulders and said, "I don't know." Mrs. Bernard then asked me if I read a lot of books. To this, I answered a resounding, "Yes." She nodded, asked me to name some of them (I'm pretty sure I answered *My Side of the Mountain*, *The Secret Garden* and *Where the Red Fern Grows*) I know I answered *The Last of the Really Great Whangdoodles*. Mrs. Bernard suddenly broke into a huge smile. Aha! Now she understood.

Mrs. Bernard then asked me, "Jenny, do you know what you are?" *What*? I shrugged and shook my head, then in a tiny-scared voice (I didn't want to get the answer wrong, but I suspected the question was some kind of trick) I answered, "A girl?" Her violent reaction to that called for an immediate do-over, so I quickly tried to recover by coughing out, "A Reader!" *No, no, no*. Mrs. Bernard shook her head. *Dang it, I knew it was a trick question*. And then, as dramatic as this might sound, came the moment that would change my entire life:

Mrs. Bernard looked at me with the most beautiful smile on her face. She said, "Didn't anyone ever tell you? You're a writer."

Whoa. That rocked my world. Suddenly I had something I'd never had before: an identity. I wasn't a girl, I wasn't a fourth grader, I wasn't an Alaskan, and I wasn't a dork. I was a Writer. And from that moment on, whenever anyone asked me what I wanted to be when I grew up, I began answering with a resounding, "I wanna be a writer!"

I didn't waste any time, either. Mrs. Bernard encouraged me to enter my school's annual Make-A-Book Contest.

I didn't tell Mrs. Bernard, but I actually spent a fair amount of my free time reading hordes of Stephen King novels. By the end of my ninth year of life I'd already devoured *IT* and *CUJO*, and was making my way through *The Stand*, and by the end of fourth grade, *Skeleton Crew* and *Night Shift* lived on my bedside dresser.

When it came to writing for an audience near the end of fourth grade, I ended up writing a horror story (huge surprise) about a black cat that curses anyone who crosses its path. I really don't remember much more than that. I won 1st place in the contest, which was apparently a big deal, because usually first place goes to a sixth grader, and occasionally a fifth grader. I might be remembering wrong, but I may have been the first fourth grader to ever win 1st place, but don't quote me on that.

I kept reading, and writing random little lines here or there. For some reason, I wrote a lot of poetry. In fifth grade I wrote another story for the Make-A-Book Contest. Again I won 1st Place. That story was about a haunted greenhouse, and as silly as that may sound, it was pretty darn good for an eleven-year-old. I still have that book somewhere in my garage. *The Black Cat* went into my school's library, and every once in a while, I wonder if it's still there, and if some random little kid pulls it out and reads it.

In sixth grade I wrote a sequel to *The Lanston Greenhouse*, but that only won me 2nd Place. Next came middle school.

In seventh grade, I was walking home from school one day with some friends when a black cat crossed the street right in front of us. My two friends stopped, refusing to cross the cat's path. Heck, one of them even remembered my *Black Cat* story from fourth grade and said that, I, especially should know better. I told her that story was just fiction, and to prove it, I walked right across that cat's path.

It was a Friday that day, and that night, my friends and I went to the roller rink, because in seventh grade, it was 1988, and everyone went to the roller rink. I had twenty bucks to buy snacks and whatever else with, that my parents had given me.

I always got a locker at the rink to keep my stuff safe in, with a little key you pull out after you put a quarter in. I put my jacket, shoes and my twenty dollars in that locker, put my quarter in and locked my stuff up.

After about an hour of roller skating, I wanted to get some soda and nachos, so I went back to open my locker and get my twenty bucks (I didn't have pockets that night, I was wearing those retarded patterned leggings all the 13-year-old girls wore back in 1988), and my jacket and shoes were still in that locker, but the darn twenty-dollar bill I'd placed directly on top of the pile was gone.

I pulled everything out. It was just gone. My friends reminded me that I'd been cursed by crossing the black cat's path earlier that day. I don't have any answer for where the twenty bucks went, to this day.

So basically, what we have here so far is the fact that the very first real story I ever wrote was about a cat, and it even won me a prestigious award. I guess we can skip over how I took Journalism in eighth grade, wrote as a reporter and even worked as Managing Editor for a couple of issues. That was my time on the Falcon Flash.

I didn't write at all in high school, except a few articles for this 'underground newspaper' a friend of mine ran. I found that appealing since I could say whatever I felt like (even swear!) without being censored. I'm sure if I could go back and read any of the articles I wrote back then, I'd cringe. I remember one article being about why no one should stand and recite the Pledge of Allegiance. I was seventeen and rebellious by nature. Good times.

I wrote tons of essays in high school. The first three years were Honors English, followed by senior year in Advanced Placement English. I can write a mean five-point essay. But somewhere along the way, I'd gotten a bit lost. I'd forgotten amidst the chaos of teenage hormones, driver's licenses, SAT's and college prep, and crushing on cute boys that never noticed me, that I had wanted to be a writer. I wrote a few poems in high school, but that was all. I never wrote one single story.

College came and I had no idea what I wanted to do or be. I'd reverted to I-Don't-Know mode. I blindly stumbled through freshman year in a foreign environment, for I'd been transplanted from my lifelong home of Anchorage, Alaska to Malibu, California, all because I'd had some fun in a few school plays back home and thought I'd enjoy being a Theater Arts Major.

I changed my mind when I got to college and realized I kind of sucked at acting. I was too shy and introverted, and being up on stage in the spotlight made me feel, well, like I was up on stage in the spotlight. I didn't like feeling uncomfortable like that, even if it did give me a rush during, and I thought it was so much fun after it was all over. The dread and negative anticipation before the auditions and shows I hated enough to drop my major. Freshman year I stumbled blindly through the basics just to satisfy core units.

One of those classes was introductory Psychology to satisfy the core science requirements.

I hadn't received very high grades my freshman year. I was averaging B's and C's, but when I took Psych, I got my first college A. I really liked it, something about it just clicked with me, and I stuck with it. Next thing I knew, Psychology was my major, but I still hadn't formed any real plan with that. I hadn't sat down and thought or realized that being an undergrad Psych major is about the same as being Pre-Med. There's the inevitable Graduate School that must come after to earn a Master's or Doctorate, get credentialed and actually become qualified to work with troubled minds.

I didn't think that far ahead. I was just happy to have a major picked out. The last two years of college I started writing again, I don't know why. I just did. The stories weren't all that good; they were sloppy and misguided; directionless, sort of like me.

Cut to three weeks before graduation. I was madly in love with my college sweetheart. My parents were scheduled to fly out for my graduation in a few weeks or so, where they would be meeting my boyfriend of the last year-and-a-half for the very first time.

Well, what do you know? I found out I was pregnant. My boyfriend proposed to me literally five minutes after I took the home pregnancy test.

I went to the gynecologist, who did an ultrasound. She pointed to the baby on the screen, that already had a head, arms and legs, clearly visible and easily identifiable. She did some measurements, told me I was one day short of eleven weeks, and gave me a delivery due date of only six months away.

Needless to say, the after graduation dinner my parents took me to lives on in infamy in my family. I dropped the marriage bomb and the baby bomb onto them just hours after I walked across the stage in Malibu and claimed my undergraduate degree in Psychology.

I got married just three months later and three months after that my amazing daughter was born. Two years later came my beautiful son. I was now a stay-at-home mother, and once again, that age-old question was being asked of me, only this time it had morphed itself into a more accusatory form. The question went from, "What do you want to be when you grow up?" to, "When are you going to work?"

Well, I finally realized with that question that I had failed to plan my life properly. Most of it just sort of felt like it happened to me, and I was just along for the ride. I couldn't work in my chosen field of Psychology because I wasn't qualified to. I didn't have the money, time, or concentration with double-diapers to successfully pull off Graduate School. I didn't even want to try fighting in that war.

Picking any random job seemed haphazard at best, utterly chaotic at worst. I eventually ended up teaching Mommy & Me classes at the same center I'd been taking my own toddlers to the last few years. After that I briefly worked as a Front Office Medical Receptionist, but was laid off due to over-staffing, along with four other people. Next I worked as a Yard Supervisor during lunch and recess at my kid's school, but it didn't suit me very well.

It was my mother, one day, who asked me out of the blue if I'd been writing any stories lately. I frowned and said, "No, what a weird question." She told me she thought that was a shame, because I always wrote such amazing stories.

She told me I had an incredible imagination. She reminded me of how much I enjoyed writing, and I guess I must have truly forgotten. She then smiled and asked me if I'd been reading Stephen King at all. Well, that at least, I had been doing religiously for two decades straight. Some things never change. But I had branched out as well, to other horror and even science fiction writers. Writers like Richard Matheson, Jack Finney, James Patrick Kelley, Robert

Silverberg, eventually Joe Hill, and even Edgar Allan Poe and H.P. Lovecraft, among so many others.

I was forced to recall that at one point in my life, and for several years in fact, I had identified myself as a Writer, and that I'd dreamed of becoming one as an adult; a professional writer. I was ten-years-old when that dream was initially planted in my mind, and at the age of 31, I sat down and wrote my first true story as an adult.

I failed to notice the ironic on-going theme, for my very first story, just like all those years back in the Make-A-Book Contest, was about a cat. Not a black cat this time, mind you, but still: A Cat.

That first story, *All Because of the Cat*, you'll find is the last story in this collection, and the namesake of the book you hold in your hands. I would go on to write at least one more story about a cat, when I wrote *Every Living Thing*. I don't always write about cats, but for some reason, when it comes to my writing, they are a theme I like to use. I suppose I have other themes (like zombies), and still others that I don't even realize. But I've been told by more than just a few people, that of all the short stories they've read of mine, they all like *All Because of the Cat* the best.

Was I destined to be a Writer? Some people joke that I am, because as fate would have it, I married into the perfect writing name. Word is my married name, although that union ended in the thirteenth year. I kept the name because it's mine, and it's my children's, and the people that joke about it aren't wrong: it's a great writer's name.

I have two cats now. I've always had cats, except for the four years I was in college, and the first few years of my marriage when the kids were too little and they would have been too cruel to a pet. I'd never had a black cat ever though, until I was 31, and that beautiful cat, Shadow (so named by my children) is the one who sat on my bed, just five feet from me in the afternoons while I wrote my first official story, *All Because of the Cat*, even though the actual cat in the story isn't ever described as black. Shadow was all black. I didn't go with that description because I thought since it was a horror story, a black cat would be too cliché.

Anyhow, I don't know if I was truly cursed by that black cat back in my thirteenth year or not. I dared to cross its path, and I did mysteriously lose twenty dollars. Previous to that, however, I'd won my first official writing award with a story about a black cat (literally titled *The Black Cat*), and when I finally owned a black cat of my own, she served as an amazing inspiration for the namesake title of this book.

I've written stories about cats, zombie cats, but also about ghosts, witches (ghost-witches, actually), The Devil, Voodoo Curses, Zombies, Sea Monsters and Sea Creatures (yes, there is a difference), Cursed Carnivals, Death (as in the Grim Reaper), Vampires, More Zombies, Unnamed Monsters, Serial Killers, Werewolves, More Zombies, and varied other supernatural phenomenon, such as the Brown Mountain Lights (in *Lightning Ball Rock*), Aliens, Angels, and Robots.

I've written in so many genres, I cannot tell people any one genre I write in. I started off with short stories that were mainly horror, but I branched out from there to drama, tear-jerkers, historical fiction, science fiction, thrillers, speculative fiction, Action and Adventure, Spiritual, and the list goes on and on.

I just write out my ideas. Sometimes they just come to me, other story ideas are inspired by different events in my life, or even stories I hear from a friend of a friend, that I change up and form into my own unique blend of imagination and creativity.

The individual stories behind my stories are found in the Notes at the end of this book. In those Notes, I also list the original publication that certain stories were printed in because, yes, many of the stories in this collection were submitted, accepted and published in various print and e-zines, as well as several anthology collections through varying presses.

I think I have something to offer up to almost any reader of any genre. I believe that with the smorgasbord of stories and genres found within this collection, there's something for everyone to enjoy. It's not all horror. It's not all fantasy. It's not all sappy and dramatic. It's not all to do with supernatural events. Heck, there's a story in here about an old man who befriends two Bald Eagles. There's a story in here that's simply about a wannabe writer struggling to find his voice and fulfill his dream.

I am not a horror writer. I am not any kind of one-genre writer. I simply am a Writer. I am a teller of tales. Although, with the cat theme that does seem to pervade my stories here and there, don't think I wasn't briefly tempted to title this book *All Because of the Cat & other* **Tails**. Too cheesy, I decided. But I digress.

There's something in this collection for every reader, I believe. I simply hope that you will enjoy this collection and find at least a few stories that stick with you, haunt you, move you, disturb you, or otherwise entertain you. As long as you read even one story within this book that makes you *feel*, or *ponder*, then I will have done my job. If any of these stories makes you care for a character, or shed a tear, or even get angry, I'll have written an effective story.

I invite you now to enter my world, my imagination, and play for a while. I can now say that I am a Writer, but I'll never be the judge of whether I am any good at it or not. If I *am* decent, though, I suppose you, (as Stephen King might say) "Dear Reader" will be the judge.

This collection of 29 stories was written over a seven-year period, and you now hold in your hands every short story I've written to date in my career. So, my Beloved Readers, turn the page, and grant me the privilege of truly becoming what I've dreamed of being for nearly three full decades now. Dear Readers, I invite you to become my audience, live in my mind, and hopefully become fans. A writer is only a writer if they are read. So, Welcome, and I hope you enjoy the ride.

February 15th, 2015
Oak Park, California

-Our Beloved Shadow-

Barnaby's Endeavor

Barnaby Wilson was forty-three years old and lived alone. He'd been married, briefly, at age thirty-four, to an older woman, five years his senior. She'd thought him a good catch, and at age thirty-nine, naturally, she'd been raring to go on the family front. She was another file clerk in his office, the same one he'd worked in for ten years.

How Charlotte hadn't put two and two together had always miffed Barnaby. How she hadn't realized that if Barnaby'd been a file clerk for ten years already, he would always be a file clerk was beyond him. It was a simple case of blind love. That and, women always thought they could change a man. Or, perhaps Charlotte thought Barnaby would want to change for her. This didn't turn out to be the case.

Charlotte was well aware while she was dating Barnaby that he had high aspirations of being a writer. She championed him and spurred him on in the evenings when he wrote on his second-hand laptop after dinner. When he proposed to her with a simple, silver ring he bought from the pawnshop around the corner, she'd cried and immediately said yes. There were never any talks about 'except,' or 'what if.' So, a year into their marriage, when an assistant position opened up in the office, and Barnaby, given the number of years he'd been in the office, was first in line seniority wise, Charlotte was irked when he let the opportunity pass him by.

It was the worst fight they'd ever had, and it set the precedent for the next two years of their lives together. Charlotte demanded to know how, just exactly how, would they support a family if both of them remained lowly file clerks? And worse, Charlotte continued on, what if she decided she wanted to stay home with the baby? How could Barnaby expect to support a wife and child on his paltry income as a file clerk? Didn't he want to become more than this?

Yes, had been Barnaby's answer to Charlotte. Of course he wanted to be so much more than a file clerk. He wanted to be an author. A writer, a published and paid scribe. It was Barnaby's dream. It was hard enough finding the time and energy in the evenings and on weekends to be creative and write after long hard days filing in the office. Becoming an assistant would mean even more work, more energy spent, and probably more hours. Hours of overtime. Hours of overtime and extra *pay*, Charlotte had intoned. Barnaby only shook his head and reiterated that he'd get even less writing done.

The fights eventually turned to the baby. Barnaby wasn't ready to become a father, not when he hadn't even become what he dreamed of becoming. He wasn't published yet. Wasn't becoming a father his biggest dream? Charlotte asked, as if daring him to answer otherwise. When he did answer otherwise, Charlotte's face broke. She sobbed and sobbed and wouldn't stop, not until she'd cried herself to sleep.

When Charlotte was forty-two and Barnaby had been married for three years, she came to him and told him it was over. Not only was it over, but she was pregnant. Not only was it over and she was pregnant, but the father was Dave Rawlings, the file clerk under Barnaby, who had jumped over his head to become the new assistant. The affair had been going on for quite some time, and Barnaby hadn't noticed his wife's distance in the evenings, as busy as he always was with his writing.

The divorce was final when Barnaby was thirty-eight, although Charlotte had moved out months before the final paperwork was finished. He'd lost his wife, but it only spurred him on in his task, his dream. If he was ever going to please a wife or become a father, he'd better get his dream going, *now*.

At age thirty-nine, Barnaby Wilson quit his job as a file clerk, a position he'd held for thirteen years. He took his meager savings, all of eight thousand dollars, and moved into a four-hundred-square-foot apartment, right next to the last L-Station on the outskirts of town. There was a shared bathroom down the hallway and a fire escape for a view. Beyond this were the railroad tracks, a flimsy metal fence and a scant smattering of Alder trees that lined a muddy creek.

The entire building shook when the L passed by, every half-hour on the hour, 'round the clock. The rent was cheap. Just two hundred dollars a month. Barnaby took on the extra expense to install three deadbolts across his door. This to ensure his second-hand laptop and used printer (found by the dumpster at his old job) wouldn't be stolen.

He scoured the garbage outside office supply stores and took used printer paper, barely printed upon. He used mostly empty, used bottles of white out to paint over sheets of paper found inside dumpsters next to offices much like the one he'd worked at all those years, and erased url's at the tops of pages.

Sometimes he even stole paper. When no one was looking, he'd enter a supply store and get a key to a printer. He'd wait, and then when the coast was clear, he'd open the tray and remove a large handful of snow-white paper, quickly stuffing it into his moldy-smelling courier bag. Then he'd replace the tray and photocopy one page. He'd lay his hand upside down with his middle finger prominently displayed. He'd pay his ten cents for this one copy.

His walls were covered with copied sheets of his middle finger in black and white. Like some sort of strange wallpaper paying tribute to 'the man.' Barnaby ate his macaroni and cheap noodles, his cold cereal for dinner and stared at his own hand, flipping off the world. He always smiled, causing milk to dribble down his chin.

Charlotte had been a good catch for him. Older, yes, but still decently attractive, considering Barnaby's looks. She'd been taller than him, and thinner, too. Barnaby was only five-foot-five. He had a slight potbelly, a rather hairy chest, and curly, short, brown hair that always looked slightly frizzy. His skin was a pale, sickly shade of white, due to his mostly indoor life. His brown eyes were always hidden behind thin, cheap metal glass frames.

Barnaby still dressed in his file clerk garb. Most days he wore a button-down work shirt, khaki pants, tube socks and patent leather (used) brown shoes. By this point, however, the shoes were rather worn down, and Barnaby could no longer justify the added expense of polish. His shoes were scuffed, shabby and worn down at the heels, because he walked everywhere he went. He'd sold his car to save on gas. He now owned a 21-speed bike with a basket for carrying groceries. The bike lived in his apartment, next to his bed, in the corner of the kitchen.

Barnaby had been on six dates in the five years since his divorce from Charlotte. All six times, he'd brought them back to his place. He figured he'd better get that part over with, right up front. Assuming that once they saw where and how he lived, women would want nothing more to do with him, Barnaby invited them to have dinner at his place. He was right, too. Dinner always ended rather quickly, his dates stating they were full, and 'my wasn't it getting late?'

Only one date had ever asked to hear any of his work. Melissa had been interested in Barnaby's endeavor. She had wanted to know how he could be so brave, as to give up everything, simply for the chance to be a writer? Barnaby had answered, "I'd rather be a failed writer than a successful office drone."

He read her an excerpt from his latest book, a science fiction trilogy he was currently 5,000 words deep into book three of. An 'Ode to Henry Kuttner,' Barnaby explained to Melissa, who only shook her head, looking lost. Barnaby shrugged. He began to read and within five minutes, Melissa began to shift and fidget in the stiff, metal chair at the kitchen table. Within ten minutes, she excused herself to use the bathroom down the hall, taking her purse with her. She never returned. That had been Barnaby's last date.

He had a handful of friends. A few were leftover from his year of community college. One fellow writer, Neil, he'd met at the local coffee shop. Barnaby had similar experiences with his friends as well. He attempted to read excerpts from his stories, sometimes even trying to read a few of his shorter stories to people. They always began to fidget or started clearing their throats. Barnaby would grow nervous, looking up repeatedly from his pages to try and read their facial expressions. When this occurred, they always suddenly broke into a forced smile, plastered on so tightly; it made Barnaby's heart drop.

One day, he asked his friend from the coffee shop what was wrong with his latest story, a short, five-pager about a Martian who falls in love with a plant. Neil turned to Barnaby and simply shrugged.

"There's no plot."

"What do you mean, there's no plot? He falls in love with a plant. It's an ode to nature and to Henry Kuttner."

"A *poem* would be an ode to nature, Barnaby," Neil said. "A Martian falling in love with a plant, that's just…well…boring."

"But it's a Martian," Barnaby said.

"Exactly, Barnaby, that's the other problem," Neil said. "No one calls them Martians anymore. This isn't 1950."

"It's an Ode, to Henry Kutt," but Barnaby was cut short.

"Yes, yes, it's an ode to Henry Kuttner," Neil said. "No one even knows who Henry Kuttner is Barnaby, okay? Secondly, Henry Kuttner is a hack writer from the 40's and 50's, and he wasn't very good."

"Have you *read* Henry Kuttner?" Barnaby stared at Neil with distaste. "Matheson dedicated *'I am Legend'* to Kuttner in 1954. Ray Bradbury dedicated his first book, *'Dark Carnival'* to Kuttner! *'The Ticket That Exploded,'* by William S. Burroughs, contains direct quotes from Kuttner about the parasitic pleasure monster from the Venusian seas!"

"But only you know these things, Barnaby," Neil said. "And quite frankly, none of that matters. It doesn't change the simple fact that your stories are boring," Neil sighed, turning a sympathetic face to his friend. "Look, Barnaby, I know how badly you want to be a writer. I know how much time you spend on your stories. But the simple fact of the matter is, nothing will change that…well…your stories just aren't that interesting."

Barnaby stared at his friend, his mouth agape, his eyes boring into Neil's. Neil began to wonder if this horrid revelation hadn't broken his friend. Perhaps he should have found a kinder way of breaking this news? Finally, Barnaby spoke, and Neil sighed in exasperation. Barnaby was a lost cause.

"Which parts?"

"Barnaby, please," Neil said.

"Which parts of my stories are uninteresting?"

"Barnaby," Neil now had the bridge of his nose pinched between the thumb and pointer finger of his right hand. His eyes were shut tight.

"Which parts of my stories are bad, Neil?"

Neil looked at Barnaby with a pained expression. His eyes pleaded to no avail. He shrugged.

"All of them, Barnaby," Neil said. "Your stories have no structure, no plot, no character development. Not any of them, not one single story, Barnaby. Nothing ever happens in anything you write. Everything is just, boring. Passé, old fashioned, a knock-off. It's like reading a poor copy of an already bad story. Barnaby," Neil shook his head. "Even your sentence structure is sloppy. Your dialogue is choppy and unrealistic. It's unbelievable. People don't talk the way you have them talking. They just don't. *And*," Neil emphasized his tone, "you make up words that aren't even real. I mean, 'evolval?' Barnaby, seriously? 'Evolval' is not a word. It jars the reader right out of the story, and your stories are already difficult to begin with. Every sentence is a new attack on the intellect and patience of the reader."

"Why don't you tell me what you *really* think, Neil?"

Sigh. Neil stood up to leave.

"No, really," Barnaby said. "Is that what you *really* think?"

Neil looked away.

"Tell me," Barnaby said, barely above a whisper. "Have you read even just *one* sentence of mine that you thought was good?"

Neil looked at Barnaby with sadness. He shook his head. Barnaby hung his own head and nodded.

Over the next two months, Barnaby fell into a sort of daze of days. He woke up late, still felt tired and only wrote a couple of hours a day. The rest of his time he spent staring out the window or going for long walks to nowhere.

Eventually, Barnaby made his way to the public library and found himself standing in the 'Greats' section. The greatest collections of novels, poems, essays, and articles lay before him, prominently displayed in the open, on top of low lying bookshelves and tables. Everything from the greatest minds that had ever lived, the most incredible philosophers and thinkers that had ever existed sat before Barnaby's eyes.

He read Matheson. He read King. He read Silverberg and Burroughs, and Kelley and Bradbury and yes, even Kuttner some more. He read Shakespeare and Jordan, and Orson Scott Card and Nabokov. He read Thomas Pain, and Jack Finney and Kierkegaard, and Plato, and Milton and Kant.

Barnaby used his dollar-fifty public library card and filled his small apartment with books. He read the O. Henry Prize Winner Collections covering a decade straight. He read Plath and Keats, and O'Shaughnessy and Bukowski.

All the while, Barnaby prayed for a miracle. He prayed for osmosis. He slept with books underneath his pillow, and later he used the books *as* his pillow. He read and read, and walked and thought. He couldn't afford a writing class, and he believed the true talent of good writing should either come naturally or not at all.

Mostly, he thought. Barnaby thought about the myriad of contests he'd entered over the years. The sheer number of entry fees he'd broken down and paid, the dozens of stories that had failed to help him make any mark on the literary world. He'd won nothing, been paid nothing. He'd received not one single accolade. And now, Barnaby had been told by a close friend the hard, cold truth, apparently; that he was no good.

Barnaby simply couldn't accept this, however. He just couldn't. He'd been a terrible husband, couldn't even procure a second date at this point with any woman. He had no real friends, no job, and no prospects for his future. He'd built (and lost) everything around this ridiculous belief that he was meant to be a writer and that he would succeed some day.

In his wildest and absolutely most desperate daydreams, he'd even resorted to believing whole-heartedly that his work would someday be published posthumously, and he'd live on as one of the greatest writers in history. He'd be lauded in classrooms, years after his death, his meager existence studied as a biography by English students, moved to lamentation at the sad fact that in life, Barnaby Wilson had been unappreciated and uncelebrated. Like the artists Van Gogh and Picasso, and Dumas, who, while still alive, only sold their paintings on the side of the road for a penny apiece, Barnaby would be loved and revered by many, one day.

All these dreams fell apart if Barnaby allowed the hard truth of Neil's words to sink in. If he recalled the look of sheer boredom and impatience on Melissa's face, and her hurried body language as she rushed out the door. If Barnaby recalled accurately (for once) the fact that his own wife had never bothered to finish a single story he'd given her to read. If Barnaby were to let the whole truth of everything sink in, he'd have to realize; he was an awful writer.

*****

Barnaby Wilson sat on the edge of his bed, the razor poised at the skin of his wrist. He was crying, despite himself. He wanted to end it all with bravery, not tears. He was ashamed of himself. He was afraid of physical pain. He sighed, setting the razor down on his pillow. He was leaving nothing behind. What a sad tragedy his life had turned out to be.

Suddenly, Barnaby was angry. He wasn't about to leave this world without telling it off. He was tired of playing by all the rules. He'd done what he thought he was supposed to do. He'd given up everything for this life of a penniless writer, devoted to his craft and nothing more. He'd read all the greats. He'd read '*The Elements of Style.*' He'd read '*On Writing,*' he wasn't an idiot. But nothing had made him any better.

He screamed. A demonic sound escaped Barnaby's mouth. His throat felt as if it were being ripped to shreds under the stress and strain his vocal cords endured.

He stood and went to the kitchen table, grabbing "*The Bell Jar.*" He took a pencil and opened the book to the last page, and there, on the blank backside, he began to madly scribble his rage. All Barnaby's emotions poured out in a deluge of broken dreams. His brain vomited forth his shortcomings and frustrations with life, with his own limited abilities to pen even one good sentence.

He ran out of space and went to the next book, "*Burning in Water, Drowning in Flame*," and again, he filled the blank sides of the pages within. He did the same inside "*Hell House*." Barnaby wrote and wrote, until his hand ached. His mind was reeling, and then it was not. Finally, his mind was quiet. He was exhausted. He no longer had the energy to slit his wrists. He laid his head down on his pillow and placed the razor underneath.

Tomorrow, he thought. *Tomorrow I'll do it, when I've the energy to kill myself.*

He was asleep before he'd even finished the thought. He awoke the following morning to a loud banging on his door. He sat up, feeling groggy, and lifted his pillow to ensure the razor was still there.

Barnaby answered the door to find Neil huffing and puffing, his cheeks rosy from the winter cold. The look of utter relief on Neil's face made Barnaby want to throttle him. He made his way into the kitchen instead, to fetch his friend a glass of water. He was all out of food or even instant coffee.

"Jesus, Neil," Barnaby said, "You needn't break my door down."

"I was worried," Neil sighed, still attempting to catch his breath. "You haven't been into the shop in over two months. I was actually sort of afraid you might have…well," Neil trailed off.

"What, killed myself?" Barnaby offered.

Neil nodded. So did Barnaby.

"Yes well, that's after breakfast. I figured I could afford to splurge on a nice meal before offing myself."

Neil only stared at Barnaby, his mouth agape. Barnaby stared back; his eyes round behind his thin, silver spectacles.

He handed Neil the glass of water. Neil set it on the table without drinking.

"Don't worry," Barnaby said. "I plan to return all my books before hand as well. Although, I suppose they'll be quite cross when they see that I've scribbled in some of them."

Barnaby shook his head, sitting down on his bed. He grabbed his copy of "*The Bell Jar*," and ripped out the last page. Neil came over and sat next to Barnaby, absentmindedly taking the page that his friend mindlessly handed to him. Barnaby took his copy of the Bukowski book and tore the pages from this as well, before standing to grab the Matheson book on the kitchen table.

"I'm not certain which is worse, returning a book to the library with scribbling inside, or pages torn out."

Barnaby shrugged, his body defunct of any real vibrancy. He looked at Neil who was frowning.

"Either way, I suppose it doesn't matter. I won't be around for any kind of admonishing or worse—fees."

Barnaby frowned at his friend's face. He walked back over and sat down next to Neil again, who was finishing up the "*Bell Jar*" page. Neil desperately grabbed at the pages in Barnaby's hand, ripping the remaining paper from his weak grip. Barnaby watched in sheer amusement as Neil fumbled with the remaining papers, to place them in the proper order. He read, then turned the papers over, then leafed to the next sheet, and the next.

Barnaby sighed. He lifted his pillow again, to check that the razor was still there. He raised an eyebrow.

"You know, you would be doing me a huge favor, Neil," Barnaby mused. "Would you consider returning these books for me? You could save me several trips on my bike."

"Sure," Neil said, still reading, not even looking at Barnaby. "Now, shut up."

Barnaby only nodded. His friend wasn't even listening. Naturally. Barnaby lifted the pillow again and took the razor into his hand, then quickly slipped it into the pocket of his khaki's. He stood and headed for the front door.

"Well, it's been nice knowing you, Neil. Come to think of it, you've saved me quite a bit of wasted time and effort. I want to thank you for that," Barnaby said. "And I'm not being facetious. I really mean that, Neil. Thanks."

Barnaby opened the door. He rounded the other side.

"Jesus," Neil said.

"Hmm? Where?" Barnaby said, without even the slightest hint of a smile. "Goodbye, Neil."

"Barnaby!" Neil shouted. Barnaby sighed, perturbed at being kept from this, his last task in life.

"What, Neil?" Barnaby fidgeted, anxious to get on with things.

"What are you going to do with this?" Neil said, brandishing the odd array of pages in his hand.

"Do with it?" Barnaby said.

"Yes," Neil laughed. "Did you write this for the annual Poet Laureate Contest?"

"Neil, really, I have to go," Barnaby said, his hand now in his right pocket, caressing the razor's smooth metal.

"Yes, yes, fine," Neil waved off Barnaby's remarks.

"But you simply must enter this into the contest, Barnaby. The first place winner gets published in the magazine, and the grand prize is literary representation and five thousand dollars! And honestly, Barnaby, if this poem of yours doesn't win, I'd be damned surprised."

"Poem?" Barnaby blinked at Neil. "I didn't write any poem. Hell, I'm not even a poet, you know that, Neil. I'm a failed storywriter. A bad copy of Kuttner, with no style, no finesse. No ability, remember?"

"Whatever," Neil said, ignoring Barnaby's remarks again. "The deadline is in two days. Come on, let's type this up properly, print it out and get it postmarked before time's up!"

"But I've plans for today already," Barnaby whined. "I'm full-up for the rest of my life…"

"But, Barnaby," Neil stared at his friend. "This is *good*. This is really, truly, amazingly *good*."

Barnaby stared at his friend. His mouth fell open. He tightened his grip absentmindedly on the razor and failed to register the pain as the blade bit into his skin. A small spot of red bloomed on the light tan cloth of his pants pocket. Neil did not notice. He was looking at his friend in complete and utter disbelief.

"Barnaby, this is…probably the best poem I've ever read in my entire life!"

Neil actually had tears in his eyes. Barnaby's heart began to dance. His mind reeled. He was lost in confusion and euphoria.

"Barnaby, forget Kuttner. Forget short stories and Science Fiction altogether. Didn't you know? Why, didn't you ever realize before now? You're a poet!"

"A poet?" Barnaby whispered.

He walked over to the kitchen sink. Barnaby removed the razor from his pocket and tossed it on the counter. He placed his hands on the counter and stared at the bloody fingers of his right hand. His shoulders hunched up to his ears. He sobbed aloud. Neil only stood, frowning, looking horrified.

"Why, it's no reason to cry, Barn," Neil said. "Look, I'm sorry if I hurt your feelings before, by saying all those things, but…what does it matter now? Why, no wonder your stories were so bad. You've just been working in the wrong medium is all! You can structure your sentences any way you want to with poetry, Barn. You don't need a plot. All you need is the ability to make people feel. And you've got that, good and plenty."

Barnaby turned and smiled at his friend. He rushed over and hugged him. Then he nodded, clapping Neil on both sides of his arms, causing him to wince in pain.

"I'm a poet," Barnaby said, as if trying to convince himself. He walked over to the window and looked out at the new day. A huge smile was plastered on his face.

"I'm a poet," Barnaby said.

"Yes," Neil laughed.

Barnaby turned and smiled at his friend. Then he walked over to Neil and gently removed the pages from his friend's hand. Barnaby sat down at his old, second-hand laptop and turned it on.

"Well, let's get this thing out there then, shall we?"

Lightning Ball Rock

Two years ago I almost died. My parents almost died as well, but I'll get to that soon enough. I'll try to explain everything as best as I can.

Let me start off by stating that my name is Theresa Catherine Huffman. Catherine was my mother's maiden name. My dad's last name is Huffman. Everyone just calls me Theresa.

I'm currently in my second year at North Carolina State, with a major in Geology. Two years ago, however, I was in my senior year of high school, visiting my grandfather over the Holiday Break, when my life changed.

My grandfather lives in Morganton, North Carolina. You have to get the setting straight. Picture a small town, population barely 20,000, filled with families and small children. Reader's Chronicle says that Morganton is one of the top ten places to raise a family.

My granddaddy owns a small farm on the western edge of Morganton, overlooking the Pisgah National Forest and Brown Mountain. Brown Mountain isn't so much of a mountain, really. It's basically just a low-lying ridge, about a mile and a half long. It's the legend that most people are excited about.

You haven't heard about the Brown Mountain Lights? I'm not surprised, a lot of people haven't heard of them. If you live around here, however, you've heard of them. Out-of-towners, a lot of times, have no idea what I'm talking about.

My whole life, I've spent two weeks every summer, and a week every Winter Break at my Granddaddy's farm. He's got a livery stable and a hay barn out back of the house. There's also tons of pastures and flat grassland all around the property. There's an old, big oak next to the house with a tire swing that I still love, even at my age.

I love the smell of hay. I used to love just walking in the barn, standing there, breathing deep. I love taking buckets of oats and carrots and feeding the horses. When I was really little, I used to lay all my plastic dolls out on the wooden worktable inside the barn and play make believe.

At night, however, we'd all sit on the porch and look up at the Ridge, hoping to see the lights. I've seen them plenty of times. I'd gotten used to them. Sipping Sarsaparilla on the porch swing, sitting with my Granddaddy, we'd always talk about it.

"Grandpa, what are the lights made of?" I'd ask.

"That there light is from the lanterns of Cherokee wives searching for their brave warrior husbands, killed in battle. Their spirits wander the ridge, forever searching for their lost loves."

"Grandpa," I'd chide, for I was already too old to believe any of that folkloric, superstitious nonsense.

Good old Grandpa would just laugh in his devious, maniacal way, slapping his knee. When he saw that I was dismayed and annoyed, he'd quiet down and give me a reproachful look, as if to say, "Now, how could you even think I was being serious?"

"Okay, missy, then try this one on for size. Those there lights are simply an atmospheric phenomenon known as Ball Lightning."

"Ball Lightning?" I looked at my Grandpa, confused. "How can lightning be in a ball? I thought it struck down like a rod?"

"Well, most of the times it does, but..." he trailed off. "Oh, Hell, I'm no scientist. Look, you can see it for yourself, plain as day. It's electric, hence the lights. And it's round like a ball."

"Huh," I said, and that was the end of it.

Lightning Ball Rock

*****

Until two years ago. We were there, my parents and I, over the Winter Break, like always. It was an unusually balmy winter, with very little snow. A cold front was moving in, however, and two days before Christmas, cold met hot, over the Brown Mountain Ridge and the Blue Ridge Mountain Range, and we got some of the biggest thunderstorms Morganton had seen in over three decades.

My family and I also got the brightest displays of the Brown Mountain Lights we'd ever seen. The lights were visible even through the sheets of pouring rain that cascaded off my Grandpa's roof. Even over the distance and through the mists and thick dark clouds. Balls of lightning that rose into the air like large Chinese lanterns, or even round Christmas tree ornaments set on fire. Lightning Balls, floating in space. Mostly red and orange, but some of them were white and even light blue. I swear one was even an odd shade of green. Couldn't rightly say how big they really were from so many miles off, but they were big enough to see with my naked eye.

Anyway, it was December 23, two years ago, when this happened. It was nearing bedtime, but I was worried for the horses. I said goodnight to my Grandpa and my parents. When everyone was in their rooms, I went down and threw on my rain slicker. I grabbed a flashlight and made my way out to the livery stable and went inside.

I quickly turned up the battery-operated lantern hanging by the door. The horses didn't seem fazed at all by the steady tap-tapping of the rain on the wooden roof. I filled a metal pail from the bag of oats near the closest stall. I took my turn feeding treats to each of the five horses.

I was feeding the last horse, Napoleon, when I noticed a light behind me. I thought for sure it was my Grandpa with his flashlight, come to admonish me for being up so late and sneaking out of the house.

When I turned around, my explanation already poised on my lips, I got the shock of my life. The light wasn't coming from a flashlight. It looked like a freestanding ball of light, just floating in the air. It was white. I squinted and raised my arm across my face, to shield my vision from the ambient assault, raking in my breath.

The horses didn't seem bothered by the light at all. I dropped the metal pail I was holding. Luckily it missed landing on my foot. I watched the white ball of light as it floated through the livery door, not even making a single mark on the wood. Then it was gone.

I turned and looked at Napoleon. He didn't offer any explanation. I smiled, feeling giddy, like I was living inside a dream.

Without even thinking, I headed out of the livery stable, keeping the presence of mind to latch the door closed behind me. I looked around and was shocked to see the same white ball of light still floating, seemingly unaffected by the pouring rain.

My heart was pounding away inside my chest. I couldn't believe myself. I dared to walk towards the light. It looked to be about the size of my own head, this close up. As I neared toward it, the ball floated away. I swear it was reacting to my movements.

Suddenly it flew, so fast, it seemed to leave a light trail behind it, a sort of afterglow of latent tracers that my eyes had trouble adjusting to. It went into the barn, passing through the wood, again leaving no marks.

I dumbly followed it, and opened the barn door. Inside, it was pitch black. I fumbled around for the lantern in here and quickly found it. Looking around, I didn't see anything. I figured the ball, or whatever it was, had gone straight through and out the back and was long gone by now. I was disappointed.

I walked over to the worktable and set the lantern down. I remember just standing there, feeling so let down, that I didn't get to see the light up more closely. It hadn't even made a sound. How could something glowing that brightly not make any sound, I wondered?

As I sat there frowning and contemplating the entire phenomenon, I became aware, somehow, of a presence. I guess that's the best way to describe it. I felt as if something was in the barn with me. Before I even saw the light again, I sensed it.

I was frozen in fear this time. From behind me and around my left shoulder, a ball of light appeared, slowly, at face level. It rounded the table, moving only a few inches a second, until it was floating directly in front of my face, on the other side of the worktable. It was light blue this time. Was it the same ball I'd seen before? I had no clue.

We sat there, just staring at each other. That's what it felt like. I felt as if the light was *regarding* me somehow. Then it jutted forward, just an inch or two, and my breath caught. It seemed to glow just a tad brighter, and perhaps, maybe even widened in circumference a few inches? To this day, I'm still not certain of this part. The barn was dead quiet, however, still no noise emanating from the ball.

Then suddenly, it just...exploded? I'm not sure if that's the right word to describe it. The light just went out, in all directions, everywhere, in a strange, circular arc, like a Tesla coil, or one of those weird Plasma ball things. Like the white-hot filament of a light bulb, only in all directions at once, this line of light went out. Still no sound, but the blast knocked me to the ground. I felt a slight buzzing all over my body, as if I'd been shocked, only everywhere at once.

When I stood up, all the hairs on my arms and neck were standing on end. I know because I could feel it. I don't know if my hair was standing up or not, but probably it was. I felt euphoric. I felt energized. I was completely happy. I should have been scared shitless, but I wasn't.

I also knew I'd get in trouble if I rushed back into the house and started shouting about what I'd seen. I'd be caught sneaking out when I was supposed to be in bed, and probably no one would believe me.

I went back inside the house and went to bed. If you can believe that, I just fell asleep.

Believe it or not, that's when things got strange. I had a dream. The most realistic dream I'd ever had. It was like I was floating in the air, much like the ball of light, and looking down at a scene from high above. I was looking at a deserted stretch of road. I saw a mangled car, completely crumpled and destroyed in a ditch. Not too far from that, I saw a huge semi truck, parked, and the driver sitting inside his cab, dazed. I could tell from the looks of everything, that he'd hit that poor car. Surely there were no survivors.

I woke up from the dream feeling really strange. I went downstairs and had breakfast. I didn't say anything to my parents or Grandfather about what had happened the night before. It was December 24.

That night, I had the dream again, only this time I seemed to have moved backwards in time a few minutes to before the accident happened. I woke up from this dream screaming. I was floating above the car, and I could tell it was my parents Camry this time. They didn't seem to be going too fast, but as they came around a curve in the road, my dad slid on a patch of ice, into the oncoming lane, just as a Semi was barreling through. I woke up to the sound of crunching metal and screeching brakes echoing in my mind. It was Christmas morning.

I opened my presents in a daze. I don't even remember what I got for gifts. The whole time I was opening presents, I was thinking. I was thinking about the fact that I didn't even really believe in the whole ball lightning phenomenon, or even the Brown Mountain Lights, despite seeing them every winter of my life that I could remember.

I had seen the lights up close now, however. And what I'd seen was most definitely not ball lightning. That ball had come down from the ridge and visited my Granddaddy's farm. That wasn't any damn Cherokee spirit searching for a long lost warrior love.

Whatever had happened to me when that ball of light exploded, it seemed to have had a lasting effect on me. Or it had given me a strange gift. The gift of prophecy? Was I actually glimpsing the future? Were my parents truly soon to die in a horrific traffic accident? I felt like I was losing my mind.

I had the dream again on Christmas and into the morning of the 26th. This time I floated down, through the roof of the car, and inside the cab. I could hear the radio playing - Jingle Bell Rock. A Christmas song, which would indicate the accident would be occurring soon.

On December 29, my parents announced they were driving into Hickory, a neighboring city in the Unifour. They were going to attend a New Year's Eve party. I would be staying with my Grandpa alone. I got a horrible, sinking feeling when they told me about their plans. How could I stop them?

I tried talking to my mother first. I told her I'd been having bad dreams about her and dad getting into a car accident. She only smiled at me and assured me that dad was a really good defensive driver.

"That doesn't matter," I tried to argue. "Dad's going to go around a corner and slide on some ice. It's not his fault, but he's going to go into the other lane, just as a Semi is coming around the corner!"

"Sweetheart," my mother took my face into her hands, "How could you possibly know that? You're being silly."

"But, mom!"

"Honey, your dad and I hardly ever go out. Don't spoil our fun."

I tried going to Grandpa and talking to him. I made the mistake of telling him about sneaking out the night of the 23rd. After that he didn't hear anything else I said.

"You shouldn't be sneaking out in rainstorms, Theresa, you could have been struck by lightning!"

"Grandpa, I think I *was* struck by lighting…or something."

"Yeah, and it's scrambled your brains, honey. You're acting kooky, you know that?"

"Grandpa, something happened to me," I pleaded with him. "Please believe me."

"What do you propose we do?"

Grandpa was looking at me with seriousness now. I was so grateful.

"You believe me?" I asked.

"I've looked at them there Brown Mountain Lights for over thirty years, missy. And they ain't no atmospheric phenomenon."

"But," I just stared at the old man, frowning.

"I ain't never been visited by any lights," he continued, "but if you say you saw it, and now you're having dreams, who am I to disagree?"

I rushed up to my Grandfather and hugged him tight. He let out one of his maniacal laughs and hugged me back.

My grandpa and I began devising ways to stop my parents from going out for New Year's Eve. We had less than two days to stop them.

"Why don't we just cut the gas line?" I said.

"How do you propose we explain that to your dad?"

"Well, at least he'll be alive to yell at us!" I huffed, crossing my arms.

We decided on sabotage. Grandpa went out after dark on the night of the 30th and cut the gas line. We were all set. I was so proud of myself and Granddaddy.

All day on the 31st, we kept smiling at each other, and Grandpa kept winking. I felt bad, whenever I played the upcoming events in my mind. I envisioned my mother spending hours getting ready, putting on makeup and curling her hair, spritzing perfume onto her shoulders.

Looking beautiful. Then I pictured she and my dad sitting in the car as the engine turned over and over but wouldn't start. I saw the sad look on my mom's face as she realized she wouldn't be going out, and I truly felt bad. But at least they'd be alive.

The late afternoon went exactly as I had envisioned. My mother took a shower and blow-dried her hair. Then she curled it and put on her makeup. Then she put on the most beautiful blue dress I'd ever seen her in. My dad looked very handsome in a jacket, vest and tie.

I kissed them goodbye and Grandpa and me stood out on the porch, after dark, watching them get into the car. I had a smile plastered on. I was already rehearsing in my head my reaction when they got back out of the car, looking dejected when it wouldn't start after repeated attempts.

"Oh, no!" I'd wail and frown. "That's too bad. But you can have New Year's with me and Grandpa!"

When the car started up without any problems, my heart leapt in my chest. I turned to look at Grandpa and saw his mouth hanging open in shock. This was no faked reaction. He was just as surprised as I was. The car drove away and I latently ran after it, slipping in the muddy driveway and falling down.

"Wait!" I screamed, but they didn't hear me.

My Grandfather came to help me up. His face was grim.

"I don't understand," I cried. "You cut the gas line, didn't you?"

"Yes, indeedy," Grandpa said. "But I guess there was still enough left in the tank to get her started. They'll run out, for sure, but..." he trailed off.

"We have to go after them," I said. "You stay here, Grandpa."

After all, I was seventeen and I had my license. I went back into the house and grabbed my Granddaddy's keys to the pickup. Grandpa appeared in the doorway.

"You know how to drive a stick, little lady?"

"No, but…" I trailed off.

"Then I'll drive," he took the keys from me.

We got in the truck and headed out, towards Hickory. When we caught up to the Camry, Grandpa started wildly honking his horn. The Camry's break lights went on, then the car slowed down. I was so happy I began to cry.

My dad pulled over on the left side of the road, since the right had no shoulder safe for parking, and Grandpa followed suit. I got out and followed the old man over. My dad got out of his car, leaving the driver's side door open. My mom, for some strange reason, stayed in the car.

"Joe, what the Hell are you doing?" my dad yelled.

"Now listen, Gabe, I didn't want to alarm you, but apparently your car is leaking a good deal of fuel. I saw a puddle of it in the mud, after you drove off. I think you may have a leak, and if that's the case, you're gonna run out of gas long before you reach Hickory, and you're gonna be stuck."

"What?"

"Go check your gage," Grandpa said.

My dad got back into the car and talked to my mom for a minute. I saw him looking at the gages on the dashboard. My mom turned and looked at me. She looked sad, but not angry. I waved at her, beckoning her to come over and get out of the car. She waved me off. I'll never forget that.

My dad got out again and came back over. He shook his head.

"I'll be damned, Joe. You're right. The gage reads on empty. Mel doesn't want to get out in this ditch. She doesn't want to get her shoes all muddy."

I sighed. I looked back at the car with my poor mother inside. Even with her back to me, I thought she looked so sad. Her dress was so pretty and she just wanted to go out and dance and have some fun.

The driver's side door was still open. I could hear the radio playing. Jingle Bell Rock was just reaching my ears. I started to feel woozy, a huge wave of déjà vu suddenly washing over me. I looked around at where we were, and realized with dawning horror what was happening.

"Grandpa?" I said.

Grandpa looked at me, saw my eyes and that's when both of us heard the screeching breaks of the Semi truck. My parent's car hadn't ever hit that patch of ice around the corner. Instead, the Semi hit that slick patch and came careening around the corner, into view, jack-knifing towards everyone.

On instinct, Grandpa grabbed my shoulders. I was turned facing the Camry. My mother saw the Semi coming at her. She just had time to turn and look back at me and my dad and Grandpa.

"Mom!" I screamed.

I tried to wrench myself free of my Grandfather's grip, but he pulled with so much force, I was raked to the left and onto the ground. The last thing I saw was my mother, reaching her hand out to me.

I heard the crunching of metal. The bending of gears and ripping of steel. It was so loud I thought my ears might burst. The Semi toppled and came to rest on *top* of the Camry, utterly flattening it. There it rested, feet from the three of us, lying on the ground, covered in mud and water. I was sobbing. My grandfather was silently weeping. My father sat there, stunned. He was silent.

*****

Two years ago I almost died. My parents almost died as well, but instead, an odd sort of fate intervened. My mother died, but my father is still alive.

Does he blame me? Sometimes I wonder. We don't go to Morganton anymore. Grandpa Joe was my mother's father. And my dad can't bear to drive that stretch of road anymore. Never again.

He'd heard, you see? He'd heard me talking to my mother, begging her not to go out that night. He'd heard me telling her about my nightmares. He'd pretended not to hear, letting my mother deal with it as she saw fit. She'd passed it off as silly, inconsequential dreams.

I knew better. I knew because the dreams had come after my odd encounter with the Brown Mountain Lights. The odd visiting of the Ball Lightning that seemed to impart some sort of temporary ability to dream of the immediate future. Did that ball of light come to me on purpose? Was it all some sort of plan, by some sort of odd paranormal entity that knew of my parents' fate?

What was the purpose, I've often wondered? What was the purpose of saving my father, while allowing my mother to still die? Or perhaps it was my failing, or my Grandfather's mistake?

They were never supposed to even be able to drive off the farm that night, yet they did. I was never even supposed to be able to dream of the future, yet I did. What if we'd reached my father's car just a few seconds earlier? Or what if my father had pulled off the road just a few feet further up, or even back?

I've played that night through my head again and again, trying to change what happened. What if my mother had gotten out of the car, instead of remaining inside? If I had only realized sooner, exactly where my father had pulled over, maybe I could have rushed over and pulled my complaining mother from her seat?

The thing that bothers me the most and keeps me up at night, however, isn't the accident itself. The thing that keeps me up nights, my mind running in circles, is my dream. I've replayed it in my head again and again. Each time I come up empty, with no answers.

Never in any of my nightmares did I ever actually see the dead bodies of either of my parents. I floated above the car, like a ball of light, and saw the wrecked Camry lying in the ditch. I saw the Semi, pulled over, the driver looking dazed. I heard the song playing inside the cab, "Jingle Bell Rock," and instead, now, I always strangely hear the words replaced with "Lightning Ball Rock," and never once do I see either my mother or my father's lifeless, bloody, crumpled body.

Who's to say that if I'd just let the accident take place the way, perhaps, it was meant to, that both my parents wouldn't have survived? Seriously injured, perhaps, but both still alive?

Perhaps my intervention *caused* my mother's death? Perhaps my interceding and changing things around actually made things worse? These are the thoughts that keep me awake at night. It's even worse on nights when there's a lightning storm.

For all I know, that Lighting Ball really did help. Perhaps both my parents would have died, and I managed to save my father.

The problem with the whole thing is that I'll just never know, will I? The crux of it all is that I'll simply never know.

Their Own Fallen

It was a crisp, peaceful morning in Jakolof Bay, the kind of Alaskan day that can inspire utter tranquility within a man's soul. Five a.m., but the sun had been up since three, and had only put itself to bed, briefly, at two. From midnight 'til then, the entire Northern Chain had been sunk in a perpetual sunset, with pink and orange hues painted on the low clouds like a still from Bob Ross.

Jack Trembley was 84-years-old and still had a decent head of hair, although it was mostly gray-white now. He kept it short. He was up every morning at four a.m., and was in bed fast asleep every evening by nine. It was mid-June and the Silvers were running. Nice summer, so far. The temperatures had been mild, mostly never dipping below 45 at night, and reaching the mid-seventies in the afternoons. Mostly sunny days, with an equal mix of white clouds and blue skies.

Jack made his coffee on that clear-cut morning, sucked it down, black, then headed to the front hallway and methodically pulled on his sweater, then his flannel jacket. His USS Arizona cap hung on the hook, exposed only after he pulled his jacket off, so this went on last.

On the porch, he had no need to stoop down for his tackle box, for he'd left it on the wide rail for easy pick-up. The wood was gray, cracked and splintery. It creaked as he walked to the outside store shed to retrieve his rod, and pull on his waterproof fishing overalls. He made his way with tackle box, reel and bucket, down the pebbled walkway in front of his cabin, until the gravel gave way to a mix of sand, dead crab carcasses, a few dried-up jelly fish and salt-smelling tangles of brown kelp.

By five in the morning, Jack was casting and reeling with his silver lure. He cursed at having to untangle fresh seaweed every time he reeled in. A few times, his rod bent and his heart jumped up a bit, then he'd slump down with disappointment when the initial pull didn't become a war. These times, he'd pull his line up only to remove dead branches, a flounder skeleton, sometimes a half-eaten Irish Lord.

The bay was quiet. Only the gentle sound of inch-high waves lapping at the sandy-pebbled shore behind him and beating against Jack's galoshes offered any real sound. Blue Jays sang as well, and squirrels chattered and argued. Flies buzzed around Jack's ears, then eventually settled on the refuse he'd thrown behind him, investigating the wet branches and fish carcasses.

A soft hiss and plop accompanied each new cast, followed by a steady, whispering hum as he quickly reeled in. Jack breathed in the cool air and hoped for a big bite and pull. His arms ached for a fight today. He had his bucket ready, as well as his net. Suddenly a loud crashing noise bombarded his ears, from down the side of the mountain, just to the right of his spot on the beach.

Jack's heart did double time, and he briefly worried about it, wondering if a heart attack might be in store for him this bright, sunny day. He took a few deep breaths, and looked in the direction the sound had come from. He didn't see anything. He waited for a Black bear to come barreling out of the brush and down the beach towards him, but nothing happened. Must have been a large rock or boulder, come loose and rolled itself down the mountain, Jack figured.

Still, he was curious by nature, and for some reason, Jack had a feeling. Couldn't quite explain (even to himself) what it was, really, but he looped the rod's hook to the end of an eyelet and placed the pole inside the chum bucket to go have a look. No boulder had actually made it onto the beach, and

Jack was infinitely curious as to what had caused such a ruckus.

He made his way down the beach-water's edge until he hit the brush. It was thick and headed nearly vertical up the side of the mountain. Jack tried to peer through the thick coverage of pines, to spy any moving thing, but failed.

He puzzled over what could have caused such a loud commotion in the trees. He never did find out, for he glanced to his left and saw a lone pine jutting straight out from the mountain, to hang just slightly over the water.

The pine was mostly stripped of its branches, having most likely fallen over sometime during the winter, and the heavy wind, snow and hail had literally stripped the tree to a bare trunk. Its thick roots were all that held it tied to the mountainside, along with healthy pines acting as support beams. It wasn't such an unusual sight. What Jack noticed, however, was that something was perched on the end of the tree. He peered with his failing eyesight. He was too far away, and it was too small to see clearly.

Jack trudged with his rubber coveralls, into thigh-deep water, to make his way closer to the tree. As he pulled up just a few yards from it, he sucked in his breath. It was an Eagle: Majestic, beautiful, stoic. It regarded Jack with a sideways eye, its white head in such contrast to its leather-black body. Its bright yellow feet appeared under the dark body plumage to reveal sharp talons gripping the branch: a Bald Eagle.

"Huh." Jack stared.

It was unusual for a Bald Eagle to remain, when a human approached it. They usually flew away before any predator could get closer than a hundred yards, unless they were picking a carcass clean. Jack often took the skeletal remains of his catch and threw it down on the beach, so he could watch the Baldies descend upon it and feast. He'd use his binoculars to study them up close. Now he didn't need them. He was looking at a Bald Eagle the closest he'd ever been, he figured. It wasn't flying away.

It didn't appear to be hurt, Jack noted. Nor did it appear to be alarmed. He dared to take a few steps closer, and the Eagle did not react. It only glared at him with its dark eyes, ringed by yellow. Jack regarded the branch it was perched upon. Then he looked at the Eagle again, squinting.

"You didn't make all that noise, did you?"

The Eagle offered no reply. Jack took a few steps to his right, closer to the mountain. He turned back to see that the Eagle had inched down the branch a few feet, as if following him. It preened and ruffled its feathers, as if nervous.

"Huh."

Jack took a few more steps closer to the shore and the mountainside, this time not taking his eyes off the bird. He duly noted that this time, it seemed very agitated. It scooted down the branch again, several inches and then regarded Jack with a scrutinizing glare.

Jack had a feeling now. This time he could definitely say what it was. This bird was not budging from its branch, for some reason; something that had to do with the mountain. Whether it had anything to do with the mysterious noise he'd heard, he didn't know, but there was definitely something out-of-the-ordinary going on. Jack followed the pine trunk along its course, back into the brush of pines and salmon berry bushes, trying to figure out what this bird was being so stubborn about.

He saw it within the bushes, just before the pine trunk disappeared into thick, green tangles of leaves. Something else perched on the branch, barely visible. It blended in with the foliage, in the shadowed-light of the hillside. It was smaller and brown, with no white. Another Eagle. An immature Bald Eagle; a Juvenile.

"Well, I'll be," Jack said. "Huh."

He turned to look back at the mother, who continued to glare at him with a mixture of anger and concern. He took a few steps back towards her, and she did not move. Then he took another few steps away from her, toward her baby, and she fidgeted her wings nervously, never taking her eye off Jack.

"So that's it, huh?" Jack said. "You won't leave your baby alone."

He turned to look at the baby again. It truly was small. He squinted and considered its plumage. There still soft, downy fuzz visible and tufted out underneath and around its light and darker brown feathers. Jack began to wonder if this bird was simply not capable of flying yet. He regarded the mother again.

"Is that it, Mama? Can your baby not fly yet?"

She did not answer Jack. Jack looked at the baby Eagle again and thought he detected an emotion in its tiny, feathered face. He thought he saw panic and fear. He suddenly felt awful. Whatever noise had drawn him over to this section of the beach, it was this Mama Eagles' worst nightmare. To be discovered by a human. He nodded to the mother and backed away, the seawater churning around his rubber pants.

"I'm sorry, Mama," he said. "I'll leave you be."

Jack went back to his fishing and caught two decent-sized Silvers by 7:30 that morning. He took his bucket, tackle box and rod up the beach and onto his work porch, where he gutted, cleaned and filleted his catch. After putting the Salmon meat into his fridge, he trudged back out to his workbench on the porch and collected the Silver carcasses. He walked back down the beach and trudged through the water again, towards the out-jutting pine trunk.

The water was now only up to his knees, as low tide was approaching. Jack scanned the branch for Mother Eagle, and didn't see her. He peered at the base of the branch, however, and saw Baby still sitting. Mama must have gone off in search of food, Jack figured. She'd be in a panic if she returned now and found her offspring alone with him. He made his way toward the beach, just under the branch, daring to get anxiously close to Baby. He spied an old rotted log, just at the edge of the brush, peeking out. He quickly laid the Silver carcasses on the log and sloshed away, back up the beach, around the shoreline.

As he rounded his way toward his cabin, Jack looked up and spotted Mama, perched on *his* workbench. He hadn't cleaned the blood or guts up just yet. He was planning on doing that next. Last. Of course, she'd gone after the Silver innards, once Jack had left his station. Probably flew around on his left, while he was busy looking to the right, following the shoreline, he figured. She'd been watching him all along, even while getting her meal.

No doubt, she'd spied him placing the carcasses on the log. With her Eagle vision, she'd have gotten a binocular-quality view with no artificial assistance required. Jack stopped up short and gazed at her. She looked back at him, hopping down the table a foot, getting ready to vacate, should he come any closer.

Jack only stood where he was, frozen, admiring. Then he stooped down, his knees popping and stayed hunkered, giving Mama her space. She regarded him for several more moments and then carefully went back to her picking at the workbench. It was not a pretty sight, watching long, sticky strands of red and black, gooey fish innards stretch from the wood table to Mama's beak. It was not a pretty sight, but it was food. It was survival. After several more minutes, Mama was satisfied. She tilted her head and seemed to give Jack one last, cautious look and then she took flight and soared directly over his head. He craned his neck upward to watch her in her full glory of flight, and was overjoyed.

She flew back to the pine trunk and he watched her disappear into the foliage against the mountain, knowing she was feeding her baby. He smiled.

Over the next two weeks, Jack made it a habit to fish every morning, and whether he caught a Silver, a Flounder, or even an Irish Lord, he kept it. If it was a Silver, he gutted it and left the carcass for Mama and Baby. The Flounders and Irish Lords, he simply offered up whole to the Eagles, on the same rotted log just off-center of the jutting pine perch.

It was also a habit now for Jack to leave the innards of his catch after cleaning, so that Mama could eat this, too. It became a pattern, quickly established. Every morning, Jack came down to the water's edge to fish. By the second week, Mama always welcomed him by appearing from out of the foliage, inching her way down to the tip of the branch, and watching him cast and reel. She seemed peaceful, as if, perhaps, concentrating. As if she was aligning the universe and sending good mojo Jack's way. After all, it was a matter of survival.

For two weeks while the Silvers ran, Jack caught one almost every day. Only a couple of times did he have only fry fish to offer up to the Eagles. The dance between them became finely perfected. Mama watched and silently cheered, and Jack caught the fish. She waited patiently for him to clean his catch and then flew around on his left side while he either placed a full carcass, or skeletal remains on the rotted log. She flew by and went to Jack's workbench to clean up the leftover innards.

Jack was highly impressed and honored to see that Mama seemed to trust him with her Baby. She never hesitated to fly to the workbench, even as he trudged almost directly underneath Baby to place the carcasses on the log.

Must be, she realizes I'm just an old codger, not worth any threat or worry at all, Jack reasoned.

By the end of the second week, Jack watched in awe and amazement as Baby's white, fluffy down disappeared and his feathers grew in. They were still light and medium brown, as Bald Eagles remain this color for four years before reaching full maturation. Baby, however, doubled in size, and on day number sixteen, as Jack placed the last Silver on the rotting log, he looked up to the sound of whooshing feathers and whistling air, to see Baby take off in all his new-found glory of flight. Jack's heart swelled.

"Good timing," Jack whispered, for the Silver run was just reaching its end.

The next two weeks, Jack fell back into his old patterns. Rising at four, making and drinking his coffee, and every Tuesday and Friday, he made his way into town in his old, beat-up Ford Chevy. He parked in his usual spot each time, in downtown Seldovia, and bought his groceries at the market, along with the paper. Then he drove back out, down the seven-mile dirt road, to his side of the island's mountain, back to Jakolof Bay.

At age 84, most of Jack's friends had passed away, along with his wife, Mira, three years earlier. Mira had loved spending summers at the cabin in Jakolof. Jack still spent every summer there. It was getting harder and harder on his body, however, trekking along the thick sand, through the kelp, and making the climb up the steep stairs from the cabin to the road. His place was nestled at the base of the mountain, just at the beginning of the spit. He spent his summers at the cabin, his winters back on the mainland in Homer. He no longer owned a boat, but flew in on charter every June 1st, and left again promptly on August 31st.

It was a lonely, isolated life for Jack Trembley, and he was shocked to discover just how lonely he truly was. He had not known, 'til now. As he watched Baby make his first flight, Jack felt a pang of heartache at losing this newfound association. Surely, with Baby now able to fly, both he and

Mama would vacate this fallen perch; perhaps even leave the bay altogether, for another destination. Ironically, two wild Bald Eagles were the only social interaction Jack had experienced in months, other than the quick banter he sometimes exchanged with the grocery clerks on Tuesdays and Fridays.

Jack left the final Silver carcass on the log, and trudged half-heartedly back to the cabin. It was just starting to rain. Some summers were like that. Some, it rained every day, for three months solid. Others were sunny the whole go of it. And some, you just got socked in for a week, and then the whole world felt as if it ended in the thick, white fog that surrounded the lower mountain and filled the bay. As luck would have it, the day Baby took his first flight, and Jack felt the first drops of rainfall on his head, would be the beginning of a two-week period where he remained indoors nearly constantly, save for his store trips.

Socked in by the heavy rains, cold, moist air, and sheering winds, Jack took to drinking his coffee and then either reading a magazine or book, or listening to the radio. On day three, he set his book down, while sitting in his recliner, and frowned. There was a scraping noise coming from the back porch.

"Must be squirrels," Jack muttered.

He usually placed his left over crumbs of cornbread, or sourdough biscuits out on the railing for the furry little rascals, but with the last three days being so wet and rainy, he hadn't thought to do so. The bread would have only become a sopping, mounded, clay-like mess on his railing, and he doubted the squirrels would eat that.

When Jack opened the door to take in the view of his back porch railing, his heart skipped a beat. Mama was perched only inches from his body, and she quickly hopped a few feet away, down the railing, but she did not fly away. Baby was perched behind her, on the edge of the railing nearest the top stairs. They both regarded Jack with expectant eyes.

"You came to see me?" Jack said. "Is that it? You want some food?"

He stared at the feathered duo, as if waiting for some kind of answer. His freezer was filled with stored Silver fillets. Jack shrugged and quickly closed the door, gently. He went into his freezer and pulled out two fillets, quickly removing them from their plastic bags, and popped them onto a ceramic plate. He then hit the defrost button on the microwave and waited.

Ten minutes later, Jack opened his back door to find Mama and Baby still there. They had not flown away. Were they aware he had been inside preparing a meal for them? Jack couldn't help but wonder. He placed the ceramic plate on the floorboards of the porch. He didn't want to risk the plate being knocked off the railing and broken by the Eagles' pecking beaks, nor did he want the fillets to end up on the ground covered in a coating of dirt and rocks.

He placed the plate down and quickly backed up, closing the door again, gently. He then went back into his kitchen and peered out his window at the porch, on his left, to catch sight of the birds eating their fill. They didn't even seem to mind that the fish had ended up getting cooked along the outer edges, in order to fully defrost the thicker meat in the center.

"Must be tough, finding good eats with all this thick fog and heavy rain," Jack muttered.

How would he survive, he wondered, if he had to rely solely on the elements, instead of just driving to the grocery store twice a week? However, he was a bit concerned about these two particular Eagles. After all, such a strong, majestic, natural hunter shouldn't need to rely on an old man for a meal.

"Well, why not?" Jack continued muttering to himself. "If there's a free meal, why not take advantage of the opportunity?"

After all, he hadn't hesitated when these two showed up on his porch, now had he? No, instead, he'd gone straight inside and fixed the Eagles a gourmet meal.

"I'm being taken advantage of," Jack smiled. He didn't mind. He only hoped the Eagles wouldn't become too reliant on his providing them with food. He hated the thought of his seeming acts of kindness doing any ultimate harm to these beautiful creatures. It had been three years, however, since Jack felt even remotely useful to any living thing.

The Eagles made him feel wanted, somehow. Needed. They had come to him for food, even. He had no children. He and Mira hadn't been able to, and they never even discussed the possibility of adopting. He was utterly alone, until now.

For the next two weeks, as it continued to rain, Mama and Baby came to his back porch every three days or so. Jack got into the habit of defrosting fillets overnight in the fridge, so as not to have the need to microwave their food.

In the second week, Jack dared, after putting the plate down for them, to keep the door open and stood there, watching them up close. They eyed him warily at first, but soon took to their meal with little agitation. Jack always simply stood there, ridiculously still, afraid to move. The Eagles soon became comfortable with his close presence, and by the end of the second week, as the rain finally tapered off, he was standing out on the porch, leaning against the railing, just feet from the Eagles.

He took to talking to them. Just shooting the breeze—anything and everything that came to Jack's mind. He told Mama and Baby all about Mira and their life together, before she died. How much he'd loved her. In a way, he was looking forward to his ticker giving out, he told them, so he could be reunited with her. He believed he would be.

Once this line of topic was fully covered, Jack began to reminisce about his childhood, in Tennessee. He told the Eagles about his hopes in life, his fears.

"Big spiders, they got in Tennessee," he told them one afternoon. "One day, I was raking up piles of hay out front of the barn. I'd gotten down to the bottom of the pile. I stuck that rake down into the last of that straw and lifted. What did I find underneath? A huge, brown spider, big as my hand. That thing was not happy about being so suddenly exposed. I swear, it lunged at me. Well sir, I dropped that rake," he laughed. "Screamed like a little girl, and I was sixteen. I ran as far from that thing as I could get."

Jack was laughing so hard, tears poured down his cheeks. Mama and Baby just kept on at their meal. They were almost done.

The rain cleared up the next day, as the Eagles ate their last meal on the porch. They seemed to enjoy the sound of Jack's voice. Or that was the impression Jack had, anyhow.

"Buster Browns," Jack said, smiling. "Back in those days, that was the only shoe there was. Everybody wore Buster Browns. You can't find good shoes made like that anymore."

Right on queue, the sun broke through the clouds, and suddenly the rain was misting down through pockets of sunshine. Jack looked up at the sky and sighed. He was suddenly surprised by Mama, fly-jumping up to the rail. He stared at her. She regarded him with one, sideways eye, and Jack swore it was her way of saying, "Thank you."

"You're welcome, dear Mama," Jack whispered. "You take good care of Baby, now, you hear? I know you will."

With that, Mama on the rail, and Baby on the floorboards both took off in unison, as if on some telepathic wavelength with one another. Jack picked up the empty plate and went inside.

The next few weeks, Jack would see Mama and Baby, soaring together, high above the spit of beach. They were doing just fine scavenging all on their own. Jack took long walks along the beach, in the newly returned sun of late July. He walked along, and sometimes Mama and Baby would join him, as if following along, high above. Sometimes they called to him, as if just saying 'hello.' Jack always smiled at this. He had found two new friends, late in life.

He still fished for Flounders and Irish Lords. Every once in a while, he caught a baby Halibut, and he always simply left his catch on the workbench, whole. Sometimes, if the afternoon turned rainy again, he'd leave it up on the back porch. During his naps, he'd wake up to hear the Eagle's talons scraping along the old, wooden boards, and he'd smile and fall back to sleep with dreams of dancing Eagles in his head.

On August 11th, a Thursday, as Jack was walking along the beach enjoying all of Alaska's splendor and beauty, he frowned. He felt a pain in his arm, near the base of his shoulder. It quickly radiated up his shoulder and down around underneath his armpit on the left side of his body. He raked in a short breath, almost knocked windless by the sudden pain shooting through his chest. His torso felt constricted and he was having trouble pulling in breath.

"Oh, Mira," he managed to whisper. Mama and Baby soared above his head.

On a deserted beach, along a spit hugging Jakolof Bay, Jack Trembley fell to his knees in the sand, a quarter mile from the cabin, and never got up again. He fell face-first into the sand and kelp, already unconscious. The last sound he heard was Mama and Baby calling out to him. He died with a smile on his face that no one could see.

On Friday, August 12th, when Jack was a no-show at the Seldovia market, the regular clerk got a bad feeling. He'd been expecting this was how things might go, with Jack. He'd already worked out a plan of action, in his mind, in just such a case. He quickly phoned the Wildlife Office in town and reported a possible heart attack, or perhaps a fall and broken hip.

Wildlife State trooper and pilot Ken Morrow flew his plane over the isolated stretch of beach and spotted the body of Jack Trembley a quarter mile down, unmoving, in the sand.

"Damn," Ken muttered. He called it in.

Ken Morrow landed and was second on scene, once he loaded up in his four-wheeler and got down to the beach. The Medevac team was already there. They stood off several yards marveling, as Ken came up behind them.

"I'll be," a paramedic said. "Look at that. I've never seen anything like that before in my life, have you?"

The other medic only shook his head. Ken took in the sight and also marveled. There was a dead man's body on the beach – fair pickings for all the scavengers, not least of which were the myriad of Bald Eagles that inhabited the island. There was a large pack of the majestic birds on the beach now, surrounding Jack's body, in a large circle.

Two Bald Eagles seemed to be holding sentry over Jack's body, however. A mature Bald Eagle, and a slightly smaller, immature Juvenile stood on the old man's back. They systematically jutted and darted forward at the attacking birds surrounding them, holding them at bay. Neither of the two guard birds took so much as a single peck at the dead man's body. They fought off and constantly warned the crowd of subsequently attacking Eagles, tirelessly.

"How long you figure they've been doing that, you think?" the first medic wondered aloud.

"I have no idea," the other medic said.

Three grown men simply stood and stared at the two Bald Eagles who appeared to be trying to keep the old man's body from being desecrated.

"I'll be darned if those two don't look like they're actually protecting him," Ken said.

"But, why?" both medics wondered.

"Beats me," Ken said. "I know Eagles protect their own fallen, but not people. Eagles don't eat their own kind."

"How you figure we're going to get near them, to move the body?"

"I don't know," Ken said. "I suppose they'll all fly off, soon as we get close enough."

For several more minutes, however, the three men simply watched in complete wonder and reverence. It didn't seem right, somehow, to disturb the scene.

The Sculptor

She looked through the window without even knowing what to name such a strange creature, and wondered if he moved with such natural presence because he somehow knew she was watching. Or perhaps he was simply graced with a self-assuredness she had never known in another. She now felt herself drawing closer, even bumping the glass with her nose in her hurry to scrutinize the beautiful creature.

He was strangely familiar, although, seeing him in motion was surreal, after sculpting him in static, frozen stances for so long. Had it really been all that long, though? Andrea thought about this, even as she watched him disappear into the sparse shadows of the forest beyond her property. She absently rubbed the tip of her throbbing nose, extinguishing the dull ache from her clumsy fumbling at the glass. She recognized him.

Andrea blushed, thinking about all she knew of him. She knew his form. She'd seen him in fine detail in her mind, her dreams. She knew every sinewy curve of his body. Including the wings. She frowned. Wings? What kind of a man has wings? Surely she was dreaming, even now. She must have fallen asleep at her stand, perhaps slumped over the table, and part of his torso. Of course, this would account for her reverie, would it not? Falling asleep across a sculpture of a dark angel would cause any artist to dream of strange things.

She actually pinched herself. Hard. She winced at the pain, staring at the deep line-indents where her nails had carved grooves into the flesh on the back of her mocha hand. She was awake. Sculpting this same form, again and again, had caused her to begin hallucinating. She already believed herself to be mad. Her friends had all told her so, in less harsh words, as well. Now they were all absent, becoming too bored with Andrea's continued obsession.

She could not abandon her thoughts of him, no matter how hard she tried. She thought about him almost every waking moment. Even when she was not aware that he'd invaded her thoughts. Her mind sought him out. He brought her peace, even in the midst of accusations of a psychotic break. She knew not his name. He was some sort of figment of her imagination, brought on by grief, and a stark, desperate need for comfort.

Tony had died. It was no surprise to anyone when it happened, yet Andrea was shocked all the same. The one person who'd been so close to him, watching Tony sink deeper and deeper into a drugged oblivion, she should have been the first to guess how he'd be found.

*****

When she woke that crisp, spring morning and tried to push the bathroom door open, it had bumped into something. She'd frowned, pushing harder. Something solid was on the floor, denying the door free access to swing open.

"Tony?" she'd said, but a hollow feeling had already settled in the pit of her stomach, and her heart was pounding away in her chest. She'd quickly rammed her face into the small nook opening of the door (much like she would later ram her nose into the glass), just enough to see an arm and a sickly pale foot.

Tony had overdosed. Everyone knew it would happen. Especially after he'd checked himself into rehab and gotten clean. He'd only done it for Andrea. She knew that, and because she knew that, she'd felt responsible for his death. If he had never stopped using, his body would have been accustomed to the dosage he'd taken. It was the same dosage he'd been on at the height of his addiction, and it was a pattern his mind (and fingers) simply returned to, his first shot back. It wasn't his fault, she'd reasoned. How could he have known his body was no longer built up to handle that? He'd only done what he'd always done.

It was her fault. She believed that with all her heart. If Tony had kept using, he'd still be alive. He'd tried to stop, for her, and that was what had gotten him killed. She had killed him.

Her grief turned her creativity off. She tried to sculpt all through the rest of that spring and summer, and nothing came. Her usual renditions of woodland creatures and statuesque pines in amazingly fine detail all crumbled into piles of polymer clay shit. She did not have the energy to chisel the needle outlines with her rasp brush. She always ended up slashing at the soft material in anger, slumping down on the floor- a complete mess.

She'd given up by fall. No new attempts to create anything. The cabin was paid for; it wasn't an issue of how to manage her bills. Sure, things would begin to get tight if she didn't produce something by next year's end, but Andrea still was not convinced her artist's block would last that long.

She didn't drink. Not usually, but on September 3rd, she bought herself a bottle of Chablis from the local market and finished almost all of it off over an evening of microwave pasta Alfredo and Tony's favorite big band music. He'd been an odd duck, she mused, smiling. She toasted to Tony in the empty chair across from her at the small kitchen table. Later, while heavily inebriated, she finally cleared out all of Tony's clothes from her closet and the bottom two drawers of the dresser they'd shared. She stuffed everything in black garbage bags and carried them out to the side of the house.

Once this task had been completed, Andrea felt cleansed, somehow. Did this mean she was finally ready to move on? She entered her work shed, the large out-structure adjacent to the cabin. As she entered and closed her eyes, smelling the strong odor of aging cedar, Tony's smile flashed across the backs of her eyes. The movie of him began to play inside her mind, of a time when he'd been completely drug free, standing high up on a makeshift scaffold, affixing rafter beams. He was always an amazing carpenter.

Andrea opened her eyes that night and frowned. Tony's image disappeared as quickly as it had debuted. She felt compelled. She rushed to her worktable and immediately went to work on the clay. Remnants of a raccoon's tail and a squirrel's paw stuck oddly out from the jumbled mass of gray clump. She mashed it all down into a moody half-pancake, then grabbed her rasp brush and began gently gliding it over the surface of the clay. After several minutes of almost hypnotic work, Andrea glanced down and saw the outlines of wings. Then she turned her head to the side of the table and threw up.

*****

As September gave way to October, Andrea began to sculpt again, only this time woodland creatures took a backseat to headless birds with giant wings. The sculptures were small and they didn't feel right. Andrea wanted to go bigger. Was she becoming contemporary in her work? Extemporaneous? She didn't know, nor did she care. She had a vision in her mind. She didn't understand it, and it was vague, but she was compelled to form it with her hands.

She needed more clay, much more. She spent a couple grand and had large, fifty pound barrels delivered to her home. A few weeks later, she'd returned them all. The clay was the wrong color. She exchanged the gray for black. Blackbirds filled her dreams now. Dark-feathered wings rasped and brushed against her skin, and every morning when she awoke, Andrea felt warm and watched, somehow.

She needed a base. She spent long hours traipsing through the woods, with a paranoid feeling of eyes boring into her back. She collected old pine logs; half-rotted, and carried, or sometimes dragged them back into her work shed. When she realized the base was still not large enough, she bored a spike into one log and mounted another on top of it. Then she began wrapping the log base in wire mesh, cutting and pulling and pushing and bending until it resembled a form she somehow knew.

She secured the cut mesh-ends in place with wire ties and soldered the edges together. Then she began filling in the form around the wire cage with black polymer clay, kneading, pounding, sometimes caressing and gently loving it into place, in the delicate parts. Her heart raced all the while and every night she went to sleep exhausted.

It took three days for her to finish the first sculpture, and when it was done, her hands were black, not just mocha, from the porcelain resin finish she'd sprayed onto her work. Her friends came to see it, at her request, and none were impressed.

"What is it?" a girlfriend asked. "It looks like an angel, but...why is it all black?"

"It's art," Andrea replied. "I guess it represents the...darkness of good."

"The *darkness* of good?" a male friend asked. "What the hell does that even mean? How can good be dark?"

"Is it a demon?"

"No," Andrea responded, feeling annoyed. "It's just...it's art, okay?"

"Why doesn't it have a face? It looks kinda creepy, Drea."

She walked up to the creature she'd created and gently touched it with the tips of her fingers, gazing into the empty face, which remained formless, like a solid mask.

"Isn't he beautiful?" she breathed.

Her friends thought she was crazy. As one sculpture gave way to two, then four, then twelve, she began to be rejected in her invitations for people to look at her work.

Andrea didn't care, however. Her solitude was a comfort to her. She enjoyed being alone. In the woods now, she felt accompanied. Once, she slipped on a wet patch of moss, and could have sworn she felt strong, invisible hands pushing against her back, helping her avoid a fall. When she looked down and behind her, she realized a sharp stick was jutting out of the ground. Surely, if she had fallen, she'd have been impaled by it.

At night now, her dreams were always filled with Him. The beautiful creature of her art. She thought now that she could hear him whispering to her, although she could never understand any of his words. His voice was soft and ensuring, however. His presence was undeniable to her, even as a mere figment of her imagination. She'd managed to breathe life into Him, feeling as if He was all around her. She knew it was crazy, but she was only lonely, she reasoned. Without Tony. She was only desperate for comfort and love.

*****

On the night of November 17, she saw Him. She was working on her thirteenth sculpture, when she glanced out the window. A shadow backed away from the glass and Andrea gasped, dropping her rasp brush. Her detailed work on His wings and hair were quickly forgotten. She slowly inched towards the window, squinting to see into the darkness, against the reflected lights from inside the shed.

She was standing three inches from the glass when it occurred to her to turn off the light. Instantly, the buzzing halogen overheads dropped into silence and Andrea was plunged into utter darkness. It took several moments for her eyes to adjust to the faint moonlight from the night sky outside. Then her eyes began to register movement and her pupils dilated into larger circles.

Just in front of the trees, she saw Him. At the edge of the clearing. His feet did not appear to touch the ground. His movements were so fluid, her head began to swim, as if hypnotized by his grace. His face remained in shadow, but he tilted his head, as if listening for something. She got the distinct impression He knew she was watching Him. Then He quickly disappeared into the trees, and in her haste to catch a glimpse of His disappearing body, Andrea pushed her head forward, rapping her nose hard on the glass.

Tears sprung up in her eyes, in reaction to the pain, and she rubbed gently at her nose, cursing herself inside her head. She really was going crazy. She'd been sculpting the same image over and over again, for almost three full months now, driving her friends away, depleting her savings, and now she was so far gone, she was actually seeing Him.

The fact that she was calling him a Him, inside her own head, did not worry her in the least. It was the simple fact that her obsessive madness had culminated into a hallucination that had Andrea so alarmed. Yet, her skin tingled. Her mind danced. She felt so alive: unbelievably euphoric. She wanted to see Him again, real or not. Her eyes wanted to feast upon his form, drinking in every detail. The face was still missing; always an empty, black oval.

Andrea sighed and closed her eyes, seeing His shadow amongst the trees. She recalled the invisible hands that had pushed her back. She thought of the wings. Suddenly her eyes flew open in a panic. It was Tony! He'd become some sort of guardian angel, surely, and was here to protect her. He'd saved her life once already, and was inspiring her to sculpt her greatest work ever.

Andrea suddenly threw the door to the shed open and ran out into the night, across the short clearing and into the woods, without a single thought for her own safety. Adrenaline coursed through her veins and tears streamed down her cheeks. Was that why everything was so dark?

Because Tony had died such a tragic death? Was he a dark angel, sent back down to earth to pay penance for his own, stupid demise? Was he denied access to Heaven, yet still elevated to some sort of supernatural level? She continued making her way through the trees, guided by the moon, as it made brief appearances through the breaks in the foliage.

She was sobbing now. And suddenly she raked in a panicked breath as she heard a familiar sound. A rasping of feathered wings floated to her ears in the silence. She heard it as if it were a bell ringing inside her own head. She'd heard the same sound countless times within her dreams, for weeks on end. She stopped moving and settled deep within herself, becoming small.

From a pine several feet in front of her, Andrea squinted and saw a dark figure round the backside of the trunk, his hand trailing along the bark. He stepped forward only a foot, his face still in the shadows and there He remained, statuesque and frozen.

"Tony?"

No answer. She could scarcely breathe. She felt dizzy. Nothing was real, and her head swam. Her knees suddenly buckled beneath her, and Drea fell in a slump onto the moist, carpeted moss of the forest floor. He also knelt down, his large, black wings lightly whispering and rasping against the pine's bark, behind him.

He moved with such grace, such amazing power, Andrea felt instant love for Him. She could feel his energy, surrounding him, emanating outward. She was now too weak to even hope to stand. His energy seemed to hold a signature, a sense of aura, of knowing. Andrea knew immediately that this was not Tony. She felt foolish in an instant for even thinking so. She knew not what this creature was, only that it intrigued her and commanded all of her attention. She was completely enraptured. When He spoke, it sounded like music to her ears, all her senses on high alert, humming with an energy that coursed through her with every sound that emanated from His mouth.

"You can see me," He said. It was not a question, not a statement. His voice gave off the distinct impression that He was impressed, even intrigued, musing over it.

"What are you?" she asked.

"You feel weak because of my energy," He said. "It drains humans. Your bodies, in carnal form, cannot abide exposure to it."

"What are you?" she asked again, determined to know.

"A dark good."

He sounded amused. She believed she could actually *hear* Him smiling, although his face remained in shadow. She said nothing, merely waited for Him to speak again. Several moments passed, and in the silence, He seemed to hear her confusion.

"You have seen cartoons, where a person sits with an angel on one shoulder and a devil on the other, have you not?"

Drea nodded. In the silence she heard Him exhale and her body felt numb.

"There are no angels, nor devils. I am not good or bad. Necessarily."

"What are you?" she dared to ask again. "Are you a muse?"

He laughed. The hair on Drea's arms and neck stood on end, as if electrified.

"I am a creature of chaos...with aspirations of order. The netherworld, the spirit world, is filled with positive and negative energy. Everything is equal. There is no Heaven or Hell, it is merely the human mind's way of understanding that which is simply beyond you to understand. You give names to things with no name. Definitions. I cannot be named, nor defined, nor planned for. I am not a muse. Muses inspire; they give. I take away. I am Nothing."

"I don't understand."

Silence. Yet, she could feel Him frowning. He was thinking; she knew He was.

"Inspiration is an angelic muse. I come, set to deceive. To make you sabotage yourself. You make excuses for why you cannot work, and I whisper them in your ear. You're too tired; you're out of ideas. I block the images from coming, simply with my presence. I cloud your thoughts. You create nothing. If you must name me, call me a Hell-Muse. If you must give me a title, let it be a Devil-Muse."

"I don't understand."

Drea repeated her statement, sounding angry now. She was daring and apologetic all at once, afraid to upset Him, but wanting clarity. Needing to understand Him, in order to keep her thoughts straight. She needed to know who He was, with some form of definition, or she felt as if her mind might slip.

"The spirit world, as you might call it, is filled with energy, in forms you cannot even imagine. Humans are drawn to this energy. They are drawn to things greater than themselves. The spiritual plane contains energy, a power that is intoxicating. It's what you may know in terms of *magic*. I come and take away. Others give. It's all I can tell you. I don't choose. I am drawn to those who are lost and full of despair."

"Why? To what purpose?"

"To take away," He shrugged. She saw his wings rise up then slump back down. She was amused. Her head still swam.

"You were surprised I could see you?" she asked.

"I wanted you to see me," He said.

"I saw you in my dreams."

"That was a mistake."

He sounded exasperated, confused. She forgot to breathe.

"You were never supposed to know me. You were never supposed to sculpt anything, ever again. Presumably, you would have lost all hope, eventually, and died, like Tony."

"You know about Tony?" Tears filled her eyes, and in her sudden sadness, she raked in sobs, finally breathing.

"I've watched you for so long," He said, his voice sad and full of wonder. "I can hear your thoughts. All of them. Even now. As if you're an open diary of live streaming secrets, emptying into my mind. So much pain, so much sadness, so much confusion. So much guilt and blame. Wanting answers, as if you need them to keep breathing. Feeling so lost and alone. I see what's inside your head. So many dark thoughts, yet, you still see the world with such beauty and feel compelled to render it under your hands. As if making your visions come into physical being will somehow fix you."

"I'm not broken," Drea said, defiant again.

"I've come to break you," He answered back. "To drain you of all your hope. The opposite of a Muse. You were never supposed to sculpt anything ever again. Imagine my surprise when you did. And *what* you did."

"It was You."

"It was something. I wasn't certain, at first, I was only miffed as to how you were inspired to create anything at all."

"How was I able to sculpt you?"

"I don't know," He said. "You were never supposed to sculpt me. Know my form. Hear my voice."

"It was you that pushed me," she said. "When I almost fell."

"I should never have caught you," He said. "I shouldn't have been able to. It was instinct. Again, imagine my surprise when I actually caught you. It's not possible, Drea."

Her senses came alive then. As His voice said her name out loud for the very first time. He felt a change as well. Energy was passed between them. She breathed in deeply and could smell Him. It was a sweet scent, reminiscent of cinnamon and burnt paper. He shuddered.

"How am I able to see you?"

"I don't know."

"But you said you wanted me too?"

"Yes, and I've never wanted anything before. So, perhaps in the wanting lies the way."

"I don't understand," Drea said.

She felt drawn to Him, like a moth to a flame. His energy continued to emanate out, toward her, drawing her closer to Him. The inclination was undeniable. Drea did not have the energy to stand, nor walk to Him. She began to slowly inch herself along the forest floor, crawling like an infant, uncoordinated in her weakness, as if inebriated.

He stood and backed up against the tree. His wings splayed outward from his body in panicked surprise.

"Don't come any closer!"

"I want to touch you," she said.

"You cannot, or you will die!"

Drea stopped short and peered up at Him on hand and knee. He was like a Winged Deity, a God standing before her, and she was lost in Beauty. Too intoxicated to care about anything anymore. She only wanted to touch Him, be as close to Him as she could possibly get. She wanted to melt into Him and become part of his flesh. She wanted to be with Him. The threat of death did not deter her or frighten her away.

"How am I able to see you?" She peered up at Him, needing to know.

"Because I wanted you to," He said.

His heart was breaking for the first time in his entire existence; a life that had no memory of any beginning. He seemed to have no memory now, save for this, for Her. He'd never wanted anything before Her. He'd never been known before. He'd never been glimpsed in all His life, not even in someone's dream, nor artistic vision. He was meant to take away inspiration, not be the source of it. Him. She had seen Him, sensed Him somehow. She'd become *aware*. He saw Her as a creature of wonder and beauty, mysterious and powerful in Her own right. She'd done something no human had ever managed before. She had made Him long for Her. He loved Her.

"You made me want you," He said. "You're drawn toward my supernatural energy, Drea, but you cannot touch me!"

He backed up against the pine, hard. He was in full physical form now, and the bark bit into his flesh, causing pain. She continued to inch toward him, bent on running her fingertips over his flesh, to feel its warmth, or lack-of. Either way, she didn't care. She didn't mind. She would die in ecstasy, if death were the cost.

"What is your name?"

He frowned down at her. He who had no name for the creature he was. Somewhere throughout the vast history of time he had occupied, he'd acquired a name. He did not know if he'd always known it, if it had been given or assigned, or if he had simply chosen it for himself, with some unknown need for self-identification. He had a name. He knew what it was. He'd never spoken it aloud before.

"What is your name?"

She asked Him again, still inching forward. Only a few feet of distance now remained between them. He wanted to tell Her. He wanted Her to touch Him. He wanted Her. It was all new to him. He was certain She would die, and yet, he wanted so much from Her, wanted Her so badly, he no longer cared. That one touch would be so exhilarating, so much agony and ecstasy, all in one moment. Perhaps a kiss.

"Zacharias."

The whole world fell away at the utterance of His name. It fell upon Her ears like warm oil, washing over her entire body, bathing all of Her being in warmth and liquid love. She rose up on Her knees in front of Him and He fell down upon his own, mortal knees, his majestic black wings outspread as if to wrap around Her and embrace Her.

He reached for Her and She for Him. His hands met her face and cradled it. Her own hands came to rest on the naked, dark flesh of His chest, and she felt His heart drumming away, beneath her fingers. As their lips met, the moonlight illuminated a scene of death.

Zacharias' wings, out-splayed and vibrant, quickly withered, like blackened paper in fire. The aviary tips curled inward, as if giving way to a tremendous heat, and lightened to a gray color, as they crumbled into ash.

It did not hurt. Zacharias felt no pain. He only felt the warmth of Drea's lips, the pressure of her touch, the joy inside his heart. As his wings continued to disintegrate, he felt nothing, save for joy. The feathers disappeared, leaving the cartilage stock naked and exposed. This, too, began to disintegrate, glowing like an ember, hotter and brighter, then collapsing with the heat, melting into nothing, from tip to husk, until the wing joints jutting from his back were all that remained.

As Zacharias reeled in Her embrace, his hands roaming over Her body, he felt the first traces of heat ignite on his skin. The traveling inferno was now past the wing joints and had arrived at the skin upon his back. A searing blaze began eating away at his flesh. He felt himself burning from the inside out, the heat-destruction entering his body cavity from two rounded holes where his wings had once been attached to Him.

The pain was exquisite. Zacharias relished it, locked in his embrace with Drea. Drea felt filled with energy, as if everything that was Him was flowing into her. He had come to take away, but He was giving all of Himself to Her. She was Becoming. The Hell-Muse had inadvertently become a reluctant Muse, through an accident of Love, Want and Desire.

As Zacharias- alive for untold centuries- winked out of existence, the last thing he felt was Drea's lips and her breath upon his crumbling skin. Ash floated upon the air, reflected in the faint moonlight.

Drea was suddenly alone, kissing nothing. She opened her eyes and blinked, looking around. As she puzzled over where she was and how she had gotten there, she did not see the last of the floating ash as it continued to shrink in on itself. Each tiny particle became smaller and smaller, until nothing remained of the beautiful creature named Zacharias. He was gone.

Andrea remained in the forest for several minutes, confused, her memory of Zacharias gone, just as He was. He no longer existed, and so, He never had.

*****

For the next several days, Drea puzzled over the odd sculptures she found in her work shed. She could not remember making them. The last several weeks seemed to be a blur for her. Perhaps she'd been drinking too much, in the wake of her grief over Tony? Drea simply did not know, and had no explanation for her memory loss, or the creation of the sculptures in her shed.

Drea did not care. The sculptures were beautiful, fascinating. Oddly hypnotic to look upon. She wondered if she could render one now, with her mind seemingly fully intact. Sober. As she raked her rasp brush over the clay of the form on her worktable, she felt oddly invigorated, as if an unseen energy were coursing through her body, from some unknown source. She felt vibrant.

She must be crazy, she thought to herself. She swore she almost felt as if her hands were on fire as they worked. As if she'd been infused with some odd form of *magic*. She laughed out loud at the silliness of her own thoughts. This was simply a case of an artist being suddenly inspired, for whatever reason, she concluded.

Who knows where creative drive truly comes from? Drea thought.

As she continued to work on what she was certain would be her greatest artistic masterpiece yet, she answered her own question with resounding clarity. She told herself that the creative Muse is merely an idea, a notion created by the human mind. That true creative drive lies within, deep inside the heart of every artist.

Drea worked with a smile. For the first time in months, she felt truly free. Tony was not on her mind, nor her own stricken fear that she would suffer from artist's block forever. The veil had been lifted, somehow. She cared not why, or how. She only cared that it was so. She felt happy and full of love for the world.

It All Comes Around in the End

The wind was chilly, a thick scud of gray clouds covering the sky. The light wind whistled through the bare trees, seeming to taunt and tease, threatening rain at every shrill note. Rachael stuffed her hands deeper into the pockets of her Trilby coat. She should have brought her gloves, but they were sitting on the passenger seat of the green Fiat. They, at least, were warm. John was walking with the farmer, Kell O'Donough, asking questions like an excited schoolboy. Rachael shivered, sighed, and then walked over to John, grimacing a smile. Her lips felt numb.

"Honey, this is amazing," John said, pointing to a headstone. "This tombstone is over three hundred years old."

Rachael smiled and nodded. Mr. O'Donough smiled back, sympathizing. He had only agreed to bring the couple out here because John had offered him ten dollars, and Kell never refused easy money, especially from American tourists. Not that he'd ever had any knocking on his door before, but that was beside the point.

The tourists blew through town, marveling at the quaint little pubs, the architecture of the buildings, staying in the few bed and breakfasts along the row. Then they left and it never affected Kell at all, one way or the other. In town, he listened to the townsfolk complain about the 'traffic,' but he noticed they never complained about the money these tourists spent on their fine establishments. Now it was his turn to reap the benefits.

He'd taken over the farm after his father died, and his father had done the same on back through too many generations to count. The graveyard had always been here, he mused. A fixture no more out of the ordinary than the trees surrounding his land. As it so happened, he was an expert on the site, so to speak. The stories, like the farm itself, had been handed down over the generations. No one had ever bothered to knock on his door asking about them, however, until today.

"There's older than that, fella. In the monastery down Cornamagh," Kell repeated. He had already told this man, John Engall, that this old, deserted graveyard was small business, if the American really wanted to see some ancient graves. John simply shook his head.

"Everyone looks at those. I want to see something no one else has seen."

Rachael sighed heavily, turning to head back to the car. Kell stopped her with his hand, smiling gently. She blushed and he lowered his hand to his side, feeling awkward.

"Now hold on, missus, if it's different you want to see, I can show you that much."

"I'm not the one who wanted to see anything," Rachael huffed. She perceived Mr. O'Donough's accent to be more of a Scottish persuasion than Irish, but then again, what did she know?

"Sorry, honey, but it's not everyday we are in Ireland. We both picked this, remember? You wanted Europe," John said.

"Paris, Nice, *Rome*, John."

Now it was John's turn to look embarrassed. He glanced quickly at Mr. O'Donough and pulled Rachael to the side, turning his back on the farmer. Kell pretended to look off, not hearing their conversation, although he heard every word.

"Honey, we went to all those places, like every other tourist, and the *crowds*," John sighed. "That's not real, that's what everyone comes to see. A McDonald's on the French Riviera! That's not Europe, Rachael. That's ridiculous. You agreed, we'd see some *real* parts of Europe, honey, remember?"

"Yes, but we've stopped at every small town for one hundred miles. They all look the same, and now you're stopping at random graveyards in the middle of nowhere…and I'm freezing!"

"I think I can settle this for the two of you," Kell said. He spoke low and gentle, as if sharing a special secret with his best friend.

"Now listen," he said, motioning to Rachael. "You're cold, and your new, eager husband is hungry. He wants to see something no one else has ever seen. Well, I can do that for you. I'll show you something no tourist has seen through these parts, and then after, you can check in at Bell's Bed and Breakfast, 'cause I know it's not full tonight. She serves the best Shepherd's pie you'll ever taste, with a warm brandy to top it all off. Agreed? It'll only take ten minutes, and you can be on your way. I promise, you won't be disappointed."

John looked at Rachael, his eyebrows raised. She sighed lightly and nodded her head.

"All right, but after this, we check into the hotel and we're done for tonight. For the rest of the trip."

"Okay," John said. "We're done…for tonight."

"John."

"Okay. If this is really as good as Mr. O'Donough says, then fine. We can be done for the trip."

Kell led the couple past the larger headstones, down an overgrown path ripe with dead vegetation. They reached the edge of the graveyard, where the trees began to take over. John and Rachael stopped, but Kell motioned them to keep walking.

"Just a bit further on, through the trees," he said. They followed him ten more yards, into the thickening woods, Rachael grasping John's arm. Kell stopped short, arriving at a large headstone that stood alone. He turned to the couple, looking sinister, and also devilish. A small grin played at the corners of his mouth.

"This is the grave of a witch, so the legend goes," he said. "Sometime around 1380, or thereabout. Ashlynn Cass was her name. Her brother entered a wager-of-battle when she was accused by a man in town. The man said she bewitched him to sleep with her. He was married, see, but if he could prove he was bewitched, his wife could not hold him accountable. Back in those days, if a woman was accused, a wager-of-battle was sometimes fought. If the one fighting on the accused side won, the charges were dismissed, and the accuser paid a hefty fine. If the accuser won, the witch was hanged."

"And so they hanged her," Rachael said, rolling her eyes, her voice sarcastic and annoyed.

"Now don't go thinking you know the story just yet, missus," Kell winked. John was looking rather interested now.

"Her brother fought the accuser in that wager-of-battle I told you about. A sword fight, it was. A drawn out affair, too. Lasted some thirty minutes or more, and by the end, both men were bloody and well cut up, but the brother stood, and Ashlynn's accuser was on the ground, without his sword. So Ashlynn's name was cleared, of witchcraft anyhow. The man paid a weighty fine, the likes of which broke his family, not to mention his wife was none too pleased with the infidelity. She killed herself, so the story goes, and her husband went mad not too long after. You can well imagine these events started some gossip amongst the townspeople. They began to say that Ashlynn was a witch after all, and that it wasn't suicide and madness that took out that married couple, but Ashlynn herself, using her craft. She was banished from town, living on the outskirts. Her brother died of illness some years later, and no one ever heard from her again."

"That's it?"

Rachael was not about to let the story end on that note. She motioned to the headstone, which bore no name or date on it. It was in pristine condition, and contained odd-looking carvings etched into the gray stone.

"This headstone doesn't look that old to me. If this is supposed to be that woman's grave, that would make this headstone over six-hundred-years old. This stone is obviously much younger than that."

"Ah, now here's the part where the story starts to get strange," Kell continued. His grin expanded, causing Rachael to grab John's hand.

"Some years after all this took place, the town was growing, pushing outward in all directions. Some townsfolk took it upon themselves to pay a visit to the old Cass home, which no one had seen in years. Take it over, they probably thought. The money won in that wager-of-battle would have run out before too long. With Ashlynn not coming into town for supplies and the harsh winters we have in these parts, no one could fathom how she would have survived. They figured her home must be abandoned by now. They found her brother's headstone back yonder," Kell motioned behind him, back towards the graveyard.

"So they knew he was dead, but they couldn't figure how Ashlynn had put up such a nice marker on his grave. They knocked on her door, 'cause they seen smoke billowing out from the chimney. Some twenty years had passed since the battle, so they were expecting an old woman to open the door, if anyone at all. What they got, instead, was Ashlynn herself, just as young and pretty as ever."

"Oh please," Rachael snorted, rolling her eyes. "Let me guess. She still lives out here somewhere, in the same little house, and at night, you can hear her cackling as she rides around on her broom in the moonlight."

"Honey, let him finish," John said.

"Now I told you, missus, don't go thinking you know the tale just yet. It was three folks from town, come back swearing Ashlynn was still alive out here, and just as young and beautiful as ever. That's how everyone finally learned that she really was a witch. That married man was telling the truth, and Ashlynn did bewitch him to lie down with her, and later, to lose his mind and his wife to kill herself. So, the people in town decided it was time to hang her as a witch, like they shoulda done all those years before. A group of men with torches and knives and ropes came back out that very night. Knocked on Ashlynn's door, and sure enough, a beautiful woman answered, looking confused. She was the spitting image of Ashlynn, see? Only she kept telling them that her name wasn't Ashlynn, it was Criona, but they wouldn't believe her. She tried to take them and show them Ashlynn's headstone, which she said was in the cemetery, just yonder from her brother's. They dragged her from the house, into the waiting woods, threw a noose over a tree branch and hung her, as she cried and protested she was not Ashlynn, she was not a witch."

"And?" John was leaning forward, eager and waiting. Rachael also looked excited now.

"Well, you can't guess?" said Kell. "She died, the woman. And the men who hung her walked back out, through the graveyard, and on their way, they spotted the brother's headstone, with peculiar words writ upon it. It said Angus Cass, loving brother and uncle. His name was Angus, did I tell you that?"

Both John and Rachael shook their heads impatiently. Kell paused for dramatic effect, then delved on.

"The men were puzzled by the word uncle, so they looked for that other grave, the one 'Criona,' had said was not too far off from Angus. They found it, the next row over- another headstone. It had Ashlynn's name on it, and it said loving sister and *mother* on it."

Rachael gasped. John merely looked at Kell with a blank stare. Kell paused again, then continued.

"Ashlynn had been with child from that affair, and had born it on the outskirts of town. She named her 'Criona,' which in our language means 'my heart,' and that little girl had been raised by her mother and Angus, her uncle. Angus died, and later Ashlynn, and it was Criona that managed, somehow, to put up the lovely headstones. No one ever knew how she afforded it, or who crafted them, for it was none from their town, as far as anyone could tell. When those folks from town saw this beautiful young woman at the door, they thought it was Ashlynn, bewitched and still young, when it was really her daughter, who, as I said, was her spitting image."

"So, that poor woman raised a child all alone, outside town, then her poor daughter was hung as a witch, all because of superstition and misunderstanding?"

Rachael's cheeks were aflame. She breathed heavily. John continued to look blank. Then his expression changed to one of doubt.

"Now hold on, Mr. O'Donough," John said. "You said the story got weird. So far it sounds like a series of simple misunderstandings and mistakes."

"It does sound that way, doesn't it though? Those men stood there, in front of Ashlynn's grave, and realizing their mistake, they went back to that tree, meaning to cut down the body of Criona and give her a proper burial, but when they got back to the tree, Criona's body had disappeared."

"This is ridiculous," Rachael said. "You're making all of this up."

"No, missus," Kell said, sounding insulted. "This story has been passed down in my family for over six hundred years. I'm not making it up, I'm only telling it the way I was told. The way my father was told. The way every O'Donough has told it, since the first one broke ground out by this graveyard, where no one else would go, all those years ago, and my ancestors got the land almost free. It's the same story I told my son, and he'll tell it to his," Kell said, his voice cracking slightly.

"She didn't mean anything by it, Mr. O'Donough, I swear," John said. "Right honey? Please, finish the story."

Kell took a deep breath and spoke.

"Like I said, Criona's body was gone, but all the growth around the tree was dead, just below where her body had hung. The men were spooked. They ran back to town, crossing themselves. It was over a year later, people began moving further out, and the original idea took hold to use Ashlynn's old place. They knew for certain now it was empty. It was after a family moved into it, their son wandered out into the woods one day and found the headstone; right on the spot where they hung Criona, where all that green growth next to the tree had died. The very headstone you are looking at now."

Kell stood silent, watching the Engall's faces. Rachael and John stared at the headstone. Rachael could feel gooseflesh spreading up both her arms and on the back of her neck. She shivered, her body shuddering. Then she turned to Kell. It was her turn to look doubtful.

"I don't mean to be insulting, but still, if this headstone is that old, wouldn't it be crumbling by now? This stone looks to be in perfect shape, as if it were placed here last week."

"That's the strange part, at least some of it," Kell said. "The headstone has remained in perfect condition all this while. Time seems not to have any effect on it. Angus and Ashlynn's graves are the same. Only difference is, this one's not marked. At least, not with anything that makes sense."

"What does it mean?"

Rachael stared at the headstone, an ominous feeling seeping into her. The markings were dark, as if they had been burned into the stone itself. How much heat would it take to do that, she wondered? The markings were foreign. Odd shapes and symbols all over it, even along the outer edges. Symbols and etchings that made Rachael feel as if she might lose her mind if she stared at them for too long. The light was beginning to fade as twilight came on. John brought out his camera.

"Do you mind of I take some pictures of it?"

"If you can take a picture of that, it's yours to have."

"What do you mean?"

"Tried to photograph it some years back myself," Kell said. "None would take."

John looked at Kell for a few moments, trying to decide if the man was joking or not. He didn't know whether to believe his story or not, and yet, Kell seemed to be dead serious in telling it. John took several photos of the headstone, checking each digital image afterwards to ensure it was clear. Then he smiled at Kell, looking relieved. The pictures seemed to prove to John that the story was a fake. He no longer felt scared at all. He took Rachael's hand to walk back to the graveyard, but was met with resistance. He tugged on Rachael's hand, looking back at his wife with only slight concern. She stared at the headstone as if hypnotized.

"Rachael, honey, come on," John said. He shook her hand in his. Rachael looked over at John, suddenly, confused.

"Huh?"

"Let's go, it's getting dark. I thought you couldn't wait to get back to town?"

"Sorry," she said. "I must have zoned out there for a minute."

"Happens all the time," Kell said, leading the couple out of the woods and back into the graveyard. He stopped momentarily to show them both the graves of Angus Cass and Ashlynn Cass, and John took photos of these as well. They both, indeed, looked brand new, although the other graves surrounding them were crumbled and broken. Many were so old the writing was worn too thin to read anymore.

They reached the house and John shook Mr. O'Donough's hand, thanking him for the tale. Kell smiled.

"I hope I gave you what you were looking for, Mr. Engall. It's definitely something no one else has seen before. My farm is not on most tourist's radar."

"You've never shown those headstones to anyone before?" Rachael asked.

"No, missus," Kell said. "The townsfolk all know about it, but they don't like to think about it. No one comes out here to look at it. I've only looked upon it three times in my life. As a child, when my father first told me the story, again, when I told the story to my son, and today, with you."

"But I thought you said you also tried to photograph the headstone," said John.

"Did I? I was mistaken. My son tried to photograph the headstone, and it wouldn'a turn out." A shadow fell over Kell's face then. It was only momentary, so brief, John barely noticed, but Rachael stepped forward, looking concerned.

"Where is your son, Mr. O'Donough?"

"In town, getting supplies," Kell answered quickly.

"What about her home?" asked John, looking thoughtful.

"Her home?"

"Yes, you said a family eventually moved into Ashlynn's home, didn't you? And their boy was the one to discover Criona's headstone?"

"Yes, that's right," said Kell.

"Whatever happened to Ashlynn's home?"

"Why, you're looking at it," Kell answered simply. John and Rachael stared at Kell O'Donough for several moments, their mouths hanging agape. Kell stared back at them, unblinking. John was the first to speak.

"You mean your family lives in Ashlynn's old home?"

"Yes, it were my ancestors who got this land near for free way back then, when no one else would have anything to do with this place. A far distant relative, a great-great-great-great-great-great grandfather, many times removed, Shamus O'Donough, who as a young boy first discovered the headstone in the woods, at the foot of that old tree. So, you see, I tell you the truth when I say this story has been passed down in my family for generations. It's the truth, every word."

"Have you ever seen anything, or…you know…heard anything in your house?" John asked. He had a twinkle in his eye. Kell grinned.

"You mean ghosts? Sure, I got my fair share of those tales as well."

"You're kidding," John said. "Witches *and* ghosts? This is too rich."

"I ain't rich, Mr. Engall, that's for sure," Kell laughed. "Stories I got, but money, not so much of."

"Well, you should really think about starting up a business with all this legend," said John. "I mean, you could charge people to look at those headstones and tell your story. Like a little tour. You could even open your own bed and breakfast. Let people stay in Ashlynn's home, like a tourist draw. You'd probably make a small fortune."

"I don't know about that, Mr. Engall. I doubt if Ashlynn would like that much, having strangers come into her home all the time."

John stared at Kell for several moments, waiting for the joke, but Kell only looked back at him with a complete look of seriousness on his face.

"You're not kidding, are you?" said John. "Your house is actually haunted by the spirit of Ashlynn?"

"Undoubtedly."

John looked at Rachael, then back at Kell, then at Rachael again. Then he reached into his back pocket and pulled out his wallet, producing several fifty-dollar traveler's checks. He handed three of them to Kell.

"I'll pay you one hundred and fifty American dollars to allow my wife and I to sleep in your home tonight, what do you say?"

"John, are you crazy?"

"Shh, Rachael, let the man think."

"Absolutely not, John. We are not pushing ourselves onto this poor man and invading his home. We've already bothered him enough."

Kell simply stood, staring, as if in deep thought. His mind was already made up.

"There's a guest room, in the back. You can stay there tonight, if that's what you like."

"Awesome. Honey, let's do it."

Rachael pulled John away from the house, arguing with him beside the green Fiat. Kell watched them closely, smiling his slight grin. After several minutes of arguing, John opened the trunk of the car and produced two small suitcases. Rachael walked back up to the house, John following quickly behind with the baggage.

"Thank you so much for doing this. I'm really sorry about my husband. It's just...when he gets something in his head, he can be sort of stubborn and even kind of crazy at times."

"I understand, Mrs. Engall. We all get that way sometimes."

"Honey, think of the stories we'll be able to tell when we get back home. How many people come back from Europe and can say that they stayed in an actual haunted house? And I can show them the pictures of the headstones, and tell them the story Kell told us. Is it all right if I call you Kell?"

"That is my name, Mr. Engall."

"John, please."

"All right, John."

Kell led the Engall's to a bedroom in the back of the house, where they deposited their bags. There was a bathroom directly across the hall. Kell explained that his and his boys' rooms were both upstairs.

"Used to be, this was only one story. My family added the upstairs long after the Cass story unwound. That guest bedroom you're in, that was Ashlynn's bedroom."

The Engalls, who had been following Kell back down the hallway, stopped abruptly.

"We're sleeping in Ashlynn's bedroom?" Rachael looked at her husband nervously.

"You're not scared, are you honey?" he teased her with a poke to her ribs.

"Of course not," Rachael said, slapping John's arm.

Kell led the couple into the kitchen, which had a small dining table in the corner. The entire house was made from wood; the support beams visible near the ceiling. It was a humble home, and walking through it gave both John and Rachael the distinct feeling of stepping back in time some two hundred years or more.

Kell put a large pot on the stove, which Rachael thought resembled a cauldron almost. She looked at John to see if he noticed this. John seemed oblivious. Kell poured water into the pot, then began chopping up potato and carrot. He pulled what looked like, possibly, a medium sized hare out of the fridge, already skinned. He began butchering this, throwing the pieces of raw meat into the pot as well. He looked sideways at the couple.

"Rabbit stew," was all he said. Rachael gave John a look. He shrugged back at her.

"I'm really sorry to be imposing on you like this, Mr. O'Donough. I mean, Kell. We really shouldn't be putting you out like this. We can drive into town and stay at that bed and breakfast, really."

"And force me to part ways with one hundred and fifty of my new best friends?"

Kell raised an eyebrow at the Engalls, who simply stared for several moments. Then Kell laughed heartily. John laughed as well, although Rachael only smiled, weakly.

"You know, I do believe I've spooked you a bit with my tale, Mrs. Engall."

"No, of course not. I'm fine. Besides, I don't believe in ghosts."

"Really," Kell said, in a daring tone.

"Well, what kinds of things have you experienced living here, Kell?" John intervened.

"Oh, the usual," Kell said, sitting down to the table. "That will need to boil low for a few hours, steep the juices. She'll be ready just in time for supper. We can sit in the living room, by the fire, if you'd like, and I can continue my tale."

"Yes, that would be great, wouldn't it, honey?"

John put his arm around Rachael, rubbing her shoulder with his hand. He hardly even noticed how she bristled at his touch. The couple followed Kell into the small living room where a fire was already glowing. Kell added two logs from a pile in the corner and stirred the embers up a bit with the poker. The couple settled on a couch directly in front of the fire, and Kell settled into a chair adjacent to them. The furniture smelled old and musty, yet it was comforting; a welcoming smell. The walls were bare, save for a portrait of Kell and what Rachael presumed to be his son. There didn't seem to be any Mrs. O'Donough.

"I hear crying," Kell said. Rachael frowned, straining to hear any wayward sounds. She heard nothing and said so. Kell smiled, understanding.

"At night, I mean to say," he explained. "In the darkness, laying in my bed at night. Sometimes I hear crying."

"Maybe it's the wind outside, or an animal, a fox?" Rachael said.

"No," Kell smiled again. "It is most definitely a woman. Crying inside the house. There are odd knocking sounds as well."

"That could simply be the house settling," John offered.

"Not the way these knocks come," Kell said, his face suddenly becoming dead serious. Rachael's heart skipped a beat, a cold chill coming over her. She suddenly didn't want to be in this house for another minute.

"You think it's Criona? Or is it Ashlynn?" John asked.

"Perhaps both," said Kell. "My son and I have also seen shadows moving on the walls. Shadows as if there are bodies in the room, but the bodies themselves are not visible to the eye, only the shadows they cast. You can hear them climbing the stairs sometimes as well, the steps creaking beneath their weight."

"Well, no offense, Mr. O'Donough, but many of these things could be explained by natural occurrence, even a runaway imagination," said John. Rachael stiffened beside him. John did not notice. Rachael expected Kell to take insult at John's remark, but instead, he laughed again, heartily.

"These are the suggestions of one who has not yet experienced what I am talking of," said Kell. "But if you do intend to stay the whole night in my home, perhaps by morning, you will have a different perspective on these things?"

"Perhaps," said John.

Rachael relaxed a little. She was suddenly angry and lost inside her own head. Damn John and his crazy need to have some unique adventure while in Europe. Europe itself wasn't enough. No, he had to go off looking for some quaint little experience that wasn't on the normal tourist destinations. He always had to veer off the beaten path. It was one of the reasons she had fallen in love with him to begin with. He never did things the way anyone else did. He was always coming up with last minute changes of plan, or just flying by the seat of his pants. She usually loved that about him, but in this particular case, it was starting to wear her down.

Rachael had agreed on Europe, instead of Hawaii or the Caribbean. She had later even agreed to this unplanned side trip to Ireland, when John had become bored with their pre-planned tour of Italy and France. It was too 'touristy' he had said. In some ways, she had agreed, although it did not irk her in the same way it did him. Now, here they were; in some small town in southern Ireland, she wasn't even sure what county they were in anymore. Heathmore, perhaps? John had the map, not that he'd been using it much. Kell continued to explain the spooky goings-on inside his home.

"They try to push you down the stairs," he said, his face growing shadowy again. "You can feel their hands on your back. And sometimes at night, you wake up feeling as if you can't breathe, and you'd swear they were trying to suffocate you."

"Are you serious?" John looked at Rachael with doubt.

"Hey, you're the one who wanted to sleep here, not me," she said.

"Oh, I'm sure you'll be fine," Kell assured the couple.

"Really?" John looked worried.

"Well, no, not really, you're the first guests to ever stay here, so who can really tell?" Kell said matter-of-factly.

When he saw the look on John and Rachael's faces, he bellowed a loud booming laugh that made Rachael jump. This made Kell laugh until tears rolled down his face. Then he excused himself to the restroom, leaving the couple alone.

After a few minutes, John left to get his camera from the bedroom, leaving Rachael alone to stare at the fire. She looked to her right, to the portrait on the wall. It was covered in glass, which reflected the firelight, as well as the dimming light from the window. She stood up and walked over to the picture to get a better look.

Kell's son was in the photo, standing on the right side of his father. The picture was taken in front of the house, and Rachael briefly wondered who had taken the photograph. She thought the boy looked bothered, something about the expression on his face looked troubled.

Rachael jumped, as she saw an image of a man in the portrait glass, reflected and moving. She turned in time to see John, frowning, holding the digital camera in his hands.

He was scanning the photos he had taken less than an hour before.

"Honey, you're not going to believe this. None of those pictures turned out."

"What do you mean?"

Rachael had a sinking feeling, remembering what Kell had said earlier. Something about his son trying to take a picture once. His face had clouded over, that same troubled look she noticed on his son's face in the portrait.

"Look at this, they're all dark, like the lens cap was still on. I looked these over when I took them, they were fine then."

"Are you sure?"

"Of course I'm sure, I *saw* them. They were perfect when I checked."

"You won't get any pictures of that headstone," Kell said, making Rachael and John both jump. John actually dropped the camera on the floor, mumbling a quick "shit!" and bending over to pick it back up.

"You didn't believe me?" Kell said with a devious smile.

"Of course I believed you," John said, cradling the camera and sounding petulant.

"No, you didn't, but I don't blame you," he said. "It's a fair hard story to swallow. Sit back down on yonder couch and I'll finish the tale for you two."

"John, I think we should leave," Rachael whispered.

John looked at Rachael momentarily, considering her request. Then she saw that gleam in his eye, the one she knew meant he couldn't help himself. There was a mystery here, and John wanted to hear the rest of the story. Rachael sighed and followed her husband back to the couch, sitting on the far side, away from Kell, who was back in his chair.

"Now where was I? Ah, right. The bumps in the night, as they like to call it, eh?"

More hearty laughter came from Kell and Rachael stiffened. John leaned forward, listening intently.

"She whispers to you in the night, while you lay in your bed." Kell seemed distant now, staring off into the fire.

His change in demeanor was so abrupt; Rachael again had that uneasy feeling. It stemmed from a basic impression that Kell was a man truly haunted. She began to feel as if eyes were on her, boring into her back. She looked around the room, feeling paranoid, then foolish. She still couldn't believe any of this was real. Perhaps Kell had snuck into their room and deleted the photos John had taken? Then he replaced them with new snapshots that were dark, she reasoned. That seemed a plausible explanation.

Those headstones, they really did look brand new. Kell probably put them there, amongst the old ones, and made up the entire story. But why would he do that, she wondered? His farm was on the outskirts of town, his home the only one for miles. Surely he didn't get that many visitors, if any at all? If this was all some sort of ruse to part tourists from the cash in their wallets, it wasn't being advertised very well. John only stopped at the farm because he noticed the old cemetery and wanted to look at it, which had annoyed Rachael to no end. None of this made any sense. She sat on the musty old couch wondering now, how she had ended up here, in the middle of nowhere, in a man's house she barely knew anything about.

"She tells you to do things," Kell continued.

"She does? Wh-What does she tell you to do?" John looked at Rachael nervously, taking her hand.

"Wait," said Kell, looking John dead in the eye. "She tells me to wait. Says he'll be coming around soon."

"Who?" John said, his voice shaking a bit. "You're son?"

"No," Kell spoke so quietly they could barely hear him.

"My son is dead."

At first John wasn't sure he had heard Kell right. He glanced at Rachael, a confused look on his face. Rachael only stared at Kell, a deep feeling of dread sinking into her.

She was frozen in place; unable to believe any of this was really happening.

"What did you say?" John spoke gently.

"I said my son is dead. Pushed down the stairs. He didn't want to go along with it anymore, didn't want to stay here. Wanted no part of my family, and our cursed generations of the damned, living here alone like this. It's enough to drive a person mad, and many a man in my family went that way, you can be sure."

"Okay, this isn't funny anymore," John said, standing to leave.

"Sit down, Mr. Engall, I'm not yet done with my story," Kell spoke forcefully. "You wanted something no one else has ever seen or heard, and you're going to get it, if it's the last thing I ever do. Now sit and listen."

John sat back down, looking at Rachael with fear and apology on his face. He took her hand and squeezed it tightly. His hand was ice cold.

"She been waiting, you see? All these centuries. Waiting for it all to come back 'round. It always does, you see? She knew that. It all comes around in the end, everything does. She drove that wife to suicide, and drove her lover mad, but they had a son, and he was shipped off to England, to live with a distant relative. She had power, that woman. Ashlynn was right strong, but she had a child on the way, and was banished from the town. Had to put her focus on that, see? Then her brother died, and she took ill. She taught everything she knew to Criona, and Criona was stronger than even Ashlynn was. Strong enough to survive death, in a way. To keep on in these parts, in this land, here on my farm.

"She was strong enough to keep my family going. Always a son, each generation. Always to keep it all going. Waiting for it all to come around. She knew, somehow. Didn't matter to her how long it took. And now, here you are. Showing up on my farm, the day after I buried my son.

She knew you were coming, could feel you somehow, I suppose."

"What the hell are you talking about? What does any of this have to do with us?"

John looked at Rachael, panicked and confused. Kell looked only at John.

"Nothing to do with her," he motioned to Rachael, his eyes never leaving John.

"You're an only child, ain't ye, John?"

"Yes, but how did you…"

"What was his name?" Rachael interrupted; speaking urgently, but softly, looking at Kell with calm, cool eyes. The fear had settled deep into her, leaving her collected somehow. It was overload, and she sat frozen, unable to move, scarcely to breathe, awaiting the answer from Kell that she already knew, in her heart.

"What was the name of the man Ashlynn had the affair with?"

"Ah," Kell smiled, settling back into his chair. "I was wondering when ye might be asking me that one."

John looked at Rachael again, imploringly. Rachael only closed her eyes, not wanting to see his face.

"His name was Connor. Connor Engall. His only surviving son was Riley Engall."

"Engall?" John said, his voice shaking.

"That's right. What I presume to be your great-great-great-great-great-great-great grandfather, many times removed. It don't matter much, though. Like she says, it all comes around in the end. Ashlynn's daughter was killed, but by that time, Ashlynn was no longer of this world. Ashlynn's lover, Connor Engall had died in a crazy-house, and his son, Riley Engall was an older man with a son of his own, living too far off for her reach. So, Criona waited.

"Time's not the same in the spirit world, s'far as I can tell. It moves differently. To her, this has all been some sort of game, taking mere minutes to play out, for all I know.

For my family, it's been centuries of madness, torture. Constantly haunted by her presence, and those damn headstones. All because my ancestors were the ones to take over this land, so cheap it was. We were the ones cursed to live out that witch's game! My son wanted out, thought he could end it all for us by simply leaving, but she would have none of it. She knew it was time, knew you were comin', even if you didn't know where you were goin' next, or how ye really got here. Drawn here, ye were. Drawn back to the place where your bloodline began. It all comes around in the end," Kell laughed, and Rachael felt sorry for him, even as sickened as she was.

John sat frozen in his place on the couch. Rachael stood facing Kell O'Donough.

"So, what happens now?" she asked.

"Now, ye go and pay your respects to Criona's headstone," Kell said to John, still not looking at her.

John looked at Kell blankly, then behind him at Rachael who had stood up from the couch and was now backing away from him. She stopped when her back hit the wall, standing directly next to the portrait of Kell and his dead son.

"Rachael?" John looked infinitely hurt. "Honey?"

"I'm sorry, John," she sighed and closed her eyes, not wanting to look at him. Her hand subconsciously went to her abdomen and settled there. Kell looked at John, waiting. Behind him, the front door of the house opened slowly, creaking, allowing a cold wind to blow in.

"She's waiting for ye, Mr. Engall," Kell said.

John walked towards the door on numb feet, as if on autopilot. His mind told him this was all some kind of elaborate joke. He was floating, as if in a dream, and all of this did indeed feel completely surreal to him. He swam through the front door, carried by an unseen force, leading the way. The door closed behind him and Kell and Rachael were alone. There was no sound but the wood crackling in the fireplace and a slight whistling of wind down the chimney. Rachael stood where she was, frozen for what felt like an eternity. Her hand still lay on her stomach. She felt ill. Kell smiled, still sitting in his chair.

Suddenly there was a loud, piercing scream, which sounded almost like a small child waking from a bad dream, and yet, Rachael knew it was John. She stumbled over to the couch and fell into it, crumbling.

"Ye did the right thing, Missus," Kell said. "She woulda taken him anyway. This way was better for everyone."

Rachael began to cry, cradling herself in her arms.

"It wasn't your fault," Kell said. "You know that, don't ye?"

"It wasn't John's fault, either," she said bitterly. "He had nothing to do with any of this. It was six hundred years ago!"

"There's no need to yell, missus."

Rachael began to sob. Her head ached.

"There is one wee bit of business yet to take to," Kell said gently. "Your husband didn't know you were expecting, did he?"

Rachael looked at Kell through her tears, her heart suddenly skipping a beat.

"I...I don't know what you're talking about," she whispered.

"Course ye do, missus," Kell said gently. "You're carrying John's child in your belly. That's why you let him go, so as not to create a commotion, nothing to harm your baby, like a good mum would. I understand," Kell said, smiling at Rachael.

"You're crazy!"

She lurched from the couch and ran to the front door, trying to open it. It was locked. She turned the deadbolt, which should have unlocked the door, yet it was still sealed tightly.

"Can't get out, missus," Kell said sadly. "My son tried, and she took care of him. If she don' want you to leave, you won't. Besides there's business yet to take care of. I can still feel her around, her presence. She ain't through just yet. John was an only child, but…"

"No," Rachael said softly. "No."

"I'm sorry, missus. No choice, really. It all comes around in the end. She don' want you, like you said. You've got nothing to do with any of this, save for what you're carrying inside, and I expect she'll take care of that soon enough."

Rachael felt sick to her stomach. A sudden pain wrenched her abdomen and she fell to the floor, doubled over. Cold, invisible hands squeezed her insides. Kell stood from his chair and walked into the kitchen.

"Help me," Rachael said, reaching her arm out to grasp his leg as he passed her. Blood was already beginning to soak the crotch of her pants, warm and sticky. Kell walked past, unscathed.

"Have to check on that stew," Kell said. "It should be ready any time now."

A knot popped in the fireplace and sparks of ember floated upward into the darkness of the flue. Outside, in the night, the chilly wind blew and whistled through the trees. All else was silent.

The Life and Multiple Deaths of Virgil Eugene

The Robot *felt*...wonderment. He stared at the rainbow-haloed, luminescent bulbs above him. The colors made him *feel*; something he hadn't been able to do for quite some time. How long it had been, he couldn't be certain. He lay on the polythene-foam boxing mat, marinating in his own sweat and stink and frowned- something else he hadn't been able to do in eons.

In reality, his last facial expression depicting any type of emotion had come just ten months prior. It was the day he was brought into the Warden's office and told he would be part of a new 'experiment'. The Robot recalled that day as if he were reliving it in real time.

"You're going to be part of a cutting edge development in human mental conditioning," the Warden said.

Inmate number 186905, previously referred to as Virgil Eugene, frowned. He opened his mouth to protest, to inquire, to defend, but the door immediately opened and he was whisked away by five guards with batons. Fighting would be futile. Of course, had he fully realized what was about to happen to him, what was about to be done, he would have fought to no end: to the death.

The Life and Multiple Deaths of Virgil Eugene

His last memory as Virgil Eugene was of being laid on a table in a sterile white room, and a musky-smelling plastic mask was placed over his nose and mouth.

"Breathe deep, one-eight-six-nine-zero-five," the technician said, in a lifeless tone.

Virgil Eugene breathed deeply. Then he closed his eyes- and died.

His next memory was hazy, as he now recalled it, lying on his back on the mat. He knew where he was, but it was like waking from a bad dream. As his memories crashed back in on him, he merely converted from one nightmare to another.

"Do you know your name?"

Inmate number 186905 only stared at the man. Tabula Rasa; he was a blank mental slate. The man smiled. Inmate number 186905- now bald and sporting an ugly-red, stitched incision laterally across his scalp — did not smile back. He wasn't programmed to.

"Do you know what has happened to you?"

Again, no response. The doctor nodded, looking pleased.

"Your brain has been altered; manipulated by a thin sheath of complex, spider-web thin wiring and something called a Motherboard, all outfitted with a transmitter: not unlike what you see in a standard RCA Victor. You're a

prototype, number one-eight-six-nine-oh-five. Your brain is now being controlled by this device I hold in my hand."

The doctor revealed a gray box in his palm, with tiny buttons and a stick in the middle.

"Your limbic system has been 'rewired', so-to-speak. This system is part of a complex set of structures that lies on both sides of the thalamus and includes the hypothalamus, the hippocampus, and the amygdala. The hypothalamus is responsible for regulating your hunger, thirst, response to pain, levels of pleasure, sexual drive, your anger and aggression, and more. Your hippocampus is the area of your brain responsible for converting your experiences into memory. The amygdala, when stimulated electronically, further controls aggression. Tiny transponders in your brain are now in place, at receptor sites, to intercept the signals your brain receives. In this way, we can effectively cut off the sensory neurons that tell your mind you are feeling heat, cold, and even pain. Do you comprehend what I am telling you?"

The inmate only continued to stare. He had no thoughts of his own. He felt nothing.

"We've attempted this with prototypes; in machines. The problem is, it is simply far too complex to reconstruct a mechanical likeness of the human body. Robots, these are called. Or, in the event of full-bodied human likeness, the term android has been applied. But my job was to take the actual human body, and simply convert the brain. Rather than build a whole robot, why not simply rebuild the human mind?"

The doctor had a mad gleam in his eyes. They shone.

"Of course, the experiments on human beings would be extensive and in most cases: deadly. There'd be an outcry, and who would volunteer for an experimental procedure such as that? No one would. But no one cares about you, do they, one-eight-six-nine-oh-five? You're a hardened criminal. And criminals die in prison every day, don't they? Shanked by fellow inmates, or simply beaten to death in the yard. Or they hang themselves with their own bed sheets, and no one even knows."

The doctor stood. Inmate number 186905 did not follow him with his eyes.

"Many have died for me to reach this point in my research. You are the first to live. From this point forward, your name shall be The Robot. It's what you are, after all. You will not feel hungry, tired, sad, or any other human emotion. You will not feel pain, or cold. You are under my control. The sections of your brain that control the production and excretion of adrenaline can also be manipulated, to temporarily increase your stamina and strength. Nod if you understand my words, Robot."

The Robot nodded. The doctor nodded back and smiled. The Robot did not smile in response.

"What you were before your conversion has been short-circuited. Your current mind has no access to previous events or memories from before today. You will not make new memories. Each day will be your first and only moment of existence."

But something had gone wrong.

For eight months, The Robot slept, ate, and worked. He made no new memories. Each day, he awoke anew and did what he was ordered to do. At first, he lifted heavy things, and his back did not ache. He built walls, structures, whole buildings. He hammered in the rain, worked in the snow, and never felt cold. He carried large boxes and handled inventory. He labored and did the work of ten men, and never became fatigued, nor did he once complain.

The Robot never spoke. He wasn't programmed to. He slept when told to. He never defecated or urinated unless told to, at regular intervals. He was kept away from the other inmates, until one day, the doctor had an idea.

"I want to test control of your aggression and strength, Robot. You will box with another inmate. You will follow all the rules, but you will hit him until he goes down and does not get back up."

In the recreation room, The Robot was put into the ring with a fellow inmate. When the time came to fight, he felt a sudden surge of adrenaline-energy flood into his veins. The usual accompaniment of euphoria was absent. The Robot simply threw his punches at the other man. They hit with great force.

He was not perfect in his technique. He took many hits. His lip split open, his right eye swelled shut, and his nose was crushed. He bled profusely, but felt no pain. For every punch he took, he delivered a hit, until both men should have lain unconscious on the mat, equally destroyed, yet, The Robot stood in the end, over the unconscious body of the other fighter, feeling nothing.

His wounds were tended to and dressed. The Robot was treated, his body healed. Then he went back to working for the Warden and the doctor. They had begun a betting pool with all the correctional officers and guards on the floor of Cell B. The Robot could not be beat, and eventually, he was fighting several bouts a week, entertaining everyone, and the Warden and the doctor were making a nice supplemental income.

Ten months into The Robot's existence, he took a hit to the temple. Unbeknownst to the doctor, something shifted loose; some vital wiring, an intrinsic part of the webbing connecting his brain to the Motherboard. For the first time in the ring, The Robot went down – and stayed down – for he stared up at the lights in wonderment at their colors.

He lay in astonishment at the sudden return of his feelings. His body ached, his wounds stung madly. He frowned. Memories came crashing back of who he was; who he had been before he'd become The Robot. Every moment of his thirty-eight years upon the Earth flooded back into his awareness. Connections were made, between the past and the present, and The Robot suddenly comprehended what had happened to him.

The Robot became *Virgil Eugene* again. He was reborn, and he recalled his death, for that was what had happened to him. He had died. Losing himself in such a way, he was never so relieved to be who he was, as in that moment, despite his mistakes and even his crimes. For, he *knew* who he was. He *knew* that he was *alive*. He *felt*, and *thought*, and was *aware*. He began to cry. There was no control.

The doctor witnessed this. He grimaced.

"Damn."

A stretcher was brought. Guards in white coats and members of the medical staff carried inmate number 186905 off the mat. The broken man could do nothing but lay in shock, drained- traumatized by the reality of what he'd been made into, and what he'd been stripped of.

Every task, every long day of physical labor, spans of days without sleep, stretches without food, followed by surges of aggressive shock, in the ring, fighting; it all came back to Virgil with a shocking clarity.

It was all a blur that drained him of every ounce of energy his body was now manufacturing again on its own, without orders. His heart, his mind, his body cried out, and He screamed in a war cry.

"I am Virgil Eugene! I am Virgil Eugene! *I am!! I am!!* I am Virgil Eugene!"

He sobbed.

By the time he realized where he was and what they were about to do to him, yet again; it was too late. He fought feebly, but there were too many guards, too many medical staff members. Too much had happened to him, and there was nowhere for him to run. He could not get away. He'd already been stripped of his rights, for his crimes. He'd disappeared from the world. Already, he had ceased to exist.

They were about to murder him for the second time.

"Breathe deep, one-eight-six-nine-zero-five," the technician said, in a lifeless tone.

With the mask covering his nose and mouth, his words were hazy, muffled and lost.

"I am Virgil Eugene. I *am...* "

Virgil Eugene breathed deeply. Then he closed his eyes, and died; again.

His next awareness was in-the-moment. The Robot opened his eyes, saw the doctor, and sat up as he was ordered to. The doctor smiled.

"Do you know your name?"

The Robot only stared at the man.

"Do you know what has happened to you?"

Again, no response. The doctor nodded, looking pleased.

"Your circuits have been replaced. It's a miracle we were able to go back in and do the work without killing you. I suppose if I were a philosophical man, I'd surmise that you were *meant* for this experiment, Robot. Your new circuits are much more deeply implanted. I don't believe they'll come loose this time around. To be on the safe side, however, we'll avoid any traumas to the head for a bit, hmm?"

The Robot only continued to stare. Tabula Rasa; he had no thoughts of his own.

"We're going to move on from boxing, Robot," the doctor said. "Let's see how you do with assassination training."

The doctor smiled again. The Robot did not smile back. He did not know humor. He did not even know his God-given name, or that he'd been born twice and died as many times. He'd been stripped of that which made him a man: his identity, his personality — his soul.

In the end, The Robot felt nothing. He wasn't programmed to.

Aunt Beck

It is commonly said that there is one crazy person in every family. I used to laugh at that joke whenever I heard it in a movie. I laughed even harder whenever that joke came up in real life. I laughed at it because I felt it was true. I felt it was true because I had a crazy person in MY family. Although crazy is really a flippant term. I prefer eccentric when it comes down to it.

Everyone in my family knew who the strange one was. I had a crazy aunt. She never had a boyfriend, always lived alone. She never had less than 3 dogs in her house. If one died, she'd go get a new one the very same day. She dressed in outrageous outfits you could see coming from a mile away. Everything was bright, flamboyant and fluorescent if possible. Neon was a plus.

My crazy Aunt Beck, short for Rebecca, never finished a complete sentence. Her stories consisted of run-on sentences that all connected. She'd only stop long enough to take a breath. It was easy to forget to breathe while listening to one of her silly tales. She had a talent for turning the simplest event, like a trip to the grocery store, into a vivid and eventful epic. She had a beautiful soul.

I remember once, her spinning a tale about the shrew infestation she'd discovered in her couch and closet. The story went on for over an hour. The first half I was laughing so hard I had tears streaming down my face. The second half of the tale was somber and morbid. That half was about the de-infestation.

Yes, my Aunt Beck was nuts. She was also funny, lively, and a mystery. There were days when she wouldn't stop shopping until she literally dropped. Then there were the other days; the crazy days where she wouldn't speak at all.

For as high as she could fly, she could fall just as low. These were the days where she didn't finish a sentence. Not because she was talking too fast for the period pause to register on your brain, but because she would simply trail off in mid-sentence, as if lost in thought, her face becoming dark.

People in my family joked about crazy Aunt Beck. We would all laugh when she wasn't around. Later in college, I studied psychology and put a name to what Aunt Beck was: bipolar. I thought I knew everything. I thought I could study the world from a book and know all its secrets.

It's funny how a person's world can change in an instant. How everything they think they know can just float away. I would forget to breathe when Aunt Beck told one of her run-on stories. She always could bring up those high-end emotions in people. Two days ago, I read a letter from Aunt Beck, and she took my breath away, yet again. Just one last time. The letter she wrote me told a story; a simple, sad story, one that I won't ever forget. The letter contained only one sentence, but that was enough. Aunt Beck always did have a talent. I'll tell you what her letter said, but first, I have to go back eight years...

***

Aunt Beck had gotten old. I had gotten older. I graduated from college and started working as a therapist in people's homes, while earning my Master's. Students are much cheaper to pay than graduates. So, I went to people's houses and worked three-hour sessions with their autistic children for nine dollars an hour. I ate mac 'n cheese or Taco Bell every night for dinner, and didn't go out to drink with friends. Drinks are too damn expensive.

During summer break, I flew home to visit the family, including Aunt Beck. I was the only person in the family who truly appreciated her personality. I always went to the movies or shopped with her. We used to have lunch twice a month before I moved out of state for school. I hadn't been home in over a year though, and when I first saw Aunt Beck at the airport (she was my ride) I knew something inside her had changed.

She was dressed in her usual flamboyant colors, a huge neon pink flower fastened in her hair, which was pulled back into a bun. She had never been a thin woman, rather a bit large. I could see as I walked out into the terminal now, though, that she had become gargantuan. Her face was pale and shiny, her makeup on even thicker than usual. I knew she was having one of her dark times. I didn't know how dark until two days later at her house.

I went over to see her new clock, one of her many shopping gems. It was in the shape of a sun, and every hour-on the hour- it played music from a sun-themed song. I arrived just in time to catch the 5 O'clock rendition of "Here Comes the Sun."

Aunt Beck had a sheen of oil on her skin so thick you could probably mop it off with a kerchief and wring it out into a frying pan to cook with. She smelled bad, like she hadn't showered for at least a few days. She had dark circles under her eyes. Her house was a mess. It was always a mess, but this time it was bad. I mean, really bad. I began to worry about my health just being in there and breathing the stale air. It was the kind of mess that doesn't just happen overnight. This had been going on for a while. Months, if not longer. There were flies in the kitchen. The counter was covered with dirty dishes piled up for weeks. I couldn't see the counters anymore.

As I continued further into her home, it looked like she'd been on a shopping spree from hell. There were boxes everywhere that were unopened. Things she had bought and just brought home to stack on top of other boxes of more things she'd bought. In her spare bedroom, there was a mountain of clothes, all with the price tags still on. Like I said, it was bad.

We sat down on her couch, which was the only clear area in the whole living room. I couldn't help but recall her story from a few years back about it being infested with shrews. I didn't sit back all the way.

We were friends, Aunt Beck and I. More than anyone else in my family. If she needed to talk to anyone about what was wrong with her, it would be me. I knew then that she had asked me over to her house for just that reason. She'd brought me into this place knowing I'd see the mess. Knowing that I would know there was something very wrong in her world. I was also educated now, with a psychology degree, albeit, an undergraduate bachelors. Maybe she thought I was finally qualified to hear what she told me that day. She didn't go into it slowly, she just launched right in.

"You know I'm not normal, Jaime." She said it as a statement. "I know you know that. I know that."

I didn't know what to say. Working with autistic children did not qualify me for dealing with statements like that.

"You're old enough to know the truth now, Jaime. I know you were only two when your grandfather died, but he was my father. I know you never got to know him at all. I have a story to tell you about him. I think after you hear it, you'll understand me a lot better."

"Okay," I said slowly, trying to sound reassuring, for Aunt Beck had already begun to dab at her eyes with her fingers a bit. "Take your time, Beck. I'm listening."

She paused for a moment longer then jumped in, as if it was one of her happy tales of shopping, or a run-in with a driver with road rage. She told me about when she and my father were kids and they lived out in the country. It was the early 1960's when there still was country. I mean, real country. The kind where it took a whole day to go into town and back.

They had lived on a homestead in the wilderness where you had to fly in by plane. Beck's father had bought a huge plot of land in northern Alaska. The story was so surreal I almost didn't believe it. My father had lived in Alaska as a kid? How could I not know that? Aunt Beck told me a story I'd never heard before. A story of a brother and sister who went fishing one day. A story about a brother who, for some reason, went to cut his sister's fishing line with an axe and accidentally put the blade through his own ankle.

"Your father almost died that day. He nearly cut his whole foot off," said Aunt Beck.

The story continued. It took a whole day to get a plane out to the homestead to take my father and his father into town where he could have his ankle mended. I didn't know where the story was going. I would soon find out. My father and grandfather returned a week later by plane. My father would walk with a slight limp for the rest of his life. A limp I had been told was from an injury while fighting a fire, for my father would grow up to be a firefighter. It is so surreal to hear a story and have it 'undo' an older story. To hear a different version of events from what you've been told. It's like having your memories half-erased. I listened to my Aunt Beck tell her story as if everything I'd known about my family was being changed as I listened, for in reality, it was.

"I had gone fishing by myself while they were gone in town," Beck continued. "I'm not sure exactly how I did it, but somehow I managed to get the fish hook stuck in my finger. And I mean *stuck*." She paused. "Grandma couldn't get it out. It had gotten embedded in the bone, and even worse, the whole damn end of my finger had swollen up to five times its normal size."

I winced.

"There was no pulling that thing out and just healing. I needed medical attention. I needed a doctor."

My aunt Beck was already starting to cry again. I still didn't know why.

"So here comes my father off the plane after being gone for a week with your dad, and his ankle's all wrapped up. Our dad had to pay cash to cover all the hospital bills. And what's worse, he'd been gone a whole week, which up where we were, was a big deal. He was trying to build a cabin for us to live in before winter, because once winter hit, you couldn't build anymore. You just couldn't. And here he goes, losing a whole week of his precious summer."

I had to interject at this point in the story. I asked Aunt Beck if the cabin wasn't built yet, what the heck were they living in?

"That's the whole crux of the thing, you see? Our dad had us living in a one-bedroom shack, since that one room was the only part of the house that had the roof on. The rest of the damn house was open to the daylight. Even in summer, that sucker got colder than hell at night. We were freezing all of the time. I think that made my finger even worse."

"Jesus," I couldn't help saying. But Beck just kept going on, as if I hadn't said anything.

"So anyway, here comes my dad off the plane, and what happens? He comes back to the homestead only to find he's got to take another injured kid back on the plane and go into town again. Well of course, he had to take me in. I mean, he could see it was bad. If he hadn't taken me to the doctor, I would have lost my finger. It would have gotten infected, and I probably would have died, even. He had no choice. But I could see that he was pissed."

Beck got up then to grab a tissue. I could sense that we were about to get to the bad part. She'd begun trembling a bit, her fingers were shaking as she wiped at her eyes.

"My dad was pissed," she said again, "and he let me know it, too. My father let me know that it was all *my* fault he wasn't going to finish that cabin on time. He had to sell the land and we ended up moving out-of-state, to civilization after that summer. But it was the summer from Hell. It changed my whole life, Jaime. My father never forgave me for ruining his dream. He punished me for the rest of my time growing up with him. Every chance he got."

I had to interject there again. I had to point out that the whole first week of going into town had been to mend my father's ankle. The trip to town for Beck's finger only took two days.

"It didn't matter, Jaime. It was because he had to turn around and go back into town a *second time*. It did something to him. It put him over the edge. And the second time was for my injury, so somehow it all became my fault. Never mind that the whole idea of a homestead, and a cabin was crazy to begin with. The whole thing was a crazy financial mishap just waiting to happen. But my dad didn't want to see that. So he found his excuse. He blamed it all on me. And he tortured me for the rest of my life."

"Tortured you?" I didn't know what she meant. "What do you mean?"

"Well, here's how it happened. We got to the doctor's and he got that hook out of my finger. He had to cut through my skin all the way to the bone and somehow he managed to work the hook out of the bone. I almost passed out from the pain. It had gotten all filled with puss from the swelling. That damn hook had been in my finger at that point for three days. They didn't have painkillers back then, not like they do now. Or if they did, he didn't use any. I often wonder if my dad told the doctor not to use any to avoid the extra costs. He was that upset with me for keeping him off his land again."

I was wincing again. The thought of my aunt Beck, a young girl at age twelve, having her finger cut open to the bone with no painkillers, just got to me. I thought that's what she meant when she said her dad had tortured her. I was wrong.

"After it was all done, I was about ready to pass out. I had tensed up so much while he was cutting. And he had to clean it out too, with all that puss. That hurt like hell. My dad just stood there watching, with this look on his face, almost as if he was enjoying it all. He didn't hold my hand or try to comfort me. He just stood there, watching."

She paused again, to dab at her eyes. It must really hurt recalling stories like that. Almost like it's happening to you all over again. That's how Beck made it seem, anyhow. I hated hearing her story, but she was only halfway done.

"We stayed in a hotel overnight. The plane couldn't fly us back 'til daylight the next day. My dad didn't want to pay extra for two rooms, so we stayed together in the same room, and slept in the same bed. It was this awful, tiny, little room, and the bed was barely big enough for one person, let alone two.

"My dad was still upset with me. That night I lay in bed next to him, and I could feel how tense he was. How mad he was at me. That was bad enough. But then, my whole world changed, in an instant. It felt like a dream. My dad was lying on his back. Then he rolled over and lifted the covers and looked at me. I was twelve, and starting to go through puberty, so I was really self-conscious about my body. My dad knew this, I could tell he did. He lifted up those covers and looked at me and said the words that would scar me for life."

She paused for a moment. At first I thought the pause was meant to be dramatic, for the sake of the story. Then I saw how she was crying and her mouth was pursed shut. She was having trouble getting out what she had to say next. Finally, she said it.

"He said it to me matter-of-factly, like it was no big deal."

Beck lowered her voice to mimic a man's.

"Lift up your nightgown, I wanna see what you got."

"What?!" I couldn't help but exclaim. I had never heard a word of this story before. I could hardly believe the first half. The story had now become completely unreal to me.

"Yeah," Aunt Beck wasn't crying now. She seemed to be upset in a different way, an almost angry way.

"That's what he said. I'll never forget it." She paused briefly then continued. "Now, I know what you're thinking came next. And I thought that's where it was going, too. I thought for sure any moment my dad was going to reach over and grab me, but he didn't. He just lay there waiting to see what I would do. I was frozen at first. That one sentence kept ringing in my head over and over again. It still haunts me to this day, because it was that one sentence that started it all. All the torture." A very long pause. Then Aunt Beck went on, in that husky voice.

"Lift up your nightgown, I wanna see what you got." She looked really angry now.

"I finally did move, after what seemed like forever, and when I did, it felt like I was moving in slow motion. I remember thinking to myself that I had to move slowly, like you would if you were staring down a wild animal or something. You know how you're not supposed to make any quick movements?" Beck didn't wait for me to acknowledge that I had heard that saying ever, before she continued on.

"I somehow knew instinctively that if I could just get up out of that bed, everything would be okay. I knew that he wouldn't come after me once I was up. I can't explain how, but I just knew that. I sat up slowly, and then I scooted down towards the end of the bed. When my feet finally touched the floor, I knew I was going to be okay. I got out of that bed, and I lay down on the floor and went to sleep."

I got a weird feeling then. Like something was amiss. Something just felt wrong. I couldn't identify what it was, but something just wasn't right. Hell, the whole story just wasn't right.

"That's what happened?" I asked. "That's how he tortured you?"

"No, that was just the start," she continued. "He saw what saying that had done to me. He saw the fear in my eyes. I could tell he enjoyed it. You see, the thing is, Jamie, he wanted me to live in fear of him. Of what he *might* do. Of what he *could* do. He didn't have to touch me to abuse me. What he did to me was almost worse. He mentally tortured me from that day forward."

"How?" I couldn't help but ask.

"Whenever we were in a room alone together from that night on, he'd look me up and down, as if he was checking me out. He wouldn't do it when my mom was in the room. He'd wait until it was just us. It got to the point where I avoided ever being in the same room with him. He'd make comments when no one was there, about my breasts, or my ass. He'd say things that no father should ever say to his daughter. Things that just weren't right. And let me tell you, Jaime. It hurts just as much mentally having your own father say things like that to you, as it would to have him go after you. You see, it was almost just as bad, knowing that at any moment he *could* come after me. That he *might* come after me. He never actually did, but for years, I didn't know that. I thought at any time it would happen. I lived every day of my life from age twelve to age eighteen just waiting for him to finally grab me, but he never did."

"Jesus," I said again, but I was breathing a sigh of relief at this point.

"When I turned eighteen and graduated from high school, I got out of that house just as fast as I could. But, see, growing up that way had scarred me. Having my own father put me through that every day for so many years. I was never relaxed at home. I was a total wreck constantly for six years. The most important years developmentally that a young girl goes through. Honestly, I could never relax around any man after what my father put me through. Every time I tried to date, or have a boyfriend in my twenties, he would eventually say something. Something 'sexy' that he would mean as a joke, like maybe, how he wanted to see me dress up for him, or strip for him, and God help me, I'd just hear that damn thing my father said to me when I was twelve."

She paused again.

"Lift up your nightgown, I wanna see what you got."

Another pause.

"He ruined my life," Beck dabbed at her eyes again. She was no longer angry. "And lately, I've been thinking about it again. I don't know why. It's just been on my mind."

I thought hard before I spoke to her. Finally, I said, "Maybe it's been long enough, and you've been thinking about it because it was time to let it all out."

"Yeah," she said, and started to cry harder. She said other things that day, and so did I.

We talked about how keeping secrets like that can hurt you even more. We talked about how keeping things like that all locked up inside you can turn it into something even more ugly than what it was to begin with. I tried to empathize with her, and tried to imagine how it would have felt if *my* dad had ever said anything like that to me. I didn't even want to think about it.

Still, I reasoned, there were lots of young girls who'd had the exact same thing happen to them, and many times even worse. I'd studied psychology for heaven's sake. I'd heard similar stories from girls in college even. Stories that involved what I imagined might have happened to Aunt Beck if she hadn't gotten out of that bed that night and lay down on the floor. Stories of fathers who *had* gone after their daughters, time and time again. I reasoned that those people (many of them) had gone on to live normal lives. Many daughters lived through that and still went on to marry and have families of their own. They still were able to grow up and have successful relationships with men.

Of course, Aunt Beck was a character, and perhaps it was just her specific personality that made it all worse inside her head. She was really sensitive, and strange. And I hadn't lived through it. No matter how she had described it to me, maybe it was worse than I could ever imagine, being haunted your whole life by one sentence. Maybe I just could never understand that kind of pain. I wish that were true. And in many ways it is. I will never know the pain Aunt Beck felt every time that one sentence ran through her head, intruding many times, unwanted, in her adult life. But I do know how one sentence can haunt you. I know that now.

"Lift up your nightgown, I wanna see what you got."

Out of nowhere, when she hadn't seen it coming at all.

I guess that's how all bad things happen to people: Suddenly. I know that's how it happened with me.

I finished my visit home that summer, and went back to my life as a student/therapist. I didn't enjoy the work so much anymore. Actually, I never really had. It wasn't what I'd thought it would be. I had wanted to help people. I had wanted to make them feel better. But all I could see now in my fake therapy sessions I did with fellow students were potentially dangerous secrets lying just behind their eyes. Whether they told me their secrets or not, didn't matter. All that mattered to me was that whatever their secrets were, whatever had happened in their lives to cause whatever damage they had accrued, I couldn't fix it. I couldn't change the bad things that had happened to people. How do you fix broken things? I thought I'd learned that from reading books. I thought I could study how to fix people's heads. I hadn't known in school, at the still childish age of twenty-two that there are ghosts in people's heads. Ghosts that are invisible, sometimes even to the people who are haunted by them.

I never made it through graduate school. I met a boy and fell in love. I got married (so now I'm Jaime Metoyer) and had two kids. I worked for a while longer as a therapist, but that ended when I had a baby to take care of. I'll go back to work eventually, I guess.

I like to make up my own stories to tell the kids at bedtime. I read them children's books too, but my stories are more fun. They smile more when I tell my own stories. My husband says I should write them down, that I seem to have a talent for telling stories. I should be writing a children's story on this page right now, but Aunt Beck's story is what came out. Funny, in a way, it *is* a children's story. It happened to her when she was still a child. Aunt Beck.

***

Six months ago, I got the call that my crazy Aunt Beck had died. She hadn't been taking care of herself. The shape she'd been in the last time I'd seen her was even worse than the day she'd told me her story, and even that had been four years before. I never told my dad I knew about the homestead, or where his limp really came from. I never asked him about Alaska, and he's never told me. It was, after all, just one short summer. Maybe he'd forgotten it.

Aunt Beck had died of a heart attack, and when she died, she'd weighed a whopping 315 pounds, at an adult height of 5'5". I thought talking about her hidden pain would help her to begin healing. I guess I was wrong. She let herself go. There's more than one way for a person to kill themselves.

Someone had to go through all of her stuff, and the condition her house was in when she died, it was no small task. No one wanted to do it, but I went in with my dad over a three-day weekend, and we cleared out all that junk. Salvation Army was very happy that week. We didn't keep much, really. The photo albums, my dad kept. I kept her sun clock. And I kept something else I found at her house, too.

In the nightstand next to her bed, she had a jewelry cache where she kept her earrings and things, at least the ones she wore most often. She had a ton of jewelry, but just this little cache of the most important pieces right next to her bed. I figured I'd keep those pieces, but when I opened the very bottom drawer there was no jewelry in it, just an envelope with my name on it. It was sealed. I didn't know how long it had been in there, or when she had written it. I didn't want to open it and read it there with my dad around, so I quickly stuffed the envelope in my pocket. My Dad hadn't seen. I waited until I was on the plane flying back home to my family to read it.

I guess I knew it was going to be something ugly. I mean, why write a letter to someone and never give it to them? I figured it must contain something in it that would make me upset. Or maybe it was something that had made her upset, too upset to mail it to me. At any rate, she hadn't thrown it away; she had kept it right there next to her bed. She had slept next to that letter for who knows how many months, or even years.

I guess she figured I would eventually find it and read it. Maybe it was the thought of what that letter contained that made her let herself go the way she did. Knowing the deepest, darkest part of her life was down on paper, and put out into the world.

I thought that talking to someone and getting the pain out into the open was a part of the healing process, but for Aunt Beck it was the beginning of a slow and agonizing downward spiral into self-destruction.

It's amazing how a person's life can change in an instant. It's amazing how one sentence can change the way you view the whole world. One sentence had been the beginning of my beautiful Aunt Beck's life changing forever, when she was still only a child. It only took one sentence for these things to happen to me, and as always, crazy old Aunt Beck took my breath away for one last time. I opened the envelope and slipped out the paper inside, folded in half. It only contained one sentence, but that was enough for me to finally understand her pain.

Aunt Beck

Dear Jaime,

I'm sorry I lied...I never did get out of that bed.

–Beck

Ava Kate

Ava Kate had often wondered what a situation like this would feel like. It happened all the time in movies or books. A seemingly ordinary trip to deposit a paycheck at the bank, interrupted by a sudden proclamation of, "This is a robbery!"

When it actually happened, she thought it was a joke at first. Suddenly thrust into an action film, she looked around at the other faces, to see if anyone else was taking it seriously. They were. She had lain prostrate on the floor like everyone else. When the adrenaline began coursing through her, she felt alive.

Glancing up at the masked man closest to her, she noted, in a surreal way, how young he must be. Only young men could look that fit and trim in a skin-tight black t-shirt. He glanced down at her, looking up at him, and their eyes met. His eyes were blue and clear, and in an instant, Ava Kate knew he was handsome, regardless of the black ski mask.

The sirens were disconcerting. It meant a definitive end to her special story. Ava Kate was not ready for her story to end, when it had only barely begun. In her mundane life, this was the most exciting thing to ever have happened to her, and she cherished it already. It would be a story to tell her grandchildren someday. If only there were more to it, she longed.

She feared for the young man in the black shirt. He would most certainly be caught. There was no escape now. When he bent low and grabbed her hand, pulling her to her feet, she felt rejuvenated. As he spun her around and placed her back against his chest, she relished the feel of his heart beating heavily. He was just as alive as she.

His heavy arm rested across her collarbone, his strong hand clasping her left shoulder. As he pulled her toward the bank entrance, she reached up her own hand and clasped it over his. On the nightly newsreels that played over and over again, she looked like a frightened young woman, clutching desperately to her captor in sheer terror, her eyes closed, not wanting to see the horror that was happening to her. A grainy image caught by a cell phone, only a very sensitive eye would ever catch the slight upward curve at the edges of her mouth, and even then, they might mistake it for a vain attempt at self-consolation, a sort of defense mechanism.

At the moment her hand clasped onto his, there was a brief hesitation from the man; a surprised sort of faltering, his hand loosening slightly on her shoulder, his breath catching for a moment. Then his breathing resumed, in deep bursts, his hand tightening again, more securely, more forcefully, yet at the same time, gentle, as Ava Kate went with his movements.

She closed her eyes and filled her mind with the warmth against her back, the steady rise and fall of his chest, and the constant rhythm of his heart as they danced together out the front door. He had claimed her as his own. She belonged to him, and that was just fine. No bullet would touch her, and as long as that were so, nothing would harm him. She would be his shield, his protection- his salvation.

For a moment, he seemed unsure of what she would do. He seemed to be giving her a choice. He did not shove her into the car. His arm dropped, as if he were allowing her to simply walk away. Ava Kate felt naked, suddenly cold. For just one moment, she felt the chill of death, which was loneliness. Then the warmth returned, as she felt his hand on the middle of her back, gently urging her into the passenger seat. They understood each other now.

He knew she would not run, and unlike the police and the stunned spectators, he also knew she was not his hostage.

An odd way to meet, he mused, but still, it would be a story to tell the grandkids someday.

His partner had never come out of the bank, but this did not concern the man. He had what he needed. This was a new lease on life, and he felt it. This job had never been his idea. In an instant, as he started the car, with this woman sitting compliantly next to him, he knew how everything should be.

As she placed her hands in her lap, her trim legs leaning in his direction, he knew he would go straight. With the money in the bag, they would drive away to some mid-sized town, get simple jobs and live ordinary lives together. Money did not matter, only this woman who had saved him, turned his life around. The engine revved and he put it into gear, not glancing at her, but feeling her anticipation, which was…

"Sweetie it's time for bed," Molly's mother said.

Molly blinked and looked at her mother. She was cross at being interrupted in the middle of her reverie.

"Are you upset?"

"Hmm?"

Molly sat dazed on the couch. Her mother looked at her, concern in her eyes. She flicked the remote in the direction of the television, turning it off.

"Honestly, I don't know why I watch the news right before bed. It tends to give me nightmares," she said.

Then she looked at her daughter, again with the concern.

"You are upset, aren't you?"

"No," Molly stated, shrugging her shoulders.

She was afraid her mother knew what she had been thinking about.

"About that awful story, with that woman," her mother went on. "You got so quiet and still after they showed that footage of her being taken by that robber."

"It didn't bother me," Molly shrugged again, getting up to leave.

"It's okay, if it did," her mother reassured her. "It upset me too, that poor woman."

Molly's mother fidgeted with her necklace. The skin around her eyes creased with worry.

"Can you even imagine what she must be going through? What she must have felt, being taken like that?"

Her voice had risen now. She was getting all worked up. Suddenly she cried out, sounding almost guilty.

"I don't even remember her name, do you?"

"Ava Kate," Molly said. "Her name was Ava Kate."

"She was so young…and he actually got away with it, too," she almost whined. "I mean, anything could be happening to that poor woman right now, absolutely anything."

"Yes, anything," Molly said.

She walked away, then hesitated, turning back for a moment. At fifteen, she felt more the parent now, if only for a moment.

"Yes, anything could be happening to her right now," she said more firmly.

Her mother looked surprised. In her upset state, Molly's mother failed to notice the sound of longing in her daughter's voice. Instead she heard the same dread and concern she herself felt. She looked at her daughter with pity and understanding. Molly looked straight at her mother, her face expressionless.

"You're right mom, you shouldn't watch the news before bed," she mused.

Molly turned and walked away, sighing. Her mother went to bed, thinking about all the horrible things that might be happening to the woman from the news story, Ava Kate, concluding that she would undoubtedly be found dead within the next few days.

Molly went to bed thinking of all the wonderful things that were probably happening to that woman, Ava Kate. She fell asleep with a smile on her face.

You Again

Cora Leigh was plagued by bad dreams for months after Andrew died. She was taken to a child psychologist and underwent extensive therapy. For two years, from the age of fourteen 'til the age of sixteen, Cora Leigh saw her doctor once a week, for an hour. They talked about anything and everything. Of course, at first, they talked about the guilt she felt over Andrew's accidental death.

Cora Leigh talked about her nightmares, about how in her dreams she was swimming in the lake and suddenly felt a cold, skeletal hand tickling the bottoms of her feet. She awoke from these dreams screaming Andrew's name over and over again. This made her mother cry, every time.

***

Her parents never blamed Cora Leigh, any more than they blamed themselves, but they blamed themselves plenty. Natalie, Cora Leigh's mother, ended up hooked on prescription Valium and heavy sedatives. She never was the same, but then again, neither was Cora Leigh. Richard, her father, became an iron door, never unhinging under the strain or pressure, never showing any emotion over the loss at all.

Eventually, Cora Leigh quit going to therapy, when the dreams had all but stopped and she had talked about Andrew enough for it to be too much. At that point she would not have thought about Andrew at all, except for the hour of therapy every week, which now forced her to think about him, and so the therapy had become more detrimental than helpful, and was cancelled. Richard and Natalie were all too happy to stop paying the bills at that point. Two years was enough time to grieve, time to move on. So, they all did just that.

***

When tragedy strikes a family, there is really no other choice but to move on, eventually. Life has a way of getting in the way, as Natalie once said, groggily. The weight of her guilty words settled on Cora Leigh's shoulders, and although she never quite realized it, she carried the weight of that guilt around forever.

***

Life has a way of moving on and dragging people with it. Cora Leigh went to college, studied art history, met a cute boy and got married two months after graduation. She went on to grad school, got pregnant, never finished school, and went to work in a small art studio in Venice Beach. Her husband, Michael, was a CPA working in Santa Monica. When the baby came, a boy, they decided on Ryan Charles. It was a nice name.

Nothing unusual occurred during the first three years that Ryan Charles was alive. As a baby, he loved baths in the small tub that fit into the kitchen sink. Later, when he was too big for the sink tub, he sat in a plastic blow up tub that fit into the larger bathtub. He giggled and cooed in delight over the bubbles. He loved to be squirted in the armpits. This caused gales of laughter, which made Cora Leigh laugh so hard, tears squirted from her eyes.

There is nothing more heart warming than the sound of your own child's laughter.

The thought glimmered in Cora Leigh's mind. For just a moment, an old familiar feeling came over her. The weight that had landed on her shoulders so many years before and sunk in (becoming a normal, undifferentiated part of her gait) shifted loose, slightly askew, and she suddenly became aware of it again. She was a mother now, discovering all the joys and tribulations of parenthood from a previously unknown angle, and her own mother came to her conscious mind.

Every parent fears the worst for their child. That something will happen, beyond their control, and their child will be hurt, or even killed. Some parents have regular nightmares about it. Others become so wakefully fearful, they shelter their children from almost everything, like little prisoners.

Cora Leigh was not the first mother to entertain those dark thoughts about Ryan Charles. Never before, however, had she ever associated those thoughts with her own parents, the fact that they, too, must have feared the way all parents do, and worst of all, it had happened to them. Cora Leigh had lost a baby brother, but her parents had lost a son, and it was only now, all these years later, when she herself was a mother that she truly comprehended the horror of what her parents had suffered. Here, of all places, while giving Ryan Charles a bath.

It was later that night that Cora Leigh had her first dream about Andrew after so many years. It was not like her old nightmares, however. It was a memory coming back.

Andrew was three years younger than her; he had been eleven when he drowned. When he was three, Cora Leigh had been six. Andrew used to follow her around wanting to play with her, and she had always been annoyed. He loved to color, and one day she discovered that Andrew had scribbled all over her My Little Pony coloring book, on every page. At age three, scribbling in large arcs and circles was Andrew's idea of artful coloring. He was very good at it. Cora Leigh was outraged and picked up Andrew's favorite toy, a red fire engine and threw it on the floor so forcefully that two of the wheels broke off. Andrew wailed so balefully that their mother had run into the room thinking a limb had been broken, or worse. Cora Leigh was grounded; Andrew received ice cream to cheer him up.

What he had done was an accident, her mother explained, it was unintentional, but Cora Leigh had purposefully upset and hurt him. She ran to her room, sobbing. She could hear her mother and Andrew through the door, singing down the hallway to the kitchen, Andrew's favorite song, 'Zippadee Doo Dah'. Cora Leigh woke up from this dream, as if on cue, the song still playing in her mind, echoing. An eerie new thought occurred to her.

That's Ryan Charles' favorite song.

***

Two months later, Ryan Charles developed a sudden fear of water. He hated the bathtub and refused to go in. Cora Leigh did not understand what could have caused such a sudden phobia. Nothing had happened, and she knew most childhood phobias came from a personal, bad experience. Ryan Charles had never had any bad experiences with water. Michael began taking him in the shower with him. Even then, Ryan Charles was reluctant to go near the water, or get wet at all. Weekend trips to the beach stopped. People stared too much when he screamed frantically each time his father tried to walk him down to the waves. Cora Leigh chalked it up to one of those weird, unexplainable things.

He'll outgrow it, at some point, she thought.

When Ryan Charles turned five, he begged for a toy red fire engine for his birthday. Cora Leigh felt a small tinge of panic at this request, and then pushed it out of her mind.

All little boys love fire engines. It's just one of those things.

The dreams had started, though. Little ones that half the time, she couldn't remember. Other times, she did. Dreams of Andrew.

She never dreamed about the day he drowned. That horrible day, when Cora Leigh had swum off a ways, assuming her parents were watching Andrew from the shore. They, too, had made the mistake of thinking that she would remain with her brother and keep an eye on him. Anyway, he was eleven, not a little boy anymore. No one noticed when he dived to swim under the dock. No one noticed when he misjudged and came up just a tad shy of clearing the other side, hitting his head on the edge, a dull thunk spreading and dissipating far short of anyone's ears. No one saw Andrew go under the second time, now unconscious. No one even noticed he was missing for another five minutes.

Cora Leigh's dreams were inconsequential, mundane memories that came back in spurts while she slept; the forgotten fact that Andrew had hummed almost constantly, which had annoyed her as a young girl to no end.

Everywhere he went, Andrew hummed; sometimes actual tunes, like 'Zippadee Doo Dah', other times, just random notes. Cora Leigh told Andrew to "be quiet!" so many times; Natalie commented that if she gave her daughter a nickel for every time she said that, she could pay her way through college someday.

Most dreams, Cora Leigh didn't even remember upon waking. Others she did, but they faded by the time she was brushing her teeth or peeing. Some came back later in the day, in an *Oh yeah, I remember that*, sort of way.

The dream where she recalled how Andrew always, constantly hummed came back to her while she was buttering toast on the kitchen counter, her back to Ryan Charles. She stopped in mid-butter, pausing, her breath catching, as she listened to her son humming some random notes that didn't seem to be any song she had ever heard. Her heartbeat skipped, then danced up a bit quicker. Suddenly, she remembered (*how could she have forgotten that?*) how Andrew always hummed that way.

Cora Leigh spun around on the balls of her feet to face Ryan Charles. Her eyes were wide and frightened. The fright was mostly caused by her sudden realization of just how much she had forgotten about Andrew. She lived with him for eleven years, spent two years in therapy talking about him, and then had suddenly put him away, like an old book on a shelf. Only Andrew wasn't a book; he was a person, or he had been, before he died.

How do you just forget a person?

Cora Leigh felt that old guilt-weight shift again, and became fully aware of it now. It had originally sat on her shoulders. Now it stood up, balancing, wobbling on its feet. She felt the weight and adjusted her own gait to help it stay on. She didn't know what might happen if it fell.

As she walked slowly over to Ryan Charles and sat down across the table from him, studying him, she remembered things. Memories began to flood back into her mind so forcefully; she felt her head might explode. The steady rush-flow of blood in her ears didn't help. Her eardrums themselves felt as if they were contracting and expanding under the weight of so many things running around, suddenly loose in her head. There was so much about Andrew that she had failed to recognize, even when Ryan Charles began to do those same things.

When the mind decides a memory is too painful, it has a way of making it disappear. It's like a magic trick, only the mind is the magician and it never gives up its secrets. The mind is so good at this trick; the person never even knows what's happening. How can someone know something is missing if they don't remember to look?

Cora Leigh saw all the things she had missed. How Ryan Charles hated eggs (just like Andrew) and loved peas. How he hummed all the time, no matter where he was, and was deathly afraid (out of nowhere) to be near water. The toy red fire engine, and how they both loved the same song. Ryan Charles loved Halloween, and so had Andrew, even more than Christmas. Andrew had a weird affectation of twisting his lip in a painful looking way. Natalie was always begging him to stop doing it and was constantly asking "Doesn't that hurt?!" Ryan Charles twisted his lip the same way. Cora Leigh had even asked him to stop as well, and, yes, she had even proclaimed, "My God, doesn't that hurt?!"

As Cora Leigh thought deeper, she realized the list could go on and on: how Ryan Charles, for some reason, didn't like to eat foods that were the color brown; just like Andrew.

"They're poop!" Andrew had once proclaimed when he was around five. This had made Cora Leigh laugh so hard she cried, and her mother could only roll her eyes. For this reason, Andrew refused to eat hamburgers, hotdogs, chocolate, or any other brown colored food, regardless of shape or texture. Ryan Charles had the same odd eating quirk.

My God, how did I miss all this?

Cora Leigh sat stunned, still staring at her son. Ryan Charles stared back, smiling. He tilted his head and stopped humming.

"Mom-my!" he sang, his grin growing even wider.

Cora Leigh smiled at him; her beautiful, perfect little boy. She loved him more than life itself. Here, at this table, she became convinced that somehow, Andrew had found his way back to her. Her baby brother, who had died while she was swimming, carefree and alone, was now looking back at her through her son's eyes. She was certain of it.

The weight of the invisible guilt-being that was standing on her shoulders stepped down, walked across the table, turned around to face her and assumed an odd position. Cora Leigh saw this in her mind. It had no face; it was merely a dark shadow; as dark as the feeling the weight had caused her all these years, even under layers of forgetfulness. It crouched, scooted backwards to the edge of the table, and fell off, onto her son. It seemed to melt into Ryan Charles and become a part of him. His smile faltered for only a moment, then burst forth, wider than ever.

"Mommy!" he proclaimed. He was playing a game with her. She was crying. She walked around the table to him, in his booster seat and cried harder, throwing her arms around him. She sobbed out his name.

"Andrew!"

"Mommy, mommy," Ryan Charles sang. "You're weird."

"I love you, honey, you know that?"

"Uh-huh," Ryan Charles played with his toast, which he was still holding. Butter stains had gotten on Cora Leigh's blouse, but she didn't notice just then.

***

They spent the day at the park, and Cora Leigh noted how Ryan Charles loved the swings, but hated the teeter-totter, just like Andrew had. Over the next several weeks, the similarities continued to jump out at her, everywhere they went and everything they did. Michael noticed that Cora Leigh was more exuberant than usual, but that was all. She, herself, felt ecstatic. She was free of any guilt she had felt over Andrew's death, because Andrew was here, back in her care. Nothing bad would ever happen to him again, because this time, she would make sure to be watching.

The Monster Across The Street

Emma stumbled down the hallway, still half asleep. Her brain hadn't quite caught up with her pounding heart. Already though, her daughter's screams were planting visions in her head, pushing out her quickly fading dreams. She imagined she might open her daughter's door to find a strange man standing over her bed.

She wished she had woken her husband to go in, instead of her. How would she defend herself against a strange man in her house? She didn't even have a weapon, unless you counted her nails. How could her husband sleep through his daughter's blood-curdling cries? She reached Jordan's door and barged in without hesitation.

"Mommy!"

Jordan reached out, crying hysterically. Emma was there in an instant, holding Jordan in her arms.

"What is it, honey, what happened?"

Although Emma already knew. This was the third night in a row. Why had she thought a man was breaking in to kidnap her child? They had been through this twice before.

Damn news, Emma thought.

Some little girl had just been kidnapped in the middle of the night, right out of her bedroom, in Utah. It had been all over the news for the past week. She wondered if, somehow, Jordan had picked up on this story and perhaps, subconsciously, this was the cause of her nightmares.

"A monster, Mommy, a monster!"

Already Jordan was calming down, however. Her voice was still shrill and panicked, but she was no longer actively crying.

"Honey, it was just a dream," Emma soothed. "It was just a nightmare."

"But it was closer this time," Jordan whined. "It was underneath my window!"

Emma's head snapped up with a start. It had never gotten that close before. She tried to sound calm, hoping Jordan wouldn't hear anything suspicious in her voice.

"I'll just look, honey, okay? You'll see, there's nothing there," she paused, "because it was just a dream."

Emma walked over to the window, pulled back the curtain, and peered down into the yard. She inched her face closer to the pane and looked directly down. Her breath fogged up the window almost instantly, but she breathed a sigh of relief. There was nothing there. Just grass. She turned back to Jordan and smiled.

"See, honey? It was just a dream. It wasn't real. There was no monster."

She walked back over to Jordan, who already looked sleepy again. She was blinking and her eyelids were drooping at half-mast. She settled Jordan back down onto her pillow, stroking her hair. Jordan's eyes closed.

"There are no such things as monsters," Emma whispered.

In her heart though, she thought she knew better. She just wasn't sure anymore.

~

She was having coffee with an old friend from college the next day, when Emma finally talked about her dream. This was a friend she trusted- the type of friend a person makes in college, and somehow a bond forms so that despite all the years that came after, Emma felt completely comfortable telling her friend this crazy thing. Years could go by without talking to each other and yet, whenever they did meet, making time in their busy schedules for the drive, they fell into conversation as if no time had gone by; as if they were still in school, living in their dorm. Liz was always the one Emma talked to about her problems, specifically because she never interrupted. She just listened until Emma was done, then took a long pause and finally commented, always with some sage advice that seemed to help. Until today.

Emma began:

She was five years old, the same age as Jordan was now.

~

She had been asleep in her bed, like she had been every night for five years. This night hadn't been any different than any other. She was sound asleep, not having any particular dreams she could recall, and certainly no nightmares. She had woken up.

~

"That's point number one to remember," Emma pointed out to Liz, before going on. "How many people dream that they are waking up? Dream that they are awake? I mean that is just too existential for a five-year-old mind, isn't it?"

~

Emma sat in her bed for a moment in the dark. She knew she was awake, but she didn't know why. She rarely woke up in the middle of the night, unless she had to pee. She took a moment to become aware of her body, feeling for that tingling sensation in her abdomen. It wasn't there. She didn't need to pee. Perhaps a noise had woken her up? She listened intently to the night. She could hear the wind blowing outside, ever so slightly.

Her bedroom was at the end of the hall, far away from the kitchen. There was no hum from any appliances to wake her up. Her bedroom was normally stone quiet at night, and even now, as she strained to hear any unusual sounds, she heard nothing.

It was fall. No birds chirped outside, even the ones that might have made noise at night. No sound of tires screeching from some bored teenager who might have been driving around in the middle of the night. She tried to think of other noises that could, or had, woken her up ever in the past. She couldn't think of any. Why did she feel so uncomfortable?

Something wasn't right. She felt it from the moment she became aware that she was awake. She had an uneasy feeling that she couldn't quite put her finger on.

It wasn't because she was in the dark- she wasn't. They lived in a cul-de-sac, just two houses in, and on either side of the circle opening, on the street corners, were two tall street lamps. They were bright enough to light up most of the circle at night. Emma's curtains were translucent pink; a thin substance of sheer linen that allowed light to pass through. There was enough light in her room every night from the lamps that she had never needed a nightlight. She could see her room well enough, and she began to take stock.

First off, the closet was closed. She always made sure it was closed before bed, because every child knows that if the closet is closed, it traps whatever creatures may be in there. Whatever plans those slithery, disgusting things may have about creeping out into your room and grabbing your exposed toes, were always ruined. It was a rule of the creature world that all children, somehow, mysteriously knew. As long as the closet door was closed, they couldn't get out.

Of course, there was never any need to worry during the daytime. They didn't come out during the day, they simply couldn't. There were rules, apparently, that even monsters had to obey. This was fair, Emma thought. This was how things stayed in order. Justice ruled supreme in a child's world, and any instance where justice was thwarted was simply inconceivable to Emma. The closet door was closed.

As for any monsters that may reside under her bed, she had taken care of that. She knew her stuffed animals were Magic. They were not just inanimate, stuffed fluff- they were Guardians. As long as she placed one at each leg of her bed, making four Sentinels in all, she would be safe.

Emma slowly leaned over the right side of her bed. She breathed a sigh of relief. She could see her stuffed elephant, Ellie, at the front post. Mr. Frog was at the foot post. That side was okay. She straightened back up, perspiring a little. She scooched over to the left side of the bed, where things were a bit darker. This side was by the corner of the room, the window being just slightly off-center of her headboard. She peered down into the dark, waiting for her eyes to adjust just enough to see the silhouettes of Mr. Shark and Mrs. Crab. It took a moment to be sure, but yes, they were there. Her bed was being guarded. Everything was in its proper place.

Why was she awake? She felt scared and didn't know why. She had a sudden thought then. It popped into Emma's head almost as if it wasn't her own thought at all, but some thought that was pushed in there; forced in from the outside.

***Outside.** She needed to look out the window. The answer was there. She somehow knew this without a doubt. She had woken up, for some reason, because she was supposed to look out her window. She was suddenly terrified.*

Emma slowly got up on the balls of her feet, her knees bent. Her cotton nightgown brushed the tops of her toes briefly. She spun around on the fleshy part just behind her toes, until she was facing her headboard and the window.

She placed her hands on the sill and slowly raised herself until her eyes were just able to see over and out the window.

It was as if she knew where to look. Her eyes looked out, and immediately down, towards the corner, just under the diagonal street lamp. And that is where she saw it- the monster across the street. It stood several feet away from the street lamp, just sitting there. It was looking up at her. It was smiling.

~

Emma paused for a moment to take a sip of her coffee. Her hands were shaking. She hadn't recalled this incident in so many details in years. She hadn't thought about it. Not until Jordan's first nightmare, three nights ago- three nights ago that seemed a lifetime away. A dream where Jordan had cried and insisted she had seen a monster outside her window- across the street. Liz hadn't said a single word yet, which Emma loved her for. She just sat there, looking at Emma expectantly, her raised eyebrows seeming to say, *go on, keep telling it. I want to know.*

So Emma went on:

"Then I started to hear something."

~

*Emma suddenly heard the thing speak to her, although not in words, but in thoughts. Somehow, the monster across the street was communicating with her. It wasn't in words, but the thoughts were there, in her head. She understood perfectly. The thing wanted her to come outside. It wanted to **play** with her. She knew it used the thought of play, but something inside her twisted. It did not want to play with her; she knew that much, no matter what it was trying to* *make her believe. It wanted to do things to her, horrible things. It wanted to* **hurt** *her. For a brief moment, she thought,* **it wants to eat me**. *She couldn't take her eyes off that thing. She wanted to, but she couldn't.*

It wasn't so big, she thought.

~

"What did it look like?" Liz asked, saying something for the first time.

The thoughts of five-year-old Emma intruded into grown-up Emma's head. She answered Liz's question as best she could in her jarred state.

It was a sickening gray color that Emma could only describe to Liz as brains. She had seen a picture of a human brain in an encyclopedia, as a child. Her parents had a full set of encyclopedia's, from A to Z, that they kept in a bookshelf in the living room. Emma sometimes looked through them, taking in the pictures, because at age five she couldn't read yet. She was just about to start Kindergarten in one week. It was a week before Kindergarten that she had seen the thing across the street- the monster.

"It was gray, like the picture of the brain I saw in the encyclopedia," Emma paused for a moment. "Only more vibrant. More *crisp*.

Then Emma continued on with her story, her memory:

~

It was bulgy and blobby. It had no arms or legs, but its shape narrowed out at the top, giving the impression of a head. It was all one continuous, bulbous form. There was no neck. It sort of reminded Emma of a Mr. Potato Head. She thought this for a moment. It had eyes, but they were slightly swallowed up by the folds of formless 'ick' that made up this ugly thing. It was vague, in many ways. No definitive form to grasp onto. It was just a thing- a gray, formless thing. Like a creation a child might make out of play dough, or even sticky mud, but they never quite decided on what it should be.

She was five, but she thought in a grown-up way. Emma looked at the thing for what felt like minutes on end, and it never spoke again after its invitation for her to come out and play. It just sat there, looking up at her. It didn't even smile anymore. There was no mouth there at all now. Emma wasn't sure if there ever had been. The smile seemed more something that was suggested in her mind than something she had actually seen.

*Alarmingly, there was a part of her that **did** want to go out and play. Part of her wanted to get closer, and see the thing better.*

Or it wanted her to think she wanted to.

*Emma did not go out and play. Something stopped her. A **smell** stopped her from even considering going outside. Whatever it was that enabled that thing to communicate with her, it had an unpleasant side effect. Emma knew this, somehow. Whatever channel had to be opened up from this thing's mind to hers in order for it to speak to her, it also, somehow, enabled a smell to come through.*

It was the smell that broke whatever hold the creature had over her. Whatever power it previously had to make her even consider wanting to go out there to play with it was gone.

~

Emma paused, troubled. Liz said nothing, she only waited.

This was the hardest part for Emma, it always had been. Over the years in her childhood after she was five, whenever she would bring this disturbing memory up in her own mind, trying to recall it, it was always the *smell* that was the most difficult to define.

"It was something I'd never smelled before," she said.

She paused, looking Liz straight in the face. "**EVER**."

She continued on, telling Liz that sometimes, occasionally in her life, she had experienced dreams that had certain elements that seemed real. Once she had dreamed she was outside in the middle of winter with no shoes on, just bare feet. She was walking in the snow, and she had woken up swearing she felt pain in her feet.

"Pins and needles," she explained, "as if I'd really been walking in the snow, and my feet were starting to get numb."

Liz nodded. She spoke for the first time in reply.

"Once I had a dream where my hand was on fire," she hesitated. "I forget why, but anyway," she continued, "I actually felt like my hand was burning. I felt the pain and heat and everything."

Emma nodded. She had experienced dreams like that, where some of it seemed to cross through to the waking world. As if the mind believed it so much, it became a physical reality.

"They say that if you die in a dream, you will actually die in real life," Emma said. "I don't know if that's true or not, but," she trailed off, shrugging. "I know the difference between a dream component, and something that is real."

Emma tried to explain the odor to Liz, but how could she explain a smell? Especially one that was new and unlike any other smell ever experienced? She went through a myriad of things in her life that had smelled bad. Things that had smelled awful, things that had smelled rotten and putrid. Garbage, rotting vegetables, burnt popcorn, spoiled milk, poopy diapers, sulfur, burning plastic; even her own singed hair, once. None of these things even came close to accurately describing the smell she had experienced that night, while looking down at that thing across the street.

~

The smell hit Emma suddenly, like a punch in the gut. Her nostrils were unexpectedly filled with a smell so foul, so all-encompassing, that Emma stopped breathing; shocked at the odor. It made her eyes water and she blinked furiously. Her heart was immediately doing triple time.

Somehow, she knew the smell was coming from that thing, just as she knew, immediately, the thoughts in her head were it, talking to her. She knew, somehow, that whatever connection it was that allowed the thing to speak to her, it had also let in this smell as well.

*Suddenly she did not want to be anywhere near that thing. The smell could not **allow** that. It was simply that awful. It was like nothing she had ever smelled before. Emma didn't know what it smelled like, only that it was **bad**.*

And just like that, the spell was broken.

Emma backed away from the window, no longer wanting to see the monster across the street. She just wanted to go back to sleep. She just wanted to go back to her normal life. Somehow, unbelievably, she had lain down in her bed, flat on her back, pulled the covers up to her chin, and had closed her eyes.

The next thing she remembered was waking up in the morning, full daylight shining into her room through her translucent pink curtains. Her first thoughts hadn't even been of the thing from the night before. In fact, she didn't think about the thing across the street until breakfast, as she sat eating her Cheerios, sweetened with two extra spoonfuls of sugar. She recalled it vaguely, like a far-off memory. She wasn't frightened.

~

"It wasn't like recalling a dream," she explained to Liz. "That's point number two."

Even dreams that Emma could remember to that day were never so complete- never so detailed. She could remember everything about that night. And what kind of child dreams of waking up, and even more so, of going back to sleep?

"That's point number three," Emma said.

She remembered waking up **and** going back to sleep. She had never dreamed of waking up or being awake and going back to sleep at any other time in her entire life.

"**EVER**," Emma stared hard at Liz. "And that *smell*," she said, her eyes looking haunted.

Over the years of her life, Emma would try to recall the thing and its smell, and try to identify it, failing every time. But if she concentrated very hard and closed her eyes, breathing deeply, sometimes (only a few times in her life after the incident) she could almost smell it again, briefly, vaguely, for just a moment. However, those few moments were so tangible, they were enough.

What she had seen had been real. She was certain of it. And now, her own five-year-old daughter, her sweet little Jordan was seeing it.

"How do you know it's the same thing?" Liz asked. "The same thing you saw when you were five?" She looked at Emma with sympathetic eyes.

"At first I didn't," Emma said.

~

At first she had thought it was just a nightmare, even when the details Jordan told her raised gooseflesh on her arms. When Jordan had said she saw a monster across the street,

Emma was able to shrug it off, and tell her daughter it was just a bad dream.

The first night, Jordan had seen the thing across the street, in front of their neighbor's house. She had immediately screamed for her mother. By the time Emma came in, Jordan said the thing had gone. She said it was just a blob and she couldn't remember much else, but it had frightened her.

The neighbors across the street, the Thurston's, had installed motion detector lights on the front of their house so that any intruders even thinking about breaking in would be scared off by the sudden flood of bright light in their faces. Even as Emma laid her daughter back down in her bed that first night, telling her to go back to sleep, that everything was all right, she had an uneasy feeling.

There was nothing outside, in front of the Thurston's house, but the lights were on. Something had made them go off.

~

"It could have been a dog," shrugged Emma.

Liz remained quiet.

"Maybe a stray dog, or some other animal tripped the lights."

~

On night two, Emma rushed into Jordan's room, again woken by her frantic screams. Jordan was at her window pointing out. It had been there again, she said, this time standing in the middle of the street. This time she told her mother that it had been gray and looked like "Jabba the Hut, Mommy!"

Jordan hadn't said it looked like a Mr. Potato Head. Jordan never said that it had spoken to her, or that there had been any communication. Emma kept telling her daughter that it was just a dream, and that there were no such things as monsters. She felt like the biggest liar in the world.

~

Emma looked at Liz, her tired eyes pleading. She didn't know what to do. She could not, under any circumstances, ever let Jordan see the fear in her mother's eyes. She could not, **ever**, give Jordan even the slightest hint that what she was seeing was real.

Emma could hardly believe it herself, but she had never told Jordan about her dream as a child. Jordan couldn't have guessed the details, and they were so similar to what had happened to Emma. She knew it hadn't been a dream, but even so, she had never told anyone about it, until now.

"Last night, Jordan saw it again," Emma continued.

It was why she had called Liz, frantically begging her to drive the hour and a half to meet with her. She needed to talk to someone about it. Her husband would never believe her, and he would probably just laugh anyway, or worse, think she'd gone crazy.

Tonight, Emma would sleep in her daughter's bed under the guise of providing comfort, but really, it was because Emma couldn't bare the thought of letting her daughter sleep alone. Not when last night, the thing had been underneath her window.

It had never gotten that close before, with Emma. And Emma had only seen it once. Jordan had seen it three nights in a row. This was different. This was dangerous, and it was real.

"Last night," Emma said, her voice shaking, "last night," She couldn't continue.

What could Liz possibly say that would make it all right? What could anyone ever say, or for that matter, do, to fix this?

She felt like she, herself, was five years old again, only there were no Sentinels around her bed warding off the monsters, keeping them under there, where they could not reach up and grab her legs and drag her under. Everything seemed to have changed, the rules thrown off to the wayside, in her view of things. Old childhood fears were awake and alive now, breathing again inside her tortured mind. This time, things were different.

Her closet door was no longer closed. Emma lay in her bed (*in her mind,*) the one she used to sleep in, in the room she lived in when she was five, and stared at the open black hole that was her closet.

The door had slid all the way open.

There was no protection this time. There was no justice. There was only the monster under her bed, in her closet, across the street.

"Last night, Jordan was crying so hard," Emma whispered, her throat constricting.

~

Jordan was hysterical on the third night she saw the thing. It had not been across the street, or even in the street. This time it had been underneath her window. And Jordan said it had wanted to **play** with her. It was no longer willing to wait outside, cajoling and convincing the little girl to come outside and play with it. It was determined to come *inside* and play with her.

~

Liz hadn't known what to say, in the end. This was different than any of the other problems she had discussed with

Emma in the past. This was not a fight with her husband, or an illness in her family. This was something completely different.

In the end, Liz focused on the fact that Emma and Jordan were both age five when seeing the monster. Her eyes looked hopeful.

"Maybe there is something about being five?"

But even that was little comfort to Emma. Jordan wouldn't turn six for another four months.

Perhaps, if Emma was there with Jordan, the thing couldn't harm her? It had seemed unable, for whatever reason, to return to Emma night after night, the way it was doing with Jordan. Perhaps Emma could keep her safe until the danger was past?

But there were so many uncertainties. When would it be safe? *Why* would it be safe? How would Emma know when that time had come? There had always been rules before for keeping scary things at bay. She had always known what to do to make things okay. But no amount of stuffed animals on guard, or closed closet doors could fix this. She didn't know what the rules were. She didn't even know, for that matter, if there *were* any rules.

Perhaps that thing, that monster, had free reign?

Tonight Emma would sleep with Jordan, even if her husband balked. She would sleep in bed with Jordan for however long it took; however long it was before Emma, herself, was sure that thing was gone. How long before that would be, she did not know.

Would she ever feel it was gone? Would she ever have the comfort and peace of mind that Jordan was safe in her bed, in her room, all alone? Emma did not know.

~

Liz only stared at her friend with deep concern and sympathy, the fear in her eyes hidden poorly; a tear trickled down her cheek.

"Last night, Jordan said she *smelled* that thing," Emma said, her voice barely above a whisper. "She told me," Emma hitched.

*"Mommy, it smells **bad**.*

Divine

I could have been an actor or an underwear model. I wear a vest and tie very smartly for the occasion. These Black Tie Events are so predictable. The office drones are eager to please. If I tell them my name with my eyebrows raised just the right way, I can actually hear their heart rates increase. I give them a look, as if to say, "You mean you *don't know* who I am?" –And then watch them *squirm*. It's fabulous.

I can pick up either male or female. I prefer female, but occasionally I'll bring home a lithe subject of the male persuasion. I'm not very tall or firmly built. I'm thin and muscular in a wiry way, not thick, or burly. It is for this reason that they have to be lithe, even the males- especially the males, just in case.

I like to be careful. You should never lure prey into your lair that's stronger than you freestanding. The tainted drinks help. In the end, they will all be weak, semi-conscious, paralyzed animals, but I like to have insurance in case of the unlikely event that their body's particular chemical makeup renders them immune to the effects of the Tetro. This has never happened before, but you can never be too careful.

I'm smart, in a scary manner; frighteningly, deliciously intelligent. I'm also easy on the eyes. I really could have been an underwear model, or an actor. These are simply professions used to procure what one wants: getting laid, money, chicks, drugs, attention, applause, love. However, I don't want any of those things. I want satisfaction.

First off, I pick wealthy victims. I attend Black Tie Events, usually Christmas parties in bought-out convention centers, where Fortune 500's gather to get drunk and blown. I enter wearing my smart attire about halfway through. By this point, everyone is well on his or her way to alcoholic oblivion. I look good to the sober eye. Through the narrowed-down vision of scotch and whiskey high balls, I look downright *Divine*.

I stroll through the crowds, putting on my performance: head held high, chin raised, a smile plastered on my face, drink in hand. I carry my drink in with me. I don't sip from it because it's been laced for my victims. I like to keep things in my favor.

I'm trolling, looking for the right one. Every once in a while something goes wrong. Someone will drunkenly bump into me, causing my drink to slosh all over the dance floor, but that's okay, because I have more powder in a vile inside my vest pocket. Once, a rather large bloke bumped square into me and actually broke my vial, but I'm smart, remember? I'm always prepared with several backup plans. I keep another vial in my left pants pocket and a small folded up paper in my wallet with another dose inside. Like I said, I'm smart; prepared.

It doesn't take long to find them, my victims usually find me. I'm like a magnet, and if they're single, they'll notice me- male and female.

Sometimes I get mobbed. I'm just that good-looking; just that magnanimous. I was made for this.

I usually have my pick and choose of several delectable items. Tonight, it's a woman: Executive Assistant to the VP of Sales. She feels the need to get her job title out up front, like brandishing a trophy, emphasizing the word *Executive*, and glossing over *Assistant*.

She immediately launches into some sad tale about getting a flat tire last week, easily revealing the fact that she drives a BMW 7-Series. It's like cue cards being read off to me. She brandishes her glass of Dom, making sure to tell me she prefers Krystal. I nod, smiling. I don't even have to say anything. She already wants me. My dress, my gait, my attitude shows her exactly what she wants to see.

I have a script, though I hardly ever need to use it. If they do ask, most of the time they don't, my quick answer is that I'm contract-to-hire for the President of Marketing. I'm contract because they simply can't afford to keep me on payroll permanently; flown in to hobnob and snob. They always laugh at that one.

Eventually, I get them a drink, laced, of course. I either give them the one I carried in, or get them a new one.

The ingestion time depends on their weight and metabolism, but I usually can count on no more than thirty minutes before they start to slur (if they weren't already) and weave, their coordination compromised.

I end up carrying them out on my shoulder. By this point, they're completely compliant.

In the parking structure, they always laugh when they see my Benz; as if viewing my vehicle is the greatest trick they've ever seen.

Tonight she laughs like a hyena. Then she begins to retch.

I quickly drop her off my shoulder, pointing her away from my S-Beauty. I point her head in the opposite direction and then look away as I listen to her vomit up her filet mignon and lightly sautéed asparagus spears in a lemon-caper sauce. When she's finished, I pull a kerchief from my other vest pocket and gently wipe her mouth and chin.

"Feel better?" I ask.

She nods and smiles, her eyelids at half-mast.

She's lost some of the Tetro dose, so now I'll need to fix her another drink, but not until we reach my place.

On the drive, she's too out of it to register the streets, nor be aware of the time it takes to reach our destination.

I park in the alley behind my high rise. I live in a penthouse, naturally.

I really am a contract employee to a certain Fortune 500 company. I leave most of these shindigs with a cool ten thousand in my right pants pocket. Remember all those drunkards that kept bumping into me, the ones I talked to for a few minutes, sizing them up? They're so drunk that their bodies are completely numb. And at these parties, we're all huddled together like cattle to the slaughter. They rarely feel me reaching into their purses, or their pockets and removing their wallets, taking their cash.

Sometimes they do feel it, though. If it's a man and I'm in their pocket, I just give a squeeze to their junk and come onto them. If it's a woman and she registers the tug on her purse, I quickly remove my hand, before she can look down, and place it gently on her waist. I look them in the eyes and simply ask if they'd like another drink.

The people who notice these things, I know are not the one. I take their money then I move on, to the ones that don't notice anything.

We enter my penthouse, and I immediately fix her another drink. I pour another, smaller dose of Tetro. I don't want to over-do it. I don't want her to be unconscious, that won't satisfy.

I want them awake; aware. Tetro does that with the right amounts; it keeps them conscious, yet unable to move. It paralyzes their muscles to the point of incapacity, yet still allows them to breathe extremely shallow. It's the perfect drug. It is poison, to be certain, but it won't kill them too quickly, at least not before I do.

I give her the drink and she downs it. Her already compromised system reacts more quickly this time.

Sometimes, I have to kiss them for a few minutes. I don't mind. I never have to fuck them. This I would mind. Sex doesn't satisfy me.

I usually turn on some slow jazz and dance with them. Even the males find this quaint. They all laugh and sway and go along with it, thinking I'm the most incredible date in the world.

When they slump against me, the paralysis fully setting in, that's when the real fun starts- for me. Whether we were dancing, kissing, or simply talking, they fall forward, their heads lolling onto my chest. Then, I know they are truly mine.

***

I quickly move her into the next room. The door was closed, so she has no clue that this room is covered wall-to-wall, floor-to-ceiling in thick plastic sheeting.

This is where she will come face-to-face with her own enlightenment.

I could have been an actor, or an underwear model, no lie. I could have been splashed all over the covers of magazines, my incredibly agreeable visage in every still frame of some love story, with a leading lady from the Hollywood A-list. I could have strangers coming up to me on the sidewalk, begging for my autograph; mobbed wherever I go. I could be getting laid every night. However, as I've stated, this would not satisfy me.

These people, they aren't really alive; they're not living life. They eat their caviar and forty-dollar steaks, drive their expensive cars and climb the corporate ladder, only fucking people with higher incomes than themselves. They are always looking forward to the next hurdle, the next chapter in their ridiculous existences. That's not living.

They always want more, more, more of everything that doesn't matter. They live their pampered lives, never experiencing any discomfort. They never truly appreciate the simple fact of waking up each day, or breathing; the basic joy that lies just in gazing at the beauty of a sunrise.

I take it all away from them: their meaningless lives, and I replace it with Revelation. I make them want to see a sunrise, even though they never get it. I make them take great joy in simply breathing, as they take their last breath.

At the moment of their death, I give these people true appreciation of the life they wasted. This newfound frame of mind is only reached moments before they shuffle off this mortal coil. I give it to them, in the only way that I know how- through pain.

The drug I administer keeps them conscious and aware. They are unable to move, but they can still feel every exquisite sensation. Their nerve endings are more alive than ever, even as their muscles remain frozen.

I gently lay tonight's choice down on the plastic-covered floor. I kiss her lips, just once, slow and sensual. I gaze into her eyes. I smile. Then, I begin my work.

I keep my tools in a box near the balcony window. I start with the pliers. The fingernails are the first to go, just in case they somehow manage to gain a modicum of control over their limbs. Their first instinct would be to scratch, and I can't risk my face getting marked- I'm too pretty for that.

One at a time, I remove her nails. Slowly, I pull. There's a threshold of pressure that has to be reached before everything lets go and the flesh gives up the fight.

I keep steady, holding my breath, until I hear that juicy, wet, ripping sound. As each nail finally pulls free, I release my breath.

My cock is hard. My breathing is elevated. The satisfaction is beginning to build.

She can't scream. Her muscles are paralyzed. However, she breathes shallowly. I look into her face and see tears standing in her eyes. More are trickling down the sides of her temples and into her hair, which is damp. She's been crying quite a bit with each nail that's been removed. Her eyes are wide, in fact. They are open, shining and *aware*. This is what I want.

I talk to them as I work. I talk to *her* tonight and explain what I'm going to do next. The fingernails are gone, but I must remove her high heels now. She is also wearing hose.

I gently reach up under her dress and pull the hose down. I assure her not to worry, I'm not going to violate her, but the toenails must be removed. She could kick, and again, I don't want to be scratched anywhere.

I go about my task, my back to her face. Hunched over, I have to apply greater pressure for the feet, especially the large toenails; they are the most resistant to being removed. I clench my fingers around the pliers so tightly my knuckles begin to ache. I relish the pain, realizing she and I are going through a sort of symbiotic experience; a dance-of-pleasure through discomfort. I'm her tour guide.

When I'm finished with her feet, again, I turn to gaze into her face. Her eyes are nearly popping out of their sockets. Her hair is soaked. The capillaries in her sclera have broken from the stress and strain and are now mostly blood red. She probably has a migraine from all that pressure. Her head must feel as if it might explode.

I still have a hard-on, more so now than ever. I tell her what I'm going to do next. She can't move or react, but I still think I can detect some sort of motion, very slight, within her eyes; they well up with more tears. Perhaps it is a latent reaction to the pain of my previous acts, but I don't believe this. The news that I will be breaking every finger on both her hands is too exciting for her to hide her emotions.

I use my bare hands. I bend, bend, bend; applying pressure until I hear the audible snap of bone at the mid-knuckle. I don't stop until every finger is pointing upwards and back, at an unnatural angle to the ceiling, as if pointing towards Heaven.

Her hair is sopping. She surely can't have many tears left. She'll become dehydrated soon. Her body will become so overwhelmed with the stress and pain; she'll lose consciousness, despite the drug in her system.

I talk to her. I make her aware of everything: all that she's been missing in her mundane, useless life; by letting her know everything she'll never have again. I make her aware that she'll never see another sunrise. She'll never watch another movie, never see any of her friends or family again.

"Did you tell anyone you loved them?" I ask her. "Because you'll never get to say that again. To anyone."

I tell her she'll never feel rain on her skin again, or have the simple pleasure of eating a meal, or enjoying a hot shower. I point out so many things she took for granted in her everyday life. I ask her then, if she had the choice between driving her stupid BMW 7-Series one last time, or calling up her mother and telling her she loves her, which one would she choose?

She's getting closer to enlightenment. She's beginning to get there, but not quite yet. I still have more work to do.

***

The largest organ in the human body is actually on the outside- it's the skin; it contains hundreds of nerve endings per square inch. Everything we feel, know and experience comes through our senses, not least of which is touch. It's how we learn. Everything she's been taking for granted in her comfortable life, whatever pain she's already been through, it's nothing compared to what she's about to experience.

It doesn't take anything sophisticated, nothing complex. A simple curling iron, plugged into the wall, set on high, is all I need.

Waiting a few minutes, I tell her what to expect. I'm going to burn her over every square inch of her skin, slowly. It will take hours, but we have all night. When she passes out, I'll wait for her to come back around to consciousness. I can tell if she's awake or not by the dilation of her pupils.

Divine

***

The smell is nearly unbearable. I have to open all the windows. Up here on the top floor, the breeze is fairly constant. Of course, I don't have to worry about gagging her. They can't scream, remember? It's beautiful. It's perfect. It's amazing. It's *Divine*.

***

Hours later, as the first rays of the sun radiate through the windows, I look down at her and smile.

She stopped crying several hours ago, too dehydrated for her tear ducts to manufacture any more tears. Her skin, once milky-white, is now charred and black. She's crisp everywhere on the top half of her body. It took forever, with this tiny curling iron. I never even made it to her backside.

Her breathing has become shallow and rapid. The Tetro is wearing off now. However, her body is far too weak from dehydration and the stress of manufacturing all that adrenaline in response to the pain. She's utterly depleted, despite only lying here on my floor for the past eight hours- the longest night of her life.

I reached orgasm and ejaculated several times, hours ago- as I smelled the smoke from her burning skin and took in the exquisite lattice structure and crosshatching I designed across her white belly. I came again (twice) when I pulled the iron way, to see her orange-red nipples had turned to blackened buttons.

I have one last gift to give her: a surprise. Her moment of enlightenment is here. I inform her that she will get to see one last sunrise.

It's happening now. No more cares are in her mind about fancy cars, or expensive meals, or who she's going to blow next underneath a desk to continue her corporate climb. All she cares about now is gazing upon that beautiful sight, the light of the sun.

The paralysis is, indeed, wearing off. She's able to move her head just slightly. Her burnt and peeling, blackened skin actually crinkles and cracks as she strains her neck to look up, behind her, towards the balcony and the light that is now streaming across her face. She reminds me of what a vampire might look like after the sun has struck it; as if she's burning up with the Holy light of the sun. This moment is *Divine*.

A small miracle occurs; one last tear trickles from her left eye, making its way through the deep crevices of her broken flesh. The salt probably stings like Hell.

I look closely at her eyes. The pupils have dilated with the light into small pinpricks- tiny pencil lead spots.

As that one final tear dissipates and spreads across the ruined skin of her forehead, I see her pupils dilate suddenly into larger discs and then freeze in place, no longer reacting to the light.

The sun continues streaming into my living room, growing brighter and illuminating the beauty of the coming day.

Here is the part where I cry. No cameras are on me, no film footage is running, to capture for all eternity the wonder that I am, but I have done an amazing thing. I have changed a life for the better. I have created an appreciation for *being*. I've done what it takes to achieve this task. I'm not afraid to get my hands dirty –or my soul. I've had my satisfaction.

I could have been an actor or an underwear model. I could have whored myself out to the masses, but I've chosen to be something else. I've answered a higher calling to create awareness in those few. What I do is not easy. In fact, it's very difficult. It's not for everyone –being *Divine*.

Every Living Thing

At first, when I heard the clawing, I assumed it was one of *them*. Even out here, seemingly in the middle of nowhere, they came around. Some, I figured, were others who had the same idea as I had; people who owned cabins in the woods, like me.

I knew "neighbors," like Pete Deutschman, who owned a cabin of his own about two miles down river of me. We got to know each other a bit, on our boats every season, pulling in the Silvers at the hole. Lots of guys around the hole, but most were on charters, or even in on a plane, from the landing. Pete was one of the few, like me, who owned a place. The others I'd only see once, since most of the charters were day-payers, or only in for a weekend. Lots of people owned cabins, yet never went there themselves, not really. They ran touristy B&B's, only coming in with their fares.

Other than Pete, there was Kent Roughy, other side of the river, about a quarter mile down from me, and Brent Trentman, up river from me a good two miles or so. When the shit hit, I knew the cabin was the only safe place to be, if that even. Thank God it happened in the fall, when all the tourists and charters had stopped running. September, and already the temperatures were dipping close to freezing at night. We would have an early winter this year, I could tell. It's like that up north. Course, north is where a lot of people headed when it hit. I guess everyone figured the cold would slow *them* down.

Hell, I just figured none of them could get to me where I was. First off, you can only get to the cabin on river, by boat. How the hell would a zombie pull that off? Even getting to the landing, the last 15 miles or so is on a bumpy dirt road, off the main highway. The only way to get to my place was if you damn well meant to go there. And everyone knew those damn things had no real thoughts going around in those dead heads of theirs. Anything they did was pure instinct, sheer luck, or just a stupid accident. I was safer than a fag on a lesbian boat cruise at my place. In other words: not fucked at all.

There's always an exception to the rule though, isn't there? Groups of people in trucks and those dumb SUV's, who happened to drive out near my way. Stupid people who headed north, without really knowing where they were going. If they made it as far as the landing, they were fucked anyway. Nowhere to go after that.

The landing was owned by Ellis Harker, who had apparently been bitten in town, then driven out to Yelts to get as far away from people as he could. This was, perhaps, before people learned that a simple bite would make you as dead as the zombie who bit you. Or maybe Ellis did know he was already a goner, but just wanted some peace and quiet. I'd like to think that Ellis figured even when he did reanimate, there'd be no one to munch on way out by the river, and so he was trying to do a good thing. Why he didn't just stick a barrel in his mouth and pull the trigger, I don't know. Guess he didn't figure on the random folks who'd come along, looking for a place in the woods. He didn't figure on the people running scared, with no real plan, stumbling upon him.

I'd taken Ellis down (one shot to the head), before getting my boat unhitched and going. As I started trundling out, a few other zombies, (some of those random people I'd mentioned, who'd been Ellis's lunch), came stumbling out onto the bank, almost as if they were seeing me off. One of them just kept on walking right into the damned river, only I guess those things can't drown. I guess he's still down there, somewhere, slogging around, being nibbled on by fish, and still going. Man, oh man.

Still, less zombies wandering around here than would be in the city. Lots less, at that. It didn't feel too good, though, knowing there was a steady, small horde of dead people (who could still eat), slowly building up at the landing. It meant I had to stay put where I was no matter what, or risk trying to put my way through them, if for some damn reason I needed to go back up river and get something. I wouldn't need to, however. The point of my place was to be on my own. I was just about to retire anyhow, when it all started, so I guess now I am. Retired.

Nothing I ever did mattered anymore. Not what I did for a job, or that I was still not married, probably never would be, and was never a dad, at least, not that I ever knew of. I guess it's possible there's some kid walking around with my eyes, my charming good looks, but not likely. But, hell, anything's possible. Gotta live with that fact now every damn day. When the dead get up, start walking around, and decide that the living would make a nice snack, you gotta realize real quick that pretty much anything is possible in this world.

With this new frame of mind, I shouldn't have been so surprised at what the clawing sound turned out to be, but still, I was. Like I said before, at first I thought it was one of them. Maybe Pete Deutschman was stumbling around out there, looking for a meal?

I figured it stood to reason that a few others, like me, had got the bright idea to come out here to the woods. I also figured maybe a couple of those (like Ellis), had been bitten while trying to get out of the city, or at some point on their way here. They probably got on their boat and got down river to their places before the fever even started. Then they just up and died, all alone. Or, if they had brought family or friends with them (probably a lot had), they munched on a few of them, and turned them, before one of the still living got up the nerve to shoot their own.

I figured there were about a half dozen cabins within walking distance of me on my side of the river. I knew I didn't have to worry about the other side. No way any zombie was going to cross the river. They would easily be swept downstream for miles before ever getting close to my side. There were only half a dozen places within twenty miles of me, since it was such an undertaking to have a cabin out here anyway. Not many people will spend the money on the land, then do all the work it takes to clear it, build on it, and get all the equipment in to run it. All this by boat, mind you. I did it mostly for something to do. Others did it for money, and any other reason to do it, well that was someone else's business.

If all roughly six cabins had people who'd beat it fast enough, (and it was a good bet that most did exactly what I did), I figured maybe only half of those had an infected with them when they reached their place. Let's just say, on average, each person had brought a wife, a few kids, and a few close friends. Each place probably had a good six to eight people in it. An infected could get about half of those before someone (like I said before) got up the nerve to shoot someone they had known and loved. That would account for a good three to four zombies in about every other cabin. So, I figured, there might be an even dozen of them shambling around out in the woods.

There wasn't much else to do during the days, but think and figure. So, I had thought about these (and various other odds) for going on about a week before I actually saw one of the damn things. It wasn't Pete Deutschman. It was some lady, instead. I recognized her though. It was Pete's daughter, Ellie.

She was all of nineteen, I reckoned. I tried to remember, from the talks I'd had with Pete at the hole. I knew she had recently gone off to college, but not too long ago. I couldn't remember if it was last fall, or just this one. At any rate, even with the decomposition, I could see she was pretty damn young. Her blonde hair was mostly in her face, with streaks of dried blood in it. At first I thought it was mud, since it was brown, but as she put her face up to the window (nearly giving me a heart attack) I saw the bits of flesh in it too, and recognized it for what it really was. It was all in the front, so I knew how it had got there. She'd been eating on someone, burying her face in them, well and deep, and had gotten plenty dirty in the process. I thought, for some insane reason, of that old Carl's Jr. ad that used to run on TV. "If it doesn't get all over the place, it doesn't belong in your face." I wanted to vomit then, but it was time for action. I could be sick later, now it was time to survive.

I was ready though, you can believe it. All those hours computing the odds and running random statistics through my head had been done in my good old rocking chair, with my trusty rifle across my lap. My good old Remington short mag, with scope. Not that I needed it at this close range.

She had seen me through the window, sitting there, and somehow, I guess on instinct (God I hope it was instinct), immediately headed towards the door. She was standing there, right in front of me, when I opened it. At first I imagined her waving and saying "howdy neighbor" the way she stood there, her mouth starting to part in what could have been a convivial smile.

Then her mouth opened up too wide, and I saw those nasty teeth, grimy and pink stained. There were thick bits of pinkish meat (person) still stuck between her teeth, and her breath smelled like a skunk's ass. Hell, a skunk's ass probably smelled better, even. She hissed at me then. Actually *hissed*, with her mouth wide open. I took a huge step back, raised my rifle, aimed it right smack dab in the middle of her forehead, and obliterated what was left of the formerly attractive, young Ellie Deutschman. Before the rest of her body could fall forward, spraying guts and old, congealed blood all over my welcome mat, I put my boot to her stomach and pushed hard.

Her body went flopping down off my porch, landing with a thud in the rocky dirt. I was feeling pretty damn tough at the time. I had too much adrenaline pumping through my veins, and nothing to do with it.

"Anyone else wanna try a go at me? You'll have to be quicker 'n that, you fucks!"

I sauntered back inside, slamming the door with my boot, at the same time wondering if the stuff in Ellie's hair had been good old Daddy Pete. Probably it was. Hopefully Ellie had done me a favor and eaten off Pete's legs. I didn't think he could drag himself over to my place with his hands. Those dead shits aren't much with the physical stamina. Not really.

Where there's one, there'll be more, I reasoned. Hell, I was surprised it took a whole week after arriving before I encountered one of them. The fact that it had been Pete's daughter only lent to my rationale about who would be up here and why. If Pete had brought his daughter (and maybe a few of her college friends, perhaps?), others would have come with their own. I thought briefly of Ellie's friends from college, (a strange, twisted version of 'Horny *Zombie* College Co-eds' playing through my mind) and it was almost funny enough to make me laugh. Almost.

If Ellie had happened upon my place by accident (I seriously doubted she had been looking for it), it could be another week before any others did the same. Or a month. If those dead bastards wandered in the opposite direction, they might never end up here. Or I could see two or three amble up onto my porch in one day, who knew? But I could handle it. I had plenty of ammunition. I had plenty of canned food. The generator was working nicely. I had a decent supply of fuel. I could live for quite a while up here. I would keep listening on my radio to see if civilization came back, if ever. If it did, I would leave, when I was sure it was safe. Until then, I would just survive.

It was two nights later that I heard the scratching. I thought it was Pete, or maybe one of Ellie's friends. I looked out the window and saw nothing. Still I could hear that scratching sound. I looked out the window, peering down at the steps. Maybe one of those things had crawled up the stoop and was lying on its belly, scratching to get in? I opened the door, slowly, expecting to maybe find legless old Pete, finally dragged his way over to get some good chow. I barely had time to register that there was no living corpse on my doorstep when I saw something flash inside, quick as lightning.

Instinctively, I closed the door, in case a zombie might be lurking out there anyway. I whirled around to see what the fuck had come into my living room. I had visions of that old horror movie, the one with the hand that gets around by itself. I thought to myself, *maybe it's **part** of one of them, can that be possible?* Then I remembered that anything was possible.

I could hear it, under my rocking chair. It had gone under there, and it was in the shadows where I couldn't see it, *scraping*. Stooping down slightly, I took my rifle and stuck it under there, jabbing at whatever it was. Then I heard the hissing sound (which sounded a *lot* like Ellie's hiss, in fact) and suddenly I realized what it was. It was a damn cat. Just as I figured this out, the darn thing darted out, between my legs and backed up against the far wall. Arching its back, hissing wildly, with all its hair on end, it looked kind of funny.

"Holy shit," I laughed. "I'll be God damned, a fucking cat."

It was dark gray with lighter gray stripes. The kind you'd call a tabby, I guess. It was actually kind of pretty. It was still all arched up, only now it was growling deep down in its throat. It was telling me, *Back off, mister, or else*.

"Okay, okay," I said, easing off.

I set my rifle up against my rocking chair and sat down. I began to figure the odds on a cat being up here, and landed on the idea that some people brought their pets with them, as well as their friends and loved ones. I should have owned a dog, myself, to keep me company, only I never got around to getting one. I was just too lazy for the effort, I guess.

I never owned a cat in my life, but I'd been around them enough, at friend's houses over the course of my lifetime. Personally, I find them too skittish for my taste. This one wasn't disproving my general idea of that particular behavior. It had settled into a sitting position, glaring at me with hateful eyes.

"Hey, I let you in, didn't I?" I said.

No reaction. Typical. I was just about to get up and lock the door (I realized I hadn't before) when I heard more scratching at the door.

"Seriously?" I said.

I looked at Tabby (that's what I'd already started thinking of it as), who was arched up again, only this time she was glaring at the door, growling deep down in her throat again. I had already landed on it being a she. Something about the way she arched, and that mistrust in her eyes struck me as feminine. Later on, when I had the chance to check, it turned out I was right.

"How many of you are out there?" I said.

I peered through the window again, just to make sure it wasn't a corpse on its belly, and seeing nothing, I assumed it was one of Tabby's friends. Well, I was half-right about that. It *was* another cat all right, but it was no friend of mine, or Tabby's. When I opened the door, what I found was a disheveled, sorry looking excuse for a cat. It was dark gray, looked similar to Tabby, only with no stripes. Maybe it was a relative of hers, who knows? The problem with this cat was that it was missing half a face. It had one remaining eye with that familiar milky-white glaze over it, like I'd seen on many of the corpses I'd encountered on my way out of the city. I don't want to think about that, though.

Its tongue hung out, lolling to the right side, resting against white jawbone. Its white cheekbone glinted in the moonlight. Of course, it was a full moon. In the back of my mind I thought, *How typical*. Half of its tail was gone too, ending in a ragged stump, about three inches from its ass. I think something bit it off, gnawing it off in several chomps, from the looks of it. Under its belly I could see something else glinting in the moonlight. It was some kind of rope hanging from its middle, dragging on the porch, and I realized with sudden horror that it was the cat's entrails, dragging along as it walked. This was no living cat. This cat surely was dead. Yet, here it was on my porch, scratching to be let in, just as Tabby had done.

"Holy Jesus," I whispered. I hadn't seen anything like this coming. The damn thing walked unsteadily into my living room, having eyes only for Tabby. It didn't seem to give me a second thought. The damn thing walked right past me, going straight for Tabby, who was backing away, towards the kitchen. Just like the dead people, this cat wasn't so fast, but it was faster than a corpse, at least. I think the only thing really slowing it down was its insides. They had gotten caught on a large splinter of wood in the doorway. Dead Cat Thing was pulling and lurching forward to get free, which gave Tabby time to high tail it into the kitchen. Dead Cat Thing's entrails finally wrenched free with a sickening, wet, ripping sound (leaving a bit behind) and it went straight for the kitchen, a bit faster this time. It seemed to be having trouble coordinating its leg movements. I figure two legs are hard enough. Dead people seemed to have trouble walking fast and running was impossible, so this animal trying to coordinate four legs at once was tricky. Dead things simply cannot run. This is a very good thing for the living. It was an especially good thing for Tabby.

I finally snapped out of whatever shocked disbelief I had been in, and went for my gun cabinet. My rifle was too big for this job, and I didn't want to go blowing holes in my cabin, for Christ's sake. I grabbed my .38 Special, which is the one I use to shoot really large Silvers, once I reel them up close enough to the surface. By this time, Dead Cat Thing had made it into the kitchen doorway and Tabby was backed up against the pantry door in the corner, with nowhere left to go. I simply marched up to Dead Cat Thing, pinned it down to the kitchen floor under my boot, bent down, and displaced what was left of its head all over my kitchen floor. Looking at Tabby right after, that adrenaline flowing again, my sick sense of humor reared its ugly head, the one that tended to get me in trouble in my past life.

"No one's getting near that pussy but me," I told what remained of Zombie Cat.

I laughed at my own joke, but Tabby seemed to miss the humor in it. I chalk it up to the fact that cats, zombie or no, don't have a sense of humor. Soon after, while I was cleaning the mess up as best I could, Tabby skittered around me and went back to hiding under the rocking chair.

She must have realized though (in her own little cat way of thinking), just what I had done for her, because later that night, as I dozed in my chair, she damn near gave me a heart attack. I jumped awake at the sudden feeling of weight pushing against my right ankle, only to realize after a few dazed seconds that Tabby was rubbing herself up against me. I could hear a low level *purr* drifting up to my ears from down below and I leaned over to see her little face peering up at me, eyes half slanted closed, looking happy as could be. She knew I'd saved her ass.

"Yeah?" I said, smiling.

She just looked at me. I tempted fate by reaching down, pretty much expecting her to jump and skitter away, but she didn't. She let me pick her up and I set her in my lap. I petted her little cat head for a few minutes, and then she jumped down and went back to hiding under my chair.

The next morning I opened a can of tuna (I actually had a case of it in the pantry), and she went to town on it. I figured I could feed her on that 'til it was gone, and after that, my scraps would have to do. It's not like she had much of a choice. If she was a finicky eater before, those days were over, that's for sure. I also took an old box and removed the lid. I filled the lid with sand from some old sand bags I'd used as weights. I cut them open and filled that lid, then placed the makeshift 'litter box' in the far corner of the kitchen. She watched me do this. I wasn't certain if she'd understand what it was for, but only a few hours later, I went to check, and I could see her little paw marks in the sand, like she was trying to decorate it and make it her own. She took to using it immediately; never had any problems cleaning up Tabby's mess.

That night, after I dozed off in the chair again (I always slept in the chair, it made me feel more safe), Tabby jumped into my lap, curled herself up into a ball and slept like that all night. The night after that, too, in fact.

That's how it's been for weeks now. I pondered over, puzzled over, the zombie cat. I didn't see any other cats after that first one, and no more came scratching at my door. Thank goodness for small favors.

I knew that it was possible for viruses to cross over from humans to animals, and vice versa, so I reasoned that must be what happened here. Somehow, whatever was causing people to reanimate (I didn't know if it was a virus or not), had somehow crossed over, and in this case, had infected a cat.

Maybe it was Ellie Deutschman's cat that I had blown away? Maybe Ellie had munched on her cat when the hunger initially set in? Maybe at first, she wasn't sure exactly what it was she was craving? Maybe Ellie ate her cat's face off (part of it, anyhow), and when that didn't quite fit the bill, she had moved on to the stomach (still not sure what she wanted), tried the tail, then she had moved on to good old Dad? Who knows how it happened, but the irrefutable fact was that I had now blown away a goodly number of human zombies, and a cat zombie on top of that. However it happened, it did, and it's over now.

I'd like to say I feel confident that it will all be over soon. Maybe those things have a short life span? I mean, how long can rotting flesh walk around, before the entire contraption falls apart? At some point, all those dead things will be pretty much useless; as good as dead again. When that happens, things can return to normal.

I'd like to think that, except that this morning, as I peered out my window at the first breaking of the dawn, I saw a deer. Not so unusual around these parts. The difference here was that this deer was eating another deer that lay dead on the ground. The deer doing the eating had some ribs visible on the side facing my window. I don't mean ribs as in, under the skin, like it was starving or something. Not outlined under the skin. I mean its ribs were *visible*. White bone was peeking out through torn flesh. In one spot, I could see clean into the damn animal and out the other side. I could see insects buzzing in the air, through what should have been a solid barrier of flesh.

Now, a single, anomalous zombie cat, I can handle. That's a concept I can wrap my head around. Whatever this thing (virus?) was, it had obviously jumped from humans to cats, which is just one species. This I can also handle. Seeing that this thing had now been affecting the deer, well that's a whole other story.

It's beginning to dawn on me now, that this thing that happened to us, to people, didn't just happen to us. It's beginning to seem more likely that it happened to everything. I mean, every living thing that walks this earth. Maybe, it just so happened, that every dead thing on earth just up and started living again, in a sense? Eating, consuming, terrorizing the still normal living, that is. If that's the case, then it seems to me that there is a war going on out there in the world, beyond this cabin, past these woods and over this river. There is an outright war going on between every living thing and every dead thing of its kind.

That zombie cat hadn't wanted me. It walked right past me. Maybe Ellie never munched on her kitty after all. 'Cause I went out there and held that rifle up to that zombie deer, and it just kept right on eating that other deer. It didn't pay any attention to me at all. *It just ignored me and kept eating the other deer.* Just like that zombie cat ignored me and kept going straight for the real prize. Whatever this is, it makes the dead only go after its own kind. In a way, that makes things even worse; more tragic, somehow.

Every living thing, possibly, is at war now with its own kind. How long before I start seeing zombie skunks, squirrels, birds? Could it affect the fish in the river? How far has this thing spread, and to how many different species? I don't have the answers to any of these questions.

I just don't know what to make of it all. Human beings are one thing, but every living thing is another. We're talking a complete breakdown of the ecosystems of the world here. If that's not the definition of the end of the world, I don't know what is.

I have no idea what's really going on out there, in the world, beyond this cabin or these woods. I don't want to know. I'll just sit here, with Tabby on my lap, and wait it all out, either way. I'm so glad I have her and that she found me. We need each other, Tabby and I. I'm just glad I don't have to wait this out all alone. However all this may end, Tabby and I will face things together.

Scottie

She was an old woman when she died, but she was immediately transported back in time to the worst day of her entire life; the day she ran over Scottie. He wasn't all that old when he was crushed beneath the wheel of her Sedan. He was only five at the time, or thirty-five in dog years, the same age as the woman.

It wasn't unusual for Scottie to run out of the doggie door and bark off a farewell to her. He always had the sense to stand off to the left of the car, in the driveway, where she could see him. She'd wave and he'd wag his tail in response.

"See you tonight, after work, Scottie!" she'd yell from behind the wheel.

His tail would wag even harder at this promise of her company in nine long hours. He'd wait, patiently, by the door, starting at around five in the afternoon. At six-thirty, when she pulled back into the driveway, Scottie would race out and greet her with paws on slacks, tail wagging into tracers. He'd lick her hands, cleaning off the day's work and the grime from her keyboard.

Dinner together consisted of Scottie's bowl of dry food at her feet near the kitchen table, and her with some varied flavor of microwave pasta and a glass of Chardonnay to unwind. Just one glass, always only one; except on Friday nights, when she would indulge herself with a second glass.

***

It wasn't a very original name, Scottie. The little dog was a Scottish Terrier, and the name was a foregone conclusion. It just fit. Scottie was 'Scottie' and she felt the name fit his personality perfectly.

On the day she ran him over, she was particularly tired. She'd stayed up a little too late the night before to watch the conclusion of a reality show. Then she had run out of instant coffee that morning, and cursed at the thought of having to stop at the store after work, making her get home to Scottie even later than usual. She should have thought ahead on her Sunday store trip, but she'd failed to calculate what remained in her instant coffee can, and that item hadn't gone on the list.

She drank some orange juice instead, too tired to notice that Scottie wasn't at her feet, lapping at her bare toes. She was simply way too tired to notice that Scottie wasn't around. She filled his bowl before she left.

As she pulled out of her driveway, she felt the slight bump underneath her tires and her heart stopped. She immediately knew what it was. As she got out, praying it was a newspaper or a kid's bike that the neighbors left there by mistake, her heart sank at the sight of blood splattered outward from the back left tire. She saw a familiar paw and her world sank.

Why hadn't she noticed that Scottie wasn't there to the left of her car, barking his farewell? Thoughts flitted through her mind, of his absence at the kitchen table, and his lack of presence as she filled his bowl for the day. She should have noticed he wasn't there; why wasn't he there? What was Scottie doing lying behind her car? What should she do next?

Despite all the blood, she gently pulled his body out from underneath the car, hoping, somehow, that he wasn't really hurt all that bad, but he was already dead. She could see that he wasn't breathing. She'd killed him.

Her mind began to reel, the guilt already mounting into a million little regrets of everything she'd failed to notice that morning. She wondered what Scottie had thought as she ran him over. Did he think she did it on purpose? Did he think he'd done something wrong and that she was punishing him? Did Scottie think she didn't love him?

***

At the moment of her death, she transported herself into her own personal Hell. She ran over Scottie again. She found his body, flattened; all his internal organs reduced to mush, and feces forced out of his backside.

She'd originally buried him in the backyard when she was alive. This time, she pulled his body out and ran into the house for a towel. She gently wrapped Scottie up, placed him into the backseat of the car, and drove to the local vet's office.

Sobbing as she entered the lobby holding his limp and crushed body, the look on the receptionist's face was one of frozen shock. Blood dripped from Scottie's mouth and landed on the white tiled floor. There was one other client in the waiting room, with a cat carrier, and she immediately covered her mouth and began to cry. This was every pet-owner's worst nightmare come true.

Pet regret; it would plague the woman for the rest of her life, marring almost every happy moment that could or should have come in all the years that would follow. She never owned another pet again, living alone for many years before finally marrying a fellow office worker.

There in the vet's office, she sobbed out what had happened. She was ushered immediately into a waiting room. When the vet came in, she asked for an autopsy. She'd regretted not getting one in her actual life. Here, in the afterlife, she was getting the chance to do what she'd only wished she'd done originally, hoping for an absolution. By the time she'd thought to get an autopsy in her real life, Scottie's body had been buried for too long, and she didn't have the heart to dig him up and disturb his grave.

The vet shook his head. Scottie was dead, run over by her car. What good would an autopsy do?

"Please," the woman sobbed. "He was lying behind my car. He didn't bother to move when I started the engine. Something must have already been wrong with him. I need to know why he wasn't at my feet during breakfast."

She was hoping and praying something else had killed him, before she ran him over. The vet told her an autopsy would be very expensive, and they may not even find an answer. The woman didn't care about costs. She'd pay whatever they charged her. She just needed to know *why*.

***

In the afterlife, she was then transported to the autopsy results, glossing over the days of waiting. Time worked differently in death. She was back in the vet's office, Scottie's body, this time cremated and in an urn. The results were in.

Poisoning. Trace amounts of antifreeze were found in Scottie's stomach. She wondered how they had figured this out, when all of Scottie's internal organs had been crushed and mushed together into a soup, but she didn't dare to ask.

"Scottie was poisoned by antifreeze," the vet said. "It's very sweet, and dogs tend to lap it up. It shuts down the entire body very quickly. This would explain why Scottie wasn't in your house that morning, and why he was lying in your driveway."

The most important question lay poised on the woman's lips for a brief, quivering moment, before she dared to ask it. Her chin trembled.

"Was he already dead before I ran him over?"

God, she hoped he was. The vet shook his head.

"That I can't tell you. I have no way of knowing."

"Please?" The woman looked at the vet with too much hope in her eyes.

He wanted to give her the answer he knew she was looking for. He breathed out and tried to deliver her some kind of reprieve.

"Most likely, he was already dead."

"Thank God." And she began to sob all over again.

***

Her afterlife Hell was not yet over with, however. A transformation then occurred. She was Scottie. She could still think in her own words, but she could also feel Scottie's thoughts, in their foreign manner, and she experienced his emotions, in all their shockingly human forms as well.

She became he. He tasted the sweet liquid lying on the ground of the neighbor's driveway, where they had changed out their own car's fluids, including the oil, but hadn't bothered to clean it up, or use a pan. It was early in the morning, barely dawn, and the woman, his owner, still slept.

It was a quick sickness. Before he was even done lapping up the last of the sweet liquid, he began to sway, having trouble breathing. His insides knotted up, feeling like a ball of twine being twisted. The pain was immense, Scottie could hardly walk, seeing double. He barely made it back to the driveway, where he knew she'd find him when she got into her machine.

Her thoughts mixed with his. The horror hit her like a million needles of regret pinning her to Scottie's soul. Connecting her to his pain, making it her own, for the millionth time in her own conscience.

Scottie lay, as the woman, trapped inside his mind, his body, behind the car. She/he heard her footsteps as she walked in front of the car and the door opened.

God, oh God, no!

I'm still alive. He was still alive. Scottie wasn't dead. She lay there, trapped inside his tiny body. She felt everything he felt. He couldn't move, paralyzed by the shutting down of his entire body. He'd soon be dead, he knew this, but at the moment, he could still think and feel. And he knew she didn't see him. He lifted his head, attempting to make his limbs work, to pull himself out of the way, but his body wouldn't work. He felt terror as the car's engine started. He knew what was coming.

This was exactly as she had feared. The pain was immense, as she felt the car's tire run over her body. As Scottie felt the tire run over his tiny, fragile body. It was quick, but not painless by any amount. A crushing torrent of agony pressed his body flat; liquefying all his internal organs, making him shit himself. His hindquarters splayed out flat as blood ejected from his mouth, spattering and splattering the concrete near the back wheel that had just reduced him to a carcass. Everything went dark in only a second.

His last thoughts were of immense pain and unbelievable fear, but she was finally released from her agony from all those years of wondering. Scottie would have died anyhow, and the pain would have been just as acute, either way it occurred. But the regret she felt, and the torture her own mind would inflict was immediately released by becoming Scottie and knowing what his final thoughts were.

The fear Scottie felt was not in the pain, or in the dying. It was in leaving the woman all alone. In a split second, he had the time to form his own regrets. He blamed himself for getting sick, although he didn't know what had truly happened to his own body. Scottie blamed himself for not moving and causing the woman to run him over.

He blamed himself. Her mind sobbed inside of his. She felt his feelings, and knew what he knew. Her heart broke. Scottie thought it was all *his* fault. Yet, she was comforted just the same. His last feelings were of warmth, pushing out the pain, just before everything went dark.

***

In a few moments, she would be transported out of Hell, and into an afterlife where Scottie bounded up to her, just as he was when he was alive, and they would live for all eternity together. In only moments, the woman's afterlife would turn beautiful, once her Hell was born out and lived.

Scottie's very last thoughts were happy. His entire life flashed before him, and they were all moments of love shared with the woman. He didn't think she was punishing him. He didn't blame her for anything. And the moment of her release came in a torrent of feeling, which ended her Hell and finally began her eternal peace and contentment.

He knew that she loved him.

Queases

Joining a sorority is what turned Jenny Koenig into a murderer. Ultimately. Or, it could be said that she just made a few bad choices. Number one, Jenny chose a school with no national Greek system. She chose (out of necessity) a cheaper school, with no intent of ever joining any clubs at all. But once on campus her freshman year, she found making new friends to be difficult, especially once she'd met a few fellow house mates who all planned to Rush. Her roommate wanted to soak in Greek Week, and Jenny found herself going along for the ride. After all, she didn't want to be stuck for the rest of her year with a roommate who was separated and alienated from her by a lack of participation.

In early October, Jenny rushed with her roommate, Joy, and found herself chosen by a local chapter of Kappa Pi Omega, to become a pledge. She didn't know the difference between a local and a national chapter, and even if she had, she still would have participated. At age eighteen, she still had the narcissistic, high school need to belong.

Pledge week was a nightmare. She was ordered, first and foremost, not to speak. All the pledges were placed on an oath of silence. They could write notes, e-mails and texts to anyone they wanted, but their mouths had to remain closed. This was tough in class, and the teachers all knew of this annual tradition and tried to make it easier for the Kappa's to get through.

The week sailed by, however, and on Friday night, October 15, the final test commenced. The pledges were gathered and blindfolded. They were told they'd be taken to a series of locations. At each location, one pledge would be instructed to enter a public establishment, and under the guidance of a 'Mother' they'd be ordered to steal something.

In her blindfold, Jenny heard her own breath catch in her throat. She could hear her heart beating inside her head. She'd never stolen anything before in her entire life. If everyone else was doing it, however, she'd have to go along. If she were the only pledge to fail at her task, she'd be socially shunned for the rest of her year at school, not to mention the next three years to follow. This was a sisterhood. The Mothers wouldn't make her do anything that would get her into any real trouble, would they? These were her future sisters. Her net, her blanket, her future friends for life. She'd already bonded deeply with her fellow pledges, including Joy.

Joy even knew Jenny's little secret. At five-foot-six, and weighing only 110 pounds, blonde-haired, blue-eyed Jenny had to find some way to keep her svelte figure. She'd begun the daily ritual of purging early in her senior year of high school. It was difficult, hiding it from her mother. She'd been so relieved to leave for college, where she hoped her habit would be more easily kept under wraps.

The dorm life, however, was far more public than she'd imagined. The first few times she'd retched in the dorm bathroom, no one had walked in, but on day three, Joy herself came in. She stopped at the bathroom stall. Jenny turned around, wiping her mouth, to see Joy's flip flops standing so close to the stall door, they were almost intruding underneath.

"Jenny?"

"Yeah?"

"Oh, that *is* you. Are you okay?"

"Yeah."

"Okay."

Two days later, when Jenny got rid of her dinner and Joy walked in again, she said nothing. Later that evening in their room, however, she'd closed her study book and looked at Jenny at her desk with a motherly stare of understanding.

"I've done it too, you know." It wasn't a question.

"Done what?" Jenny never looked up from her own book.

"Made myself throw up."

Jenny only shrugged. She already knew making an excuse would do no good. Especially if she was going to live with Joy for the rest of the year. This was before they'd planned together to rush Kappa.

"It's no big deal," she continued. "Just, be careful."

Jenny turned to look at her then, her eyes full of shame.

"I won't tell anyone," Joy smiled. "And you're not the only one. I'd do it myself, but…I wasn't very good at it."

"Do you want me to help you learn how?" Jenny was scared to even ask this.

"No," Joy said. "I exercise a lot. Plus, I sort of don't eat very much."

Jenny nodded. Joy had her own problems with food. This was her way of telling Jenny she understood and she wasn't alone. They bonded that night, in a short conversation, where not so much was said, and yet, a lot was understood. When Joy asked Jenny two weeks later to rush Kappa with her, she agreed, feeling comfortable. She wanted to remain close to Joy.

*****

The girls were loaded into two vans, still blindfolded. Jenny sat next to Joy, holding her hand. The vans started and as the drive commenced, everyone remained quiet.

At the first stop, a half-hour later, no one got out, except Kelly, one of the pledges. She was gone for about twenty minutes. When she returned, she was allowed to remove her blindfold. The van commenced driving.

Kelly whispered to the other pledges. Everyone listened intently.

"You guys, it's easy. It's no big deal. You only have to steal a tiny thing. Easy."

Jenny breathed out, feeling just as nervous. She wasn't comforted by the words, 'it's easy'.

The van stopped several more times. Joy went on stop number three. Again, she was only gone for about twenty minutes. When she returned, removing her blindfold, she took up Jenny's hand again. She whispered in her ear.

"I was in a shop in China Town, I think," she breathed. "I had to steal this tiny little jade ornament thing. It's no big deal, Jenny."

She nodded. The van drove on. Ten minutes later, it stopped, and Jenny was ordered to get out. Outside the van, she was walked for several yards then instructed to remove her blindfold. She looked around, blinking.

She was on a street. The smell of incense, or some sort of perfume pervaded her nostrils. She looked around for the van, but didn't see it. Her 'Mother' was smiling at her. The older girl took Jenny's hand and walked with her down the street, filled with tiny shops and open food carts. This wasn't China Town, but something like it, Jenny realized. Little Haiti, perhaps?

They entered a shop. Inside, it was dark and foreboding. Tables lined with odd artifacts and crystals, rocks and geodes met Jenny's eyes. A very heavy odor filled her nostrils, almost burning. It was like oranges and kelp, and a bit of rubber all mixed together. Shelves filled with jars full of powders, granules of god-knows-what, and various colored liquids made Jenny feel very uncomfortable. She was a lapsed Baptist, but her upbringing cried out from the depths within her. She knew what this was. It was blasphemy. It was witchcraft.

Jenny gasped as she continued walking through the small shop. In the corner, closest to the checkout counter, was a large, open-air cabinet of some kind. On the bottom shelf, a bowl sat. As she looked inside, she found the source of the overwhelming smell that singed her sinuses. The bowl was filled with some kind of thick liquid. It looked brownish red, and Jenny thought it might be congealed blood. Steeped within the liquid was an upturned chicken's foot, the talon-tips singed black and still smoking.

"Ew." She felt as if she might vomit. Her stomach lurched.

She'd purged that evening, however, before leaving on this expedition. Her stomach had nothing to offer up. She swallowed and released a tiny burp. Then she looked over at 'Mother' who only glared.

Behind the counter, from around a dark curtain, a very old woman suddenly appeared. She looked ancient. Her eyes were sunken deep within their sockets. Her brown skin was so wrinkled it made Jenny think of a Shar-pei Dog. Her hair was thinning and the old woman's scalp was showing through in spots. The woman seemed to read Jenny's mind, so it would seem to her, and immediately raised her knotted hands to begin tying a thick scarf around her head. She smiled at Jenny, and several teeth were missing. The woman's gums were brownish pink, and again, Jenny's stomach flip-flopped.

'Mother' turned her back on the woman and looked into the dark cupboard again. Surrounding the bowl of blood and the smoking chicken's foot, there were several large, opaque jars arranged in a semi-circle. They formed a wide, arcing crescent around the front of the bowl, almost looking like a smile. Each jar had something hanging around it. A necklace or charm of some kind adorned every container. Jenny looked away from the cupboard and the blood. She walked several feet away to peruse the tables and other shelves.

There were books and candles, and packets of something. Jenny had no idea what, but she picked up a small envelope and shook it, and the sound that issued from inside sounded like sand.

'Mother' walked behind Jenny and perused items as well. After several minutes, the old woman seemed satisfied that these two customers were only looking, and weren't going to buy anything. She disappeared back behind the curtain. The older girl sidled up behind Jenny, quickly, and whispered in her ear.

"Take a trinket from one of those jars," she whispered.

It didn't need any more explanation than that. Jenny immediately knew what 'Mother' wanted her to do. She knew which jars she was referring to. She knew which trinkets as well. Suddenly, any pretense of motherly concern or love evaporated away from Jenny. She felt cold and untethered. Left to rot. She looked at her future 'sister' and her eyes were filled with dread. She began to shake her head, but the older girl shook back, answering her with her eyes. *Do this or else.*

None of the other pledges had failed, Jenny knew, including Joy. She couldn't room with her new best friend all year, while not in the same sorority. It would be Hell. She knew this. Joy would have no choice but to shun and avoid her as much as possible. They wouldn't be able to attend any of the same social events, as Jenny would not be invited. 'Mother' quickly left the shop. Jenny had to do this all on her own. She'd been given her orders.

She turned and looked toward the counter. It was still abandoned. Suddenly, her phone vibrated. She pulled it from her pocket. It was a text from Joy.

You can do it!

Jenny sighed, holding her phone in a shaking hand. She made her way over to the cabinet. Without thinking, she set her phone down, shakily, and allowed her hands to hover over the jars, sailing them in the air above. Which trinket should she take?

Just take any one, and get out of here! Her mind screamed.

Her hand stopped over the jar closest to her body, the one right in the middle of the crescent. The necklace dangling from this jar was made of twine rope, it looked like. Tied to the middle of it was some sort of charm. A small wooden figure of a person crudely sculpted in some kind of dark wood. The eyes were two X's that appeared to have been chiseled and burned. The trinket on the thin rope simply lay around the jar. It was not even tied on.

Jenny glanced over her shoulder, certain the old woman would have returned. She was sure she'd see the old lady's gaze boring right into her, knowing what she was about to do. The counter was empty, however. Still.

Jenny turned back to the jar. It was now or never. The woman had been gone for too long. Surely she'd return any moment. Jenny could not fail at this task. She quickly removed the twine necklace and shoved it into her pocket. Her heart was racing in her chest. She'd just become a thief.

She quickly turned away from the cabinet and headed toward the shop's front door. As she put her hand on the doorknob, she heard a creaking noise. She turned to find the old woman standing almost directly behind her. Jenny frowned. Her eyes went to the counter. How had the old woman gotten so close to the door? Had she seen what Jenny had done? The old woman was smiling. She didn't look angry at all.

The old woman was tiny, she realized. Jenny was five-foot-six, and this ancient lady only came up to her shoulder. Taking one step forward, the woman slowly reached her weathered, leathery right hand up to touch Jenny's face, covering her mouth, gently. Her left hand simultaneously settled, palm flat, on Jenny's stomach.

She was terrified, frozen in place. Time seemed to slow down. She stared into the old woman's eyes, transfixed. The old woman continued smiling. Then she opened her mostly toothless grin and whispered.

"Queases."

Quickly, the hands were removed. The woman backed away and walked to stand behind the counter. Jenny only continued to stand in her spot, dazed. What had just happened? The woman stood behind the counter and nodded at her, continuing to smile her motherly, knowing grin.

Jenny broke her paralysis and quickly turned back to the door. She yanked on the knob and flew from the shop. 'Mother' was waiting outside, pacing. She saw Jenny come flying out and merely put out her hand expectantly. Jenny angrily marched up to her and dug inside her pocket for the stolen trinket. She thrust it into the older girl's hand and continued on her way. The older girl caught up to her, yanking on her shoulder.

"Hey!"

Jenny spun around to cast an angry glare on the girl. The girl only smiled and shrugged.

"Welcome to Kappa Pi Omega...Sister."

That night, no one failed, and twelve new pledges were inducted into the sorority. Drinking and partying ensued.

*****

It wasn't until the next day that Jenny realized she'd fucked up big time. She'd gotten dressed while Joy still slept her inebriation away in her dorm room bed. Jenny couldn't find her phone anywhere. She retraced her steps, trying to break through the drunken haze of memories from the night before, during the induction. She didn't remember anything about her phone at the party. She pushed further back, into her memories, and her eyes suddenly widened. Shit! She remembered, far too late, taking her phone out to read Joy's text. Then she realized what she'd stupidly done. She'd left her damn cell phone right there in the cabinet, next to all those jars.

"Fuck!"

Joy looked up from her hangover slumber and groggily peered at Jenny.

"Wassamatter?" She closed her eyes again.

Jenny sighed, looking down at her friend. She couldn't go back to the shop. She didn't even know where it was. She certainly couldn't ask her sorority sisters for directions on how to get back there. Not without divulging why she needed to go there. She couldn't admit a stupid mistake like that to them. Maybe they'd decide to revoke her membership? Could they do that? She was too embarrassed to ever admit her mistake, anyhow.

Jenny worried all day about the old woman. Surely she'd see the phone sitting there in the cabinet. Next, her eyes would move to the single jar in the array that was missing its trinket. Jenny had practically left a thief's calling card behind. Would the woman use her phone to report her to the police? Could she really be arrested for stealing something so small (and surely not worth much) as a twine rope and a wooden trinket? How much could the thing have cost, anyhow? There wasn't even a price tag on it. In fact, nothing within the cabinet had contained a price tag, Jenny realized. Everything else in the shop had, however. Was it considered stealing if something had no price tag?

At any rate, she reasoned, she was simply in a bind. She couldn't tell her sorority sisters anything. She didn't even want to tell Joy. It was all too embarrassing. She couldn't get her phone back, nor would she ever be able to find that shop. She didn't even have the trinket to return, in order to apologize. Her 'Mother' (whom she was now allowed to call Monica) had taken the trinket away. What had Monica done with it? Jenny didn't know, and she wasn't going to ask.

The only thing she could do was wait. And hope. Hope that nothing would happen. She went out and bought a new phone later that afternoon. She reported her old phone stolen. She had to get a new number and spent the rest of the evening sending her new information out to friends and family, via phone calls and e-mails.

Jenny was plagued by worries for the next several days before her brain's incessant whirring finally began to fade away. As October bled into November, she was busy with midterms, Sorority parties, binge drinking (followed by puking) and binge eating (followed by more puking). By the time Jenny made the drive home for the Thanksgiving Holiday, she was proud of herself for evading the famed 'freshman fifteen', returning home weighing five pounds less than when she'd left.

*****

Her mother looked at her with concern, but said nothing. She simply tried to feed second helpings to Jenny all of Thanksgiving evening. Jenny ate to make her mother happy. She purged in her own comforting bathroom upstairs to make herself happy. Luckily her bathroom was connected to her bedroom, for optimal privacy.

As she lay in bed that evening, staring at her old TV, her phone vibrated. She picked it up and frowned, her heart leaping in her chest. Was this a joke? Had one of her Sorority sisters figured out (or known all along) her embarrassing secret? She'd been alone in that shop with the old woman. Not even Monica could have heard or known. As far as Jenny knew, only two people on the planet knew what had been said inside that shop; she and the old woman. Jenny stared at the text, her entire body feeling like a block of ice.

Queases

She tried to see what number the text had been sent from, but it was blocked. Her old phone couldn't be working, could it? She'd reported it stolen, so it should have been shut off. There was no way the old woman could have texted her on her new phone. How would she have gotten the number? Jenny smiled at the image of the nearly toothless, wrinkled old woman composing a text. In her ancient and leathery hands, picturing a phone, black, sleek and shiny was almost laughable. Combined with the image of the woman's knotted and gnarled fingers clumsily typing the word "Queases" made Jenny actually laugh out loud. Then she emitted a tiny and unexpected, acid-laced burp from her doll-like lips.

She suddenly reasoned, sitting up in bed, she must have drunkenly admitted to the strange encounter in the shop, during the induction party after her night of thievery. After all, there was a substantial blackout section from that night, she now recalled with a distinct feeling of paranoia. There was no way that Joy would play a mean trick like this on her. She was certain of this. Most likely, it was Monica-the-bitch herself. Jenny's stomach suddenly did an unexpected flip-flop so violently she'd swear something was alive inside her.

She was still holding her phone, staring at that confusing word, when Jenny realized she was going to be sick. She dropped the phone onto her coverlet and ran for the bathroom.

No purposeful attempt at purging her Thanksgiving dinner was necessary this time. She barely had time to flip her toilet's lid up, before her mouth was forced open by the projectile contents that lurched from her stomach. She felt as if she were being ripped and turned inside out. A jagged, stabbing pain followed the contents as it made its way from her stomach, back up her esophagus, moving forward into the back of her throat, into her mouth, and out into the bowl, with a wet plop. It felt as if she'd just thrown up a jagged shard of glass. Her throat burned. She would swear she'd been ripped open in one, long seam. She retched again, and watched in horror as a thin line of bright red blood ejected from her throat. A thin line of red and pink-tinged saliva slowly dripped from the tip of her tongue. Tears leaked from the corners of her eyes.

As her watery vision began to slowly adjust away from the line of pink still hanging from her tongue, she followed the bloody string down to the water in the bowl below her, and got a good look at what she'd just barfed up. She had to be seeing things.

As Jenny swallowed hard, however, another burning sensation in her throat and all along her insides, reminded her that she'd been injured somehow by what she'd thrown up. As she continued to look at it inside the bottom of the bowl, she now understood why.

It was brown. Slightly wrinkled. Bulbous. And it had a long, sharp, jagged edge, slightly yellowed and cratered at the end. Jenny covered her mouth with her hand, feeling woozy. It couldn't be what it appeared to be. It couldn't. It wasn't possible. What she was looking at appeared, for all intents and purposes, to be a human big toe. It was housed in skin the same shade as that of the old woman from the shop so many weeks ago.

Queases

Jenny thought about the text. She'd received it only moments before being forced into the bathroom. She couldn't have been sick from Thanksgiving dinner. She was certain of it. Besides, she'd already rid herself of all her Thanksgiving overindulgence. And she certainly would have recalled if she'd eaten the nasty, big toe of a black (or perhaps Haitian) woman.

The old woman had done this. Surely. And Jenny knew why, although now she reasoned that the punishment, in no way, fit the crime. For stealing a trinket surely worth no more than a few dollars at most, she was now throwing up human body parts?

Jenny became angry. She stood and flushed the toilet, walking to her sink and turning on the faucet. She rinsed her mouth thoroughly with water and spat several times. She swallowed several short gulps of cool liquid, feeling them burn her throat as the water came in contact with her scratched and damaged esophagus. Had she been cut so badly? Did she need to go to the hospital? How would they treat a wound on the inside of her body like that? And how would she explain that she'd thrown up a human toe? They wouldn't believe her anyhow, and the evidence had already been flushed away.

She wiped her mouth and stomped her way back into her bedroom, to her bed, where she picked up the phone. Without reading the texted word again, she blindly hit delete and got rid of it. She pushed the entire ordeal out of her head. If the old woman had wanted to get her revenge, well then, there. She'd gotten her revenge. End of story.

Jenny was unable to eat for the next two days, however. She dreamed about human toes. In her dreams, they showed up everywhere. She'd sit down to pour a bowl of cereal, and toes would come pouring out of the box. She'd open the fridge to get out the milk, and a toe would be sitting where the milk jug should be. She'd throw a ball to her pet dog, Billy, and he'd bring back a toe between his little doggy canines.

"Drop it," Jenny would say in her dreams. She'd wake up in a slathering sweat every time.

When she left home to return to school, she'd dropped another two pounds. Her mother was very worried and made Jenny promise to eat while away at school. She promised her mother. She returned to school believing everything would be okay. She was wrong.

Two days into the resumption of classes on campus, Jenny woke up to her phone vibrating. Joy was already gone. She picked up her phone and read the text. She dropped the phone onto the floor as if it had burned her.

Queases

She ran for the bathroom. A large, compact ball was already making its way up her throat before she even had time to kneel. In the stall, she threw up into her mouth. Something long and rope-like dangled down from her mouth and danced across the top of the toilet water. It was pink and slimy and it was still stuck in her throat. Jenny grasped the soft tissue-cord and began to pull in desperation. She was having trouble breathing. Her throat constricted around the solid mass and she began to choke. She pulled desperately against her tightening esophagus, and began a tug-of-war, slowly inching the long, slippery tendril through her windpipe. With a desperate and final tug, she pulled the end through her mouth and allowed it to drop into the toilet, where it coiled into the bottom of the bowl like an albino, eyeless snake. Intestines. She'd just thrown up what she presumed (after the toe) to be human intestines.

She quickly flushed the toilet and went on with her day. At lunch in the cafeteria, she was unable to eat. Monica sat with her, happily munching a tuna salad sandwich. Jenny glared at her as she smiled with a full mouth.

"What did you do with all the things we stole that night?"

"What?" With her mouth full, Monica's question came out sounding like 'watt'.

"The trinkets we all stole on pledge night," Jenny said. "What happened to them?"

"Who cares?"

"I care," Jenny tried not to cry. "I'd like my trinket back, please."

"You can't have it back," Monica said. "It's not yours."

"It's not yours, either."

"Drop it," Monica said, and all Jenny saw in her mind, was Billy, wagging his tail and dropping a human, brown toe onto the floor of her old kitchen.

"I'd like it back, Monica," Jenny said. "Otherwise, I'm going to report your act of hazing to the Dean of Students, and Kappa Pi Omega's charter will be revoked."

"What the fuck is wrong with you?" Monica stared.

"I'm not a thief."

"Um, I hate to break it to you, honey, but, yes, you are."

"I want the trinket back," she said. "And I want the directions to that shop you made me steal it from, so I can return it."

"You've got to be joking me!"

Jenny stood up and headed for the cafeteria entrance. She heard Monica's chair scrape hastily against the floor. A moment later, an angry, clawed hand was on her shoulder, spinning her around.

"You're not really going to go to the Dean, are you?"

"Yes, I am. Right now."

"Okay!"

Monica took Jenny to her own dorm house, on the other side of campus, opposite the freshman dorms. In her room, she opened a drawer in her desk and rummaged around through several small trinkets. Jenny saw a jade green animal of some kind and remembered Joy's words from that terrible night.

"*I had to steal this tiny little jade ornament thing. It's no big deal, Jenny.*"

Then Monica clasped something in her hand and spun around to glare at Jenny. She thrust her hand out in front of the younger woman, waiting. Jenny held her own hand open, palm up and felt an icy, electric stab flow through her, as a twine rope with a wooden figure fell into her palm. She quickly closed her fingers around it and clasped it tight, as if it were a wild mouse that might try to scramble from her grip. She thrust the trinket into her pocket and glared at Monica, waiting.

"The instructions to the shop."

"If you say anything about Kappa Pi Omega, I will string you up and whip you 'til you bleed to death, do you understand me?"

"Perfectly," Jenny said.

Monica turned back around and scribbled on a magenta post-it note. She handed the pink square to Jenny. As she turned to leave, Monica imparted her with a warning.

"And from now on, consider yourself on probation. One false move and you're out. You don't fuck with the sisters of Kappa Pi Omega, bitch."

Jenny never looked back.

*****

Inside the dingy, dark shop, she could smell the pungent odor of burning flesh and this time recognized it for what it was -smoking chicken's foot. She walked straight to the old wooden cabinet and removed the trinket from her pocket. Gingerly, she placed it back around the middle jar, closest to her body. Behind her, she heard floorboards creak.

"Not that easy," the old woman's voice came.

Jenny turned with tears in her eyes. She looked down at the old woman, pleading.

"I'm so sorry," she said. "I didn't want to do it. Please believe me. I'm so sorry."

"You come back?" the woman sounded almost reverent.

"Yes."

"What be done cannot be undone. Not that easy," the woman repeated.

"But, I gave it back."

"Curse be out on you. Cannot be undone."

"B...But," she stammered. The woman shook her head. If she didn't know any better, Jenny would swear the old woman looked sad.

"Jar be filled with Mister's parts. Talismans keep him safe. You remove his protection. I have no choice but to bring him back."

"Bring him back?"

Jenny's eyes widened at the realization of the woman's remarks. She'd thrown up parts of a human being. Would she continue to do so, until she'd regurgitated an entire person? She shook her head.

"I can't," she whispered. "I can't go through that anymore."

"Mister be brought back. Piece by piece. No stopping."

"Then what?" Jenny's stomach felt queasy.

Queases.

"Then mister come back to me, and I re-protect."

"But I flushed him down the toilet! How could he come back?"

The old woman smiled. "Pieces find each other. No protection. And he take you life once he all together."

"What?!"

Jenny's head spun. This wasn't real. She turned and ran to the door, fumbling at the handle, sobbing. She barely heard the old woman's next words.

"Cannot be undone…can be transferred to *another*."

Jenny's hand fell limply to her side. Her breathing ceased. The floorboards creaked again as the old woman came to stand behind her. As she turned, she and the old woman were in the exact positions they'd been in on that fateful first night.

"Transferred?" she whispered. The old woman nodded. Jenny swallowed, her throat audibly clicking. She was going to die, murdered at the hands of a regurgitated, zombie-corpse, for something she hadn't even wanted to do.

You don't fuck with the sisters of Kappa Pi Omega, bitch.

Jenny sighed, nodding.

"You leave phone. Need something from *her*," the old woman said.

Jenny blinked. Then she nodded again and removed the tiny pink square that was crumpled up inside her pocket.

"Will handwriting work?" She looked at the woman, her eyes filled with soulless hope.

The old woman nodded. Jenny blinked again. She didn't have to think about it. She had become a thief against her will. In this shop where blasphemy seemed to give way to another world full of nightmares, impossibilities and outrageous horrors, she would now consent to becoming a murderer.

She reached her shaking hand out to the old woman, whose wrinkled brown hand was already open, palm up. The ancient woman smiled an endearing and almost toothless grin.

Releasing the breath that she'd been holding, Jenny transferred the paper and the curse out of her own hand.

Althea's Mistake

Althea arrived in Hell on August 23rd at 1:17 p.m. She should have arrived in Purgatory, save for one small mistake. She'd committed murder, not just suicide. Now, instead of Purgatory, she would be spending all of Eternity in fire and torment, as opposed to just floating in blackness.

The difference for Althea between residing in Hell, versus Purgatory, was a simple lack of uttering three simple words. Her mistake was simply that of *silently* jumping to her death, inadvertently taking another life with her. As opposed to the simple courtesy of yelling, "Look out below."

Incident Report

"There are zombies chasing me!" the lady screamed.

That's how it all started. I'm not kidding. We had just pulled into the Sierra Madre Station. The doors opened, and the lady jumped in, howling her head off. She was all sweaty and her face was pink. She kept heaving and trying to catch her breath.

I remember looking around at the other Metrolink passengers. They all had the same look on their faces, which I imagine is the exact same look I had on my face. As I looked at each person around me, our eyes locked for a short moment, and one guy even laughed and shook his head. When he smiled, he had dimples in his cheeks, and I remember thinking he was actually pretty cute. Everyone had that expression on his or her face. That, '*Yeah, right*' look.

Then suddenly there was a loud scream from out on the platform, and the lady who was heaving let out a loud 'squawk!' Then she fainted dead away. Probably the shock from all that running, then suddenly stopping. Her lungs couldn't get caught up, and her brain just said, '*Okay, that's it, we're done for a while.*'

The scream came again, and I looked around at all the faces in the car once more. Again, even without words, I could read everyone's thoughts, just from the looks on their faces, and their physical reactions. Everyone still had that smile on their face (it had only been a few seconds since the lady first came on board), only now the smiles looked frozen, plastered on. No one moved. People's shoulders and torsos went rigid. Then slowly, the smiles began to fade and fall away, being replaced by a new expression of dawning horror and complete disbelief.

Everyone's face seemed to be saying, *'Wait, really? Could it really be true?'* Then the wave began. That's really the only way I know how to describe what happened next. It was like one of those waves people are always starting in stadiums, only this one was a panic wave. It started in the back of the car, furthest from me, and worked its way up to where I also sat, frozen, unbelieving.

People began to stand up, some of them craning their necks, trying to see out the compartment windows. Some looked like they still didn't believe, while others looked like they believed fully with no doubt or reserve at all.

Somewhere out on the platform, the screaming continued. It was shrill and high. It was another lady. In the car, the first lady lay crumpled on the floor. No one went to help her. Everyone ignored her and rushed to the windows to see what the hell was going on.

I still didn't believe. And even if I had, I couldn't have made it to a window to see. Not then. In a matter of about two seconds, there were too many people crammed up against the windows for me to even hope to get a good look. Instead, I settled on watching the faces of the ones who were watching. That's when I started to believe.

One lady looking on put her hands to her mouth and just started biting her fingers. It would have been comical, except for the fact that I had to watch a slow, steady trickle of yellow liquid appear on the floor at her feet and begin spreading outward around her black boots. I watched in disgust as the puddle slowly spread until it reached the unconscious lady's hair and tangled into it. I'm sure I must have grimaced then.

"Holy shit!" a black man yelled. "Holy fuckin' shit!"

"Oh my God," a teenage girl said. She began to cry, but all I could think about was wondering why she wasn't in school at 10 a.m. on a Tuesday.

"It's eating her!" the girl said, her voice high and warbly. "It, it's eating her!"

Then everyone screamed as the loudspeaker dinged its warning to stand back, because the doors were closing. The 'pee lady' stepped back too quickly, and tripped on the unconscious lady. She fell backwards silently, hit her head on the floor with a loud, sick thud, and I watched as a new puddle of liquid began to spread around her head. This time it was red.

The Metro car began to move then. Everyone was still standing. Several people fell into their seats. Others frantically grabbed at the ropes above them, or the poles next to them, for balance. I finally stood then. I don't know why, but everyone looked at me. I was the only one moving at the moment. I didn't want to be near the two unconscious ladies anymore.

I made my way past everyone, toward the other end of the car. As luck would have it, this was closest to the 'dimple guy'. I stopped in front of him. He only stared at me.

"Do you mind if I sit down next to you?" I asked. I felt completely stupid. The guy only nodded his consent.

No one spoke for what felt like forever. Then the black guy spoke, making several people jump.

"Is she dead?" he asked.

"Which one?" a Chinese guy said.

"The one who's bleeding," the black guy answered, sounding annoyed.

"How the hell should I know?" Chinese guy yelled back.

"Check her pulse," Mr. Dimples said. His voice was soft and gentle, but it carried through the car. I felt warm all over.

"You have to check her pulse," Dimples repeated.

No one moved. Everyone just stared at Mr. Dimples. After several seconds, he sighed heavily and stood up. I watched him walk over to the bleeding lady. He gently stooped down and placed two fingers at her neck. His back was facing me, but I could see his fingers at her neck. I was in love.

Mr. Dimples stood up and faced the black guy and the Chinese guy. His eyes darted back and forth between them.

"She's not dead. She has a pulse."

Mr. Dimples walked back over to me and sat down. He didn't look at me. He didn't see me smile at him, trying to comfort him.

"What's your name?" I asked, feeling extremely shy.

"Devon," he answered, almost like it was a question.

"Are you a doctor?" I asked.

"No," Devon smiled. "I saw that on TV," he laughed.

"Oh." And suddenly I was laughing, too.

"This isn't funny," the black guy said, walking over.

"I can't help it," I laughed. Devon laughed harder.

"What the fuck is wrong with you?" Black guy said. His eyes were round and huge. They kept darting back and forth between Devon and me. The two of us just cascaded into more gales of uncontrollable, shaking hysterics. Devon grabbed onto my shoulder and buried his face there. Tears began streaming down my own face. My stomach was beginning to hurt, and I was having trouble breathing.

"Jesus, you two are loony, you know that?" Black guy said.

"What's...Your... Name?" I managed to choke out.

The black guy only stared at me for several moments, seeming not to comprehend my question. Then he softened a bit.

"Eric," he said. Then he shook his head and a smile broke out on his face. A big, beautiful smile.

Eric turned to the Chinese man. He put his hand out offering for him to shake it. The Chinese man looked baffled.

"I'm Eric, my man," Eric said. "What's yours?"

"Mine?" Chinese said.

"Your name, bro," Eric said.

"Oh. It's Randall."

Silence filled the car. It hung on the air like thick, acrid smoke. Then Eric began laughing, large tears suddenly squirting from his own eyes. Devon had stopped laughing, but his face remained buried in my shoulder. I could feel his body still spasming.

"You're name is Randall?" Eric said. His voice was suddenly very high. He sounded like a woman, almost. The teenage girl, who I had forgotten all about, suddenly giggled.

"My name is Kate," she said.

"I'm Maggie," I answered her.

Devon pulled his face from out of my shoulder and looked at me with an apology. I smiled at him. He smiled back.

"What about the other lady?" Kate asked. She motioned past the 'pee lady,' who was really now the 'blood lady,' to the original lady. The one who seemed to mark the start of the whole mess.

Devon moved to get up, but I pulled on his arm. For some reason, I didn't want him to go back over there. He looked at me questioning. I only shrugged.

"Sh-she passed out, right?" Kate said.

"It was shock," Eric said. "Had to be. I mean, no wonder."

"Did you see?" Randall said. "Did you see what happened on the platform?"

Everyone nodded, except me. I was the only one who hadn't seen. A Latino guy spoke then. He had a thick accent.

"She said it was zombies, man."

"Nah," Eric said. "Gotta be some other explanation."

"Well, how else do you explain it, huh?" Latino yelled. "That thing was eating a lady! Eating her!"

"There's gotta be another explanation," Eric yelled. "Other than zombies. I mean, come on people. This is real life. This is fucking L.A."

"Well, what then?" Kate said. "Why would someone do that…At a Metrolink?"

"Jesus, lady, don't you know nothing," Latino said. "This is how it starts. I knew it, I fucking knew it." He was now talking to himself.

"Knew what?" Eric said. "This is how what starts?"

"Revelation, dude," Latino said.

There was a collective groan from everyone on the train. Even Kate shook her head and released a small, "Jesus," under her breath.

"Hey, don't laugh," Latino said. "My cousin studied this shit. He knows all about it. Whatever is supposed to happen is already under way. So this is it, huh? Gotta be."

"What's your name, dude," Randall said, easy enough. He was smiling.

"Rafael," Latino answered, sounding extremely defensive.

"Okay, well, Rafael? Let's just focus on the problem at hand, hmm?" Randall looked at everyone then. "We appear to have a slight problem on our hands."

"A slight problem?" a man in a suit said.

He'd been sitting in the far corner with a briefcase and a newspaper the entire time. I hadn't given him much notice. No one had. He stood up then and addressed everyone. His eyes were narrowed down into slits. He had salt-and-pepper hair. He seemed shrewd and sharp. I could immediately picture him in a huge meeting, where everyone was listening to whatever he might be saying in complete and utter rapture.

"That guy could sell shit on a stick, I bet," I said to Devon, who snorted his approval.

"My name is Mr. Betterman," (I kid you not, that was his name), he said. "And saying that we have a slight problem? Well, I'd say that's a slight understatement."

"Way to keep everyone calm, Mister," Randall said. He sounded hurt.

"Well, while you all were so concerned with the lady who hit her head, I was a bit more interested with the woman who came on board screaming that there are zombies outside," Mr. Betterman said. "In point of fact, we all witnessed what appeared to be a zombie, feasting on a waiting passenger."

"Look, like I said," Eric said, "There's gotta be another explanation for all this."

"Like what?" Rafael said.

"Let's hear it," Randall overlapped.

"Occam's Razor," Mr. Betterman said. "The simplest explanation is usually the correct one."

"Oh, and zombies are simple?" Randall said.

"A woman ran on board screaming there were zombies. Then she fainted. Then we all witnessed a carnivorous human devouring another living human being," Mr. Betterman said. "Who wants to come up with another explanation using random information not already related to the topic, hmm?"

"Huh?" Randall said. No one else spoke. More silence.

"Okay then," Mr. Betterman said. "Because while everyone else was busy playing the name game, I was busy playing the save-my-ass game. I was busy asking myself, 'why was this woman running from a zombie?' What events unfolded in her life, prior to her entering our Metrolink car, that allowed her to reach the conclusion that a zombie was chasing her?"

"Dude, what the fuck?" Rafael frowned.

I put my hand on Devon's arm then and squeezed. For some reason my heart began beating a little faster.

"No one bothered looking at this woman, did they?" Mr. Betterman said.

I looked at Mr. Betterman and for a moment our eyes locked. He was grimacing. He shook his head, and I felt like he was my father, reprimanding me. Although he'd said nothing, I could read his thoughts. Or felt as though I could, anyhow.

"She passed out, from the shock," I said.

"No, she did not," Mr. Betterman said.

He reached down gingerly and used his newspaper to push the woman's skirt up a few inches, revealing her thighs.

"Hey, don't be a pervert," Randall said.

"Shut up," Rafael said, walking over. He looked very interested.

On her leg, just above the woman's left knee, the milky white skin broke and gave way to mangled flesh. Rafael stared at it intensely, his face full of fascination. Mr. Betterman looked up at Rafael, nodding. Rafael shook his head.

"She's been bitten," Mr. Betterman said. "She's infected."

"Wait, what?" Kate said.

"Hey, you don't know that," Eric said. "This ain't Dawn of the Dead, you know?"

The train was beginning to slow down again. We were coming up to the next stop. We'd reached Alameda. The loudspeakers began their dinging again. Everyone groaned.

"We have to tell the driver," I said. "That woman needs to go to a hospital."

"She's infected!" Rafael said. "We have to kill her!"

"What?" Kate began to cry in her seat.

"Well, fuck you all," Randall said. "This is my stop."

"Wait, you're getting off?" Eric said. "What if there's more of them outside?"

"There are no such things as zombies," Randall yelled. "You said so yourself."

"No I didn't," Eric argued.

"You said there had to be another explanation," Randall said.

"Well, *some* crazy shit is going on," Eric yelled. "I'm not saying it's zombies, I'm not saying it ain't. Either way, you sure you wanna get off this train?"

Everyone stared at Randall, waiting. Randall swallowed, hard. He looked around at everyone, thinking. Finally he spoke, just as the train came to a complete stop.

"I...I don't know what the hell is going on. But I know I can't stay on this fucking train all God damned day, now can I? And not with her!" Randall pointed to the bitten lady. "I'm sorry. I wish you all the best of luck, but I'm getting off."

The doors opened. Everyone rushed over to look. A woman got on, took one look at the two women lying unconscious on the floor, and quickly got off again. Randall peered out at the platform for a few more seconds. Then he turned and smiled at everyone, shrugging.

"Good luck," he said. Then he walked off the train.

"We need to tell the driver there's an injured passenger," I said.

"Maggie's right," Devon said. He took my hand and squeezed it. "Pull the cord."

Eric pulled the emergency cord. We all knew this meant the train would not be moving on again. We were stuck. An alarm began to buzz, low. Still it was annoying.

"Ungh." The Pee Lady was stirring. Perfect timing. She sat up, slowly, holding the back of her head in her hands.

"What...what happened?"

"You fell. Hit your head," Eric said.

He helped her to her feet, where she swayed. Eric walked her over to an empty seat, on the other side of the car, across from Mr. Betterman. The woman pulled her hands away and stared at the blood.

"Oh my God," she said.

"Hey," Rafael said, walking over to Mr. Betterman. "You sure you wanna stay over here, so close to the infected lady?"

"Who's infected?" Pee Lady said, sounding offended.

"Sorry ma'am, not you," Rafael said. "Her." He pointed.

"What's she infected with?" Pee Lady said, sounding woozy. No one answered.

Just then the driver appeared inside the car. He took one look at the woman on the floor and pulled his walkie-talkie out from his back pocket.

"Central, this is 1080 at station 4D. We need medical, over. What happened?"

The driver looked around at everyone. No one said anything. He looked at the Pee Lady, who had blood on her hands.

"Ma'am, can you tell me what happened?"

Pee Lady shook her head. I wondered if hitting her head had given her amnesia. Then I wondered what the hell we were all going to tell him. I decided the simple truth was best. That and no one else had bothered to speak up. I cleared my throat, then explained everything the best I could. When I was done, the driver only stared at me. Then he looked around at everyone else. Then back at me.

"Did you hit your head, too?" the driver asked me. I shook my head.

"It's true," Rafael said, nodding. I smiled at him. Devon was still holding my hand. It was so warm.

"Okay," the driver said. "Well, I'm going to need everyone to fill out an incident report."

"Are you serious?" Eric said. "An incident report?"

"All incidents that take place on the Metrolink have to be documented," the driver said. His voice was monotone. I got the impression he'd delivered this speech a few times already during the course of his employ with Metrolink. Although I doubted he'd ever heard this particular set of events before. Then again, you never know. It *is* L.A. The driver continued his speech.

"Especially ones that involve injuries. I need everyone here to fill out a report that clearly states that this woman was not injured on this Metro car. For liability reasons."

"Wait, there's zombies out there, and you're worried about Metrolink getting sued?" Eric said.

"Hey, I don't know a God damned thing about any God damn zombies, all right?" The driver said.

"There was an attack at the last station," Kate said. "Just call them up. All hell was breaking loose when we left there, right guys?"

"Well, I don't know," Rafael said. "It was only the one lady. And she got ate, so…"

"But, someone must have seen her there," Kate said. "Other people will have happened upon her body by now."

"Look, I don't know anything about any damn body, or any damn zombies at the freakin' Sierra Madre stop, okay?" the driver said. "What I *do* know, is that I have a schedule to keep. I need to get this train moving again. To do that, you all need to simply fill out an incident report and we can all be on our way."

Everyone looked around at one another. Ten seconds later, a paramedic team came on board and loaded the zombie lady onto a stretcher.

"Do you need medical?" the driver asked the Pee Lady. She shook her head. The driver nodded.

"Just make sure you put that in your report. I offered you medical and you refused."

The driver went with the paramedics as they exited the train. Once again, silence filled the car. I turned and looked at Devon, worried. Devon only smiled, those dimples appearing, making my heart melt.

"Do you remember anything?" Eric asked the Pee Lady.

The Pee Lady only shook her head. Her face looked fearful, however. I wondered if she really did remember, and just didn't want to say. Mr. Betterman only shook his head. He sat back in his seat and crossed his arms over his chest.

A few minutes later, the driver reappeared with a stack of papers and some pencils. He handed them out to everyone.

"Okay, just fill these out for me, please. Make sure you mention that the lady was already hurt before she got on the train, okay?"

Everyone filled out their incident report. Then we handed them back to the driver. Once he'd collected them all, he left. Within two minutes we were moving again.

"What do you think is going to happen next?" Rafael said. No one answered. Mr. Betterman had gone back to reading his newspaper.

At the next stop, Rafael got off. He waved to everyone, told us all to 'take care,' and then simply left. At the stop after that, Mr. Betterman got off. He didn't say anything to anyone. Kate got off at Santa Ana. Pee Lady got off at Alamos. She also said nothing before leaving.

Eric came over and sat down across from Devon and me. We were the only three left. New people came on and filled the seats of the others who had exited. They had no idea. Eric smiled.

"Helluva day, huh?" Eric shook his head. "My stop is the next one."

We rode in silence after that. When the train stopped again, Eric stood up, still smiling. He paused before getting off though, looking back at Devon and me.

"Still don't believe in zombies, you know?" Eric shook his head and got off.

As the train began moving again, I looked at Devon. We'd been holding hands the entire time.

"Which stop is yours?" I asked.

"Whichever one you're getting off at," Devon said.

"I'm supposed to have lunch with my friend," I said, feeling shy.

Devon only looked at me, his eyebrows raised, his smile bringing up those beautiful dimples again.

"So, have lunch with your friend," he said.

"Okay," I said. "I will."

We rode on in silence for several minutes, intermittently looking at each other, smiling, and then looking away. Eric was right. It was a helluva day. Suddenly I frowned.

"What did you say on your incident report?" I asked.

"You mean, did I put down that I saw a zombie chomping on a lady on the Sierra Madre platform? And did I put that another lady came on board who appeared to have been bitten by the same zombie?" Devon said.

I nodded my head, feeling stupid. Devon only smiled and squeezed my hand more tightly. My heart burst with joy.

"On my incident report, I wrote I didn't see or hear anything," Devon said. "I was too busy checking out a cute brunette."

"You did not write that," I said, laughing.

"I did," Devon said, laughing back. "Why? What did you write?"

I only looked at Devon and smiled. It was far too early in the relationship to do so, but I didn't care. I leaned over and lightly brushed my lips against his. I never did get around to telling him what I wrote on my incident report.

Two/One

When we reached the cabin, there were only *two* of us left out of our large group. *Two*. She couldn't hide the fever, however. You can't hide sweat.

I found the bite wound on her upper arm, as she lay unconscious, hours from turning. She'd tried to hide it. She had tried.

I made it quick and painless. *One* bullet, while still asleep. *One*. At least she won't become *one* of them.

I wonder, though, what will become of me? Of the world, of humanity?

Our large group had been the only *one* we ever knew of, and as far as I know, when it was down to just the *two* of us, we were humanity's last hope.

If I am the only *one* left, I should lay by her grave with *one* bullet. If...

Splish-Splash

"There's something living in my toilet," Mary blurted out.

She felt stupid saying it like that, but she didn't know how else to put it.

Ally, Mary's best friend, just sat staring at her for a moment. Her glass of water remained poised, halfway to her lips. They were having brunch at a corner café on a Sunday morning.

Ally's eyes squinted, seeming to try and size up if what her best friend had just said was supposed to be a joke, or if she was really being serious. Mary fidgeted in her seat, uncomfortable at the sudden silence. She waited for a response.

"Um...what?" Ally's water glass finally made it to her lips, and she drank gingerly.

"Well," Mary sought the right words. "I mean...there's *something* in my toilet."

Ally laughed.

"Don't laugh, I'm being serious. It started about a week ago. I keep waking up in the middle of the night to these *splashing* noises coming from my bathroom toilet."

"Okay," Ally nodded. "Then you have a plumbing problem. You need to call a plumber."

"And tell them what, exactly, that there's some sort of...*something*...living in my toilet?" Mary stared at Ally, waiting for a proper response.

"Okay," Ally said matter-of-factly. She was always the logical one. "You're hearing some sort of watery, what...a splashing noise, you said?"

Mary nodded.

"Okay," Ally continued. "Then there's some sort of problem with your toilet. Maybe it's leaking, or maybe it's about to back up or something. It's probably just filling up in the middle of the night."

"No," Mary interrupted. "This isn't the toilet *filling* up. These are **splashing** noises, like something is swimming in my toilet at night."

"It's bubbles coming up to the surface of your toilet," Ally retorted. "There are probably a dozen logical explanations for the noises you are hearing. Jumping to the conclusion that there's something *alive* and *swimming* in your toilet is...."

"Is what?" Mary already felt insulted. She knew what she had been hearing at night, and she was having a hard time describing it to Ally.

"Look," Ally hesitated, searching for the right words. "I want to put this as gingerly as possible. I'm not trying to insult you, it's just...Roger has been gone now for over two months. You're all alone in your house now, and maybe you're just not used to being alone. You know how it is...suddenly every creak of the house is the boogeyman waiting in your closet. Every moan and settle of the wood of your foundation is a monster trying to get in. Every scrape at your window is a serial killer come to get you. It's your imagination playing, and it's getting the best of you."

Mary sighed. Ally continued on.

"Look, I know how it is, okay?? It's like after watching a scary movie in your living room in the dark. Suddenly all your senses are heightened, your imagination is in overdrive, and every noise is a ghost or demon trying to kill you. I get it. That's how I was right after seeing Paranormal Activity. I was convinced after coming home from the movie theater that every noise I heard was a demon trying to possess my soul. Jake laughed at me, but I was truly frightened and on edge."

"This isn't because Roger left me," Mary insisted. "I've been alone now for nearly two months, and why would I suddenly now start hearing splashing noises coming from my toilet?"

"Because you have a plumbing issue," Ally repeated. "Just call a plumber, have him look at your toilet, and everything will be fine. It will turn out that you have a leaky valve or something. You'll probably save money on your water bill."

"Fine," Mary sighed.

"Just," Ally paused. "Just don't tell the plumber that there's something living in your toilet, okay? Just tell him the water is bubbling and making funny noises. Okay?"

"I said fine," Mary snapped, although she didn't mean to.

***

That night, she heard it again. She was sound asleep, dreaming peaceful dreams, when the splashing started up in her master bedroom bath. She woke up to it, and quickly sat up against her headboard, already laboring for breath. Her heart hammered away in her chest as she listened to the now, unfortunately familiar noise of what sounded like some tiny creature splashing and jumping in her toilet bowl.

Splash…floosh. Flop. Sploosh. Splish-Splash.

That's not a leak, or bubbles floating to the surface of my toilet, Mary thought. *That's something **swimming** in my fucking toilet!*

She had never had the courage, yet, to go and look. Tonight, before calling the plumber in the morning, she decided she would brave up and go finally see what the hell was making that splashing noise. Before going into the bathroom, however, she grabbed the baseball bat that Roger had always kept next to the nightstand.

Roger didn't believe in guns, but he'd always been adamant to keep some sort of weapon handy, in case of a break-in. Mary had once argued with him, about what use a baseball bat would be against an intruder with a gun (she always assumed the intruder would have a gun), and Roger only rolled his eyes at her. He'd left the bat behind when he moved out. Now she was utterly relieved to have something to defend herself, although, how a baseball bat would do any good against a scaled and tentacled water monster was beyond her.

She'd already decided it would be scaled and have long tentacles that would snake out of the toilet and grab her by the ankles, yanking her to the floor and slowly dissolving her flesh. Perhaps she did have too active of an imagination, she thought to herself now.

She inched her way along the wall next to the bathroom, bat poised above her shoulder, ready to strike at whatever was splashing in the toilet at the moment. She could still hear the water sloshing. In the mornings, she'd find puddles of toilet water on the floor all around the base. She'd mop it up with towels, ever fearful that whatever had made the mess would suddenly jump out of the toilet and suction itself to her face, smothering her. She really needed to get ahold on her thoughts; they kept running away from her.

"Probably is just a leaky valve," she whispered to herself. She was now at the bathroom door, but the light switch was several inches in, along the wall. She should have thought to keep the light on. Now she would have to reach her hand into the dark room, feel along the wall for the switch, and pray to heaven that whatever was in her toilet stayed there, and didn't somehow grab her wrist.

She inched her hand inside the room and felt along the cold, painted wall. There! She felt the switch. Just as she flipped the light on, she heard one last, large splash coming from the toilet. The light flooded the bathroom with sudden brilliance, so bright against the darkness of her room; she squinted and shielded her eyes with the hand not holding the bat.

She looked at the toilet, and in a moment of sheer audacity, she rushed up, now gripping the bat with both hands, poised overhead, to peer into the water of the toilet. The water still roiled and settled from the movement of whatever had been swimming in there only a moment before.

Was it Mary's imagination, or did she see a green-finned tail quickly disappear into the toilet's mouth? She gasped and dropped the bat in utter surprise. YES, she had definitely seen some sort of green-finned...*something* swim back up the toilet pipe.

"Oh my god!" she yelped. She slammed the toilet lid down and fled the bathroom, turning the light off, as if that would make everything go away. She ran and jumped into her bed, her heart doing triple time in her chest. Ally could make fun of her all she wanted, and throw a dozen different theories her way, about Roger leaving her, her over-active imagination, loneliness...whatever to explain the noises, but there was no getting around what Mary had just seen. There was definitely something living in her toilet.

She set herself on calling the plumber in the morning. If there was something in her tank, or her pipes, a plumber would surely find it and get rid of it, right? It was settled. She'd take the day off work, call in sick if she had to, and wait all day to let the plumber in, and get this problem taken care of once and for all.

***

The next morning, she called Mike's Plumbing Services from the Yellow Pages that had been left on her doorstep before Roger had ever left. He had chastised her for keeping the phone book.

"People don't use the Yellow Pages anymore, Mary, they just do a search online," he'd opined. She didn't care. She was old-fashioned and still used the Yellow Pages for any services she needed.

Mike himself answered the phone and gave her a service time of between noon and four. She told him she didn't mind waiting. She called in sick at work, feigning a fever and vomiting. She felt bad about lying to her boss, but this problem needed to be solved immediately. The sleep deprivation alone, along with bad dreams, was enough to make her want to get rid of this problem as soon as humanly possible.

***

Mike showed up at 1:45 p.m., with all sorts of equipment that meant nothing to Mary. He was slightly older than her, pushing his late thirties, but fairly trim (she'd expected a heavyset, bearded type with sagging jeans revealing a butt crack), but Mike's jeans were snug, and he had no beard, only a day's worth of appealing stubble. She made idle chitchat with him, asking about his equipment, grimacing mentally at her unintentional innuendo.

Mike told her one of the items was a 'snake' that would get rid of any clogs she might have deeper into her pipes. She didn't care. She just told Mike that her toilet was making 'weird water noises at night', and left it at that.

Mike went to work on her toilet. He flushed it, and it seemed to work just fine. She told him it made 'bubbling' noises at night.

"Probably you've got a leaky valve," Mike said, and it reminded her of Ally and her logical explanations. Mike used the 'snake' to see if there were any blockages further along the pipe.

Mary watched as the long arm of the snake disappeared deep into the toilet's mouth. Mike cranked the snake and rotated it several times. He frowned. The cranking stopped.

"Huh," Mike said. "The snake is stuck. There seems to be something clogging your pipe down in."

"Can you fix it?" Mary was hopeful.

Suddenly the snake started to thrash in Mike's hand, as if something inside the pipe had gotten hold of it and was yanking on it.

"What the Hell??" Mike gripped the snake and tried wrenching it out of the bowl. It wouldn't budge.

"It seems to be stuck. This is weird."

Mike put his hand into the water bowl and reached down to try and dislodge the snake from the pipe.

Oh, don't do that, Mary thought. *It'll get you,* but she was mindful not to say anything, lest she sound like a crazy woman.

Mike's hand disappeared into the toilet's mouth, trying to grip and free the snake. Mary waited, with baited breath. This all had to be over with soon, she hoped.

Mike suddenly pulled his hand back, grimacing. There was blood dripping from his right index finger, from some sort of gash-wound.

"Dammit!" He held his finger up to his mouth and sucked on it. "The fuck?" he cursed. Suddenly he slumped to the floor, as if inebriated. Mary didn't know what to do.

"Mike?...Mike?!" –But Mike was unconscious on her bathroom floor.

***

There was a bubbling sound coming from the depths of the pipes now. Mary looked down, and saw from around the snake, the familiar green-finned tail of a creature blossoming into the mouth of the toilet.

She screamed. She tried to back away, but Mike's body was there, and she tripped, falling backwards and landing in a thud on her back. She hit her head on the tiled bathroom floor and saw stars. Meanwhile, she could hear the water splashing and broiling up, as the creature, whatever it was, continued making its way to the surface of the toilet.

The last thing Mary saw before succumbing to the throbbing of her head injury was green fins and scales reaching over the edge of the white porcelain of her toilet bowl, before she passed out entirely.

***

Strange dreams invaded Mary's mind. She was on the floor, and something was playing with her genitals. She could feel the soft suction, as something attached itself to her clitoris and sucked. She moaned, unable to control the ecstasy that suddenly rocked her body. She felt something thick and slimy enter her. She arched her back, filled with pleasure and pain at the same time. The tentacle continued its way inside of her, the suctioning on her vulva increasing, as she reached an orgasm more powerful than any she had ever felt before. As Mary came, she fell back into a drugged slumber so deep; she would not remember her dreams when she awoke.

***

At 2:27 p.m., Mary awoke on the bathroom floor to find herself alone, and naked from the waist down. Someone or something had removed her underwear and wrenched her skirt up around her hips. Mary reassembled herself, pulling her underwear up and righting her skirt.

Mike was nowhere to be found. Mary was paranoid that Mike had raped her, but then she remembered him passing out, after something had bitten his finger inside the toilet.

Was the toilet fixed? She wondered. This seemed like an odd thought, after everything she'd been through. *What happened to Mike??* she wondered. Her answer was on the dining room table downstairs. Mike had left a bill for $137.00 for his services.

What had he thought, Mary wondered, when he'd come to and found himself bleeding from his hand, and her, Mary herself, half-naked on the bathroom floor and unconscious? Whatever his thoughts were, Mike had decided to get out of Mary's house as quickly as possible.

She thought of Mike's bill and laughed. What a jerk. He'd charged her for his services without fixing a damn thing. Unless...she wondered...maybe the problem was fixed?

Only time would tell. Mary went to bed that night praying that the splashing noises from the toilet would not return. She hoped with all of her being that the whole ordeal was over with.

***

It was seven months later, and no sign of the creature from Mary's toilet. Mary didn't care, however. Her belly had grown, starting a few months after the 'incident' involving Mike the plumber. Mary's period was late, and she secretly assumed that Mike had raped her, but she didn't dare tell anyone. She didn't remember her crazy dreams from that day, of the creature entering her and pleasuring her at the same time. She only remembered Mike passing out, then herself waking up half-naked. And then she was pregnant.

Mary toyed with calling the police to report the rape, but she didn't have any proof. Mike was long gone, and she had showered later that same night, in the downstairs bathroom, too shocked and disoriented at the time to realize she'd been invaded and attacked. She wasn't in any sort of pain, and she was still reeling from the fact that Mike had been attacked by something that had bitten his finger, and that she had somehow passed out on the tiled floor of her own bathroom.

***

Mary told Ally it was from a one-night stand. She felt oddly protective of the baby, and didn't want to report the rape any longer; she only wanted to bring her baby into this world in a safe, healthy, and sheltered environment. She had already decided on a home birth, in the bathtub.

No hospitals.

Ally thought that Mary was crazy. She insisted that Mary register with the hospital, but she refused.

"At least hire a midwife, then," Ally continued.

"Women have been giving birth since the dawn of man," Mary intoned. "And they didn't need hospitals or midwives. They did it all on their own. I want a *natural* birth, in my *own* home, in my own *bathtub*."

Ally had given up on arguing with her best friend. Truth be told, she'd gotten a little crazy lately, and Ally was just about done with her. First, it was that nonsense about something living inside her toilet. Then Mary was knocked up by some mystery date that she refused to talk about or identify. Now she wanted to give birth in her own bathtub, alone, with no medical intervention whatsoever. Mary had gone absolutely crazy, Ally decided. She'd abandoned her best friend in utter frustration. There was no getting through or reasoning with her.

***

It was in the middle of month seven after the attack, that Mary had an inkling of what had really happened to her. Mike showed up, knocking on her door one night, after midnight. In the darkness, Mary had a hard time identifying who it was. Her belly was already round and tight, and she knew the baby would be coming within a few short months.

The knock came at exactly 12:52 a.m. Mary was asleep, but was awoken by a banging on her front door. She cursed as she tripped out of bed, half-asleep, to see what asshole was bothering to knock on her door after midnight.

She made her way downstairs and to the front door. She flipped on the porch switch, but no light came on.

"What the hell?" she whispered. "Where's my light?"

The knock came again, even more urgent this time. Was it teenagers playing a prank, Mary wondered? She instinctively held her own growing belly, ever mindful of protecting the baby inside of her. She was already a mother, loving and nurturing. She debated whether she should even answer the door at all. After all, any knock that comes after midnight can't be a good thing. But the knock came yet again, this time shaking her door. And then she heard a voice that made her blood freeze.

"Mary, it's me, Mike…the plumber?"

The plumber. Yes. The one who had done this to her. She ripped the door open, suddenly; exposing her own burgeoning belly in her white night dress, ready to accuse Mike of his wrongdoing and evil ways.

It was pitch black on her porch, the light still not turning on. She squinted into the shadows of her own porch, trying to pick out Mike on the front steps. She could barely see his shadow there. It looked misshapen and *lumpy,* somehow.

"Mike?" her voice trembled. "Is that you?"

"Yes, it's me," Mike answered, only his voice sounded hollow and oddly *bubbly,* as if he were speaking under water.

"I can't see you, my porch light won't turn on."

"I know," Mike said. "I shattered the bulb. I didn't want to frighten you away before I talk to you."

"You…you broke my porch light?" Mary was perplexed. "Why?"

"Because I didn't want to frighten you," Mike repeated from the safety of the shadows of the bottom steps, his voice still watery and hollow, somehow. "I didn't want you to scream at the sight of me, like so many others. I can't even go outside anymore. My business is gone. And the doctors..." Mike sobbed. "The doctors don't have any answers for me. They only want to stick me in a lab and run a bunch of tests on me...and I won't have that. I'm not a lab rat."

"I...I don't understand what you're talking about, Mike," Mary said, holding her belly tight. "You...you attacked me that day, didn't you?? You violated me."

"I what?" Mike slogged. "I never did anything to you. There was something in your toilet. Something that bit me. I passed out, and when I came to, I wasn't certain what the hell had happened...to me, or to you. But I was dizzy and my hand wouldn't stop bleeding. I just wanted to get out of your house. I'm sorry I left you there that way."

"What the hell are you talking about?" Mary's voice had risen now. She was no longer afraid, but angry at Mike's denial of his attack on her.

"I went home and bandaged my finger, but it never really healed. It just kept...spreading. I started growing scales on my finger around the cut...and they just kept growing, further and further up my hand, then my arm, then my torso...until I was totally covered. And then the *fins* started to grow. It hurt so much, like the worst growing pains I'd ever had. And then one night, my neck opened up, and I was in the bathtub, but I could *breathe*, you see?? Under the bathwater...I could *breathe.* And I had to stop working, and the doctors started wanting to lock me up...and I had to go into hiding. I never saw the doctors under my real name, thank goodness, and I always used the wrong addresses and phone numbers...a fake social security number. They can't find me, but if they ever do...I'll be a lab rat forever. And it all started from something that bit me inside your toilet. I just thought..."

Mike hesitated, bubbling and squishing.

"I just thought maybe you could tell me what the hell happened?"

"What the Hell happened is that you raped me, Mike," Mary spat. "You took advantage of me while I lay unconscious on the floor of my own bathroom, you bastard!"

"What?" Mike sploshed. "I never touched you!" He sobbed, the sounds watery and distant.

"Then how do you explain this?" Mary said, and stuck her belly out even more than it already naturally protruded from her body. She was already twice the size of any normal pregnant woman.

There was silence from Mike for a prolonged amount of time. Then he stepped forward, up the steps, and the light from inside Mary's house suddenly fell upon him, in all his glory and horror.

"How do you explain *this?*" he asked, spreading his finned arms out in front of Mary, almost like an aquatic bat, or some sort of antiquated creature from a bygone era. Every inch of Mike was covered in green scales, and darker green fins grew from his armpits and inner thighs, like some sort of hybrid between a betta fish and a shark.

Mary couldn't help but think that Mike was actually sort of beautiful. Majestic and ancient in his vestige and appearance, although, alien and frightening at the same time. She felt an odd sort of maternal instinct to shelter him as well. To hold him to her protruding belly and take him in as her own. She wanted to take care of him.

She no longer held him responsible for her own condition, but rather, felt sorry for his own state of being. He was helpless and afraid. Mike was alone and terrified and being hunted down by scientists who wanted to poke and prod him in a lab, and find out what he really was.

Mary ushered Mike into her home and kissed him gently on his scaled cheek. She caressed his soft, slimy fins and quickly fixed him a nice, tepid bath in her master bedroom.

He acquiesced with no arguments at all. He lived with her from that moment on, hidden and protected from harm.

***

Mary knew who her baby was, and who the father truly was now. She was not repulsed, but rather, intrigued. This would be an entirely new species, a cross between man and some ancient being that had somehow survived all these millennia, to end up in the sewers, and finally, in her own toilet, in her own home. It had survived all these millions of years, to try and replicate and survive by crossbreeding with the human race.

She couldn't explain how she knew all this, but she did. And apparently, one bite could infect and transform a human into a crossbreed...but why would the creature impregnate her, instead of just biting her, like it had bitten Mike?

She asked Mike this, at one point, and he asked her how many babies she thought she was carrying. Mary understood immediately what Mike was getting at.

"Why bite people and transform them one at a time, when you can impregnate one mother and have several babies at once?" he'd reasoned.

Mary knew he was right. Mary's attack was propagation of the species in the quickest way possible, with the highest numbers of offspring.

But what about the creature that had attacked her? And...

How many others were out there, somewhere, she wondered? Was the one that had attacked her the last of its own kind? If so, then she and Mike were the only surviving remnants of a lost breed, and the parents of a new hybrid soon to be born.

The creature from Mary's toilet had disappeared. Had it died? Perhaps after mating with her?? Mary didn't know, and she didn't care. She would be a mother soon. Roger was gone, he had left her, but Mike was here, and he desperately needed her love and attention -and her protection. She would do anything and everything she could to take care of her new lover, and her new babies.

***

Mary went into labor on a Saturday afternoon, in week thirty-seven of her pregnancy. It was a bit early for a regular gesticulation, but this was not a normal pregnancy. Mike sloshed in the bathtub, his usual place. He'd been living there for two months, happy, content – safe.

Mary's contractions started suddenly, just after she'd eaten her breakfast of raw clams and lobster tail. The labor pains bent her in half, they were so intense. She felt as if she were being torn apart.

She quickly made her way upstairs and into the master bathroom, where Mike was in the tub, swimming freely in the shallow water. He was completely scaled and finned now, and had trouble breathing regular air for very long.

They would need to make their way to the waterways soon, Mary knew. For she, also, had begun growing scales and fins, the last four weeks of her pregnancy. Whatever infection Mike had, she now had it as well, but she didn't mind. All the more fitting to look like her own babies, and be the mother that they needed to take care of them.

***

The contractions built, until Mary thought she would burst open from the inside out. Then she felt a slipping sensation, as the first of her newborns made its way out of her womb. She ushered Mike out of the tub, briefly, and let loose a finned creature into the tub, beautiful and glorious in its new nature. The others followed shortly.

***

They would make their way to the waterways outside of town in just a few hours, the newborns already able to breathe underwater. The last thing Mary saw before losing her own humanity completely was a green-finned and scaled tentacle emanating from her vagina, curling and vibrating, waiting to be born into this world.

--END--

Zombie Survival

"Look, all I'm saying is that women wouldn't survive," Alicia said. She sipped her Chardonnay quickly and set it down primly.

"That is not true, that is absolutely not true," Christie responded.

"It *is* true, and I'll tell you why," Alicia continued. "Women don't know how to fight."

This caused an uproar among the two other women. Christie and Jeanine both began talking at once. After a few moments, Jeanine quieted and Christie went on.

"Women know how to fight, we wouldn't have gotten as far as we have if we didn't. We're tough, obviously tougher than you think. I mean, do you have any idea what those iron teethed angels had to go through, just so we could gain the right to vote?"

"It's iron jawed," Jeanine politely and quietly corrected. Alicia continued without losing a beat:

Alicia- Oh sure, the right to vote, but that is not what we are talking about here. That's not survival. I'm talking about really doing what it takes to survive. We're talking cataclysm here, okay?

Christie- And I think that you're wrong. I think women would rise to the occasion spectacularly. I mean, what's the main difference between men and women? Strength, that's what. Physical strength. But that wouldn't be an issue with zombies, because everyone knows that zombies are weak. It doesn't take muscle to overcome a zombie.

Alicia- Well, it takes guns, and do you own a gun? Do you even know how to use one?

Christie- I don't, but I'm sure lots of women do.

Alicia- Sure, but I'm willing to bet that, percentage wise, far more men own a gun and know how to use one than women. This automatically puts us at a disadvantage. The majority of women would have no weapons on hand to defend themselves, and they'd get eaten.

Jeanine- But the men with the guns would probably be protecting their women.

Silence filled the table. Christie and Alicia stared at Jeanine for several moments. Alicia's mouth hung open.

Alicia- Oh.My.God. You see? This is what I'm talking about. Women wouldn't survive, and in this case, according to *Jeanine*, our lives would be dependent on men to live through a zombie attack.

Jeanine- But then, we *would* survive.

Alicia- We wouldn't survive anything. The men would survive, and we would be riding around on their coattails. And anyway, that is not what I was talking about in the first place.

Christie- Then what were you talking about?

Alicia- I'm talking about *survival*. Let's just say that a woman managed to get out of the city, away from the major zombie hordes, and, I don't know, stumbled upon an abandoned cabin in the woods. There's a generator in the shed out back. She's screwed.

Christie- Um, why is she screwed?

Alicia- Do you know how to run a generator?

Christie- No, but it can't be that hard.

Alicia- Ah-ha! You don't know, but men do. Men just know these things, because, I don't know, their fathers teach them, or something. Just like men know about machines, and the insides of cars and electronic junk. It's like some special knowledge gets passed down among them, like some secret club or something. Males take shop in high school, females don't.

Jeanine- Well, they could take shop though.

Alicia- But they *don't*, do they? Just like women don't own guns. This is my whole point. Women don't possess the know-how to survive a zombie epidemic.

Christie- For your information, I know for a fact that lots of women own guns.

Alicia- Oh yeah?

Christie- Yeah. Female cops. They own guns and know how to use them.

Alicia- Okay, so a few female cops have a slightly higher chance than the rest of us.

Jeanine- And the girls who took shop.

Alicia- Not funny, Jean. But if I was to go along with what you're saying, it only proves my point, again.

Christie- The point that women wouldn't survive, but women cops and shop girls would?

Alicia- No, the point that the very few women who do survive only do so, basically, because they act like men.

This statement caused another uproar from Christie and Jeanine.

Christie- What?

Jeanine- You've got to be kidding me.

Christie- How is being a cop acting like a man? You can't sit there and say that the profession of being a cop belongs only to the realm of the male sex, can you?

Alicia- No, no, but you have to admit that these female cops, come on, you've seen them on TV and crap, do tend to act, nay, even look kind of masculine. They are not going to win any beauty contests, and frankly, many of them look downright butch. Admit it girls.

Christie- Oh, so now I get it. Any action taken on by a female that even remotely seems masculine automatically makes them gay?

Jeanine- You know, my sister is a lesbian, Alice.

Another bout of silence filled the table. Alicia looked embarrassed, her cheeks flushing. Christie looked back and forth between her two friends, waiting for the hot wind to cool.

Alicia- (a smile playing on her lips) Isn't Hazel on the force?

Another round of loud exclamations followed, this time laced with giggles. All three women took sips from their wine glasses.

Jeanine- Anyway, I can solve your generator issue for you, Alice.

Alicia- Oh yeah, Jean, how's that?

Jeanine- Wikipedia. Learn how to run a generator now, before the zombie epidemic begins.

Christie- Yeah! That's great. And don't forget, after groups find each other, which they inevitably do, it will turn out in the end, that men will be the ones who can't survive without us.

Alicia- Enlighten us, oh sage one.

Christie- Well, who's going to run the cabin? Men don't clean, we all know that. And who's going to garden and grow the food?

Jeanine- The men would hunt for game.

Christie- But the women would grow the vegetables, and you can't survive on meat alone.

Alicia- Women could do the hunting, men could grow the garden. Why not switch it around?

Christie- Oh, so now it's okay for the women to act like the men? When did that happen?

Alicia- I'm just saying, in a post-apocalyptic world, the slate would be wiped clean and women could start all over again.

The past is gone. It wouldn't be them acting like men anymore. It would be women acting like they do in a new era.

Christie- So, it would take a full-blown zombie invasion and ninety-nine percent of the world's population being wiped out for you to finally stop being a sexist?

Jeanine- Ouch…but she does have a point.

Alicia- I am not a sexist.

Christie & Jeanine- Yes, you are.

Alicia- I am not a sexist. How can I be? I am a woman.

Christie- And yet, you won't defend your own gender. You seem hell bent on proving how weak and useless we all are, and when we're not, you say we're being masculine, acting like men, and that we must be lesbians if we know how to use a gun.

Alicia- (ignoring Christie's comment) Okay, forget your stupid Wikipedia idea for now, because if a zombie plague broke out right now, in this very restaurant, what would you do? 'Cause I doubt you'd have time to run home and look things up on the Internet.

Jeanine- No one has a gun in this restaurant, so, male or female, we'd all be on equal ground.

Christie- And even if you're right, and some men in here survived, while all us females were devoured, this doesn't prove your point.

Alicia- It doesn't?

Christie- No, because your point, if I'm not mistaken, is that in the event of a zombie outbreak, women basically wouldn't survive, because…we're women? Do I have that about right?

Alicia- Yeah, pretty much.

Christie- Well then your point disproves your point altogether, because if no women survive, then ultimately, no men survive either, because eventually they'll grow old and die. And without women to help them repopulate the earth, it wouldn't just be women that don't survive, but all of humankind.

Alicia- (grimacing) Well. thank God you didn't call it mankind, at least.

Silence filled the table for a third time. The three women looked at each other, looked down at the table, sipped their wine, and checked their cell phones for non-existent text messages. Eventually one of them spoke.

Jeanine- I really do miss you guys. We need to get together more often.

Christie- Yeah, I mean it's not like we live that far apart from one another.

Alicia- (nodding) I need to make more of an effort to see you guys.

The subject turned to other things: their jobs, their boyfriends, Jeanine's husband and little girl, the weather. They talked for another half hour or so before calling it an evening. As they waited for the waiter to bring the check, a middle-aged blonde who had been sitting in the booth next to theirs came up to the table.

"Excuse me, but I couldn't help over hearing your conversation a bit earlier. I used to go camping with my father when I was a kid. He actually showed me how to run the generator at our cabin. He also taught me how to hunt with a rifle, and I've been known to be a pretty good shot. Although I'm not a cop, I am a parole officer, and when I was in college, a friend of mine was date raped. The mace she attempted to use didn't deter him well enough. After that I bought a small handgun, a Smith & Wesson .38 special to be exact. I applied for a permit to carry a concealed weapon, so now I am legally allowed to carry said gun in my purse."

The woman opened her purse and quickly showed the gun to the three women, who sat and stared. The blonde smiled sympathetically.

"Rest assured, I am not a lesbian. I'm married to a wonderful man and we have three beautiful children. My husband is an accomplished marksman in his own right. In the event that a zombie attack occurred right now, I would save both our asses in time to gather our children up and get someplace safe. With the help of my husband, we would work as a team to survive."

With that, the woman walked away from the table, leaving the women to talk amongst themselves. Alicia was the first to speak, but the other two women nodded their agreement.

Alicia- (barely above a whisper) God, what a bitch.

Carnival of Thrills

Todd Wilson and Caleb Dennis hopped the fence and skirted their way past the tent poles and generators, trying to blend in with the whittling crowd that soon appeared around the Carnival canopies. It wasn't nearly as hard to sneak in as they thought it might be. After all, this was just a second-rate, traveling Carnival. Security was lax.

They probably could have found a way to sneak past the front gates, even, if they'd been daring enough to try. Jumping the fence on the back-East side proved to be easy enough, however.

Their small town didn't lend much to entertainment, and Todd and Caleb, both sophomores in high school, decided the visiting Carnival might be a nice distraction from the mundane day-to-day of their small town's sleepy ambivalence.

With a population of barely 20,000, there wasn't a whole lot of action on the teenage scene. There was one main drag way through the middle of town, with a liquor store far too familiar with spotting fake I.D's, and a billiard house on the West end that was the only real entertainment for teens, besides the small, 3-theater Cineplex, that liked to play last year's films for a dollar a-piece.

The Carnival was the most exciting thing to come to Pleasanton Falls in a long time, and Todd and Caleb weren't going to let money, or lack of, get in the way of their chance at some real fun. The freaks were what Caleb wanted to see the most, although, Todd wanted (or rather hoped) to see the belly dancers. He knew there were strippers that worked the Carnival scene. Caleb wanted to see the bearded lady, the fat man, and the deformed monstrosities that lay waiting within the shrouded tent walls. Todd could care less about the freaks.

They snaked their way through the crowd, ever paranoid that somehow they would be figured out. They didn't have ticket stubs to prove they had paid. They could just say they'd dropped their tickets by mistake, or lost them. That seemed a good enough explanation. No one questioned them, however, as they made their way through the milling crowds of people, towards the tent that read "Special Attractions."

"The belly dancers and strippers will be in there, I bet," Todd said. "Probably your freaks will be in there, too."

"More likely, the best you're gonna see is the 800-pound lady," Caleb joked. "I wouldn't hold my breath on the strippers, Toddy-boy."

"Shut up, this is a class-act Carnival. *All* Carnivals have belly dancers."

"Yeah, well, we'll see about that."

The two youths made their way toward the "Special Attractions" tent, where a line was formed, snaking out and around the tent for several yards.

"Shit! There's a long line," Todd complained. "We'll be waiting for hours to get inside the tent."

"So? A, it's not like we paid to get in here, and B, it's not as if we have anything better to do with our time tonight. You got anywhere better to be, Toddy-boy? 'Cause I sure don't. Let's get some popcorn and munch on it while we wait in the line. This will be worth it, I promise."

"Fine," Todd said. "We'll get some popcorn. But stop calling me Toddy-boy, you know I hate that."

***

An hour later, the line had barely moved. Todd and Caleb had eaten two bags of popcorn each, plus a churro. The people were being brought into the tent in groups of ten, only. There were still a good forty people ahead of them in the line. Todd turned to Caleb and sighed.

"This is bullshit. We've been here all night. We're never getting to the front of this line."

"What else can we do? We just spent all our money, the little that we had, on popcorn. We can't afford the ride tickets, and this tent is FREE. And this is what we came here for. It's pure entertainment. The fact that each group spends so much time inside the tent proves it's something good to look at, right? I know it's a long wait, but I bet it'll be worth it, once we get to the front."

"But this is bullshit! My feet hurt!" Todd shifted his feet for emphasis.

"Come on, dude, don't be a total douche-bag wimp on me, Toddy-boy. Or should I call you *Potty*-boy? Give me a break and stop complaining like a sissy-girl."

"Fine," Todd sighed. "I've got two dollars left. Go get me another fucking popcorn while I keep your place in line."

Caleb went and got the popcorn. Two hours later, they were finally at the front of the line. They were in the next group scheduled to go into the tents. They had been waiting for so long, neither Todd nor Caleb even cared anymore about what they might see. They were sick to their stomachs from all the stale popcorn they'd eaten, and their foot soles ached and throbbed from the uneven fair ground littered with piles of hay.

Finally, their group was ushered into the fore-tent. A Dramatic Gentleman with a top hat and a flowing, curled mustache bellowed from on top of a box.

"Ladies and Gentlemen! What you are about to see may shock you. It may turn your stomach sour! You may have nightmares for weeks, after the monstrosities and deformities you are about to behold! I warn you now, so you can turn back, if you so wish! Now is the time. If you have a weak stomach, or a stilted constitution, I'd advise you to turn away now, before it is too late! Enter at your own risk, and be forewarned: What you are about to see is not for the faint-hearted. Move forward, please, or exit the line."

A few people opted to exit the line, which surprised Todd and Caleb, after how long everyone had waited in line just to get to the front. They weren't about to exit, not after all the waiting they'd done. Besides, the foreman was simply being dramatic. Todd figured the worst they'd see was a scaled man with fake reptilian regalia super-glued to his skin.

Everything in these Carnivals was fake, everyone knew that. There were no REAL freaks, and definitely no REAL monsters. There were no such things as monsters, Todd knew.

***

They entered the first tent, which housed a dwarf. They weren't all that impressed. The next tent over held a 'giant' at seven-foot-three, but Todd told Caleb that there were NBA players easily that size, and that this guy was nothing special.

Next came what Caleb had been looking forward to: The bearded lady. But Todd said the beard was probably just fake and spirit gummed on. There was no way to tell for certain. It looked real to Caleb, but Todd insisted it was fake, and that was enough to ruin the effect for Caleb.

Next came the 900-pound man, who looked to Todd and Caleb to be only maybe around 500 pounds. They'd each seen worse on TMC.

"Dude, the guy in that movie, *Seven*, was bigger than this dude here. And that guy's an ACTOR. You know??"

They weren't impressed. Next came the Merman, which Todd fully could tell was fake, the werewolf man, which might have been real (that was a real disease, wasn't it?), and the half man-half woman, which, again, wasn't so shocking.

Todd and Caleb were about to give up on finding anything worth the wait time they'd endured, when they reached the final tent. Inside, was a skinny man, who looked to be in his mid-thirties. He didn't look like a freak at all. He looked completely normal. He was dressed in light brown trousers, a white button-up shirt and dark brown suspenders.

Todd and Caleb exchanged glances, and Todd shrugged. The thin man introduced himself.

"Hello, my name is Madrigal. How are the two of you doing tonight?"

"Um…fine," Todd answered. "What are you supposed to be?"

"I am the gate-keeper," Madrigal replied. "I decide where everyone goes next."

"Where everyone goes?" Todd said. "There's only one way out of here, and that's through the exit tent."

"That's what *you* think," Madrigal smiled. Then he winked. "Tell me, what was your favorite attraction here at the 'Special Attractions' tent?"

"Well, I was hoping to see some belly dancers," Todd replied, with reserve. "But there weren't any."

"Well, I'm sorry for your disappointment," Madrigal sounded genuinely apologetic.

"I guess I'd have to say that the Merman was my favorite, though" Todd pondered, "Even though I could tell it was fake."

"What makes you think it was fake?" Madrigal sounded contemptuous now.

"W-Well," Todd stammered, "I mean…everyone knows there are no such things are mermaids or mermen. It was a fake tail suit or something."

"Really?" Madrigal said. "But that was your favorite?"

"Y-Yes," Todd said.

–Instantly, his vision changed. He was no longer staring at Madrigal in the final tent, but rather, he was looking at a crowd of people staring back at him, some of them looking perplexed, others entertained, and still others, completely apathetic. His lungs were filled with liquid. He felt like he was drowning. Instinct took over, however, and he found himself taking in the cold liquid, deep into his lungs. It felt refreshing and invigorating. He was breathing under water!

He looked down and saw his own body, which was covered in fins and scales. He realized where he was and panicked, swimming in the shallow tank with fury and sheer energy. The crowd watching gasped and backed away.

The Dramatic Gentleman appeared and bellowed at the crowd. They all turned towards him, enraptured.

"Ladies and Gentlemen…the Merman is at times untamed and violent. They are not the gentle creatures that Disney Cartoons have made them out to be. They are wild monsters that eat the flesh of the living. What you are looking at is not something from a gentle fairy tale, but a dark creature from a bygone era, intent on killing and surviving in any way that it can. Move along, folks, to the next shocking attraction!"

Inside the prison of his Merman body, Todd's mind shrieked, *No!* but his gills prevented him from speaking English. He wondered where Caleb was at that very moment, but he soon dipped down beneath the waters and slept in the comfort of his tank.

Instantaneously, at the same moment that Todd was being transformed into the Merman's body, Caleb answered the same question that Madrigal had posed.

"What was your favorite attraction here at the 'Special Attractions' tent?"

"The Wolfman," Caleb said.

"Why?" Madrigal asked.

"I don't know," Caleb shrugged. "I guess, just because it's cool. An actual Werewolf, man. What's not to like about that?"

Instantly, Caleb was looking at a crowd of people, staring back at him in shock and horror and disgust. He looked down at his own hands, or rather, paws. He saw the sharp talons and the matted fur, and he howled in lament.

***

Todd Wilson and Caleb Dennis were reported missing on August 2nd, 2006. They are presumed to be teenage runaways, although, their parents have never stopped looking or hoping for their lost boys. Their whereabouts remain a total mystery.

House Call

Lydia Grange first saw it when she wheeled out to see Tilda leave. The red Taurus disappeared around the bend, and *it* stepped from behind the trees: a dark, shadow-figure, all in black. Even its head was covered. It reminded Lydia of an executioner's hood. What did they call that? A Junco? She shivered in her chair as the figure raised its hand, palm up, as if waving. Gasping, she turned and wheeled herself back into her home.

Next day, she told Tilda, who gasped and said, "At your age? My family is superstitious, and you know what they'd tell you? -That it's *Death* coming for you."

"I may be old, but if it's Death calling, I'll be damned. Not yet. I'll spend it all, first. None for the Taco Muncher."

Lydia grimaced. Tilda frowned.

Later, while watching Tilda leave again, *it* stepped from behind a tree on the furthest corner of the lawn.

Closer.

***

She'd been confined to the wheelchair for the last three years, her congestive heart failure keeping stores of oxygen tanks in every room. She was 72, but determined to see a birthday that began with an '8'. Mr. Grange had been a very fine banker and left a hefty sum behind -enough to keep the secluded lake house and Tilda, who was Lydia's private nurse.

It was an isolated life for Lydia Grange. Tilda was her sole means of social interaction, and she called every afternoon.

Lydia's daughter, Samantha, had 'come out' to her mother after her father's death, and they'd had a falling out. Sam was still named in the will, however. Mr. Grange would roll over in his grave if Lydia cut out his sole child. If Lydia lived long enough, however, she might deplete the tidy sum Sam was to inherit.

I'll leave nothing for the deviant, disgusting dyke, Lydia thought with smug satisfaction. In her head, she saw her daughter rollicking naked with another woman, both lathered in sweat. She saw her daughter's head disappear between the faceless woman's thighs and felt revulsion.

***

At dusk she heard an owl screech and looked out. Peering out the living room window, middle of the drive, in fading light, she saw *it,* yet again; the dark figure.

Closer.

She closed her curtains.

***

After dinner, Lydia couldn't help herself. Again, she looked out her window and gasped. The dark figure stood in her front yard. Her heart pounded and she wheeled to her tank, sipping sweet, canned air.

***

Before bed, she dared look out the window one more time. Her heart froze. The figure stood directly at her window. They were only inches apart.

Death!

Fear paralyzed her. She choked in struggling breaths.

Death reached its hand out and hit the window, palm flat.

Thud.

House Call

She convulsed. Lydia Grange went into cardiac arrest, slumped in her chair, and in less than one minute, she was dead.

***

The figured entered the house.   It stood over Lydia, caressing her cheek. Removing the black hood, Sam smiled.

"Thanks for everything, mom. I'm glad you met my fiancée, Tilda, before you went.

Lonely and Dead

e-mails to: SexyVixen@hotmail.com
e-mails from: LonelyAndDead@yahoo.com

12:16 a.m.-

How can I miss you this much already, when I'm barely gone? And you? Never moved an inch.

I should have known better. Better than to meet you. I knew you didn't believe me, when I told you who I was. WHAT I was. You, you SexyVixen. You really are, you know? A sexy vixen, I mean.

12:47 a.m.-

Why won't you answer me? I'm waiting here, desperately, for your words. I'm hoping. Even praying, although the words hurt me. You know this.

What did you expect, anyway? Going into a Gothic chat room? Saying you wanted to meet a 'dark man.' Someone who's into things the way you are?

For months I tried to tell you. Convince you. Make you see. But you wouldn't. You thought I was joking around. Playing a game. Silly, silly you.

I should have known better, anyhow. Going online. It was an accomplishment for me, you know? Growing up when I did. When. That's right. I told you. You didn't believe me....

I know there were others. Others who told you the same thing. You wanted me to post a profile photo of myself. I explained to you why I couldn't. Your first tip-off that I was the real deal. Vampires don't cast a reflection, so how could I possibly pull off a picture of myself?

The others, you should have realized were fakes. They all had photos of themselves. Plus, they really couldn't have been all that convincing, could they? Most, I'm certain, were very unoriginal in their delivery. Trying to sound 'old world.' Spinning tales about their history. But they couldn't know history, not like I do...

Some were not even trying all that hard. Like that one guy you told me about. The one who tried to convince you he'd lived through the Holocaust? Been changed right before marching into the gas chamber? But there was no gas chamber at Dachau, you know? Only furnaces. I would know. I WAS there. Feeding off the dead, as they lay dying in their bunks. But you didn't want to hear about that, did you? Too dark, too close to home, too real.

Did you want a fantasy? Is that why you played along with all the others? Is that why you continued to play with me?

The others didn't know their history very well, did they? I told you how it really was. Seeing the gentry hanging from the gallows, and the hissing slice of the guillotine. Yes, I was there, too. Some of the others wouldn't even venture beyond the 19th century. I took you so much further back...

2:55 a.m.-

I've been around for quite a while. Lived through (if you can call it living) some of the darkest periods of humanity's history. I'm not evil. I only lived off those who were going to die, anyway. I never murdered anyone.

I tried to make you see what a gentle, unbeating heart I have. So, it only took me a few decades to catch on to this whole 'technology' thing. It's 2010 and I finally learned how to type. Stole a computer from a dead man in an alley. Sorry, a laptop. But I didn't understand Wi-Fi. So, finally, I found a 24-hour Internet café. You know I can only go out at night.

3:23 a.m.-

How did I find you? You already know. Gothic chat room. SexyVixen caught my eye. You had a photo. Your raven black hair appealed to my undead eyes. Your milky-white skin practically glistened and glowed off the screen at me. If I could breathe, I think I would have forgotten for a moment or two.

When I first saw you, if my heart was capable of skipping a beat, it would have. Oh, how we talked. Talked and talked-or should I say, typed?

When I finally felt comfortable enough, I told you what I was. You laughed. You lol'd, actually. How cute. I had to ask you what it meant, remember? Along with TMI, when I tried to describe to you the feeling of sheer exhilaration when feeding off warm blood as it still beats in a victim's veins. The warm, gushing feeling as it slips down my throat, fills my belly and seeps, slowly, into my shriveled veins. The vitality that resumes...

BRB was another one. When you were too shy or embarrassed to admit needing a bathroom break. I don't need those, either. But you are my age. In bodily years, anyhow. Mentally, you're still a child. Technically, I'm 1,100 years your senior. Small numbers, really.

5:27 a.m.-

When you finally asked to meet me, I was delighted. Yet, I tried to warn you. I knew you didn't believe me. Even after everything I'd told you. You still didn't believe. But what is the saying? 'Seeing is believing?' Indeed.

Of course, I could only agree to meet you at night. And you played along; with what you thought was a game. I tried to warn you of my appearance. I'm dashing, in my own right. But pale. So pale, you can see the blue, spidery veins underneath my skin, like an intricate latticework of webs. They carry the blood-life through me. I tried to tell you. How pale-white my lips are. How sharp my canines, so I avoid smiling, even when alone.

I made certain to feed before meeting you. To quell the hunger, decrease the risk to your fragile health. So much fragility in the human condition. It really doesn't take so much blood loss, before the heart has no pressure to keep on beating. Once the pumping stops, the blood no longer gushing into my mouth, the sucking must begin. I know, I know, TMI. You didn't want to hear it...I have to stop writing now, as the sun is about to come up. I'll write you again when night falls...Oh, Sexy Vixen, please let there be an answer from you waiting for me tonight.

***

9:36 p.m.-

Still no answer from you. I am deeply saddened....

I asked you, before meeting me, why it was you felt the need to converse online with a 'vampire.' I asked the question I so longed for an answer to. Are you hoping to become like me? I can do that for you, you know? I can make you like me.

I can also make you 'like' me. I could have, you know? When you stood there, in the dark doorway of your own home, staring at me in complete and utter horror and revulsion. You said nothing, so of course, no invitation to come inside. You wouldn't move from your spot, safe within your own doorway. I stood just feet from you, your porch light casting an eerie glow on the reality that is me. You saw...

10:18 p.m.-

You didn't move an inch. I took in your beauty, up close. You truly are ravishing, my dear. I spoke to you. You did not reply. You only continued to stare. I apologized for frightening you; did you even hear my words?

It was difficult, I will admit, despite having fed only an hour before. Hearing your heartbeat, deep inside your chest. Hearing it speed up at the sight of me. I could smell your fear. I could have stopped it, you know? As I've already told you. I could have made you 'like' me. I could have worked my effervescent charms on you. My magnanimous attraction trick. That wouldn't have been real, though, now would it?

10:56 p.m.-

I want real. Real love, real attraction. But no one will. Not even you, I guess. I had hoped. After everything we've talked about. After everything I've said to you. After everything you've told me.

You said you wanted to be like me. Were you only joking? 'Playing along,' with the charade? I described it to you. Told you how much it would hurt, being bitten. Being drained of so much blood, until your heart slows to a crawl. I would still be able to hear it, though. You know that? The last remnants of a beating chamber, holding on until the very end. It's such a beautiful, tragic thing. And just when the final beat is about to resound, I'd slice open my own wrist with my jagged teeth, and feed it into your hungry mouth. I'd let it drip down your tongue, pool into the back of your throat, and kiss your lips as you lightly swallow my sadness. My hope. My love…

11:28 p.m.-

You could be like me. You could be with me. But you really thought I was joking, didn't you? Until last night. Until you saw me with your own eyes…

12:02 a.m.-

The chat room ended weeks ago. We moved to e-mails. No more interruptions from other 'suitors.' -I keep checking my inbox, you know it? Hoping you'll answer me. I'm sorry to keep sending these messages. I know I frighten you.

I know, however, that if you could just get over the shock of it all, you'll come to your senses. Once your mind has had the time to process the reality of everything. Once you've replayed the last several months' worth of typed conversations between us. –

Perhaps that is what you are doing right now? Perhaps you are going back into your messages and re-reading everything again? Reading the truth in my words. Seeing the weight of it all…Please answer me!!

1:16 a.m.-

Were you only playing when you told me you loved me? Because I was telling the truth, when I told you that I love you. 1,100 years, I've been searching for you. Waiting for the right woman to capture my heart. I'm tired of living alone. Being without companionship. You said you felt the same way. You wanted to live for all eternity, with me. You said that. I believed you, SexyVixen. I truly believed you…

1:52 a.m.-

I won't give up, you know? I'll keep writing you. I'll keep waiting. I've waited all this time, 1,100 years. A few more hours, or days, surely can't cause any harm….

How long will it take, before you realize you really do love me? How many more days will I have to wait? How many more log-ins will I have to make, checking my inbox, for a reply from you?

2:14 a.m.-

Just one reply, and I will know. I'll see your address in my inbox, and I'll know that you've changed your mind. I'll know you want me to come straight to you, and you'll allow me to embrace you, and give you an ever-lasting gift. All my love. I'll know....

2:47 a.m.-

If you truly love me, as much as I love you, you'll send a reply. In the subject line, you'll write, "Yes." -Is it a deal?? I won't even need to open the message. Everything I need to know will be right there, in the subject line. Everything I need to know, to have you. Forever....

3:21 a.m.-

I've checked again. Nothing.... I've said everything I have to say. I know your real name, SexyVixen. Because you told me. And you know mine. Did it frighten you? You thought I was playing around. You thought I was joking....

3:56 a.m.-

Still nothing. It's been sixteen hours since I saw your face. Your beautiful, porcelain visage, a face of Helen-of-Troy. You could launch a thousand ships, you know? Or one vampire's immortal soul, you could set to soaring, if I had one. If I had a soul, it would belong to you. You belong to me....

4:07 a.m.-

I could make you love me, but I want you to choose. I never got to choose. My love, I want you to decide. I'm waiting for you. I'll wait forever...I'm off again for another day. I'll check again tonight....

***

Message from SexyVixen@hotmail.com sent at 11:04 p.m.:

-Subject line, "Dearest, My Love – YES."

***

Last message to: SexyVixen@hotmail.com:
From: LonelyAndDead@yahoo.com:

11: 20 p.m.-

My heart soars!! My undead, unbeating heart! It took you two days to sort through everything, to decide…I am coming for you my dear. -My beloved, I fly to you now. Be ready for me. Be waiting and be ready.

-All my love, forever and forever. –Vlad

Six Degrees

I'm here in the police station about to make a report. I didn't go anywhere else before coming here. They're making me wait. They didn't ask me what it was about; I just told them I needed to report something.

"A crime?"

"Yes."

I didn't know how to say the actual words, so they told me to wait here, until an officer is free to take my statement. In the meantime, the sergeant at the desk tells me there's a vending machine down the hall, so I can get myself a soda while I wait. He smiles at me, but I just look away. He doesn't know what I saw tonight, doesn't know how I *feel*.

Funny how the mind works after a trauma; little things bring me back. As I near the soda machine, I feel a slight drop in temperature. I raise my hand, palm flat, and lay it on the cold plastic casing. It makes me think of how the armrest felt beneath my arm, in his car. That was before he pulled over and got out, and...

Someone behind me drops something. It hits the floor with a light fwap, but I hear the sound of twigs breaking as a body is dragged through dead grass. I hear a light tap-tap-tapping of someone's shoes. They're behind me, waiting impatiently, but I haven't prepared my change. The tapping of their foot sounds like the popping of gravel under the weight of a dragged body. I heard that tonight, too.

I let them go in front of me and pull loose change from the bottom of my purse; three quarters. The person in front of me–a man, gets his drink and leaves, but not before throwing me a look of annoyance. His eyes quickly flit to my chest then back up again. He smiles, but all I see is a sneer. He could be just as capable of committing the crime I witnessed tonight. He *could.*

The mind grasps onto inane thoughts in the wake of a trauma, doesn't it? Behind me, I hear the desk sergeant call my name, telling me they are ready to take my statement now, but I barely hear him. I'm frozen in place, staring at the three coins in my hand, lost in the oddest thought. They say every person on the planet is only separated from the next by six degrees. If that is true, we have all touched evil without even knowing.

I look at the coins in my hand, and can't help but wonder. Six degrees of separation; the odds are slight, but perhaps one of these quarters was once in the hands of a thief, a wife beater, a murderer...

Or perhaps my rapist.

Hungry

My name is William B. Hensfield. I am a retired lawyer of the California court of appeals. Yes, I used to work as an Appellate Attorney for the 4th District Court of Appeal, in Division One, located in San Diego, which holds jurisdiction over matters from Imperial, and San Diego Counties.

I was born in 1979. In 2001, I graduated and moved on to Law School. I was twenty-one then. When I was twenty-five, I passed the California Bar and went to work as an associate in the Law Firm of Weston, Beal and Oremor. That was in 2005.

Eight years later, in November of 2013, I was emergency sworn in as a commissioner of civil marriages. It was simply a formality. I was thirty-three. A year earlier, my wife had just given birth to our first child, a son, that we named Jackson.

Jackson Hensfield was born on October 12, 2012, already dead. On October 15, during the funeral, little Jackson began to cry. At first, everyone thought it was the wind. It was low and muffled. Although, the day was bright and sunny (such a juxtaposition to the mood) and thinking there might be wind whistling through the oaks of the cemetery really made no sense. But still, several people later told me that they all thought that's what it was at first, as did I.

Until everyone heard the light pounding coming from inside the tiny coffin. I never knew they made coffins that small until little Jackson passed away. He didn't stay inside for very long. Melissa (that's my wife, or should I say was) became frantic.

"He didn't die! Jackson is alive!! They made a mistake!! He's *hungry*!"

Her words will forever haunt me. Jackson was *hungry* all right; but he wasn't alive. Not in the true medical sense. October 15, 2012, is when it all started.

***

No one knew then, and they still don't know today, what caused it or why some were affected and others weren't. It's worldwide. I only write this down now, because future generations may not understand this. Sure, it will be in all the history books, but that won't explain the *experience*.

Imagine: not knowing if *you* will become one of them. A bus could hit you, or that nasty smoking habit could catch up, or you could get into a lethal barroom fight while defending your girl. Next thing you know? You've got a serial walking impediment, you're socially ostracized and your penchant for chewing on human flesh rages out of control.

It isn't like all those old movies said it would be. Romero only got part of it right. Zombies *are* real. They *do* like to eat human flesh, and their rotting bodies are a serious hindrance to societal functioning. However, once reanimated (in that mystery way that no one can seem to explain), they can still think, sometimes talk - at least until their teeth fall out and their tongues rot away - and even work.

It sucks, plain and simple. America just got a whole new set of social challenges heaped upon it. Some of the ones that come back (especially drowning victims) don't even look all that gruesome. Some people are happy their loved ones come back, while others are horrified (rightfully so). Some get jealous when their loved ones don't show back up knocking on their doors, while their neighbors get half the family plot showing up. You just never know what you're going to get.

And some people have had to deal with real heartache. Like a newborn (stillborn) coming back to life in its tiny coffin at the flippin' funeral.

Melissa went a little nuts. She was never the same after. When the coffin was opened up, little Jackson had been dead and decomposing for a couple of days. Plus, he'd been dead inside the womb for over a week, even though we hadn't known. We just thought Mel was going into labor a couple of weeks early, we had no clue Jackson had died with the umbilical cord tangled around his neck; Mel's body was trying to flush out the dead fetus.

Jackson was a nightmare. And before anyone could stop him, the officiating Priest had grabbed a stick lying on the ground, and thrust it through the little soft spot that all newborns have. Jackson died again on October 15, 2012. This time, he stayed that way.

That was just the beginning. Six years later, and the legal battles rage on. Those that had a spouse who died and came back, sometimes wanted to stay married and deal with the hassles. True love. California surprised the entire country by becoming the first state to recognize human-zombie marriages.

Of course, we didn't legalize zombie marriage. But, for those human couples who were already married, and one person just happened to die and come back, we created special laws for 'recognizing' those unions as still valid. It appeased the majority of the left wing, and the right wing could accept that. Thank goodness.

That's where I come in. I was emergency sworn in as a commissioner of civil marriages, remember? As a formality, I already stated. I never imagined when I went to Law School that this would end up being my career. I was emergency sworn in and then sworn in again, in a new position created in conjunction with the amended California Marriage Laws.

My official title is a Solemnization Consummation Authority. S.C.A. God, what a job. You see; for those couples that find themselves zombifically challenged, it's my job to bear witness to certain, ahem, 'acts'. Personally, I think the California Supreme Court Justices are a bunch of perverts. But the damn laws passed, and my commission was created. It pays well, too, let me tell you.

What do I do? Well, as a Solemnization Consummation Authority, a.k.a. agent, I preside over the final decree that a human-zombie marriage is, in fact, valid. California decided that any human-zombie couples that wanted to remain together and married could do so, provided they could supply proof of consummation of the marriage post-zombification. It's a crazy world we live in.

Solemnization simply means: To celebrate or observe with dignity and gravity; or to perform with formal ceremony. It's my job to observe the successful consummation of a human-zombie union. If the couple in question cannot perform the deed, their marriage will be annulled. They get three chances to successfully perform this act in my presence, otherwise, no dice.

I know, I know, you're probably curious. I get asked these questions all the time - from friends, family, and curious partygoers at random shindigs and gatherings. The most common question I get asked is: What constitutes 'successful' completion of the act? Does the zombie in question have to reach climax?

The laws spell it all out in detail, and they've been quite fair. No, the zombie in question does not have to reach a climax. Male zombies don't always produce enough 'liquid' to pull off successful ejaculation. However, some continue to produce live sperm, if you can believe that. And yes, there have been some human-zombie pregnancies (most end in miscarriage) and even a few zombabies are born. Most of those die within a few days, but again, everything is so random.

The news occasionally reports (with freak enthusiasm every time) about a human baby miraculously born from a zombie father.

It's always a zombie father, however, since, for some reason, male zombies can still manufacture sperm, but female zombies seem to lose all their reproductive capabilities. Medicine (as usual) can't figure this out, either. Maybe all the eggs dry up and die?

Climax is not required. Especially since females, classically, don't reach climax during intercourse nearly as often as men do, and if it's a female zombie in question, that wouldn't be fair, now would it? I'm told that female zombies almost never reach orgasm. Sucks for them.

So, no, I answer people when they ask, zombies don't have to reach a climax. They simply have to successfully perform intercourse; meaning- a penis (whether human or zombie at this point) has to enter a vagina (again, human or zombie) and, well…everyone knows how that works. The couple in question can move around for however long they want. There's no specification on how long things have to last. And, again, no climax is required.

The challenge for the majority of these couples is simply in the logistics of the act. First off, zombies want to eat human flesh. Cow's brains and pig's feet will do the job, but, they still want to eat people, it's their top choice. And even though these 'people' can still talk and 'reason', their deep urge to cannibalize leaves them struggling with great difficulty to not eat even their most cherished loved ones.

They work, too, but in shackles…like morbid chain gangs, cleaning up garbage along busy highways and recreational parks. They wear muzzles. Zombie suicide is prevalent. Who would want to live that way? But some do. And many want to remain married and have it recognized by the courts. There are significant tax breaks to being married to a zombie.

So, my job, as unbelievable as it is, is to go to these people's houses, on official business, and witness their sexual act. I can't believe this is what I do.

It would seem like some sick, twisted fetish, wouldn't it? Trust me, the Zombie Porn industry is bursting, no pun intended. I can't believe how many sick perverts actually get off on watching this stuff. Me? I don't get off on it. It's just my job, remember?

Mel had a hard time dealing with it. After Jackson, and the associations, I don't blame her. But the money was too good to pass up. She refused to get pregnant again. She was too terrified the baby would die in utero again, and I knew she wouldn't remain sane if she had to go through that even one more time. It was too much of a risk.

We talked about adopting as well, but...since no one knows who might or might not live or die, again, she couldn't deal with it. What if the little tyke contracted childhood leukemia, or got hit by a car, but didn't stay dead? Mel didn't want any zombie kids running around, muzzled inside our house.

Truthfully, I think what freaked her out the most about my new job, was the thought that it could happen to us. I've often wondered what she would have done if I had died and come back. Would she have stayed with me? Would she have loved me enough to visit the courts, pay those fees and fill out the paperwork? Would she have been willing to have an S.C.A. agent watch us have sex? Because that, folks, is true love right there.

A lot of people say the whole thing is just sick and wrong. Other die-hard romantics swoon and say it's...well, romantic. I'm on the fence. I watch zombie sex acts (and attempts) all week long, so the shine and allure of romance often dulls. I try to keep an open mind, however. I mean, whatever goes on behind closed bedroom doors is really no one's business. Except for me, it is. It's my business.

***

It didn't affect me at first; the first few times I watched it. Often times, the couple asks me for help or advice. I'm allowed to talk them through it, and even 'coach' them a bit, but I can't physically intervene. I sit in a chair, next to the bed.

Let me explain a common scenario. We'll do, say, human male vs. zombie female, okay? That one is actually much more common. Husbands seem to want to keep their zombie wives around much more often than female wives want a zombie-husband. It makes sense.

So, I come into these homes, and typically, the wife is tied or handcuffed to the bedposts. Her feet are usually tied as well, and she's muzzled, so she can't bite her lover's neck out. Sometimes she has a bag over her head as well; I presume because she's rotting in the face too much to want to look at.

The room is usually heavily laden with perfume, Febreze, or burning scented candles and incense. It often smells very pleasant, actually, with a bit of sickly-rotten fruit smell, just underneath.

Sometimes it takes the husband a bit of time to 'get excited'. Other times, it doesn't take any time at all. You can see their excitement poking through their pants. Some of them actually seem to get off on having a witness.

Anyhow, as I was saying, the common scenario with a husband vs. a zombie wife is simply that he gets naked (she is always already naked and tied up before I get there), he climbs on top of her, and they do it. It usually doesn't take

271

very long, as the male is almost always very excited. In these cases, climax is a definite.

I mark it down on my clipboard (among many other notes) and check off the successful completion box. Wham, Bam and Done. Again, no pun intended.

When it gets a bit more complicated is when it's a zombie husband vs. a human wife. Again, when I come in, they are already tied up. This is a specification before I show up on an appointment. The S.C.A. agent is never supposed to be put into any situation where they might be in danger of an attack. There are heavy fines if I show up at a residence and the zombie is not already contained. Before the appointment, of course, we get the zombies' agreement to events, so don't go thinking this is all happening against their will or anything.

If they are capable, they sign a consent form. If they are able, they verbally consent. This all happens at a special set of offices downtown. It's the human spouse's responsibility to safely transport their beloved zombie significant other to the premises, shackled and muzzled, in order to fill out this paperwork. Like I said, it takes dedication. The courts figure that anyone willing to go to that much trouble must really be doing it out of love. But I digress.

When I enter the bedroom, the male is tied up (usually with chains, since male zombies are stronger), and he's naked. So is the woman. Modesty seems to fly out the window in most of these cases. I've only had a few wives be shy, and they simply removed their underwear, while wearing long skirts that they hiked up.

Anyway, the problem with a male zombie is that they don't always get excited. The husbands can simply lube up with their zombie wives, and there's no problem there. But with a zombie husband, sometimes a little creativity is called for.

Zombie men become aroused by blood. So, if the zombie husband isn't already sporting a boner, the wife will often times need to dangle a raw steak over his face, or some animal brains, or a pint of pig's blood. When this happens, it's like watching a tent being pitched.

Then the wife climbs on board and does her thing, dangling the raw and bloody morsels in front of their husband's face the entire time. Sometimes they suspend the meat from the ceiling on a hook, so they can keep their hands free to touch themselves. But, again, climax isn't required. As long as successful arousal and penetration occurs, the marriage is deemed official.

They only have to do it once. As soon as I check off that box, they're married for life. Or unlife, as it were. Whatever problems will arise for those couples from that point on - that's their business. The divorce courts have their own new laws for dealing with human-zombie splits. Again, no pun intended.

I don't care about that. I only care about my part of the job. A lot of people tell me I'm the luckiest guy in the world. I get paid to watch sex all week long. And no matter how smelly, foul, disgusting or gruesome it might be, they all say it still beats the nine-to-five grind in some corner cubicle farm. I suppose they're right.

But if that's the case, why is it so hard to keep the numbers in my position? They keep raising the incentives, increasing the salaries and bonuses with every year an S.C.A. agent stays on board. If it's such a great job, why is the turnover rate so high?

Yes, I know, it messes with your personal life. My wife had a serious problem with it. She was embarrassed to tell any of our family or friends at first. I couldn't hide it forever, though. And I've seen the scared look on people's faces when they find out what I do.

A lot of them are curious and ask questions, but many others simply disappear to the other side of the room. Even the ones that ask the questions quickly lose interest, once I begin to relay the gory details. The ones who don't leave and remain interested are the people who scare me the most. They get this greedy-wet look in their eyes, like they wish *they* were in *my* position. As if they think they would appreciate it more than me. I can tell these are the types of people who would need to excuse themselves after every appointment to go whack off in the bathroom.

And in case any sick perverts are wondering, of course, as an S.C.A. agent, I have strict guidelines I must follow. If I do get excited while watching an 'act', I'm not allowed to touch myself. I certainly can't masturbate in front of the clients. Masturbation, even in private, has to be done away from the client's residence. I'm not even allowed to do it in their bathroom. No masturbation is allowed on the premises, and that includes in my car, parked in their driveway.

It's a respectful job, with as much tact and aplomb as is possible, under the circumstances. No one is made to feel dirty or ashamed. It's simply a formality.

But there are drawbacks. Like I said, the social ostracizing is difficult. It's gotten to the point where I don't tell people what I do anymore, or I lie. And it does mess with your head a bit.

Mel tried to tell me that once, but I told her she was full of shit. I mean, after Jackson, we weren't exactly doing it, you know? Her hormones were all messed up, not to mention her head. Plus there was this crazy zombie shit all over the news. It went on for weeks, months. Then the world had to deal with it and adjust.

New laws were passed, new organizations, support groups sprang up. New industries were born. Zombie-porn, specialty butchers shops, a whole new branch of social services, etc. Special court buildings had to be constructed, new registration offices opened to deal with incorporating back into the system those who were legally declared dead, but were now walking around again. Special schools were opened to try and help those zombies who'd lost the ability of speech. Fucking zombie sign language. Someone invented that.

***

People have gotten rich off of this catastrophe. Others have been devastated. I got a job out of it, with a really nice pension package and a whole new set of issues in my fucked up brain.

Yeah, Mel tried to tell me once that the job was messing with my head. She said it was 'changing' me. Eventually she couldn't deal with it. She left a few years back. I was too numb at that point to care. If I did feel anything, it was anger. Fuck her for leaving. I'm the one that has to deal with this shit every week, every day, in fact.

I mean, so what if after a few months of this job, I couldn't get it up anymore? So fucking what? And who cares if I got desperate to sport a woody, and figured out that watching that stupid zombie-porn was the only thing that worked?

I never asked Mel to watch it with me. I told her I could just watch it for a few minutes downstairs alone, then come into the bedroom and please her. She told me I was sick and demented, however. She asked me if I thought those zombie-girls were hotter than her. Pff.

I mean, to her credit, she did try a bit. At one point, she did get really drunk and smear herself with some bloody juice from some raw steaks in the fridge. Before that, she'd tried fake blood from this Halloween costume kit, but it smelled like sugar, and that's not what zombies smell like.

So what if I started needing a few rotting pieces of day old, rancid meat to be kept in the room? The smell just seemed to help with my arousal time, that's all. It was no big deal. I don't know why she freaked out and left, I really don't.

So what if I once asked her if I could tie up her arms and legs and put a bag over her head? I don't know why she got so upset that one time I tried to suspend a cow brain from the ceiling. It was kinky. You'd think she'd be willing to be a little more open-minded. Couples have to work at this stuff, you know? It's difficult.

But she left. It's okay, though. I'm fine. I'm perfectly healthy.

I've seen my therapist. I had one specifically assigned to me for the job. How 'bout that? Every S.C.A. agent gets his or her very own, personal shrink. He tells me there's nothing wrong with me. He says my reactions are perfectly normal, given the situation. He says my job has to come home with me, and that this is one of those cases where work simply will bleed into your personal life.

They tell you not to take it home with you, but in this case, that type of removed categorization would be the unhealthy thing to do, my doctor assures me. The fact that it is affecting my personal life is a good thing, he says.

He really seems to enjoy hearing about my job. During the appointments, he asks for lots of details, tells me it's healthy to talk about it all. Everything is confidential, of course. And it's his job to listen, but I really do feel as if he's not just doing a job, he truly cares. He likes to hear about every appointment I go to, so I know he's not just checking out during our sessions. He's a really good therapist. He takes tons of notes. I'm a really lucky guy.

So, my therapist says I'm just fine. Some people simply don't have what it takes to stomach what I do. I'm sure I'll find a new wife at some point. First, I need to secure a girlfriend.

I had one, briefly. I lied to her and didn't tell her what I do. I just said I work for the courts. I have a lot of money, so she didn't seem to care beyond the basic explanation. But she seemed to take offense at some of my sexual preferences. When she finally broke up with me, she told me I had an 'unhealthy fetish' and that I should go see someone. She told me I needed professional psychiatric help.

I would have told her I already had that, and that my doctor tells me I'm totally normal, but she ran out of my apartment too fast. I really don't know why she freaked out, just because I told her I wanted to have someone sit in a chair and watch us do it. That's not so weird. Lots of people are into voyeurism.

But, whatever; as my shrink says, I'm perfectly normal. He says I just need to find someone who's a good match for me. I need to find someone who is into what I'm into - someone with the same tastes as me.

***

A lot of new industries popped up with the zombies. This whole thing has really changed the world. As I've said, the butcher's shops, the courts, the schools, the pornos. Not all zombies who come back were married, either. And not all of them want to work the chain gangs picking up garbage. And with all those pornos being made, there's a new industry in the escort business as well.

Pimps got in on the action, just like everybody else. Where there's money to be made, people will flock. And zombies need to make a living, too.

My shrink says it's perfectly normal. Everyone has their specific tastes, and no one can judge or say what is right or wrong in the areas of sexual preference. I mean, it makes sense.

Shrinks are supposed to remain objective. He can't anymore tell me I'm sick or perverted for my 'fetish' as my ex-wife called it, than he could if I was attracted to other men, or wanted to engage in S&M. There's no judgment in that guys' office. As long as I'm willing to talk about it all, not hide it, share the juicy details, he tells me I'm totally normal.

***

So, my wife left me, and so did my girlfriend. My one and only son was a newborn zombie. No biggie.

I have a really good psychiatrist, and a cushy, secure job as an S.C.A. agent. All in all, I'd say my life is going pretty well. But I am a human male, and men have their needs. No one seems to be willing to help me out with these things.

The job hasn't gotten to me. This whole zombie thing hasn't really affected my life all that much, other than providing me with lifelong security and a nice retirement. So, I'd say that all in all, this whole phenomenon has been a positive influence on my life.

I have plenty of money, and there's nothing wrong with me. I do my job, and occasionally, I need physical release. Fuck having a girlfriend or wife. Clearly, these human women can't understand my needs.

But I know a place to go.

I know I can find a woman who won't have any trouble being tied up, or having a raw cow brain hung in front of her face. In fact, I know a place where there are girls who will buck and thrash even harder from that.

A little blood dripping onto their face?

-That will only make them *more* excited. And that's what I want. It's what I need. I want them excited. I want them *hungry*. Hungry for *me*.

***

Hungry

The thing my ex-wife and my stupid ex-girlfriend could never understand is that I need a woman who truly acts as if she *wants* me. These zombies, sure, they want to eat people, but the thing is, they *want* people. I get it now, why these married couples want to stay together. I get why the human spouse wants to stay married to their zombie partner. They come back from the dead, and they *want* their living spouse in a whole new way they never did before.

Being wanted that way - it really does make a person feel loved and desired. In love stories and erotic poems, scribes always talk about the *longing* of love - the *voracious appetite of attraction. The lusty hunger and the desire for flesh.*

In my opinion, zombies are the epitome of human desire. They are the ultimate answer to everything. That's probably why all of this happened. People need to stop being so uptight and embrace the beauty of what's happened to our world. I have.

***

I know what I need, now. And I know where to go to get it. I love my job, and I also love myself. Tonight, I'm going to love something new. Tonight, for the very first time, I'm going to feel what it's like to truly be wanted by another being that is *hungry* for me, for my *flesh*.

I am an S.C.A. agent. This is what I do, but it's not who I am. I just have certain needs now. My name is William B. Hensfield. I am a retired lawyer of the California court of appeals, and I couldn't be happier about that.

TELLCORD

Cordelia Whitmore had been dead for eight months when she sent an e-mail to her granddaughter, Shelley. It began on a lark, one day, as Shelley was sifting through her inbox, deleting obsolete messages.

She had friends with e-mails going back for years, but this was not her personal style. She liked things neat and organized. Any more than three pages of e-mails were too much. She periodically went through her inbox, about every two months, and got rid of anything she no longer needed.

*****

Her current ritual cleaning was put off by several months, which was very unlike Shelley. She had been distracted. Her family had moved across the country, from California to Texas, and one month into the move, her grandmother unexpectedly died of a stroke.

Shelley experienced an odd sort of grief when Cordelia Whitmore passed away. It was not so much grief over losing someone she had loved, so much as losing someone she *wished* she had loved. The relationship between Shelley and her grandmother was a strained one, for the older woman was very abrasive and cold. Shelley spent most of her childhood being afraid of the woman.

Cordelia Whitmore was, in all honesty, the type of woman most people would describe as a cold-hearted bitch. That was how Shelley's sister described her. Neither of the girls ever successfully connected with the woman, no matter how hard they tried.

Shelley had tried, in earnest. Just the summer before Cordelia passed away, Shelley took a trip to her grandmother's Oregon beach house, with her two children in tow. Cordelia had not seen her great-granddaughter since shortly after her birth, and had never met her great-grandson, nor had she ever expressed any interest in getting to know them, until recently.

Shelley had a mixture of feelings over the first e-mail she received from Cordelia, asking about Scott and Jenna. She immediately called her mother, and asked if she had given Cordelia her e-mail address. Shelley's mother said she had, because Cordelia had asked for it.

"I didn't even know she had e-mail," Shelley mused.

Her mother explained that Cordelia bought a computer and was now hooked up to the Internet. Shelley, in truth, would have much rather received an e-mail from her grandfather Frank instead, whom she actually liked.

As a child, although her grandfather was a bit abrasive as well, he at least took the time to talk to Shelley, albeit in curt form, and enjoyed sharing stories of his own childhood. When he saw Scott and Jenna's light-up shoes at the last visit, he went into a dreamy-eyed ramble about how, when he was a boy, the only shoes he could buy were "Buster Browns. That's all they had. Everybody wore Buster Browns."

He taught Shelley how to play cribbage on that visit, and his eyes gleamed as he played against her and won. It was on that last visit that Shelley pinned all her hopes that finally she could get closer to her grandmother.

The e-mails were frustrating and encouraging, both at once. All of Cordelia's messages inquired after her great-grandchildren, yet they never once issued forth any questions about Shelley's life at all. Perhaps the old woman had decided it was too late to try and forge any relationship with her grandchild, and had decided to start over fresh with the next generation? Shelley puzzled over this with her sister, Rebecca. Reba only grumbled and complained that she hadn't received any e-mails at all.

*****

At first, Shelley did not reply, feeling snubbed by her grandmother even more than before. How could that woman expect her granddaughter to write to her about her own children, when she had never bothered to be friendly to her at all? It seemed to presume a level of closeness that Shelley simply did not feel. Cordelia was trying to use Shelley as a link to her great-grandchildren, when Cordelia had never done anything to secure that link.

Shelley was angry, and constantly complained that it was "too late now," for her grandmother to try and become a caring, loving person. For the first two weeks after receiving her grandmother's e-mail, Shelley did not reply. Then her mother called to tell Shelley that Cordelia had suffered a stroke - that she was all right, but she had lost the vision in her left eye.

"Things don't look good, honey," her mother spoke gently. Shelley wondered if her mother actually expected her to be upset.

"She could have another stroke at any time. The next one could kill her."

Shelley felt bad when her mother began to cry, and told her how sorry she was. Her mother sniffled and asked if Shelley had ever e-mailed her back. The first twinge of guilt hit Shelley then. She made her excuses about how busy she had been, and when her mother fell silent, she recovered by saying she would e-mail her that afternoon. Her mother brightened a bit.

She didn't get around to writing to Cordelia until the next day. It was like writing to a stranger. She was telling personal information about her children to a woman she did not know. It was terribly polite, detailing Jenna's favorite foods, TV shows, Scott's best friend in preschool, how Jenna liked to sing, and Scott liked to draw, etc. What else could she tell this woman?

The responding e-mail was cold and curt. Cordelia thanked Shelley for sharing the "tidbits" about the children. She then asked Shelley to write a letter from each of the children, "in their words." Cordelia demanded that Shelley write it verbatim, so Cordelia could "get a feel" for how the children spoke.

"If Jenna pronounces it sketti, instead of spaghetti, don't correct it, just spell it out exactly the way she says it," Cordelia wrote.

Shelley was furious. The e-mail, like the woman herself, fairly demanded her to do things the way Cordelia wanted them done, and yet, she had a mysterious way of telling Shelley what to do, while masquerading as asking. Cordelia never asked anyone to do anything, however. People were always told what to do. That was simply how Cordelia Whitmore was.

"Can you believe the nerve of that woman?!"

Shelley fumed to Reba that afternoon.

"I barely even know that woman, and she e-mails me out of nowhere, wanting to know about my children. She barely took the time to get to know me while I was growing up, but suddenly she wants to know all about her great-grandchildren? Doesn't she realize she can't go through me, if she didn't bother to treat me decently growing up? I mean, really. How does she expect me to do what she wants, when she treated me like crap as a kid?"

Reba just sat and listened. When she finally spoke, her words were measured.

"Honestly, Shell? I think she is getting old, and she's realizing she doesn't have much time left. She's probably looking back at her life and seeing how she was with us, and now she wants to try and be different with her great-grandchildren."

"But it doesn't work that way, Reba. She can't expect me to bend over backwards for her when I hardly even know that woman. She can't just skip over me, and go straight to my kids. Why would I even try that hard?"

"I don't know, Shelley. Like I said, she hasn't even e-mailed me. At least she's trying to get closer to you."

"But she isn't, Rebecca," Shelley sighed. "She still doesn't act like she gives a crap about me. She only wants to get to know my children."

*****

Two days later, Shelley was angry with herself, for she sat down with Jenna, who was the eldest, and asked her many questions about what she liked, her favorite color, her favorite animal and why, etc. She even found herself spelling everything out phonetically, exactly the way Jenna said it. She was disgusted with herself. Why was she doing this? Why was she actually meeting the demands of that woman?

Deep down, however, Shelley knew why. If her grandmother did indeed have only a short time left to live, and Shelley didn't do what she wanted, she would have to live with that guilt for the rest of her life. She didn't want that kind of baggage hanging on her. No matter how infuriating that woman's demands were - she felt the need to meet them.

These events all led up to last summer's visit. The e-mails were short and polite, but no real headroom was made, in Shelley's mind, towards getting closer to Cordelia. The woman wrote to Shelley once a week or so, asking about the children, and demanding to know information about them. She never called Shelley on the phone. Shelley hadn't spoken to her grandmother in years. Cordelia also never wrote to the children. When Shelley mailed the letter to Cordelia that Jenna had dictated, Cordelia merely sent a short "thank you" e-mail a week later. The children never got to know their great-grandmother at all.

Then one day, in March, Shelley received an e-mail from Cordelia asking her to come and bring the children for a visit. Shelley ignored the message for two days, then received the phone call from her mother saying that Cordelia had suffered yet another stroke. This time Cordelia lost the use of her left ankle and was now using a walker everywhere she went.

Shelley felt that old twinge of guilt resurface. After all, what was she so afraid of? Cordelia Whitmore was nothing more now than an old, frail woman, who was blind in one eye and could no longer use her legs properly. Surely the woman had very little time left in this world. No matter how the woman had treated Shelley as a child, this was family. The children deserved to have the chance to meet and get to know their great-grandmother while they still could.

Shelley sent a message off to her grandmother saying she would love to come and visit in the summer. It was a short message, painstakingly worded. She even signed it "Love, Shelley," and quickly sent it back to "TELLCORD." It was a user name that implied a false relationship, as if Cordelia Whitmore was an old friend of Shelley's. The username itself seemed to be a demand, as if Shelley would actually tell Cordelia anything truly personal at all. Tell Cord. Indeed.

*****

The visit went badly. Shelley allowed herself to believe that in her failing health, the old woman had changed, grown softer in some way, and perhaps even a bit less controlling. This was not the case. As it had been when Shelley was young, Cordelia demanded that the children in her house remain utterly silent. They were not permitted to run or yell, and if they happened to laugh a bit too loudly, they were sent outside. Shelley was now thirty years old, and yet, the moment she set foot into her grandmother's home, she felt as if she were a child again.

She told herself before bringing her children into the home that she would stand up to the old woman, should her treatment of the children prove similar to her own treatment as a child, and yet, she crumbled under the woman's stare. She allowed Cordelia to talk coldly and rudely to Jenna. When Scott did not want to eat the chicken salad Cordelia prepared for lunch one day, Cordelia sent him out of the house. The rest of the visit, Scott was relinquished to a side table away from the main dining area. Shelley did not argue. She was ashamed of herself.

When the time came to leave, Cordelia said goodbye to Jenna and Scott. They politely shook her hand. When Shelley went to say goodbye, an odd voice in the back of her mind whispered, *this is probably the last time you will ever see her.*

Shelley felt relieved, even happy at the thought. The visit had broiled up a deep anger within her. She couldn't wait to leave. Yet at the same time, she was deeply disappointed and saddened that the visit had been such a failure.

Cordelia Whitmore, although very old and frail, was still the same cold, abrasive woman she had always been. Shelley convinced herself that the woman had changed, and yet, she treated her grandchild and great-grandchildren as if they were nuisances in her home. Why had she even invited them to come at all, Shelley wondered? Cordelia was still the same controlling, seemingly unfeeling woman as ever.

Shelley leaned forward and threw her arms around the woman to hug her. She didn't know why she was doing it, other than a last ditch effort at some semblance of closeness to a woman who made Shelley feel so utterly rejected, she could not help but take it to heart that her own grandmother simply seemed not to love her. She had tried all her life to gently abstract some love, in whatever form she could get. Now, at this moment, she decided she would take it. If the woman would not give her love, then Shelley would take it from her. One hug, one embrace, an act of kindness and affection.

It was like hugging a cardboard figure. The old woman hardened in Shelley's arms and seemed to grow physically colder against her touch. Then, suddenly, Cordelia Whitmore pulled her arms up, placed her hands on Shelley's shoulders, and shoved her away. It was not rough, but it was decisive. Shelley spent the next several weeks in disbelief, replaying the scene in her mind again and again. Her own grandmother had actually pushed her away. She tried to hug her, and Cordelia had pushed her away.

*****

For the next several months, Shelley heard nothing from her grandmother. Then one day she received a message from TELLCORD. Cordelia wanted to know what Jenna wanted for her birthday. Shelley was surprised that Cordelia even knew Jenna's birthday was approaching. She had written the woman off. She expected that the next time she heard anything about her grandmother, it would be to receive the news that she had died.

Shelley sighed and simply sent a quick message saying that Jenna was beginning to enjoy art now, so anything to do with art would be a good bet. She did not sign it love, but merely with her name. Two weeks later, Jenna received an art set in the mail. In December, TELLCORD sent a message to let Shelley know that a package was on the way with presents for Scott and Jenna for Christmas. Again Shelley sent a quick thank you reply.

For Christmas, Jenna received a clay model set, and Scott received a build-your-own-volcano project. Among all the other gifts received, the volcano model was set aside and put away with the board game boxes in the hall cabinet.

In February, Shelley received a letter in the mail from Cordelia Whitmore. There had been no further e-mails since before Christmas. The letter simply read, "Has Scott built the volcano yet? Please let me know how the children enjoyed their Christmas gifts. Internet down, snail mail will do."

Shelley frowned at this. She was angry. That woman was still trying to get closer to her great-grandchildren, while ignoring Shelley altogether. She was treating Shelley like a lackey, a go-between. This woman who had refused to even hug her, was still making demands of her. Shelley decided enough was enough. She did not write Cordelia back. She decided she was not going to "tell Cord" anything.

In March, Shelley received the phone call from her mother that Cordelia had died. Shelley felt nothing. She felt empty. There was no anger, nor relief, just simply nothing. After all, she would not have felt any differently if a total stranger had died, would she? Her one thought at that time was of her grandfather.

Frank Whitmore had lived with Cordelia for 58 years. How the man had stood her, Shelley would never understand. It probably helped that the man was almost stone deaf. He had spent the last thirty years barely hearing the old woman nag at him. As a child, Shelley barely spoke to him, because his hearing aids could barely register her small voice. But he always smiled at her and winked. He took her fishing, and he never said anything mean to her. He never scolded her for laughing too loud.

While she wasn't particularly close to Grandpa Frank, she was not afraid of him. Shelley also never doubted that he loved her. There was never any contact with Frank, for he was too old fashioned and had never used a computer in his life, and with his bad hearing, telephone calls were moot, but every year Shelley received a birthday card with his signature on it. Good old snail mail for Frank.

*****

There was no funeral for Cordelia Whitmore, because that was how she wanted it. She ordered her body be cremated and that no memorial services of any kind be conducted. Good old Cordelia; even in death, she was calling all the shots. Shelley did not see her grandfather after the loss of his wife. She sent him a sympathy card, and signed it "Love, Shelley."

A month before Cordelia died, Shelley's husband transferred with his company and the four of them moved to Texas. A new state, a new city, a whole new way of life. New schools for Scott and Jenna as well, so Shelley was busy for a while. It was several months before she sat down one afternoon and began her ritual inbox cleaning.

There was a small pang of sadness that Shelley did not expect to feel when she saw the old username on a message. TELLCORD was still there, the old messages not having been deleted. It was only a few, the messages Cordelia had sent in October and December, before her connection had gone down for whatever reason. Shelley opened each of the messages and read them quickly, for they were only a few sentences long, combined. Then she went on with her cleaning, but she left the messages from TELLCORD unchecked. She decided to keep them for a while longer. They were, after all, all she had left.

Later that afternoon she found the letter Cordelia had sent the previous February. Again, Cordelia asked if Scott had ever made the volcano? Shelley felt guilty. Here the woman was, dead for several months now, and Shelley wasn't even sure where the volcano set was. She immediately began looking through cabinets and found it in with the checkers and Candy Land. Scott was at school, but that afternoon Shelley made it a priority to work with him on the project.

*****

Shelley was beginning to feel more and more guilty. Cordelia had been cold, but perhaps she didn't know any other way to be? Had Shelley been any less cold, really? She wasn't sure. She knew very little about the woman, including how Cordelia had grown up, or what her own childhood had been like. People don't just become cold like that for no reason, Shelley thought. Whatever the reason for her grandmother's cold behavior, it probably wasn't her fault.

Several days later, the finished volcano sitting on the dresser next to her desk, Shelley sat at her computer looking at the messages from her grandmother. She clicked on the last one, from December. She never wrote her back, not really. She had sent a quick reply, but Shelley had never really attempted to write the woman anything heartfelt. She wished now that she had. What would have happened? Probably nothing, she mused. Probably the woman would not have even bothered to reply. At least she would have tried though, Shelley thought. At least then she would have known.

Before she even knew what she was doing, Shelley clicked the reply button and was staring at a blank page. She blinked in surprise. This was silly. What good would it do to send a message now?

In the back of her mind, however, she remembered reading a book once on grief. Shelley could not even remember why she had read the book, but she did recall a chapter on recovery. One of the things it suggested was that the person grieving should write a letter to the deceased, saying everything they wanted to say.

Sometimes these letters were left on the people's graves; sometimes they were even put into a glass bottle and thrown out into the sea. Other times the letters were simply burned. The whole point was to take all the things that were stuck inside, roiling around and causing pain, and get them out. It was a means to an end. It was part of the grieving and coping process.

Shelley didn't think she was grieving, for she hadn't cried over Cordelia's death at all. Yet, still, there was something here. Some kind of unexpressed emotion was inside her needing to come out. She could write a letter and burn it, or throw it out into the sea. Or, she supposed, she could send an e-mail. This time Shelley decided she actually would tell Cord.

*****

She wrote the letter in a blur of emotions. As she wrote, she got angry, then sad, then furious, and even found herself at times laughing and smiling.

She told Cordelia all of her memories from her childhood. Her memories of how she feared the woman, and how she respected her. She explained how she felt about Cordelia's attempts to get to know Scott and Jenna, while continuing to show no regard for Shelley at all. She mentioned her confusion, her absolute inability to understand the woman at all, and ended with her high hopes for the visit last summer, when everything seemed to go so wrong.

She yelled at Cordelia, she cried at her, she begged and pleaded with her, she asked her for answers. Shelley told Cord everything. At the end of the letter, she asked one simple question. She asked Cordelia Whitmore if she had ever loved Shelley at all. Then Shelley signed it, "Love, Shell."

With a trembling finger, she hit the send button, knowing the message would go into oblivion, for it would never be read by Cordelia. Cordelia was dead. The letter would sit in an invisible inbox, that wasn't even a real inbox, but was just emptiness, in the surreal world of cyberspace. Then she recovered herself and went on about her day.

*****

Two days later, she opened her own inbox and sat staring in disbelief at the highlighted reply from TELLCORD. At first Shelley thought her message had been sent back. *Obviously,* she thought to herself, *Cordelia is dead, so her account has been shut down.*

This was not her message sent back, however. The regard did not read "failure to send; invalid address." She had gotten messages like that before, and this was not one of them.

Shelley then figured it was a valid message sent through Cordelia's account, probably from the domain informing her that the person the account belonged to was no longer living. An automated response, perhaps. Did they do that, though? Shelley wasn't sure.

How would Yahoo even know that Cordelia Whitmore was dead? Wouldn't someone have to notify them of that? Shelley couldn't imagine anyone in her family thinking to contact Yahoo to let them know that Cordelia had died. She knew Grandpa Frank wouldn't have, because he literally didn't know how to use a computer. Whatever it was, regardless of where the message said it came from, it was definitely not a message from Cordelia Whitmore from beyond the grave.

Shelley finally became disgusted with herself for even believing for a moment it could actually be from Cordelia. She sighed, annoyed at herself and clicked on the message to open it. Then she sat -absolutely stunned- as she read the first line.

Shelley Dear,

I am so sorry for all the pain I have caused you. I never realized how you felt, all those years. You must try to understand that I did not knowingly, nor intentionally try to hurt you. It would take years to try and explain to you my life, or why I was the way I was. Please just know that I tried my best, and I am so sorry that my best was not good enough. I regret many things in my life, but mostly, I regret not getting to know you, my beautiful granddaughter, and I am also greatly saddened to not have truly gotten to know my great grandchildren either. They are wonderful, beautiful children. You are a wonderful mother to them. I don't have much time, and it is with great difficulty that I am even able to send you this message. I must go soon. I will not be able to send you another message than this. I will be moving on to another place where I will not be able to contact you. Dear Shelley, I leave you with this.

I always loved you.

With utmost regard,

Cordelia

Shelley sat with tears brimming over her eyelids and down her cheeks. Cordelia had loved her after all, and as Shelley suspected, she had never meant to hurt her or make her feel unloved. It was all a mistake. Shelley quickly hit the reply button and wrote a short message.

It's okay, Grandma, I forgive you. I am not mad at you anymore. I know you love me, and I just want you to know I love you, too.

Love,

Shelley

She hit the send button. A few minutes later, her message came back from the mail daemon. TELLCORD was no longer a valid address. Shelley wondered if her original message had been sent after all, or had perhaps been intercepted in the ether of the afterlife - some sort of strange, cosmic e-mail from beyond. Yet, here it was, in her inbox. A message from her dead grandmother - one message that had gotten through on either end, and that was all. She looked at the date. The message had been sent to her that morning.

Shelley logged out of her mailbox and left to pick up the kids from school. She turned off her computer with a smile on her lips.

*****

Frank Whitmore sat in the early hours of the morning, weeping. He never learned to use a computer, but the neighbor next door had helped him. His wife, Cordelia, had written her username and password in her address book, which she kept on her desk. Frank knew Cordelia had used e-mail as her main way to communicate with friends for the last few years. There were people who still did not know of Cordelia's passing. Frank needed to access Cordy's e-mail in order to let some of them know the news. Once that was done, he would cancel her account. He didn't want it out there in existence when Cordelia was not. It was simply something he needed to do.

His neighbor had come over a few nights before and showed Frank how to pull up Yahoo, and how to log onto Cordy's e-mail account. He taught Frank how to hit reply and send new messages to people. Frank spent the rest of the evening systematically going through Cordy's inbox and sending messages out to anyone who didn't already know that she was gone.

He continued this work the next morning and was surprised to see a new message had arrived from his granddaughter, Shelley. It was just sent that day, by the date. Why would Shelley send a message to Cordelia after she was dead? He clicked on it and read it, his eyes filling with tears.

*****

It took him an entire day to process what Shelley had written to Cordelia, to fully understand and absorb the pain involved. When Frank finally decided to write a reply, it took him nearly an hour to type it. He wept the entire time.

Twerp

The Twerp parked his bike outside the 7-11. He didn't worry about locking it, he didn't even own a lock, no one was going to bother stealing a piece of shit ten-speed that was a rusted hand-me-down from two of his older brothers.

He was there to steal, again. He didn't have any money, but that never stopped him from taking what he wanted.

Inside the store the clerk, Ricardo, eyed him warily from behind the counter. He'd never been able to catch him stealing yet, but the punk had never paid for anything, and he came in several times a week. What the fuck was he always in there for, if he never bought anything?

The clerk knew he was stealing. Today he would demand that the Twerp empty his pockets before leaving the store.

The Twerp went to the back. He'd steal cans of beer if they weren't so bulky under his jacket. Same problem with bags of chips. He always ended up taking the long bars of wrapped taffy, 'cause he could fold them in half and stuff them in his pockets, all four of them. He didn't like taffy, but tough shit. It was free.

"Holy shit!" Ricardo yelled.

Twerp didn't care what he was yelling about. He stuffed taffy into his pockets with abandon.

"Jesus fucking Christ!"

Twerp smiled. His pockets were full. *Time to motor*. He walked to the front doors, but just as he was about to go through, a hand jerked him back.

Fuck! I'm busted! he had time to think.

He expected Ricardo to look pissed when he turned to look at him, but instead, the Mexican was crying. *Crying.* He looked scared or something. His chin shook.

"D-Don't go ou-out there, m-man! D-Don't you s-see??!" He pointed a shaky finger toward the glass.

Twerp followed his hand, thinking, *this is some kind of a joke*, and he saw pandemonium outside.

How he hadn't heard the loud sounds coming from the street 'til now was a mystery. Now he heard screaming, and tires screeching, and saw smoke flying up from rubber wheels. Gunshots barked off in the distance. People ran in all directions. Cars racing in panicked lines crashed into each other. Twerp laughed - a nervous reaction.

"What's this shit?"

He turned to look at Ricardo, but the Mexican dude was gone.

A hand thudded loudly against the glass, and Twerp jumped, turning back to see a woman, roughly around age 30, he'd guess, press herself up to the glass, like she wanted to melt her way into the store.

She whapped her hand against the glass again.

"You knocking?" Twerp laughed. "Try the handle."

He pointed. She didn't listen.

Her skin was droopy. It hung off her body like a loose shawl. It looked like a roasted marshmallow when it starts to melt off the stick. She looked like one of those dogs with the foldy-droopy skin.

A Droopy Dog.

Twerp laughed.

"Dude, -the fuck happened to you, Droopy Dog Lady?" he laughed again. "Did you get roasted??"

She did not laugh, she did not seem to think the Twerp was funny in the slightest. She moaned.

–And whapped the glass again.

"Don' let her in!" Ricardo screamed. He had magically reappeared, and was behind the counter holding a sawed-off shotgun.

"Aren't those illegal?" Twerp frowned.

Ricardo did not explain the legalities or otherwise of his weapon. He just shrugged. He pointed the barrel at the lady.

"She is pretty ugly, dude, but I don't think you can shoot her. She's outside the store. And I failed History, but I think I remember learning you can only shoot someone if they trespass on your home property. This is a 7-11. It's public. Anyone can come in."

"Not if their fuckin' skin's melting off, they can't!"

"Okay, Ricardo, okay…chillax. I'll tell her to go away."

The Twerp was just glad he wasn't going to be busted for stealing the taffy. Which gave him an idea…he pulled a taffy bar from his back pocket, opened it and started eating it, thinking hard.

It was banana taffy.

"That's it!" he told the woman. "You look like taffy! You're a taffy-skinned-Droopy Dog! What happened?"

"Them," she rasped.

Her thwapping hand rose off the glass and pointed backwards. She still looked at Twerp. Her eyes rolled around in their sockets.

"What, you got eyes in the back of your head?"

He looked behind her. There were still cars careening 'round corners, more people running. He saw a few others that were carrying stuff draped across their arms, which looked strange to him. He looked again.

Oh, nope, he realized. *That's just more of those Droopy Dog people. I thought they were carrying tan towels or something, but it's just their skin hanging down.*

He shrugged.

"So…what? You can't come in here, you know."

She rasped again, her finger pointing back towards the street behind her.

"Yeah, over there, so…? It's a panic, obviously," he nodded.

"Move outta the way!" Ricardo pointed the shotgun at Twerp's head.

"Dude! Remember? Chillax! I'll clean Droopy-Dog-Taffy-Lady off your glass, 'kay? Point that at your own feet."

"Them..." she rasped again. Her hand was pointing behind her now at a very bad angle. No way her wrist should go that far back in that direction.

"So...your bones are droopy too?" he asked her.

"Them....!!" her voice rose.

"Fucking...who? Crazy-ass bitch! Get offa the glass, or my buddy Ricardo is going to blast your droopy ass to China!"

"Fuck you callin' buddy?" Ricardo spat. "Outta the way."

"You are just bent on blowing her ass away, huh?" Twerp nodded. "I hear ya, I get it. Too many video games, that's what my Ma would say. You play WOW much, Ricardo? City of Heroes? What's your damage?"

"Outta the way..." Ricardo steadied the barrel.

"Okay then." Twerp dove.

BLAST!

Shattering glass rained down on him. He screamed like a little girl. The actual female disappeared, but soon Twerp was rained on by misty red spray, some of it speckled the broken glass and he thought of rubies.

He jumped up. Droopy Dog was gone. Mostly. What was left of her slumped to the ground without a head. Her spaghetti-arms lay on the ground in S shapes. Twerp frowned and cringed.

"Aliens!!" a woman yelled while running down the street.

Aliens? Twerp frowned. He turned to Ricardo.

"You hear that shit? You think aliens made you go bat shit and shoot that Droopy-Taffy Lady?"

Ricardo stared at Twerp. The gun lay on the counter. Twerp got up into his face, discerning him like a cop.

"You think aliens turned you into a murderer Ricardo? 'Cuz you just murdered some spaghetti-armed lady, instead of letting her in. How does that feel?"

"Sh-she could have b-been...sick."

"Oh, yeah." Twerp nodded, taking a bite of his candy. "Sure, she was sick all right. And now I'm covered in her blood...so, whatever she got, I have now too, probably. What do you think about that, good ol' Ricky?"

Twerp slapped his hand on Ricardo's shoulder and dug in deep.

Ricardo jerked away, but Twerp, fast as lightning, had the barrel in his own hand, swinging the stock around. He held the shotgun on the shop clerk.

"How does that feel, huh, Ricky? So...you think I could get away with blaming aliens for when I shoot you? I wonder..."

Ricardo pointed behind Twerp, out into the street. Screaming continued...crashing cars. Car alarms blared. Fire truck and ambulance sirens sounded in all directions. Crashing noises. Breaking glass. Crying. Explosions. Twerp shrugged.

"All hell is breaking loose, I guess, huh?"

Ricardo still pointed. His hand shook wildly.

"I'm not falling for that shit, Ricky. What?? Something is right behind me?? You want me to look...? And when I do, you steal the gun back and blast me away, right? You think I'm that stupid, Ricky? Mexican shithead."

Ricardo backed away. He still pointed.

"Yeah, you can back away from the gun all you want, Rickster. Won't do you no good. Guess what I do when I'm not busy stealing from you? I play video games too."

He steadied the gun and squinted his aim at Ricardo's forehead. Ricardo's eyes were wide with fear.

Behind him, Twerp heard a rasping-scraping noise. From somewhere, a brown, tentacled-thing snaked its way into the shop, over Twerp's shoulder and with a lover's caress, whipped quickly back, across Twerp's cheek, to find the orifice of his ear.

Twerps' last thought was –*Taffy*!

Halloween

"God, this is so embarrassing," Lindsey whispered. She was a thirty-year-old dark angel wandering in the night, with a white grocery bag that exclaimed 'Ralphs' in red letters. The bag was empty, and in the darkness, it billowed in the wind, like some strange sail, leading her on. Her daughter, Alyssa, all of four-years-old, was already knocking on another door. She was dressed as a white angel with blow-up plastic wings. They glittered in the dark. Lindsey had wanted them to shimmer. She sprayed hairspray all over them, and then threw glitter onto them before the wet stuff could dry. She didn't think it would actually work, and was happily surprised when it did.

Alyssa had been thrilled. She put the wings on and danced all around the living room. She really did look like an angel, with her pale-white, delicate face and her slightly-pinked cheeks. Her tiny-little pug nose, perfect, tiny teeth and that little, cute voice completed the image. Alyssa was shaping up to love Halloween almost as much as her Mommy.

Now, here she was, an old lady by her own standards, actually trying to trick-or-treat. She couldn't help it. She loved Halloween. Always had. Maybe it was because her birthday was the day before. That explained it, right? Perhaps. Maybe it was the costumes. It was the only time of year where people put on tons of makeup, wore masks, and pretended to be somebody or something they weren't.

Except Alyssa really was a little angel. Her costume was the physical, ocular embodiment of everything Lindsey felt about her little girl. Did this mean that Lindsey was a dark angel? Not really, she just wanted to wear something dark, so she could blend in with the night. Alyssa had wanted them to match, but white would have made Lindsey look fat. Black was slimming. So, they were light and dark angels, and this had appeased Alyssa.

*****

The little girl Lindsey, who was all of five-years-old, was sitting patiently, as her mommy put cold, thick, pasty stuff all over her face. Later that night, when it warmed to her skin and dried, it would feel as if it were shrinking, pulling at her skin. It would make her afraid to smile, or even speak, because any movement of her face would cause the thick stuff to crack. Even at five, little Lindsey already felt completely consumed by the magic of disguising herself. She didn't want her makeup to crack, and risk ruining the effect. She was supposed to be a clown. When the makeup was finished, her mommy adorned her with a huge, multi-colored wig of curly strands. Her baggy yellow suit, complete with pompom puffs in bright red for buttons down her front, jiggled with every step she took.

Little Lindsey hadn't wanted to be a clown. She had wanted to be a witch. Or even a red devil, with horns and a tail. Her mother insisted she would look so cute as a clown, and besides, everyone went as a witch or a devil. Lindsey's costume would be different. Lindsey didn't argue with her mom. She was a good, obedient little girl. She was eager to please. When her costume was complete, when her mother had placed on the wig, and pulled away, squealing in delight, exclaiming how absolutely cute she was, Lindsey received the reward she wanted.

She loved Halloween. Halloween meant her mother and father's undivided attention. It meant a shopping trip sometime just before the big night, and plans, and talking. It meant her mother, actually stopping and regarding her closely. Looking straight into her face. On the big night, it meant pictures being taken, just of her, in whatever cute little outfit she had on that year. At age five, Lindsey knew all these things, though not in words. She knew all these things as feelings inside of her. They were feelings of warmth, and love- feelings of attention, and wantedness. They were feelings of hope.

Hope came in many different shapes and sizes. It came in shapes without names, inside a five-year-old girl, living in a house that she didn't know her parents would be forced to sell just two months from then, because money was too tight to continue paying the mortgage.

*****

Grownup Lindsey hurried up to her own little angel just as she knocked on the next door.

"I'm not going to say it this time, okay Alyssa?"

Lindsey fidgeted her feet nervously, wondering and waiting to see if anyone was even home. Their porch light was on, and a pumpkin was carved and lit on their doorstep. Somewhere from deep inside the cave of their home, padded footsteps came to Lindsey's ears. They became crystal clear, crackling steps as the door opened. A middle-aged woman opened up the door, an expectant smile on her face. She was already looking downward, in anticipation of the little child, or children she expected to see at her door. She glanced briefly at the grown woman, then back down at the little angel. The little angel held the straps of her bag open with both hands, shyly saying, "Trick-or-trick," in her singsong manner.

"My, aren't you adorable," squealed the woman.

She was already holding a bowl of candy in her own hands. She let Alyssa reach in and pick out what she wanted. Her porcelain little hand rummaged through the candy corns and tiny snack sized M&M packets, the little Butterfingers. She found what she was looking for, single cup packages of Reese's - always the favorite of tiny children anywhere. Even for Lindsey at her age.

"Only one," Lindsey chided. "Save some for the other children."

She hated sounding like a mom on this night, while wearing this ridiculous costume. The woman glanced up quickly, looking reproachful.

"Oh, that's all right. You're only the second trick-or-treaters to come tonight."

Lindsey felt a reversal in roles, as the woman talked to her in a tone that made her the mother now. With a stranger's permission, and against her own mother's, Alyssa reached into the bowl again, as it was thrust just under her face. She fished around for another Reese's, found one, and brought a package of M&M's with it. Her bag was already halfway full. Alyssa backed away, and looked up expectantly at her mother.

So, Lindsey shied forward and sheepishly said, "Trick-or-treat," in that same singsong manner she'd been using since she could remember. The same way all kids say it. The woman raised her eyebrows in surprise for a moment, and then smiled in an understanding way that made Lindsey feel completely stupid. The woman reached into her own bowl, fished up a Butterfinger, and placed it into Lindsey's bag.

It was the same reaction she'd gotten all night. Sympathetic, surprised looks, at seeing a grownup ask for candy. Why did Lindsey feel so foolish? She only wanted to enjoy the evening with her daughter. She only wanted to feel that magic and excitement as each door opened. As each new bowl of mystery candy appeared and revealed its contents to her. She hadn't expected to feel this way. To feel dread as each new door opened. To feel her heart speeding up, as Alyssa finished with her question, and Lindsey had to step in and ask. *This is the last door*, she told herself, even though she knew Alyssa would be disappointed.

*****

Little Lindsey walked holding her mother's hand, as they passed groups of children and parents going in the other direction. Halloween was so exciting. It was like the whole neighborhood came alive. There were children everywhere, all in different disguises. Every house was lit up, and every doorstep had a gleaming Jack O' Lantern smiling to greet her as she walked up the steps.

*Halloween was the longest Lindsey ever got to hold her mother's hand - A few hours in a row - **in a row**! She always got so much candy, too. Every house, someone was home. Every house, there was a giant bowl of candy filled with her favorite treats. Almost everyone had those little packages of Reese's. By the end of the third street, Lindsey's bag would be brimming full, and almost too heavy to carry. They never had to go too far from their own house - Still in their own little neighborhood. Halloween was alive...*

*****

They only passed two groups the whole night. It was like this every year now, Lindsey thought sadly. Less and less children trick-or-treating. Most people went to the mall, where you could trick or treat inside. The candy was safe, everything was well lit, and it was warm. But it was so crowded. There was no real anticipation. No knocking on doors, and waiting for things to be revealed. No walking through the neighborhoods in the darkness, feeling stealthy and invisible. No camaraderie, as you passed other groups of children, and feeling some sort of sense that everyone was in on the fun. It just wasn't the same.

So, this year, Lindsey had decided to skip the mall, and go trick-or-treating the old fashioned way. Surely people still did that, right? Half the houses they passed were dark. A third of the houses with lights on had no Halloween decorations. Most of those that answered had no candy. One man seemed to feel bad about being ill prepared. He disappeared for a moment, and then came back to the door with a trail mix bar, singly wrapped.

"This is all I have, sorry," he said. "I usually don't get enough trick-or-treaters to justify buying bags of candy. I just end up having it all left over."

Lindsey nodded in understanding, even though she was confused. No, she didn't understand. Why were there people who weren't home? Why would people not put up decorations, or at the very least, carve a pumpkin? That wasn't so hard to do, was it? She didn't ask for her own trail mix bar.

*****

Little Lindsey was sad when they moved from their nice house, in their nice neighborhood. She didn't know why they were moving - she just knew she would miss all of her neighborhood friends. The new place seemed nice, but she didn't know anyone. When fall came around, and Halloween arrived, she was six. Her mother dressed her up, this time as a witch. Her tall, pointed black hat kept falling off her head, until her mother secured it with bobby pins. They pinched her scalp and hurt.

Lindsey didn't know what to expect this year, in this new neighborhood, but she turned out not to be disappointed. Another neighborhood where tons of children roamed the streets at twilight, toting heavy bags full of candy. Every house was lit up, and every house had a carved pumpkin, and candy. It only took two full streets, and one hour until Lindsey's bag was full. She only got to hold her mother's hand for an hour. But Halloween was a success, and she went home that night satisfied.

*****

Three hours later, Alyssa's bag was about two thirds full. She was getting tired, and bored. They were quite a ways from their apartment now. It would take a while to walk back, and Alyssa was complaining that her bag was getting heavy. Lindsey carried it.

"Did you have fun?"

Lindsey was filled with a strange, new hope. The kind of hope that was 'wanting to share.' She wanted her daughter to love Halloween the same way she did. She wanted her to feel that same magic. She knew she had failed. Things weren't the same now, or here. Maybe it was where they lived? Or maybe times had just changed?

Halloween wasn't the same anymore. She remembered it like that scene in E.T., where Elliot, his brother and little Gertie walked the streets, as the sun set, bright golden yellow all around them. There were children everywhere. E.T. turned to look at one child who passed by, wearing an alien mask. Everyone was out in the neighborhood. Everyone was having fun. This was how her neighborhoods had been on Halloween. This is how she remembered it, every year, until the last.

*****

Year seven, and little Lindsey was having something new. A Halloween themed birthday party, the night before Halloween. Her parents had gone all out. They decorated the two-car garage. There were yellow, orange and black streamers hanging everywhere. A baby pool filled with water, and apples floating for the game of bobbing for apples. There was a table covered in a paper tablecloth; white with yellow and orange striped candy corns on it. Bowls filled with chips, and punch with ice cream floating in it. A huge half-sheet cake, covered in black frosting, with a witch sailing through the sky on a broom, an angry black cat arching its back on the tip of the broom behind her. A huge pumpkin piñata hung from the ceiling for the kids to batter later on.

Her parents had allowed Lindsey to invite her entire class of twenty kids to the party. Every other year, her birthday had consisted of one or two friends over to watch her cut her Halloween themed cake. It was always a Halloween themed cake. Why her parents threw her a huge party this year was something little seven-year-old Lindsey never wondered. She didn't think about things like that. She didn't even think about why her parents yelled at each other every night. It was just something that was. She was used to it, and it had been happening for months.

Even the sound of breaking glass, or the occasional thud, as someone seemed to fall down didn't faze her. She was busy watching this new channel that had just come out, called MTV. There was a guy on there that made a really cool, long video where everyone dressed up in Halloween costumes. It was a Halloween video. The guy was black, and he seemed to be some kind of zombie. He and all his zombie friends were dancing, and trying to scare some black lady, who kept opening her eyes really wide, making Lindsey laugh. She hardly noticed the sounds of things breaking above her, in her parent's bedroom.

*****

By the time Lindsey and Alyssa got back to their apartment, she finally noticed how much lighter Alyssa's bag was. She held it up to her face in the dim light of the porch light and discovered it was half empty. She inspected the bottom, and found the hole. Alyssa was upset. They retraced their steps, and followed a steady trail of candy. How had Lindsey not noticed this? Two streets back, they found some candy that had been squashed under the tires of a car. It was ruined. Four-year-old Alyssa was crying.

No, this can't happen, Lindsey thought. *She can't hate Halloween.*

Alyssa wanted to go back and knock on doors again, and get her lost candy back. Lindsey wasn't even sure which houses they had gone to, they had stopped at so many. She didn't want to knock on doors now, and bother people. It was late, and no more trick-or-treaters were out. They were the last. They walked, and managed to recover most of the candy. Not all, but most. Lindsey said Alyssa could have her candy as well. Her bag was not even half full, but it would make up for the candy Alyssa had lost. This seemed to please her.

They headed for home again, all of the candy in Lindsey's bag, which had no hole. Lindsey was sad, disappointed. Her feet hurt. She just wanted to go home.

She was sad at the realization that she just wanted this year's Halloween to be over. This was what it had come down to. It was the death of a Holiday, the death of a certain kind of hope. It had probably died years ago, but Lindsey had refused to accept that. Or at the very least, she didn't want to give it up. She wanted to pass it on to her own daughter. She could live without that hope herself, as long as she knew she had passed it on, given away that legacy of magic.

*****

The party was incredible. It was three hours of games, and candy, candles and songs. Little Lindsey and her classmates danced for over an hour to a record of Halloween songs her parents played. She remembered the song 'Monster Mash' playing, and that song would be one of her favorites for the rest of her life. She would never hear it again after that night without smiling and feeling just a little bit warm. She never noticed the entire night that her parents were never together. They were both there, but on separate sides of the garage.

When the piñata broke, and candy went flying everywhere, there were twenty screaming, laughing children filling their paper lunch sacks with as much candy as they could grab. There was pushing and shoving, but in a friendly way. Lindsey laughed harder than she ever had before. That party would make her popular in her class. The rest of the school year, she would have tons of friends. That was a good thing.

*****

When they finally got home, Lindsey allowed Alyssa to dump her bag of candy out on the living room floor and partake of her booty. This was a tradition from her childhood. Alyssa would probably go to bed feeling a little sick, and her teeth wouldn't appreciate it much, but it was all part of the fun of the night. Alyssa was tired, though. She only ate two pieces of candy, and began nodding off. Lindsey slipped her white, shimmering wings off her back, and carried her into her bedroom, still wearing her beautiful white gown. She let her sleep in it all night. It didn't matter. She would never wear it again, anyway.

*****

The next day, after her amazing party, Lindsey went trick-or-treating with her mother for the last time. She didn't know it was the last time. All she knew was that her life was terrific. She'd had the best birthday of her entire life, and now, the very next day, her favorite night of the year was here.

She was seven, and dressed as a red devil. Her mother had let her be what she wanted this year, with no arguments. They held hands, and again, it took less than an hour before her bag was filled to the brim with candy. They walked home, this time, not holding hands. Lindsey didn't even notice.

*****

Lindsey trudged tiredly into the bedroom, where her husband was on the computer, playing an online game. He didn't care about Halloween. It hadn't been a big deal to him growing up. Lindsey had tried to explain to him, and make him understand. Again, she tried to pass on that wonder and magic of the night. She wanted to make her husband love Halloween as much as she did. But he did not. He didn't get it. She was all alone.

She had failed to pass on the magic to her own daughter. She alone held that wonder and magic in her heart, and it was fading now, to her numbed shock. She went into the bathroom and washed her face. With a wet washcloth, she rubbed the glitter from her cheeks. Later she took off her black wings and black clothes and put on her pajamas. She brushed her teeth, got a glass of water and placed it on the stand next to her side of the bed. She said goodnight to her husband, and turned out the lights.

*****

November first, and the dull, gray morning had brought sadness to little seven-year-old Lindsey. Sadness because it was all over for another year. It had been the best year so far. The best Halloween. The best birthday party she had ever, or would ever have. And today it was all over. Every November first was sad for Lindsey. The magic was gone, in hibernation for another eleven months, and three weeks, roughly. She did not know that Halloween had gone into hibernation forever. She did not know that today, the magic would slowly begin to die.

She got up, went into the bathroom to pee, then went into the kitchen to get a bowl of cereal. But before she could even pour the milk, her mother was there, telling her to come sit on the living room couch. She obeyed, and found her father there as well. They each sat, her mother and father, on opposite sides of the tandem couch. Lindsey sat in the middle of her own couch all alone. Her parents told her they were going to get divorced, that they would no longer be living in the same place together. They told her she would have to decide whom to live with, and she had one week to decide.

At seven-years-old, Lindsey didn't really understand what was happening. The day had been gray already. Now it was just a little bit darker. A week later, when she was still confused, and back on the couch, with both parents looking at her expectantly, she cried, and mumbled, "Daddy," then burst into tears. Her mother - she would remember for the rest of her life - would slowly walk out of the room, and go upstairs.

An hour later, her mother would call her to the front door. There were two suitcases, one on either side of her. Lindsey would remember crying and hugging her mother. She would remember saying she was sorry. She would remember her mother looking sad, yet slightly cold. She would remember thinking that her mother was mad at her. Then she was saying goodbye to her mother, and staring at the door as it closed.

Eight-year-old Lindsey would not even go trick-or-treating that next fall, but she did not know that then. She did not know on that gray November 1st, that her mother would not be coming back. She did not know that next Halloween, there would be no mother to take her out trick-or-treating. She did not know then, that on that day, she had sent her mother away.

*****

Grown up Lindsey lay in bed in the darkness, thinking that her daughter would never understand her. If she couldn't understand why Halloween was so much fun. If Alyssa couldn't fully experience the magic, the same way Lindsey had, then there would always be a part of her mother that Alyssa would never be able to touch. But that was okay now. Lindsey knew there would always be a part of her that her daughter would never know, and perhaps that was how it should be.

Mothers were always, ultimately, strangers to their daughters, weren't they? And vice versa. No one could ever truly know another person, could they? And that was how it should be, because that's how it always was. No matter how hard she tried to change it. It was as much out of her control as this Halloween had been. She couldn't control who was home and who was not. She had no way of knowing how many kids were not trick-or-treating out in the neighborhoods these days. Times had changed.

Perhaps someday, they would pendulum back the other way. Maybe when Alyssa was a mother, and took her own daughter trick-or-treating? Maybe, someday, Halloween would be alive again, like it used to be? There was always that hope, still. And that hope, for a Halloween far off in the unknown future, is what put Lindsey to sleep. There was still hope, and that was all that counted.

Enjoy Your Stay

Cassie hated her roommate from the very start. On the first day of her freshman year at college, an odd feeling came over Cassie Roberts when she met Ella Moore. It was an unfamiliar feeling, one that could only be described as disdain. A small town girl from northern Washington, Cassie was simultaneously awed and disgusted by Ella's cheerleader-verve and Valley Girl mannerisms. As she would later tell her sister on the phone, "She's like a walking, talking stereotype. An absolute, living cliché."

Cassie would have never believed a real person like Ella existed, until she met her. She watched in fascinated horror all that first semester, as Ella preened herself each morning, parading through the dorm; walking back from the showers, into their room in a towel, opening her dresser drawer and slipping on a pink thong. Ella would rake through clothing neatly hung in her closet, and then spritz her carefully chosen garments with Chanel before putting them on. She shamelessly lectured Cassie on many a night of her wily ways, almost as if it were a tutoring session.

"Going dancing is the quickest way. You rub against them during a sexy song, and then just when they think they can't stand another minute of it, you grind against them. It makes them want you so bad."

These statements always confused Cassie.

"Then what?" she inquired.

Ella's stare was blank.

"Then nothing. You have them right where you want them."

"Which is where?" Cassie said, exasperated. For none of these men, these various "dates" were truly of any interest to Ella.

"You have them wanting you," Ella sighed, clearly annoyed.

"But, what for? What's the point, if you don't even want to be with them?"

Ella sighed again, even more annoyed, which made Cassie angry. It was partly out of sheer disgust over this young woman's heartless behavior, and yet she knew it was also because a part of her was jealous. Jealous of Ella for having the nerve to dress the way she did.

Cassie's conservative dress hardly turned any male heads on campus. She was jealous of Ella's incredible, effortless ability to flirt with almost any male, of any age, while Cassie found herself, most times, tongue-tied. She was jealous every time she had to listen to Ella describe her dates. Dates Ella had while Cassie stayed in, studying.

Cassie was sick with jealousy by all the male "friends" who drove Ella around, and carried heavy boxes for her, and bought her meals. She could pretend all she wanted that it was really because she felt sorry for the men, some of whom might get their hearts broken. To a point, Cassie did feel bad for some of them, but only to a point, since they all seemed to come back for more abuse every week.

"The point is, Cass, that once they want you, they'll do almost anything for you."

"But you're just using them."

Cassie was furious, yet calm.

"Cass, wake up. Men use women all the time. They only care about one thing."

Cassie could no longer hold her tongue.

"Yeah, and you're using that one thing against them like it's some sick game."

Now it was Ella's turn to be angry.

"It is a game. You either use them or be used. You'd better decide which, Cass."

"I'm not like you, Ella," Cassie shot back. Ella turned a dead eye on her.

"I know. That's why I'll always have men falling all over me, and you'll be all alone."

Ella flipped her hair and walked out of the room.

***

It was not more than a week later that Cassie began conversing with a young man in her speech class. They had been assigned to interview one another, and then give a speech to the class about their fellow classmate. This was how Cassie met, and began dating, Evan. Within two weeks, they were inseparable. The lectures from Ella on how to snare a man ended. Ella went about her preening most nights in silence, ignoring Evan and Cassie, canoodling, giggling and cuddling in the bed, or on the dorm room couch. Their silent war seemed at an end, and now, a truce.

As the weeks passed into months, Cassie's jealousy faded and was forgotten. Then one day, in the spring, Cassie walked into her dorm room to find Ella in a compromising position with Evan. The 'how-could-you' and the 'you-make-me-sick' statements ensued. Ella wasn't interested in Evan for anything long term, and so he disappeared, but the animosity between Cassie and Ella had grown into a raging monster inside Cassie. She hated Ella. She felt it from the very beginning, and now she was certain of it. She hated her on the spring night that Ella died.

***

It was at a school party, at a house off-campus. Cassie saw Ella there, flirting with a procession of men, bringing her drink after drink. Each one hoping to be the one she would leave with. But Ella never left that house. She was found on a couch in the living room the next morning with one of her young suitors. He was still drunk and unconscious. Ella was dead. The coroner reported her blood alcohol level at .48%, five times the legal limit, and a lethal amount for Ella.

Of course, the questions ensued. There was an investigation. Had Cassie seen Ella there? Who did she see her with? Everyone wanted to know and try to understand how such a tragedy could take place. The students renting the off-campus house where Ella had died were reprimanded for serving alcohol to minors. Students were put on probation; others left school, or were expelled. Cassie was comforted and many sympathies were offered. Yes, she recounted to everyone, she had seen Ella on the couch. She had sat down next to her while the young man she was there with that night was getting her another drink. Yes, she would later tell friends and family, Ella was definitely drunk, but didn't seem to be in any danger.

"Lots of people at the party were drunk, even me a little," she would guiltily recall. Ella asked for a glass of water, and Cassie went to get it. When she returned to the couch with the glass, the young man was back, and Ella seemed okay.

"She was laughing, and so was the guy," Cassie explained.

Ella had been hungrily sipping the drink the young man brought her, the water seemingly forgotten. Cassie decided to leave the party soon after that.

"I'm not really a big partier, you know?" she told the authorities.

Cassie awoke the morning after the party to the news that her roommate was dead, and of the cause. In the weeks that followed, Cassie would flash back to that night, and the image of Ella with a drink in her hand, and the young man holding two drinks while flirting with her. His drink, and presumably Ella's next. Cassie saw Ella throw her head back in laughter, flipping her hair, as the young man leaned in closer. Cassie saw all this in her mind, and felt nothing. She felt no sympathy for Ella, or even Ella's parents. She was not sorry Ella was dead. Her jealousy and anger had turned to hatred, and her only thoughts upon the news that Ella was dead of alcohol poisoning were, "serves her right."

***

"Serves her right," Cassie mumbled as she sat in the airport terminal on a late spring afternoon. Freshman year was over, and she was flying home for the summer. Another roommate would be assigned to her next year. All Cassie wanted right now was to go home and put everything from that year behind her, and move forward.

"I'm sorry, did you say something?"

A conservatively dressed, middle-aged man was looking at Cassie inquisitively. Sitting next to Cassie, she had taken little notice of him when he'd sat down next to her earlier. Her only thought had been *nice suit*. He was dressed in a business suit, but had no briefcase. Other than that, he may as well have been invisible. Cassie broke out of her reverie with a sudden start. Had she really just spoken out loud?

"Huh?" she flushed slightly, her heart speeding up.

"Did you say something to me?"

The man smiled warmly at her, his eyebrows raised. He seemed friendly enough, and was fairly attractive for his age, Cassie thought to herself. He was handsome and he smelled good; some sort of men's cologne.

Ella would probably know the name of it by smell, Cassie thought disgustedly. Then, she worried that somehow this strange man might be able to read her thoughts and she flushed again.

"No, just thinking out loud, I guess," she stumbled.

"Ah, well," the man reassured her, "I do that all the time."

He folded his Weekly Journal in half and tucked it under his arm.

"Too often, probably," he chuckled.

Cassie smiled politely to go along with the quip. Deep down she was alarmed at the thought of actively hating a dead woman, and she was equally shocked at her paranoia that this man, and perhaps everyone in this terminal, could somehow see how horrid she was. Horrid for feeling no sadness over the seemingly untimely and tragic death of a woman Cassie had lived with for almost an entire school year. That everyone around her would somehow, intrinsically know that she hadn't shed a single tear over Ella's death.

"You needn't feel ashamed," the man soothed.

"What do you mean?" Ella shot back, a bit too quickly.

She tried to steady herself, and quiet her paranoia, but failed. Why would this stranger tell her not to be ashamed, unless he knew she had something to feel ashamed about?

Why am I being so paranoid all of a sudden? Cassie thought. It was a new feeling that had come on so quickly- it alarmed and shocked her.

The man was smiling warmly at Cassie and seemed completely calm.

"Sometimes when we're thinking too hard, thoughts just come out." The man gestured with his hand, to signal the flying away of thought, like a bird flapping its wings. It was disconcerting to Cassie, although she couldn't understand why.

"Oh," she nodded. "Right."

This is getting ridiculous, she thought. *Pull yourself together.*

Maybe this was finally her true feelings coming to the surface, she reasoned? She hadn't shed a tear over Ella's death, and now she was feeling guilty for being such a cold, uncaring person. And yet, still, she hated her. That feeling never left her. It had become ingrained in her subconsciousness, like a virus. Cassie would never shed a single tear over Ella's death. She knew this with a certainty that was both alarming, and comforting to her. She was a different person now. Hating Ella had changed her. The shy, quiet person she had been when she met Ella that first day of freshman year was gone.

Ella's death had somehow been a rite of passage for Cassie. In some weird recess of her mind, Cassie even believed that part of Ella had come to inhabit her. She flipped her hair, and smiled at the man sitting next to her, her recovery from earlier complete. She laughed.

"Well, forgive me for allowing my thoughts to fly out. It was unintentional." Cassie smiled winningly at the man, keeping his gaze for only a moment, and then looked down demurely. Was Ella's ghost still offering tutoring lessons to Cassie even now? She wondered. Then she dismissed the thought as absurd. The terminal speaker announced the pre-boarding of their flight, and Cassie turned her attention away from the man to gather her backpack and purse.

"Well, I guess that's us," said the man, still smiling. They both stood at the same time, and then laughed. The man walked away. Cassie queued up in line. She glanced behind her and saw the man enter the men's room.

I don't blame him. She hated using airplane lavatories. She would even hold it, when possible, and wait to use the airport bathroom upon landing. Something about the loud whoosh of air when depressing the flush handle had always frightened her. She was now up to the front of the gate. She handed her boarding pass to the attendant along with her ID.

Soon, she was on the plane, settling in. She was in the window seat, and gazing out at the luggage still being loaded onto the plane when she heard the man's already familiar voice.

"Well, what a coincidence," he said as he slid into the seat next to her. "How 'bout that?"

Cassie smiled politely.

"Yeah, how strange."

"Well, I guess introductions are in order, now," said the man, offering his hand for Cassie to shake.

"I'm Robert Carrington."

"Cassie Roberts." She offered her hand back.

She noted how warm his hand was as he shook hers, although, it was not moist, as she would have expected from such a warm hand. It was dry, but felt down right hot.

God. Maybe he's sick and has a fever. I hope I don't get what he has.

Robert settled into his seat and began reading his Weekly Journal again. Cassie pulled down the window shade and closed her eyes. It had been a very long few weeks and she was tired. No more thoughts went through her mind as she drifted off to sleep.

***

She was jarred awake again by sudden turbulence that shook the plane. She sat up, pulling in a breath, a tiny squeak of surprise escaping her throat. Robert chuckled.

"Just a bit of turbulence. It's fairly common during takeoff and ascent."

He put his hand over hers and soothingly rubbed. Cassie was white knuckled and clutching both armrests of her seat. Again, she felt the odd sensation of warmth in Robert's hand, and actually felt the heat begin to spread throughout her fingers and slightly up her wrist. He had to be sick, she thought to herself. He had to have a fever. At least 101, she figured. Yet, he didn't look ill.

He was dressed in a fine suit, jacket and all, yet his face wasn't flushed, and there was no sweat on his brow. He looked vibrant and healthy. His smile spread even wider at the way Cassie was now staring at him, wide-eyed. Robert let go of her hand, and put both of his hands together, lacing the fingers. It was oddly masculine and feminine at the same time.

"There, you see? It's over now," he said.

He went back to reading his paper. Cassie continued to stare at the man. Her eyes noted his shaven face, with just a hint of stubble growing in. Just enough to give the beginnings of that sandpapery look. She found it sexy and appealing, and again, she noticed how he smelled so good. She breathed in deeply and closed her eyes. A sudden flash of her and this man, locked in a passionate kiss, invaded her mind, and her eyes flew open, only to find Robert facing her, staring back at her wide stare. She flushed, for the third time under this man's gaze. Robert seemed amused.

"Fear of flying, I'm guessing?"

He stared back at her, expectantly. Cassie's earlier paranoia that Robert somehow knew what she had been thinking briefly returned. *Of course he couldn't know what I was thinking, that's impossible.* She played off his assumption, now assuming the role of the damsel in distress, seeking comfort. Another Ella tactic Cassie had seen her play to perfection on more than one occasion.

"Y-yes…" she stammered. "I guess so."

"Well," Robert purred. "Everything is all right, you know. Planes hardly ever fall out of the sky."

He laughed, this time very loud. Something about his laugh was disconcerting to Cassie. Robert put his hand over hers yet again, and she felt that same warmth spreading. The laugh disquieted her, but the warmth radiating from his hand was somehow comforting. She didn't know what was happening to her - her thoughts, her paranoia, and her strange attraction to this man, her shameless attempt to flirt with him. These were all unnerving occurrences that Cassie couldn't fathom.

I'm losing it, she thought. *The strain of everything I've been through this year has finally built up, and now I'm snapping.*

The warmth from Robert's hand was spreading beyond her wrist now, beginning to radiate up her arm. She found herself closing her eyes again, breathing in Robert's cologne. She felt a stirring in her loins, and a sudden heat there. Her eyes flew open, and she realized that Robert had gone back to his paper, his hand no longer on hers. She was flushed and hot, and her breathing was hasty. She was ashamed of her feelings, and shocked by them as well.

This is Ella's doing. Ella's endless lectures on men, and lust, and how to stir it all up within them. How to tease them. How to give them almost everything they wanted, but not that final prize. Ella's incessant speeches on how to let them touch, and where. What to give away, and what not. And her admissions to when to finally give in, and simply enjoy things. Ella hadn't denied all the men she'd dated. Some of them were generously rewarded. These came back for more as well. Many would follow her around for weeks, even months, hoping for another helping. It had made Cassie sick. It had disgusted her. Yet, part of her had wished she could have the nerve to be so in control.

Who's in control now, Cassie thought smugly. *One of us is alive; the other is a dead woman.* Cassie stirred in her seat, amazed at her own brazen thoughts. Yes, part of Ella now lived inside of her, and was rearing her ugly head. She was now two separate people inside, and they were having a war. The stronger side appeared to be the new Cassie; the Cassie who suddenly wanted to flirt with strange men she hardly knew. Cassie realized she wanted to flirt with the man sitting next to her, who was old enough to be her father, but ten times more charming and handsome.

And why the hell not? Cassie thought, still shocked, and yet thrilled at her own aggression. *They do say older men make better lovers. Older men know what they are doing.*

Cassie glanced over at Robert. He was still reading, completely oblivious to her thoughts regarding him. He was smiling slightly, perhaps at something he was reading.

Or could it be that he is smiling at you, silly girl? Cassie thought. *He does know what you are thinking, and he's smiling at the absurdity of it. You, barely legal, and still dressed far too conservatively to catch any man's eye, regardless of their age.*

Cassie quickly turned her head to look out the window at the clouds far below.

Shut up, she thought to herself. *Shut up, shut up, shut up.*

Was she going crazy? Her emotions were on a roller coaster, and she was having a hard time not panicking. Here was a perfectly nice man, who was unfortunate enough to sit next to a loony on his business trip.

Besides, her darker half quipped. *He's probably on his way home to his wife and kids. Did you even bother looking for a ring?*

She turned quickly toward Robert, only to find him facing her, leaning forward into her seat space with an inquisitive look. She turned so quickly, they were face-to-face for a moment, so close, her eyes couldn't focus on his clearly. So close, that her lips almost touched his. Their noses brushed instead, and Cassie gasped. Robert laughed.

"You really are a nervous flyer, aren't you?" He patted her hand a few times. Not enough for the heat to take hold and spread as it had before.

"You were doing it again, you know."

Cassie was staring wide-eyed at Robert, unable to breathe. She was disappointed that he had pulled his hand away. The search for a wedding band was momentarily forgotten.

"Doing what?" she asked. Robert turned an amused gaze back at her.

"Thinking out loud," he looked at her with a sudden intensity that unnerved Cassie.

"I was?" she blinked in total confusion.

"I hope so," Robert trailed. "Otherwise, you just told me to shut up."

Robert gazed at Cassie with a compassionate, yet stern look, one that reminded her all too much of her father. A chill went down her spine.

"I said that out loud?" Cassie's voice raised more than she expected. Robert laughed.

"I guess it wasn't meant for me, then," he replied. "What a relief."

"Why would I tell you to shut up? You didn't even say anything." Cassie paused. "Did you?"

"No," Robert retorted. "I haven't said anything to you."

"I'm sorry," she said. "I didn't mean to say that out loud."

Robert turned his gaze upon Cassie again.

"Is something wrong?" He looked at her comfortingly. "You've seemed nervous the entire flight. Even in the terminal."

Robert put his hand over Cassie's once again. She felt the old familiar warmth begin to spread, and welcomed it. Her nostrils dilated, and she breathed in his cologne again, this time deeper than before. Her eyes remained open, and she found herself gazing straight into Robert's blue eyes with a feeling of total surrender.

She wanted to tell this man everything she was thinking. She wanted to tell him about her year, and about Ella, and even about the party, and Ella's death. She wanted to tell him she found him extremely attractive. She wanted to invite him into the airplane bathroom with her. She wanted to tell him that if he were married, she wouldn't tell his wife; it could be just between the two of them. She wanted to take Robert's hand and place it on her breast, and feel his warmth spread throughout her whole body. She wanted to tell him how much she hated her dead roommate, even now. How glad she was that Ella was dead. How shocked and amazed she was at the thoughts she was having, even at that very moment.

She closed her eyes, and envisioned herself and Robert naked, groping and feeling for each other. She pictured them in the bathroom lavatory of the plane, squeezed into the tiny space, pushed together. She could feel his hands running over her body, and she could feel his breath on her neck. She could feel him inside of her pushing. The warmth was everywhere now, and she was completely enveloped by it. She turned to whisper in his ear, telling him how good he felt, and how much she wanted him, as he grabbed her thigh to pull her into a tighter position. She felt him pushing deeper inside of her, and an explosion of heat and pleasure filled her midsection. She cried out in ecstasy, and then breathlessly whispered into his ear.

"I killed my roommate."

She felt such thrilled relief at her words; there was a delayed pause before her eyes flew open, alarmed at what she had just said. She was still sitting in her window seat, and Robert's hand was still on hers. They had never been in the bathroom together, had never touched beyond his hand upon hers. She expected Robert to pull his hand away from hers in disgust. She expected him to develop a look of shock and surprise at what she had just said. Cassie fully expected Robert to give her a look that said *you're absolutely out of your mind.* She expected him to then signal to the flight attendant that he needed some assistance, and when she arrived, for him to demand he be moved to a seat as far away from this crazy young woman as humanly possible. But Robert merely smiled at her in understanding.

It was a strange, unnerving smile, that spread still wider at the obvious amazement and surprise that was now registered on Cassie's face. Erupting, his smile continued widening to an almost impossible length. He leaned forward in an intimate manner, still smiling that impossibly wide grin, his breath now warming the skin of Cassie's face. He leaned yet closer, almost as if to kiss her, and just at the moment that his lips should have met hers, he whispered.

"I know."

Robert's once lovely blue eyes now slowly filled in. It gave the illusion that his pupils had dilated and grown to an enormous size, covering all of the blue until it was gone. Cassie gasped and pulled back, her heart leaping in her chest. Robert's hand was still upon hers, and it tightened, preventing her from pulling it away. She could feel the heat again, this time hotter than ever. It was radiating up her arm again, only this time, the feeling wasn't comforting, nor did it stir any feelings of lust or desire. She felt fear.

The heat was uncomfortable. It was the feeling of being stuck inside a sauna, wanting to get out, and finding that the door was locked from the outside. It was the kind of heat that made it hard to breathe. And she could smell something in her nostrils that almost seemed to burn into her. It entered her nose and traveled upward deep into her nasal passages. Then she felt it searing down into her mouth and throat, burning the way stomach acid does when it comes up with vomit. She felt this new type of warmth and heat move downward still, into her lungs. As she breathed in, she felt the contamination as whatever it was she was breathing in was introduced into her blood stream along with the oxygen her lungs had infused into her globulin. She even mused briefly that she could feel this crud in her bloodstream pumping to every extremity. She could feel it spidering through all her veins, reaching every organ, every cell inside her body.

It was like she was being pumped full of raw sewage, and all this from the smell of what had once been Roberts' cologne. It no longer smelled rich and sweet, but vaporous and putrid.

Cassie tried to pull her hand away again, and Robert gripped it even tighter. This time, the heat from his hand actually seared her flesh. She grimaced in pain, and tried to speak but nothing would come out. She was on the very brink of losing consciousness from the inability to breathe in a single lungful of fresh air, when Robert let go of her hand, and Cassie felt a sudden rush of chilling cold cover her body. It was like stepping from a boiling sauna into the Antarctic. She breathed in, gulping fresh, cool air, unable to move for a few moments. Then she turned to look at Robert. He smiled at her, in a completely normal manner. Nothing seemed unusual or out of the ordinary. Cassie felt as if she was completely crazy. She felt as if sanity was slipping away at astronomical speed. She had imagined the entire thing, just as she had imagined her and Robert together in the airplane bathroom. She was losing her mind. She turned to look out the window, then turned back quickly to Robert in a sudden panic.

"I didn't say something just now, did I?"

She was sweating a little, remembering what she thought she'd whispered into his ear, in what she thought had been the airplane bathroom, during what she thought was a clandestine rendezvous of the mile high club.

"Yes, you did," Robert smiled, completely calm.

Cassie's mind flew into a panic. She had said it out loud. She had actually said it out loud, to a total stranger on a plane. He heard her say it, and now he knew. Cassie was sweating profusely now. Robert looked at her compassionately, and smiled again - not nearly as wide as she had imagined before. His bright blue eyes twinkled as they caught the late afternoon light coming in through the plane window.

"You asked me if you had just said something," he smiled. Cassie blinked, not understanding.

"That's what I said," she mused. "I didn't say anything before that?"

Robert turned back to Cassie again, sighing in consternation.

"You turned to me and asked if you had said something just now, and by saying that," he paused, "you had."

Robert raised his eyebrows at her, as if to say, *I've had enough of your silly mumblings,* and then he turned back to his paper and began reading again.

Cassie felt a sudden surge of embarrassment. She hadn't said it out loud. She hadn't been with this man sitting next to her. She hadn't just experienced what felt like all the garbage of a city landfill entering her body. And she most certainly had not confessed to the murder of Ella Moore. She had said nothing, and done nothing but sit in her seat on this airplane looking out the window, clearly going mad. It was the pressure, she thought to herself - the pressure of knowing the truth.

Of knowing what I did to Ella.

***

It was true that Ella had died of alcohol poisoning. And it was true that Cassie had seen her there on that couch, with a young man, and the young man did leave to get Ella another drink, which was already one too many for her. But what no one knew about that night was that Cassie had been more than just a little bit drunk. She had been a lot drunk. Drunk enough to decide to go sit next to Ella in that empty spot her date had left, and tell Ella exactly what she thought about her.

She sat down next to Ella and told her she was a bitch. She sat there next to Ella and told her that she hated her. She told Ella she was a user, and a cold-hearted cunt. And when she was all done telling Ella that although she had men lined up now, she was going to end up an ugly older woman all alone, she looked Ella deep in the eyes, and saw nothing. Ella was too drunk to even fully grasp what Cassie was saying to her, much less remember it in the morning. Cassie was furious. She hated Ella in that moment more than ever. Ella had suddenly laughed, and in her drunken state, she motioned to Cassie and remarked about her dress.

"You wore that to a party? Cass, Cass, Cass," Ella had slurred. "No wonder you are here alone."

Cassie's anger had welled up inside of her. She turned to slap Ella, but Ella suddenly looked like she was going to vomit all over the couch and all over Cassie. Cassie shoved the drink she was holding into Ella's hand and commanded her to drink it. Ella had obeyed. Then when the threat of sickness seemed to pass, Ella turned to her and asked for a glass of water. Cassie couldn't believe the gall of this young woman. To insult Cassie the way she had, and then ask for a glass of water? To ask her a favor?

Cassie stood up angrily to leave, and that's when the thought flickered into her head. Just a small lick of a thought, and then it was gone. The impression had been made, though. The thought had been seared into her consciousness. She turned and looked down at Ella on the couch. Her low cut dress exposing the tops of her breasts. The short hem of her dress riding up to expose far more thigh than any modest young woman would be comfortable with. Cassie looked at Ella and saw her for what she was.

A waste, she thought then. *A complete waste of a human life, with no regard for the feelings of others.*

It was at that very moment she decided to obey that little suggestion in the back of her thoughts.

Yes, she thought to herself. *I'll get you a glass of water.*

Cassie went into the kitchen of that house, and found an empty plastic cup. She saw the myriad of liquor bottles littering the counter. She grabbed the vodka and poured a ridiculous amount into the tall cup. Then she added a few ounces of water, for no real reason. She even grabbed a few ice cubes from the freezer to cool the drink. Then she took the cup back to Ella, who at first appeared to have already passed out. The young man still hadn't returned. Cassie sat down next to Ella and lightly slapped her cheek. Ella stirred, barely, and without thinking another moment about it, lest she hesitate, Cassie brought the cup of liquid up to Ella's lips and tilted it slightly.

"It's your water, Ella, drink it," Cassie commanded.

Ella tried to pull away, fighting it at first. The liquid from the cup spilled out from the sides of her mouth. Cassie shook Ella's shoulder forcefully and kicked her foot even harder. Ella stirred a bit more, then she drank deeply, more of the liquid running down the sides of her mouth and landing in little droplets on the tops of her breasts.

"No, Ella...drink it *all*," Cassie had scolded. She tipped the glass forward again, and Ella drank what remained. As she finished drinking, her mouth fell open, and her head lolled back onto the couch. She was unconscious, and Cassie stood up to leave. As she exited the room, she saw Ella's young suitor chugging beer from a keg with his pals. He was so drunk he could barely stand. Cassie quickly left the house, drove back to her dorm on campus and went to bed.

A part of Cassie had wondered if Ella would really die from the alcohol she drank. Or perhaps she would just wake up with one hell of a mad hangover. Part of Cassie mused that Ella might slip into an alcohol-induced coma, and end up some sort of vegetable for the rest of her life. Part of her was disappointed the next morning to learn that Ella had died, and that she wouldn't be spending the rest of her life hooked up to life support machines in some hospital bed. But she never shed a single tear, and she knew she never would.

***

Now, sitting on the plane next to this man who seemed to be having an odd effect on her, Cassie wondered if she couldn't handle the strain of what she had done. She didn't feel guilty about what she had done. She merely lived in a constant state of wonderment at what she had done, and the incredible realization that she had gotten away with it. Until now, she had never even come close to telling anyone what had really happened that night to Ella at the party. And now she breathed a sigh of relief at the fact that she had not just confessed to killing Ella to a total stranger sitting next to her on a plane. While she had no explanation for any of the hallucinations she'd been having since boarding the plane, she was certain of one thing; this man, Robert Carrington, did not have any clue as to what she had done.

So you can stop all your paranoid thoughts right now, young lady, Cassie thought. *No one will ever know, or they would have said something by now. You are going to live the whole rest of your life scot free.*

It was at that moment that Robert Carrington turned to Cassie and spoke in the calmest voice.

"Tell me, Cassie," he paused briefly. "What exactly does *scot free* mean?"

He raised his eyebrows at her, inquisitively. Cassie just stared, not understanding the question. There was no way she was going to allow herself to go down paranoid-alley again. Not on this flight, not ever.

"Hmm?" Robert quipped. "I'm waiting for an answer, young lady."

Cassie continued staring at him, unable to speak. Was this another one of her delusions? Well, she would simply ignore it until it passed. Robert raised his hand and let it linger over hers for a moment. Cassie braced herself for the contact, preparing herself for the sudden warmth. Robert paused; allowing his hand to hover for just another moment, before putting it back in his own lap again. Once again he laced the fingers of his two hands together. Again, it seemed both masculine and feminine at the same time. He spoke again, and chills shot down Cassie's spine.

"Would you consider yourself off *scot free*, even if you knew what lay in store for you?"

He turned a dead stare on her and smiled, this time looking somewhat taxed.

"You see, Cassie. What most of you think of as getting off *scot free* is really only a small snippet of the big picture."

He gestured with his hands, reminding her of a musical conductor and continued.

"You people think that if you don't get caught, and you don't go to prison, that you got away with it."

Robert shook his head in consternation.

"But none of you, no not a single one of you," he paused dramatically, "Ever considers *me*."

As he growled this last word, Robert did place his hand back on top of Cassie's, and again, that terrible heat spread up her arm. Again, that horrible, vaporous odor filled her nostrils, and again, Cassie found it hard to breathe.

"Who do you think gave you the suggestion to do what you did in the first place, Cassandra Roberts?"

He sneered, leaning ever closer to her face. She could feel the heat radiating off his skin.

"Who do you think inspired you?"

He took her hand now in both of his.

"You see, a door has to be opened. And that door always goes by two names: Jealousy and Hatred. Once that door is opened," Robert purred delicately into Cassie's ear. "I walk right in."

She couldn't breathe. This had to be another one of her hallucinations. This couldn't be happening. It wasn't real. The sewage was pumping through her veins again, and she felt as if she were about to vomit. The skin over the entire length of her body felt like it was on fire. At the same time, she felt painful pins and needles all over. Every prick, every jab, made it feel as if her skin was about to split open and ooze out all of her insides. She wanted to die; the torment was so unbearable. She felt so disgusting all over, she wanted to stop the pain any way she could. Removing her own skin would be a good start, she briefly thought. She was unable to move or speak, somehow paralyzed by the heat that was coursing through her, pumping in her veins.

Then, it stopped. Cassie did not wake up from one of her hallucinations as she had before. She did not find herself staring out the airplane window. Instead, she found herself staring unbelievingly at Robert Carrington, who had simply taken his hands back off of hers and was now folding them back in his own lap, once more. He smiled at her. It was a sick sort of smile; one that suggested that he was toying with her, and Cassie knew it.

She knew this time had not been a hallucination. And suddenly, she was certain none of the other times had been, either. Whether they had all played out silently in her head or not, they had all been real, and this man, Robert Carrington, was responsible for everything. He looked at her the way a father lovingly looks at his child. It made Cassie feel sick.

"You see, Cassie," Robert remarked. "I'm here to let you know that you are not going to get off *scot free*."

He paused for a moment.

"I'm here to make you understand that what will happen to you will be far from it."

She glanced around, wondering if anyone else had seen or heard any of the crazy things that were taking place in these two airplane seats high up in the air.

"Cassie," Robert snapped his fingers in her face, and it seemed to echo, bringing her back.

"It's important that you grasp exactly what I'm saying to you right now. Nod if you understand what I'm saying."

Cassie stared in wide-eyed disbelief at this man. Had she thought he was good looking before? Now he seemed only menacing.

"Cassie," Robert reprimanded. "I'm waiting for an answer. And if I don't get one, I may get a little angry, and trust me…" he looked deep into her eyes. A cold chill crept up her spine.

"You do not want to make me angry."

Cassie looked at Robert for another long moment, the full reality of what was happening beginning to sink in. Then she swallowed, her throat clicking audibly, and nodded her head. Her eyes brimmed with tears.

"Well, look at that," Robert smiled, and produced a handkerchief from his front jacket pocket. "Cassie Roberts can cry. I didn't think we'd see that one so soon. After all, you didn't shed a single tear after killing Ella, now did you?"

He chuckled. Cassie looked around, alarmed that he had just spoken those words out loud.

"Come now, Cassie, do you really think anyone else on this plane can hear me but you? Do you think any of them will even remember my face once they've left this plane? For that matter, do you think any of them noticed that I got up to go to the bathroom just a moment after you did, or that any of them happened to notice that we went into the bathroom stall," he paused, "together?"

Cassie started, her heart pounding faster again. She thought she had imagined the two of them in the bathroom. She didn't remember actually leaving her seat. Surely that hadn't really happened. It was impossible.

"Do you remember anything after I first took your hand, Cassie?" Robert purred. "Because I do. I distinctly remember you thinking about how attractive I am, and how you wanted to take me into the airplane lavatory and have me. I distinctly heard you say you killed your roommate. You whispered it in my ear just as you came, my dear."

"That didn't happen," Cassie whispered.

The tears now spilled down her cheeks. She was shaking all over, uncontrollably.

"Oh, I beg to differ," replied Robert. "Like I said, you opened the door. I just walked in."

Cassie was startled by the loudspeaker. The flight attendant was announcing that they had begun their initial descent, and to please put all tray tables and chair backs into their full, upright positions. They would be landing shortly.

"Looks like our time is almost up." He sounded artificially sad. "For now."

He smiled painfully at Cassie and moved to take her hand again. She retreated violently into the corner of her seat.

"Stay away from me," she trembled. "Don't touch me again."

Robert stared innocently at her. He mocked her.

"Come now, Cass, must you be so difficult?"

He shrugged his shoulders.

"Well, my job here is done, anyhow. Now that you've seen what's in store for you, I'm sure you'll enjoy the rest of your..." he paused momentarily. "Life."

"This isn't happening," she whispered. "This isn't happening. You're not really here, and none of this is really happening."

Suddenly Robert hissed and pushed his face into Cassie's. His breath was putrid, and her stomach lurched.

"This is real, Cassandra. Oh, you'd better believe it is. Just as real as the drink you handed to Ella, which wasn't water, now was it, Cassie? No, it wasn't. This is as real as that, and you can count on it. And the pain and agony you felt a short while ago, was just a small glimpse, a taste, if you will, of what your eternal life with me will be like, after I get my hands on you once and for all."

Robert chuckled lightly and rested back into his seat. The fasten seat belt sign had been illuminated.

"I do believe we're landing now, sweetheart."

***

Cassie turned to look out the window. They were amongst the clouds now, and the view had gone a foggy white. She still told herself this was all a dream. That there was no man sitting next to her named Robert Carrington. That she hadn't seen, felt or smelled any of the things she thought she had. It was all some sick hallucination of a mind that had clearly snapped. Yet, she could feel herself sitting in her seat. She could feel the cushioning on her back and beneath her legs. She knew exactly where she was. But perhaps Robert had been a figment of her imagination? Perhaps he was her tormented subconscious popping to the surface and eating away at her?

***

Cassie closed her eyes tight and told herself there was no one sitting next to her on the plane. It was empty. When she opened her eyes, there would be no one there, just an empty seat beside her.

She opened her eyes slowly, and even more slowly, she turned to look at the seat next to her. It was empty. She breathed a sigh of relief. Then she looked down and saw a copy of the Weekly Journal lying on the seat. She picked it up, her hands shaking. The edges of the paper were charred.

Another announcement came over the loudspeaker. The stewardess thanked everyone for flying with them and began instructing passengers who had connecting flights to make. Cassie closed her eyes, and all she could think about was how much she still hated Ella. She hated Ella for this.

"We hope you've enjoyed your flight; and wherever your final destination takes you, we hope you will enjoy
    your stay."

All Because of the Cat

It was all because of my damn cat. That damn cat was the whole reason I was even up to see it. She hadn't always been that way, waking me up like that, but for the last couple of months, she had. She gets it in her head that things should be a certain way, like cats do (and women, actually, hah!), and if she doesn't get what she wants, look out.

Sometimes I'm already awake when she starts to complain, like on Fridays (which it was a Friday night I saw it, but we'll get to that in a minute) because that's the night I always stay in and drink. By the end of the week, I'm wiped out, so I always leave work, drive straight to the local 7-11, and buy myself a couple of six packs of Beck's. Yeah, that's the shit I like, so what's it to you? I always get the Beck's on Friday nights and sometimes a movie from Red Box, too. I'll go home and drink, and yeah, I'll get pretty drunk. It's my business.

Come to think of it, this whole damn thing really started around the time Stacey broke up with me. Huh. I don't know if that has anything to do with it or not. Probably not. I'm not the kind of guy who believes in that transcendental bullshit about destiny, or things happen for a reason. That's just for people who don't like to be scared of the unknown. If people think it ain't unknown, at least to somebody (a.k.a. God, ladies and gentlemen), well then, somehow, that's enough for them. But not for me. I'm not an atheist, per se, but I don't believe that whole *it's-not-a-coincidence* thing. That's just dumb.

Sometimes shit just happens. That's all. So, do I think it's a little weird the cat started this crap around the time Stacey left me? Maybe. Do I think it's a little weird the cat had impeccable timing? Sure. But so what? Just let me tell the story.

Anyway, like I was saying, a few nights a week, I am awake at midnight, but most I'm not. I have to clock in at the shop at 7 a.m., Monday through Friday. On work nights I like to be asleep by ten. Occasionally I can't sleep, for some odd reason, and I'll be awake when she starts to complain, but usually she wakes me up. I'm not complaining, just telling.

I love that damn cat, I really do. We understand each other, you know? We both come and go as we please. She doesn't tax me out; you know what I'm saying? Sometimes she'll jump up in my lap wanting to be petted, and that's fine. Most times, she just lies down next to me on the bed, where Stacey used to sleep.

It doesn't bother me that she used to be Stacey's, or that Stacey just left her here. She never liked her own damn cat, how about that? Cat doesn't remind me of Stacey, although you'd think she would. Stacey had this stupid name for her, "Allie" (like in Alley Cat? Only spelled regular), but that's just stupid. Cat's personality told me right away that she was no damn "Allie." She's just "Cat," and that's all. She looks at me when I say "Cat," she knows I'm talking to her. That's all fine and dandy.

Cat and I get along fine. Except for this one thing. For some reason, a couple of months ago, she decided she wanted to eat at midnight. Don't ask me why. Even when I gave her a full bowl of wet food when I got home at six, she still freaked out. And let me tell you, that cat can howl. There's no ignoring that noise. Not at all. If I'm awake, it's fine. I go out, marvel at her empty bowl, and the fact that she's apparently hungry again, and I give her what she wants. The dry food obviously won't do. If I just put more dry into what's already there (you know to hint?) she'll start nipping at my ankles. If I start to walk away, it's an outright *war*. Claws out and everything, tearing into my flesh.

All Because of the Cat

That cat can have a serious attitude when it wants to. But I still love her, 'cause most of the time, we understand each other. So what if she has this one little personality quirk? I learned to deal with it after a week or two, when it kept up. She liked to eat at midnight, okay? Except when I'm not already awake (which is more the case than not), she'll get right up into my face in bed and start yowling her head off. She'll stand on my chest if I'm on my back. If I'm on my side, she'll push her little wet nose right up against mine, and yowl her smelly cat breath right up my nostrils.

**

I kid you not, the first few times I was a little miffed. Cats can't tell time, can they? I've heard that animals have senses that humans don't, and maybe that accounts for it, because I kid you not, when that cat wakes me up, it's midnight. If I bother looking at the clock (I did at first, out of sheer curiosity, but I don't anymore, 'cause I already know what time it is), it always says 12:00. Not 11:59, and definitely not 12:01. Always exactly midnight, on the dot. How does the cat know? Don't ask me, but when she wants me up, she can get me up, let me tell you. No matter how heavy I'm asleep, there is no ignoring her, period.

So, now we're to the reason I'm always up at midnight, every night. And now you know why I was up that Friday night at midnight. But you still have no idea, let me tell you. I forgot to tell you something else, otherwise this won't make sense. Okay, another little ditty.

My crappy little apartment is on the ground floor. It's a basic rectangle with two windows on the east side, the patio glass doors on the south side, and a window in my bedroom, also on the south side. There are no windows on the west side, because the next apartment is on that side. I'm on the end though, so on the east side, there's a sidewalk leading from the parking lot to the north, out to an adjacent sidewalk to the south. This sidewalk either goes to the left, out to the street, or to the right, which takes you to the leasing office, pool and hot tub, and the mailboxes across the street. You get me? It's really hard to explain the layout of a place without you seeing it. Just do your best to picture it, okay? I'm sure you'll do fine.

My point is, there's this stupid sidewalk running all along the whole right-hand side of my apartment, and people are always walking by, from the parking lot to get to their place, or go to the pool, or check their mail, or just walk their ugly dog. I hate this, because if my blinds are open, people can just look into my place. It just makes me uncomfortable, you know?

I like my privacy. So, I usually keep my blinds shut a lot. The light can be a bitch, though, being on the end of the building like that, and the windows all on one side. In the winter, with the blinds closed, and no lights on, I live in a cave. Pitch black without the lights on. In the summer though, when it stays light out until after eight, it's okay. If I open my blinds all on that side (including the patio blinds) there's enough light to see really well without turning on any lamps. Hey, it saves on electricity, okay?

I actually have a pretty low electric bill. It's kind of amusing, seeing each month if I can get it to an all-time low. So, even if people can look in, I open the place up. Forget them, if they don't have anything better to do while walking by than glance into someone else's apartment. They're the ones invading, not me. Most of the time, I'm in my bedroom anyway, watching TV while lying in bed. But after dark I always close those blinds, because I don't want people looking in, and at that point, there's no outside light, so there's no point. My point is that the blinds are always closed at midnight. That's all I wanted to explain.

Well, there's always an exception to the rule, right? Sure there is. Life is all about the exceptions to the rules;

otherwise, we'd all be bored all the damn time. That's my own sage little ditty.

Well, on the Friday night I'm trying to tell you about, the night that started it all, I drank my Beck's in bed, with a plate of take out from Panda. I, as usual, got very drunk, and fell asleep with the TV on. I usually don't fall asleep so early (I want to say I was asleep by ten, but I can't say exactly, but around ten seems right), but I was dog-tired after that week. We had been slammed with people bringing in their cars to be looked over before family vacations and road trips. You gotta love spring. Lots of oil changes, which are easy, but when you've got 20 of 'em lined up in a row, it gets exhausting, you know?

I was asleep and I'd left the blinds open, instead of closing them after dark, okay? That's all I'm trying to tell you. So, when Cat started in at 12:00, and I staggered out of bed swearing at her, and went into the kitchen, (stubbing my toe on the corner as I turned the hallway) the window was open, or rather the blinds. I flipped on the kitchen light and the view out the window disappeared. All I could see in the pane now, was my own blurry reflection.

Everyone knows how that is, right? When it's dark outside, and your inside lights are on, you just can't see outside. Every Tom, Dick and Harry outside can see in at you crystal clear, but you can't even tell they are there. You have to remember that, because that's the part that freaks me out the most. I don't know how long that thing was looking in at me, before I finally saw it.

The really scary thing is, I don't know how many nights it may have been there, at my window, before all the stars lined up, and I finally saw it. Hell, forever could have gone by, and I would have never had a clue, but of course, all the horses had to be lined up in a row.

I don't believe in any preordained crap, though, like I already said, so if you're gonna tell me this was meant to be, I'll just quit telling you my story right here and now. It was just a set of unfortunate coincidences that led to my discovery. Man, what a discovery.

Yeah, I happened to be awake, and this particular night, the first I can remember, really, the blinds were open at midnight, exposing me and my home to the outside world. But like I said, I couldn't see anything out that kitchen window while the light was on, and obviously the light was on the whole time I was in there feeding Cat. I only flipped the light off again when I was done and ready to feel my way back down the hallway. I didn't need a light to see. Electric bill, remember? And of course, I was still kind of drunk, half asleep, and not giving a damn at this point, so I had left the blinds open. I figured I'd close them in the morning, you know?

***

I don't know why I looked back. To this day, I'll never know why, exactly. Maybe I thought I heard something? Maybe I just had a feeling, you know, like I was being watched? I get that sometimes, and I think most people know what I'm talking about there. For whatever reason, I did look back, right out my kitchen window. Of course, I wasn't expecting to see anything, so I was glancing away again before my mind could even register that I'd seen anything. I kind of had to play it back in my mind, you know? Like watching TV. Don't forget, I was still a little tipsy, and my reflexes were a bit slower than usual.

My head snapped back up at the window with a start, my heart pounding away like a jackhammer. Adrenaline already spurting into my veins, getting me all wired up. It's crazy how quick your body can react, even while inebriated.

I knew right away what I thought I'd seen. I could see the picture frozen in my head. I mean all this happened in the blink of an eye. When I looked out that window again, there was nothing there, plain and simple, but here's what I thought I saw- a face. A face looking in at me, pushed up against the glass, the way a kid does when they want to open their mouth wide and blow. We all did that as kids, didn't we? I mean, it was plastered to the glass, like it really wanted to get a good look. It wasn't any normal face, either. It was messed up. I guess it was human, but it was one screwed up looking human, let me tell you.

First off, it had no hair. The thing was stone cold bald. Its eyes were big and buggy and round; totally round. It had no eyebrows, I remember that, too. Its nose was long and curved, and the way it was pushed up against the glass, it bent downward into the mouth, kind of making it look like some weird bird beak. That had to have hurt the thing, having its nose pushed downward like that, bending the cartilage. At least, I would have thought so. As if I give a good goddamn about whether that thing felt discomfort. It took Eric. But I'll get to that eventually.

Anyway, the mouth was the worst of it all. It was huge, and it was smiling. I know that just because of the shape, the way it was curving upward on the sides. I have no idea what its lips looked like. All I saw were teeth. Two rows, top and bottom, razor sharp. Filed to a point, I guess, or maybe they just grew in that way on this thing, who knows? I swear it was salivating, too, but I'm not so sure about that, either. All I know is those teeth *gleamed*. And they were white, man. So white, they floated in my mind for a while, like an afterthought. Like the damn Cheshire cat's teeth floating in the air. Only these were floating in my mind. I wish I could get those teeth out of my mind. If only.

Well, of course I've got common sense, I'm not an idiot. By the time I got the front door open, I was ready to ream the crap out of the idiotic teenager wearing the Halloween mask in the middle of April. Only, as you can probably guess, there was nobody there. That little shit was fast. I decided I'd had enough of this and headed back to bed. Cat was still chomping away at her Friskies salmon dinner, and that was okay. I locked the door, STILL didn't close any blinds, and went to bed. It took a few minutes to fall asleep; I still had that adrenaline circulating, but eventually I did.

***

The next morning it all seemed fuzzy, like most memories do through too many beers. Saturday nights were for the guys. Friday I liked to drink alone (not healthy, I know), and get a good night's sleep, but Saturday was always my night with the guys. It was Eric and the gang. Eric I knew since we were kids, growing up on the same street. The gang was three guys Eric befriended in college, and I ended up befriending them too. I didn't go to college, of course, but oh well. Eric and I stayed good friends. We had that vibe. He was a great guy, man. A real great guy. That thing. I hate that ugly thing.

Saturdays we usually went to O'Malley's on Tenth Street. Sometimes we hung out at The Grill. They had a nice bar, next to the restaurant side, and cheap, but good appetizers.

Sometimes we'd end up at my apartment later, drinking Miller, or Coors. I drank that stuff when I was with the guys, I didn't mind.

Eric would sometimes stay over, if he was too drunk to drive home, which was usually every other Saturday or so. That was cool. We'd have a nice hangover-morning-after beer, and eventually some Lucky Charms or whatever. We'd talk about the old days, in elementary, or remember our weirdo neighbors. We'd always get to laughing our asses off. Sometimes we'd remember old girlfriends, or a crazy one-night stand. It was fun, you know? Eric was an okay guy. A really good friend.

We'd been going to The Grill the last several weeks. I think maybe it was because I'd broken up with Stacey (with the guys, it was always ME that broke up with her, you know?), and I'd met Stacey at O'Malleys, and that turned out just grand, let me tell you. I didn't want to run into her there, and the place just wasn't as cool anymore, you know? So, it was The Grill that particular Saturday night.

I was drinking at the bar with Eric and the gang and the next thing I know, I'm telling them about this punk-ass teenager last night who scared the shit out of me, and if I ever found out who he was, he was really gonna get it, because that shit just wasn't cool, you know? I'd decided it was a mask for sure, by then. I could even laugh about it. Ha, ha....

It was just another story, but by 11 O'clock, I was ready to go home, funny stories or no. I just wasn't feeling it, you know? Eric, bless him, drove home with me, following behind my Chevy. We were both okay to drive, I think. We usually didn't get back into our cars until we were, although there were a few nights where, if we had gotten pulled over, I think we both might have failed the Breathalyzer test. But I digress.

We were back at my place at 11:30. Just sitting around, shooting the breeze, when Eric says, "What time did that punk come around here last night?"

I said midnight, 'cause I was feeding Cat. Eric knew about the Cat thing. He was amused by it. Damn, Eric...

At 11:59, Eric felt the urge. Beer shit, you know how it happens, right? I know, I know, don't start that shit. Another odd coincidence, he just happened to need to take a dump at the right time. Believe me, I know. If he hadn't been sitting on the toilet, he would have seen that thing at the window, seen what it looked like, and maybe thought twice about going out there the next night. Maybe.

Eric was in my bathroom, stinking it up. I heard him laughing his ass off in there when Cat started yowling away. I got up to go in the kitchen and looked at the closed blinds of the window, wondering. I had only seen that damn kid because the blinds just happened to be open the other night, and now I wondered how many other nights he had been slinking around out there? That thought creeped me out, but not as much as the next thought. It just popped in there, you know? From wherever thoughts come from.

Maybe he's out there again, right now? I wondered. And of course, I just had to do it, didn't I? I walked over and grabbed the stick. The one you turn counterclockwise and the blinds slant open.

I forgot that you can't see out with the lights on. It didn't matter. With that face pressed right up against the glass, it was still visible, it's just that it was framed all around the edges with kitchen light; reflection, whatever. The face was framed, like a damn Hallmark card photo or something.

I was closer this time, right in front of the window, instead of back in the hallway, so this was much worse than before. It was pushed up against the glass again, its nose bending painfully down toward its mouth, only this time it was aslant, sideways. It reminded me of Gonzo's beak, man, no kidding. I could see, with it sideways, its nostril on the left side. It was HUGE. Like a little black hole. It was breathing and its breath fogged up the window a bit.

It didn't just disappear this time. I got a pretty darn good look at it. It felt like I stared at that thing and it stared back at me for minutes on end. Who knows, maybe we did? Then I snapped out of it.

I ran to the front door, already yelling my head off, "I'm gonna get you, you little fuck!" Of course, by the time I'd wrenched the door open, he'd run away. Like I said before; fast little fucker. Too fast. I was still yelling into the night, sure he could hear me. Probably giggling his ugly little head off while running off into the night, thinking he'd really got me good.

Eric came running out then, still zipping up his pants. I doubt he'd washed his hands. "What the fuck?" He was still tipsy, more than I was. Probably shouldn't have driven behind me, but oh well. That was past. I told him the kid had been at my window again. I opened the blinds, and there he was.

"Shit," Eric said.

"Yeah," I said back. That was an entire conversation right there.

We went to bed, and on Sunday, over cereal at noon, we talked about it. Two nights in a row, that punk had come around at midnight. Maybe he'd been walking the neighborhood a while, and at some point, noticed my kitchen light came on every night at the same time. Thank you Cat. Maybe that's what brought him around like that-what attracted him to my place. I thought that was pretty unlikely though, because most nights, up until two nights ago, he would have been staring in at blinds. I never opened my window.

Eric said maybe the kid only bothered with the joke on the night he walked by and saw my blinds open? If he knew, from other times, that I came in at midnight, he knew this time I'd see him. Again, I thought it was unlikely that he'd prowl around with a mask on just waiting for the night I might happen to see him. Eric shrugged. "At any rate, he's got your number now," he said.

"Bullshit," I said. "I've got *his* number."

That's when I came up with my brilliant plan. I would have Eric hide under the stairs by my window, the ones that led to the upstairs units. It was dark there, and the kid wouldn't be able to see him. Eric could hide there, and I'd get him right up at that window, leaving the blinds open. I'd wait in my kitchen until the little punk walked up. He'd stayed a while the last time, and he'd been so intent on staring in at me, trying to make me shit my pants, I guess, I doubt he would have noticed if someone sneaked up behind him.

If Eric could be quiet enough - it had to be Eric, because I had to remain inside, to lure him up to the window. That's how it came to be that way. Eric was all for it. The thought of grabbing that punk-ass kid and making HIM shit his pants instead, was just too good. Eric wanted to be the one to nab him. I could be the one to knock the wind out of him. That was fine.

Even though it would have to be a work night, neither of us minded. Eric was too amused by all this shit. This was the kind of story you ended up telling over and over again at the bar, for years to come, you know? We were having fun.

For some stupid reason, I'd decided it was a mask, after all, even though this time I'd seen it up close, for a long time. I'd been able to study that face, and looking back now, I knew there was no way it was a mask. I think I tried to justify this by saying it was a good stage makeup job. Latex and prostheses and whatever, like movie makeup. That stuff always looks real. Only how could some punk-ass, teenage kid pull off a professional makeup job like that? I never got around to answering that one.

It all happened so fast. Hell, isn't that what people always say? I had only seen the face on Friday for the first time. On Saturday I saw it again, while Eric was taking a shit. Now, on Sunday, here we both were, at my place, planning a stake out of sorts. Not much time to go wacky on the supernatural train. I didn't believe in that stuff then, you know? I do now. Holy shit, I do now.

At 11 O'clock, Eric went out and hid, crouched under the stairs. I took a good look, standing outside at my own window, to make sure Eric was totally invisible. He was. My porch light was always off, so it was pitch black under those stairs. He had a six pack with him to keep him occupied.

We'd already agreed I wouldn't be able to stick my head out to talk to him, or shoot the breeze. The kid might catch on. I wasn't sure exactly what time he would first come around; only that by midnight, he was at my window. Of course, that was if he even came tonight and I wasn't sure he would. It was fun, though, you know? The anticipation of it all; it was funny. By 11:30, I was getting bored and antsy. I risked cracking open my door and checking on Eric.

"Psst," I called. "How ya doin'?"

"Sshhhh!' was all Eric said.

That was the last thing he ever said to me, except for what he screamed at me later, and it wasn't even a word, really. It wasn't the last thing he ever said, but it was the last thing directed at me that was normal. I wish it was the last thing I ever heard him say. That would have been better than the words I still hear him screaming in my head at night.

***

It started at midnight, right on the dot. Cat was yowling, and I stood in my kitchen, waiting for that bastard to show up, and he did, right on time. I don't reckon he ever wondered why I was already standing there, just looking out my window, or wondered at the fact that my blinds were open this time, again. He had his own agenda, I suppose; tunnel vision. And Eric got in the way. Big time.

He came up to the window. This time I saw him coming up, instead of just being there, you know? I took note, in the back of my mind, at how he kind of seemed to glide up. There was no slight side-to-side as his feet stepped. He just remained even kilt, you know? *Floating.*

I only had time to think about this vaguely in the back of my mind though. My heart was already pounding again, and I was frozen in place in front of my window, marveling again at that amazing makeup job. Then I heard Eric shout, "Aha!" I saw his face just behind that thing's. His arms were thrown around its shoulders, and for a moment, it seemed like that little shit was caught.

For a moment, I thought everything was gonna be okay. We could laugh about it for years to come.

Then that thing spun around in Eric's arms. Fluidly, effortlessly, and Eric wasn't a little guy. He was 6'2", but this thing was just as tall, maybe a little taller. How did I ever think it was some scrawny, adolescent kid? Eric worked out at the gym a few days a week. He had strong arms, yet this thing just spun around on him.

I had nothing to do but watch from my spot in the kitchen. The look of surprise on Eric's face would have been comical in another situation, perhaps, but not now. Not here. The thing lurched its head forward, and I saw it sinking its teeth into the flesh of Eric's neck.

That surprised look never left Eric's face. He screamed. Boy, did he. Loud. It must have woken up the neighbors, but by the time anyone bothered to look out their windows (if anyone did) Eric was gone. So was that thing. No longer a punk-ass kid, in my mind.

I think it was the blood that got me moving, popped me out of my dream state. The blood that spurted up in jets around that thing's teeth; it looked like some lousy special effects from a B-level horror movie. I guess those spurting blood effects aren't so unrealistic after all. Real gore is pretty fake looking, who knew?

I suddenly turned from my spot in the kitchen and headed for the door. It only took a second to get there, couldn't have been much more. I had left the door unlocked so I could yank it open quickly and drag the kid inside, to trap him.

I had the door open in a flash, just in time to see that thing's feet (naked, webbed and long-clawed) gray and glimmering in what little moonlight was out tonight. Just above its feet, around the ankle area, dangling, I saw Eric's feet.

That thing was carrying him off. Eric was still alive and he must have seen me coming out after him. It was dark, and all I ever saw of him was his dangling feet before darkness enveloped them both. That thing's pale, gray, shiny feet and Eric's dangling, blue All Stars. I imagine (not that I want to, but I do) that he reached his arms out, back towards me. He screamed for me.

"Mike, help me! Help me!!"

His voice was bubbly sounding, from the blood that was pooled in his throat, I guess. It sounded like he was trying to talk while gurgling mouthwash. My stomach turned.

–And, suddenly, there was just night. Darkness. Eric was gone. I ran down the sidewalk a ways, and saw nothing. It was dark, but even so, they were just gone. In the vague moonlight, I could see silhouetted outlines of bushes and trees along the walk. I could see the stairs to the right, leading up to the adjacent sidewalk. On the left, I could see the parking lot. The carports, which were lighted underneath the roofs by fluorescents, lit up the parking lot. Nothing. Like I said before, that thing was fast.

No one came out, either, like I also said. Maybe some people looked out their windows, who knows? They probably went back to sleep thinking to themselves, *Good-for-nothing-kids.*

I went back inside, closed the door, and collapsed on the floor, right there on the front walkway linoleum. When I stood up a few minutes later, to call the police, the blood rushing back into my legs must have been too much or something, because I passed out. Never even got all the way back up onto my feet. My head, thankfully landed on the carpet, my feet still planted on the linoleum. When I woke up, it was morning.

***

The daylight shining around the sides of the blinds seemed to illuminate my mind. If I had managed to call the police the night before, I would have been stupid enough to tell them that a "thing" had taken my friend away, after biting into his neck. That got me to thinking.

I opened the front door and looked outside. Sure enough, right there on the concrete in front of my window, were little droplets of blood. They continued away from the window to just out onto the sidewalk, where they simply stopped. It looked to me like that thing had somehow just disappeared from that spot. I looked in the bushes and grass on the other side and didn't see any droplets on the leaves, or anywhere else. That thing had either disappeared into thin air; otherwise, it went straight up. Those were the only two options I could think of. And neither of those was helpful, or good.

Now, it may sound crappy and unfeeling to you that I was thinking of myself at a time like that, and maybe it was, but that's just how it was - self-preservation and all that. I didn't call the police, because I knew if I told them the truth, they'd lock me up in the loony bin. If I called them and told them my friend had simply disappeared, they would take one look at the blood (and wouldn't you know it, my shoes had smeared some of the droplets when I ran out there that night leaving nice little shoe prints), and charge me with murder. Either way, I would be screwed.

I did the only thing I could think to do. I got the hose from my backyard patio, the one I used to water the few plants I had out there (also leftovers from Stacey), hooked it up to my kitchen sink, and sprayed down that concrete all around my front walk. The blood was dry, and at first it didn't go anywhere. I had to spray for a while before those drops seemed to re-liquefy and begin dissolving away. Even so, I thought that if a CSI person came to check, with those special lights they have, they would be able to see the droplets, even if to the naked eye, you couldn't see them anymore. I watch too much TV.

With the blood gone, I thought about Eric's car. His keys were inside, on my living room coffee table. I took no pleasure in doing this, let me tell you, but I got in his car, and drove it back to his place on Sycamore Street.

I parked in his driveway, and after wiping down the steering wheel and the inside door handle with the bottom of my shirt, I got out, also wiping the outside door handle, and hoping no one would see me there. If the police found any other prints in Eric's car, I could just say that I had obviously been a passenger in there before, and that would explain it. Hell, I could even tell them I'd occasionally driven his car for him, when he'd had too much to drink, and that would be the truth.

I beat feet out of that neighborhood, and I didn't see anyone. It was Monday, and people were already gone to work. I wasn't even thinking about that. I walked three blocks before calling a taxi from the parking lot of a 7-11; the same one we always bought our beer from.

I took the cab straight to work, still in the jeans and t-shirt I'd worn the day before. I was an hour late, and I guess I didn't look too good, 'cause when I told my boss, Rick, I wasn't feeling well, he took one look at me and shrugged. He told me as long as I didn't yack in the garage, I'd better get to work, so I complied. I'd never been late to work before, not in the whole five years I'd worked there, so Rick let it go.

I worked on cars all day, mostly changing oil, a few lube jobs, changed some filters, whatever. The day went by in a blur. At 5:30, I called another cab, and went home. When I got there, I sat on my couch in the living room and just blanked out.

When I went to sleep that night, I wasn't thinking about anything. I'd gone numb. I felt like the whole last three days had been a dream. Maybe I tried to convince myself they really were just a dream; that if I called up Eric at his place, he would answer and want to know what was up with me, where had I been, why hadn't I called him to go out this weekend? I didn't call Eric's place though, I just went to sleep.

When Cat started yowling at midnight, I got up and fed her, my back to the window the whole time. I didn't dare turn the blinds. I didn't want to see if that thing was out there, waiting for me; waiting with that sick smile - only this time, I imagined it would have dried blood on its teeth - Eric's blood. I didn't need to see that. I went to bed.

Amazingly enough, I actually fell asleep quickly and easily. I felt exhausted. I think I was suffering from that post traumatic stress thing, but who knows?

***

On Tuesday morning, I discovered, while putting my shoes on, that there was, indeed, dried blood on the soles. I hadn't realized that, even when I saw my own shoeprints in the blood on Monday morning. I wondered, briefly, if anyone walking on the sidewalk that morning had seen those shoeprints before I got out there to hose them off.

No one ever said anything though, so I guess not. I stared at the blood on those soles, and felt sick. I chucked them into the dumpster, knowing they would be gone by the time I got home from work. The trash guy emptied the dumpsters in the complex every Tuesday and Friday, and believe me, the residents paid for it. The garbage bill was horrendous every month. We paid for "trash service" there, if you can believe that.

Nevertheless, I still expected David Caruso to show up any day now, dangling those bloody shoes off the tips of his fingers in one hand, while tipping his sunglasses down with the other, asking me, "How do you explain these, mister?" in that low, purring voice of his. Horatio never showed up. There was a visit from the police, however.

They showed up at my door about a week after Eric disappeared. When he hadn't shown up at his office for several days, and hadn't called in sick or anything, his boss had called them. Eric hadn't been answering his phone, or returned any of the messages his boss had left, and Mr. Burke was concerned. After all, it wasn't like Eric to do something like that.

The gang had tried calling a few times too, but they weren't too concerned, until they got calls from the police. Everyone got the same questions. How long had it been since we heard from Eric? When was the last time anyone saw him? Did he seem all right, or was he upset about anything? Could anyone think of anyone who might be upset with Eric, or might want to cause him harm? Everyone said the same thing. No one had seen him after Saturday night when he left The Grill.

I told the police he had followed me home, which he sometimes did, then he had waved to me out his window after I'd parked, and that was the last time I'd seen him. I told them that as far as I knew, he'd gone straight home. They, of course, confirmed this when they saw his car was in his own driveway.

They didn't suspect me, any more than they suspected the rest of the gang. The gang didn't know Eric had stayed at my place Saturday night, or that we'd spent all day Sunday hungover together. They certainly didn't know Eric had stayed at my place Sunday to try and catch that punk-ass kid. That was something only Eric and me knew; and now only I knew.

Eric didn't have a girlfriend at the time, and thank God. He lived alone in his house, which he could afford with his plush post-college job. There was no one checking up on him, or worried when he didn't come home. That was good.

I talked to Eric's parents, whom I'd known since I was a kid, too, obviously. They asked all the same questions as the police. I answered them the best I could. I lied to them, the same way I'd lied to the police.

***

Things went on for a while. Life went on. I worked, ate, drank, slept. I fed Cat when she yowled. I bought groceries. I hung out with the gang for a few weekends, but without Eric, it just wasn't the same. I stopped hanging out with them after three weeks or so. I think they understood.

Everyone must have thought I was just really depressed about Eric. I mean I was, don't get me wrong, but I was just plain old numb. I was in shock. You would be too, if you'd been through what I went through.

Believe it or not, I never looked out my window again. Every night I got up to feed Cat, I just never looked. I didn't bother opening the blinds. What would be the point? I didn't want to know if that thing was out there.

I couldn't tell anyone, no one would have ever believed me, you know? And Eric was gone. Nothing would ever bring him back, although I had nightmares those first several weeks.

I dreamed that Eric was at my window, all pale and grave looking. His eyes looked vacant and haunted. He looked in at me, the way that thing had. His face was pressed up against the window. His eyes looked at me, accusingly, and he spoke - just one sentence, always the same one. His voice was gurgly with blood, like it had been the night he was taken, and as he spoke, his mouth overflowed with that blood, spilling over his chin, and dripping down his chest, staining his green polo.

"*It should have been you, Mike*," he always said. That was always the point where I woke up screaming. Then I would sit in my bed and cry.

I'm sorry, Eric. I'm really sorry, man, I would think. It wasn't my fault. How could I have known? How could anyone have ever known?

***

For all I know, that thing was at my window every night, just waiting for me to see it. Maybe it had been waiting for me to come outside and chase it off? Perhaps that had been its plan all along? Maybe it was some sick hunting game, and that's how that thing got its kicks? I don't know. I have no clue.

How many nights had that thing been at my window, before that fateful night I happened to leave my blind's open, before I just happened to see it? I just don't know.

In the end, I just couldn't live there anymore, and I guess no one could blame me. I still had three months on my year's lease, but I paid the fee to break it. I quit my job, moved all my stuff out in one day, and loaded it up in a U-Haul.

I had no plan, really. I just wanted to get as far away from that thing as I could. I wanted as far away from the memories as I could get.

I literally drove for two days, stopping at Motel 6's at night. I drove across two state lines, and ended up in Ohio, if you can believe it. I settled in a decent sized town, called Lebanon, and found a job at a local auto shop. It wasn't hard to find work. People always had cars that needed fixing. Everyone drives these days.

I got a new apartment in a ratty little neighborhood, and Cat and me settled in. If it looked suspicious to the police, or the gang, or Eric's parents that I just went and took off, I didn't care.

I wrote a letter to Eric's parents saying I just needed to go someplace new. I needed a change of scenery. Maybe they understood, maybe not, but I doubt they ever suspected that I had anything to do with Eric's disappearance.

I don't even know what happened with all that. Maybe they eventually declared him dead, after so much time had passed and he never turned up? I don't know.

His parents have sent me some letters, but I haven't read them. They are in my ratty bookshelf, collecting dust. The police have never contacted me, since their first time questioning me, so that's okay, I guess.

Cat must have decided to change her routine when we changed apartments. In the new place, she immediately took to wanting dinner around 10 p.m. That was fine. I could feed her before going to bed and not get woken up in the middle of the night anymore.

Not that it really mattered. I woke up every night with nightmares, anyway, so a good night's sleep was still out of the question.

***

I don't have any friends here in Lebanon. I'm not really interested in making any. They would eventually want to know where I came from and why I'd decided to move out here, and I just don't feel like making stuff up. I don't want to lie, so I just keep to myself.

One of the guys at the shop, Joey, has asked me to get beers with him a few times, but I've gracefully declined, each time. I don't even give a reason; really, I just say I'm not up for it. He stopped asking after a few times, so that's fine, too.

-Things have been going swimmingly, I guess. I have a new life here in Ohio, and I'm only having the nightmares about two nights a week.

I think, eventually, I won't have them anymore at all, maybe. But for now, Eric still visits me at my old kitchen window a few nights a week, and he always tells me it should have been me. I can't say I disagree with him. If I could make it be me that got taken, instead of him, I would have switched places with him in a heartbeat. You know I would.

***

A few weeks ago, I fed Cat at ten, like always now, with our new routine, but damned if she didn't start yowling at me to get up and feed her again. It had only been two hours, so what the heck? I looked at the clock, my heart sinking when I saw the old, familiar digital-red 12:00 staring back at me.

Old habits die hard, I thought to myself. Cat was only hungry; it was nothing more than that. So, I went out into the kitchen of my new place, which does have a window, but on the second floor. It looks out over landscaping around the place.

The blinds in this apartment are the kind where you pull the string straight down, and the blinds go straight up. I hate those kind - always have, because they never seem to go up evenly. One side always slides up higher than the other. I really hate that, but beggars can't be choosers, now can they?

The blinds were closed that night, as they always are now, day or night. And Cat was getting her food, so she was shutting up, which was good. My back was to the window, but for a moment, I got that feeling - like I was being watched. Everyone knows that feeling, don't they?

I wondered if it was even possible that that thing could be out there? I'm on the second floor though, and the only way that thing could even be at my window, was if it was hovering in midair.

That's impossible, I reasoned to myself. Except I know that isn't true. If that thing could effortlessly carry Eric off and just disappear, perhaps even going straight up, then it sure was possible it could be floating outside my second floor kitchen window. Sure it was, especially when I remembered how it seemed to *float* up to my window the night it got Eric.

Of course, there was only one way to assure myself that thing wasn't outside my window. All I had to do was pull the string and raise up the blinds. Then I would see that there was nothing there. Then I could feel relieved and go back to sleep with no worries.

I went over to the window, and grabbed the bottom of the string, and then I sat there, frozen, unable to pull down. Did I really want to see what was out there? If there was nothing there, I could feel okay, for a little while. But, then again, if there *was* something out there - what then? And even if there was nothing there that night, well, what about the next night - Or the next, or even the next? What about that, huh?

I just stood there, after midnight, in my little kitchen, hearing the squelching sound of Cat eating her Friskies, and I couldn't move. My hand stayed on that string, and I wasn't able to pull it down, so I eventually just went to bed.

***

But darned if Cat didn't start waking me up every night at midnight again - and there was no Eric to help me formulate a plan. I had run, and, perhaps, that thing had followed me? If it could find me once, it would always find me.

***

Eric was gone, my life was in shambles, and I was living in fear. I had hours, each night, though, to think about things.

I began asking myself the most basic of questions, while avoiding sleep, as the nightmares had increased again, with Cat's schedule reversion.

What are the facts?

What do I know?

Not a whole lot, I reasoned, but maybe just enough to do *something* about my situation. With Eric, both he and I didn't know any better at the time; now I do.

That thing can *fly*.

I'm on the second floor, but Cat has reverted to her midnight feeding schedule. It took several months - which is the time it took that thing to somehow track me down, I guess - but it did.

Again, I started asking myself the basics, and listed out my limited knowledge, which turned out not to be quite so limited at all, once I looked close enough.

The facts:

It only comes around at night.

So I figure it must not like sunlight. It ain't no vampire, that's for certain, but it definitely is nocturnal.

The facts:

It waits outside my window.

It doesn't try to find a way in. Maybe (again with the vampire analogies, weird) it can't come inside my home? Maybe it stays outside its victim's window hoping they'll come out, just the way Eric did? Maybe it keeps coming around my place trying to lure me out? At any rate, I actually have surmised that I'm safe as long as I don't go outside at night.

The facts:

It has some sort of odd effect on Cat.

For whatever reason, when it comes around, she gets hungry. Voraciously hungry, and only when it is present. She can *sense* that damn thing.

These are things I know now, that I didn't realize while planning my stake out with Eric: I believe it's out there. I believe it cannot come inside. I believe it must hunt at night, and that it has no choice, for whatever reason, but to wait outside for me to make a mistake.

***

For two weeks, I thought about these facts, and formulated my plans. I couldn't spend the rest of my life haunted by Eric's memory and living in fear of what might be just on the other side of my window pane. Who could ever stand to live like that?

My plan was simple. Almost as simple as the one Eric and me originally devised.

I bought a few simple items from House Haven; suspension cords, electrical extensions, tripping sensors wired to metal halide ultraviolet bulbs. I did my research. Metal halides produce abundant light in sheer darkness. They produce up to 125 *lumens* per watt. It's like turning night into day, in a split second. I jury-rigged an upside down crescent of those babies, suspended underneath my second story window, on a 1000-watt HPS (that's high pressure sodium to you) backup unit, in case the halides didn't do the trick.

All of this was wired directly up to high-end motion detectors that I paid through the nose for. I set them in place, sensors surrounding the window, half way down, so that thing wouldn't trip the light 'til it was directly in front of my window.

It was a real bitch, rigging it all up, let me tell you. I almost fell out the window at one point and nearly broke my neck, but once I got it all set up, that fucker would have no clue the lights were even there, in the pitch blackness; not until it was bathed in superficial sunlight.

***

I bought everything, planned it all out, and set it all up on a Sunday, midmorning, while off work. Then I waited. I had flashbacks of Eric underneath my old stairs, in the darkness. I'd turned out all the lights in my apartment, even the kitchen, but sure enough, at midnight, Cat started her yowling.

I was already in the kitchen, sitting in the darkness, waiting, no sound but the faint electric buzz of my refrigerator and my own heavy breathing; trying to gain some modicum of control over the situation; desperately attempting to regain a life for myself - one not lived in constant dread and fear.

Then, outside my kitchen window, two stories above the ground, from around the blinds, suddenly daylight poured into my kitchen. A square of luminescence suddenly framed my kitchen window, like Heaven pouring in from nowhere.

That's when I heard it *scream*. My blood nearly froze from that God-awful sound. It didn't sound human, or animal. It was not so much a roar as an angry, surprised screech. It lasted far too long, but in all reality, was probably no more than five seconds or so, but it felt like an eternity. I remember smiling at the pained sound it made. I had been right in my surmising of why it only came around at night. Indeed, it couldn't abide daylight, for whatever reason.

I didn't kill it. I know that much. It flew away. I know that much as well. The next morning, when real daylight was out, and I had the nerve to open my blinds, I found a suspicious green, dried-up liquid on my windowsill. I had to open the window and punch out the screen (again) to get a decent look at it.

The sill was covered in it. More was in droplets and gobs in the shrubbery on the ground below my window, when I ventured to go look outside. Best of all, the lamps and bulbs themselves were coated in it. I was a bit pissed, 'cause when I unscrewed the bulbs to gently wipe them down, trying to clean the viscous green gel off them, it was dried on; caked on so hard, I broke some of the bulbs, and had to throw others away. So, I had to buy all new bulbs to replace the ruined ones, but I don't mind this, because I don't think I'll have to buy any more after that second round.

***

I doubt that thing will ever come back; not now that it knows that I know its secret. And if it does, I think I've learned one other crucial fact that it won't know that I know.

***

All Because of the Cat

You see, it's all because of the cat. She woke up when that thing started coming around. She was always hungry, even after I'd fed her. That thing won't ever try to break inside, or come in to get me. It waits for me to come outside, in the dark; like a coward–or something that's *afraid*–something that has limitations.

Well, they say every monster has a weakness, don't they? Or maybe that's superheroes, I'm not certain anymore.

It was all because of the cat, from the very beginning. She was trying to tell me something. Why that thing picked me to haunt - to hunt - to prey after, I'll never know. I have no idea why it picked me to begin with, or why it followed me after I moved. For whatever reason that thing had a hard on for me, I'll just never know.

***

Perhaps it should have picked someone with a dog. My girlfriend left her damn cat with me, can you believe that shit? Well, I sure am glad. You know, that Monday morning I punched out my screen and then had to deal with all those ruined bulbs; I came back up into my apartment and made a discovery of a new fact, if you will.

Cat was up on the kitchen counter, hunched on the sill, going to town on that dried green liquid like it was *cream*. She licked and licked and worked away at that nasty stuff, like it was the best thing she'd ever tasted. Her barbed little tongue scrubbed away at that dried goop until it was all gone. It took her *hours* to clean that sill.

I figure the UV lights, acting as sunlight, had hurt that thing. They injured it. That green stuff? That was its *blood*; and Cat *loved* that thing's blood. She's always hungry when that thing comes around - *voracious*. So, if it decides to come around again, and if my UV rig isn't enough to keep it away permanently, I think I have one more weapon to hoist upon it.

Next time Cat yowls at midnight for me to feed her; *I will*. I'll feed her something *really tasty*. Something she'll absolutely love. *—If* it ever comes around again, which I doubt it ever will.

***

So, that's my story. It was all because of my damn cat. That damn cat was the whole reason I was even up to see it. She was the reason I discovered that horrible thing to begin with, but only because she was *hungry*. Now, because of her, I might be able to sleep at night in peace.

Afterword

I don't know how useful this section will truly be. I am not one of those Readers who eagerly devours the after-sections in books, not even the notes (and not even the notes by Stephen King!) I pretty much just want to read the stories.

I'm not even certain I've encountered a whole lot of fiction books with an Afterword, or Notes, but I wanted somewhere to list the rest of my tale, as well as my previous publication credits, since the stories that actually made it to print in vehicles previous to this book deserve that shout-out, as do the publication entities themselves. But I digress. To the rest of my story, in a nutshell.

*A quick note on the whole publication carousel. A fair number of the stories in this collection were accepted and published elsewhere first. However, a fair number also were not, and not for lack of trying. I finally stopped submitting (for the most part) and querying (for the whole part) about two years ago. This coincided with my going to work outside the home full time, following my divorce.

Simultaneously, I began suffering from writer's block and general lack of passion or interest in writing anything new, and so I haven't, in all honesty. This may turn out to be my one and only collection of short fiction I ever write, and if that is the case, I can live with that, so long as these tales already writ, are out there and (hopefully) being read and enjoyed by even a handful of readers.

All that being said, I'm certain that not only my venture into full-time work, but also the fact that by the end, I could have literally wallpapered my entire home with the number of rejection slips I'd received over a period of querying a submitting for five years with nothing to show, probably had the greatest part to do with things.

That is not to say that I gave up. The fact that you are holding this book in your hands and reading these very words is testament to the contrary. I didn't give up. I simply changed the plans in my own personal playbook. After all, they say the definition of insanity is doing the same thing again and again, yet expecting different results.

The bottom line is, I submitted and queried tirelessly for over six years, in fact, with nothing to show for it but a few handfuls of acceptances into smaller, or lesser known publications, e-zines, and boutique press anthologies. None of these acceptances paid any cash for the rights to my stories. I never received any royalties afterwards. I did receive a check for ten dollars for one story in this collection, but I won't tell you which one, and two other stories that appeared in anthologies netted me a free contributor's copy, and that's all.

As for trying to gain literary representation, I rode that carousel until it rusted and broke down. For a good two years, I queried agents in batches of 10-15 a week. Finally, after those two years of slow querying, I went on an all-out crusade to get an agent, querying 70 agents a week, over a three-week period of time. I had to finally stop querying when I simply ran out of agents to try. Most never even responded. Some responded with a resounding "no thanks", while still others never even directly rejected me, but merely had their assistants send the rejection notice with an apology.

I've attended three separate Writer's Conferences, and shamefully paid to have literary agents read the first 20 pages of three separate novels. Each of those three novels was submitted to three separate agents. A few resulted in invitations to send the full manuscript, but none resulted in an offer of representation. I've spent hundreds of dollars over the years merely for the chance to sit with agents for 20 minutes a pop and pitch my work, and myself, my stories. Nothing has ever come of it except rejection.

I could probably write a whole separate book on the state of modern-day publishing, and how I believe that it is much more difficult in this era for an up-and-coming but relatively unknown writer to actually ever get anywhere in the business, but I won't. I've just said as much, so there's no need to go any further on the subject.

I didn't come this far, write this many stories (over one million words and counting, and that's just my fiction alone), and harbor this dream of being a writer for almost 30 years now to simply give up just because others in the business, (who, honestly, haven't truly bothered to read my work, and therefore, cannot know if I'm even remotely talented or not) have rejected me. I say that they cannot truly know, because it's true, and I'll tell you a quick story about that, which ties into the state of our modern-day publishing environment:

A few years ago, back when I was still trying to query a specific project (a sci-fi trilogy series I'd written called The Society), I sent out over 70 queries a week (just for that project, separate from the other all-out crusade I've already mentioned), for two weeks, so 140 agents queried. They all said no, or didn't reply. Except for one. One agent, who will go un-named actually responded to my query, and not only that, they asked for the full manuscript!

I was elated. I'd been keeping my dwindling spirits raised with a constant mantra each day I faced my rejection war, that I was meant to be a writer, it was my fate, my destiny, my purpose. I kept myself going, kept the hope alive, by repeating to myself that I am at least competent at writing stories, if not actually decent (I've never thought that I am good, and definitely not exceptional), but I kept telling myself I'm mediocre or better, which in my mind isn't so bad. I told myself I have a natural talent for this writing thing, and eventually someone will see it. They'll read it in my query, for God's sake.

So, here comes the e-mail back from my query to The Agent, the one I immediately became convinced I was fated to cross paths with, who would sign me and find a way to pitch and sell my novels to the Big Publishers. And what's more, they were asking for the full manuscript! Not a partial, but full! Well, I sent the full manuscript off to this agent, and of course I knew I might have to wait through weeks, if not months of agony, for their reply, but I was confident this was it; that whenever the agent did reply it would be to sign me.

Imagine my shock and surprise when I received a new e-mail from this agent just nine minutes later with a resounding and very harsh rejection. I remember reading the overly generic rejection letter, stating that the story just wasn't right for them; they just weren't feeling it, yada-yada. I remember sitting at my desk, staring at my monitor, pondering how it was even remotely possible that this agent could make such a resoundingly absolute assessment of my entire novel, after having only spent all of nine minutes or less reading it! I concluded that there was absolutely no way that my book had received a fair reading in that short an amount of time, no matter how fast-paced the business may be nowadays.

My book hasn't changed much from that time to when it was finally published, first by an indie publisher I finally went with, and later, a new second edition put out by me under my own imprint EMP Publishing. (*An update on that: I've pulled the entire Society series to do major revisions. All three new editions of those books will be released in the spring of 2016, much improved, yet again. But the first two chapters of book one remain unchanged). If any readers really want to delve deeper into this particular saga, (there are still a few of the old first and second editions for sale used on Amazon), feel free to pick up a copy of The Society Book One: Genesis. I invite you to read chapter one and two (the agent could not have possibly read further than that in just nine minutes), and then decide if you think the agent was a total idiot for not reading further. If you ask me, they passed (all of them) on a pretty cool book, and a fairly decent series, if I do say so myself.

So, you see, I haven't given up, I've just decided not to continue with the same old actions of an insane writer. That way would have kept me hidden away in my room; typing and querying away 'til I turned gray, pruned up and died.

A HUGE side note. I'd be withholding a major motivational factor here, if I didn't also mention that in the Fall of 2010 – Winter of 2011, I begun suffering from mysterious physical symptoms of a baffling nature, that continued over the next several years to progress, to a debilitating level. I've lived through (and am still fighting) an incredible war with my own body's immunity and frailty, that has played the largest part in my quest to simply self publish all my work.

I've lived with the belief that my lifespan and life expectancy will be greatly shortened for quite some time now. On October 20, 2014, I finally received a name (at least) for what ailed me: Chronic Lyme Disease Complex. I was more recently diagnosed, in April of 2015 with a co-infection of Anaplasmosis, which, if left untreated, can be fatal.

That is about as far into my medical saga as I care for, or wish to, delve at the moment, but I'd be remiss to not inform you, Dear Readers, that my health has played the greatest part in my quest to take the reins and assume full control of my own writing career.

I decided instead to stop asking others for permission to become what I've dreamed of being all these years. I've written a fair amount of fiction, in varying genres, and so that makes me a Writer. I was a writer before I ever queried a single agent, in fact. I've always been a writer, even before that fateful first story for Mrs. Bernard back in the fourth grade. Now I want to be a Published Writer, and I'm not getting any younger, and nothing's changing in the business (or, unfortunately, my health, so far). So, I realized that I needed to change.

I, who, in all admittance, am only moderately computer illiterate (I won't quite go so far as to say I have an actual *phobia* of anything dealing with computers or software programs), have tirelessly researched and self-educated myself in the proper and accepted formatting of books in the Publishing World, and I've tried to emulate that, to a certain degree. Although, I've taken the liberty to break from some traditions, simply because I can. After all, I'm the one in control of this book. Not some Agent, or an Editor, or a Publishing House, and it turns out in the end, that suits me just fine.

I taught myself how to professionally format. I tirelessly studied professionally published book interiors, scrutinizing every last, little detail (practically going blind in the process, and definitely a little bit stir crazy), and learned how to design my interiors accordingly. I found where I could upload my files and publish them for free, yet the services I use are very high quality. I registered my own imprint, EMP Publishing, with Bowker, and am now assigned ISBN's under my imprint banner. In the end, it turned out my dream wasn't just to become a Writer, or a Published Writer, but also an Editor and a Publisher myself. I am the owner and Managing Editor of EMP Publishing. No more months or years of querying and waiting, hoping and fighting a losing battle. I'm calling the shots now. My next step is to add to my growing resumé with the title of Marketing and Publicity Specialist.

So, that's where we're at, Dear Reader. If you enjoyed this book even remotely, please find my other works listed in the front of this book under Also By Jennifer Word. Not all titles are released yet, but all of them will be out by the end of 2016, with any luck.

I also encourage you to find my books and purchase them specifically through the Createspace e-store, as I receive 50% royalties from sales through that channel, and only 25% through sales on Amazon, and even less through other channels. And, most importantly beyond all of that, Amazing, Beloved Reader, if you like my work, please tell others about it.

My greatest ally in this war (for that truly feels like what it is) is You. I need readers, a fan base that supports me and continues to buy my new releases as they come out. I need allies in my publicity. Find me on Facebook and Twitter. Follow me, subscribe to my Pages. Tweet links to the Createspace e-store for my books, tell people you like my work. Together, I know we can do this.

***

If you have made it this far, and you've read all of this, then lastly, Phenomenal Reader, I have to thank you.

Thank you for reading my stories, for you have breathed life into my tales and caused them to truly exist. If you've read my words, then the effort to dream them and write them hasn't been for naught.

So, Thank You. I am eternally grateful. And now the stories behind the stories, otherwise known as: Notes.

JENNIFER WORD

April 25, 2015
Oak Park, California

Notes

*The note on the story TELLCORD contains a spoiler for the **Amazing Stories** episode *"Grandpa's Ghost"*. If you haven't seen that episode and don't want it spoiled, skip that note.

"Barnaby's Endeavor"- There's not much of a story here. Barnaby is sort of my alter ego, I suppose. All of his hopes and dreams were mine while writing this story, and there are some definite parallels between his life and mine. That's all I can tell you.

"Lightning Ball Rock"- I wrote this story for an anthology contest, but it didn't make the cut. The theme for the anthology was simply 'paranormal phenomena' and I believe some of the examples they listed in their open call were things like: Bigfoot, Area 51, Lochness, etc. Well, I didn't want to write about something common, lest my story be swallowed up by all the other entries dealing with the same specific paranormal topic, so I went on Google and researched 'paranormal phenomena' hoping to find a topic that interested me, yet was something you don't necessarily hear about all too often. I wanted something more original. When I read about the phenomena of the Brown Mountain Lights it was a no-brainer; I knew I'd found my topic, and Lighting Ball Rock was born. Once I had the phenomena picked out, the idea just popped, and there you have it.

"Their Own Fallen"- Jack Trembley is based on my grandfather, Will. The setting is very much real, down to the isolated island in Alaska, to the roughly two-mile-long spit where his beach house exists. The back bay where Jack does his salmon fishing is a real bay, and it's not too far away from actual Jakilof Bay (that bay just happens to be on the same island about a quarter mile away from my grandfather's bay, if you care to play the sleuth and figure that one out). That beach house is one of my favorite places in the entire world, in fact, and I have many wonderful memories of fishing, hiking, beach combing, working the crab and shrimp pots with my grandpa, and bird watching, specifically the hordes of Bald Eagles that would descend upon the beach at low tides to scavenge. And I did just happen, on one particular visit, to spy a mama eagle on a strangely bare and jutting branch off the mountainside, guarding her little baby eagle hiding against the tree base amongst the mountain foliage. My daughter was with me at the time, and we only investigated because we heard a large crashing noise. Perhaps it really was a boulder come loose and rolling down the mountain. To this day, neither myself or my daughter know what the noise actually was. It was a special experience that trip, sharing all my childhood memories of summers at the beach house, and showing my daughter that part of my life, made even more special by the eagle family we briefly discovered. So, I took that experience and combined it with the frequent thoughts I would have of my lonely grandfather, who now spends his summers at the beach house alone, a widower, and suddenly Their Own Fallen was born.

"The Sculptor"- This story was an experiment during one of my struggles with writer's block. I asked a friend if he would play along and simply write one sentence about anything that took his fancy. The idea was that he'd send the sentence to me, and no matter what, I'd use it as the opening for a story and go from there. The opening sentence of The Sculptor (the entire opening paragraph, in fact), was not penned by me, but in fact by a friend of mine, and from that first sentence, I came up with the main idea and premise of the story and went from there. It was a fun little exercise and it did produce a short story during a heavy bout of writer's block.

"It All Comes Around in the End"- This story was originally published in the anthology *From Beyond the Grave: A Collection of 19 Ghostly Tales. Compilation Copyright © 2013 Grinning Skull Press.* I like anthologies because the idea or theme is already given to you and all you have to do is work within that structure. I don't always come up with a workable idea, but if the theme appeals to me, I really enjoy writing in that mode. In this particular case, the theme (if I recall correctly) was to be about ghosts, and I had already been kicking around a witch story I wanted to write. When I saw the open call, my brain just connected the ghost theme with my witch theme and I simply came up with a tale about a ghost witch. I actually spent some time in Ireland when I was 19-years old, and I remember being enchanted by the old graveyards and crumbling, aged headstones with dates from as far back as the 1500's, so the setting pretty much just popped in there and this story was born.

"The Life and Multiple Deaths of Virgil Eugene"- This story was originally published in *The Storyteller Magazine, Volume 17, Issue 1. Jan/Feb/March 2012.* I originally wrote this story for another anthology contest, one where the writer was supplied with the opening sentence "The robot felt…" and it had to end with "In the end, he felt nothing. He wasn't programmed to." The writer held the freedom to fill the space in between with whatever tickled their fancy. I figured a lot of people would write about actual *robot*-robots, ones made of metal and the like, and always the daring one hoping to write something different that might stand out, I decided that 'robot' didn't have to mean what the word would necessarily suggest. I decided it could just be the main character's name, but then I pondered over why the heck anyone's name would be 'the robot', and the idea for this story was born. So, this story was rejected by the original anthology I wrote it for, but I later submitted it to *The Storyteller* and it was accepted and printed there.

"Aunt Beck"- I hate to remain mysterious on this one, but I really can't tell you much about it. I reserve the right. However, I will admit to you now (and hope that I don't get in trouble for this), that I was inspired by Stephen King's *'The Last Wrung on the Ladder'*, and that last line in the letter he reads really packs a wallop. I wanted so badly to write a story that performed the same feat. I wanted a story that was emotionally disturbing and moving, and I wanted a letter that ends it all with a heart-wrenching shudder. So, I used that structure, and took bits and pieces from my life and the lives of others and wrote a sort of hodge-podge mixture. My studies in Psychology played a huge role in this story as well, and some of the anecdotes are ones I came across in my Psych texts, that I took the liberty of fictionalizing and playing with.

"Ava Kate"- This story was originally published in *The Storyteller Magazine, Volume 16, Issue 4. Oct/Nov/Dec 2011*. Originally, it was simply titled, "Ava". I sent this off to *The Storyteller* and it was accepted. Other than that, I don't recall exactly how or why I wrote this, or where the idea came from. Perhaps it was inspired by the difference I noted between my old-person, pessimistic view of things in the world vs. the young-person optimistic view my daughter always has. Nothing makes you feel more old and curmudgeonly than your own youthful, exuberant offspring.

"You Again"- I really have nothing to offer up on this one. I just got an idea to have a grown woman begin believing that her son is her dead brother reincarnated. I did have one reader tell me, though, that the scene where she sees the shadow go into Ryan Charles made him think she was dealing with a tulpa. I had never even heard of that word before, and I'm still not certain I fully understand the premise of it, but what the woman sees may indeed be a tulpa, even I'm not certain. What I am certain of, however, is that a lot of subtle Psychological subtext is laced throughout this story, and any Psych 101 students out there should have a heyday with this one.

"The Monster Across the Street"- This story (I'll tell you a little secret here) is based 100% on an experience I had when I was five. To this day, I'll never know if it was a dream or not...but I can tell you that even if it was a dream, the smell was very real, which has always freaked me out. To this day, I've never smelled anything like it ever again, and I cannot compare it to anything I've ever smelled in my waking life, nor in my dreams - except for this one.

"Divine"- This story was originally printed in *Dark Moon Digest e-Magazine #2. Aug. 4, 2011*. The e-Zine was immediately re-named simply *Dark Eclipse* in the following issue #3 and forward. I have a love-hate relationship with the latest horror genre known as 'torture porn'. I am mostly talking about cinema here. When torture porn first hit the theatres, I was slightly fascinated, but soon disgusted as it morphed itself into low-level shock value faire, and not the large scale struggle for survival that I felt the early films had, which gave the genre its vitality, in my opinion. I had seen enough torture porn films for my taste, but it got me to wondering if the genre could be done on paper? So I endeavored to write a torture porn horror story, and *Divine* is what came out.

"Every Living Thing"- This was originally published in eFiction Magazine, Oct. 2012. Copyright © 2012 eFiction Publishing. I love zombies. I love zombie movies, zombie stories, zombie books (my all time favorite is *The Zombie Survival Guide*, shout out to Max Brooks!), and zombie anthologies. I wanted to get in the game and write my own zombie story, but I wanted it to have a unique spin to it, which is no easy task in our overly-zombinated culture these days. So, I thought about it a bit, and hit upon the fact that zombies are usually human. At some point, while reading the slush pile for *Dark Moon Digest* (part of my job as an Associate Editor), I ran across a story about a 'Zombie Bigfoot', I kid you not. Not the best story I've read, to be honest (also not the worst), it gave me the idea that if Bigfoot could be a zombie, why couldn't pretty much anything? Or *everything*. So, I turned to my trusted Cat theme and wrote a story that mostly revolves around a zombie cat, along with a few other zombie-things.

"Scottie"- I wrote this story for another anthology contest, the theme being anything to do with 'Life After Death'. This is what I came up with. Not my own personal favorite, I'll tell you, and of course, it was rejected by the anthology. But I've known some pretty ardent and hardcore animal lovers in my time (I'm one of them myself), and I've also heard some absolutely heartbreaking tales from pet owners about their animals getting sick or hurt, or even killed due to their own ill judgment, miscalculations or random accident. I've also seen first hand the guilt some of these pet owners suffer from. I've seen a grown man cry for three weeks *straight* over the loss of his beloved best friend. So, when the rejection letter came back with a personal note from the Editor saying he just didn't believe the premise; he didn't buy that a woman would be that guilt-ridden and distraught, nor that the incident with Scottie and her car would haunt her to the extent that it does, I just shook my head. I know for a fact that is not the case, sadly.

"Queases"- I love it when story ideas are handed to me, or in this case, texted. Yes, I literally did receive a random text on my cell phone one afternoon, from a number I didn't recognize. The word Queases appeared on my phone, from a total stranger. Needless to say, my imaginative and horror-prone mind quickly jumped past the creepiness factor and immediately began fashioning a tale around this strange word. I looked up the word queases online and discovered, apparently, that it is Spanish slang for beautiful. I still don't know who sent me that text. They never texted me ever again.

"Althea's Mistake"- This was originally printed in the anthology Slices of Flesh: A Collection of Flash Fiction Tales From the World's Greatest Horror Writers, Copyright © 2012 DMB. I was fairly proud that my little flash fiction piece was chosen to be in the same book with some impressive horror writers that I admire. I'm not at all certain I belonged in there, but the Publisher decided my tiny tale was deserving, so I guess I'll stop arguing now. I don't know how I came up with the idea for this one, other than, it had to be 100 words or less, and that's what I could come up with in such a limited word count.

"Incident Report"- Another zombie story, but I decided it would be cool if the zombies weren't actually in the story, but only rumored and gossiped about. I wanted it to be a story more about strangers banding together for a brief period of time, in an odd sort of camaraderie that effects a feeling of nostalgia when the group just as quickly breaks apart. The love story wasn't planned, but I thought it best to leave off on a note of mystery. Did she never get around to telling him what she wrote on her incident report because it simply didn't matter? Or did she never get the chance to tell him because the zombie apocalypse, indeed, took place once they left the Metrolink...? I haven't decided yet.

"Two/One"- This was just a random flash fiction piece I wrote. I tried getting into this genre, but it doesn't suit me very well. The bottom line is, I write LONG. Always have, even back in fourth grade when I was ten. We used to have to write in a journal every afternoon, and a lot of the other kids hated it, because they never knew what to write. Not me. Who knows what crap I wrote, but every afternoon when it was time to do our journal entries, I'd be scribbling away, filling a whole page, turning to fill the second one. I remember one time this boy sitting at the desk directly across from me just sat and stared at me, his mouth agape. When the teacher called time and everyone closed their journals to put them away, I finally looked up to see his stare. He just shook his head and asked me, "How do you always write so much?!" Good times. I'm long-winded, I know this. So, flash fiction isn't my thing, but here is one I did manage to write, and guess what? It's about zombies.

"Splish-Splash"- I wrote this for yet another anthology contest. This one had a theme of B-movie horror. I haven't seen a whole lot of B-movie horror. Does *Attack of the Killer Tomatoes* count? I saw *Kingdom of the Spiders* with William Shatner once when I was a kid; at least, I think that's what it was called. But I digress. My sister lives in Nevada and whenever I go visit her, we always go out one night to play penny slots, because it's fun. This one casino we go to used to have a really fun slot machine called *Creature From the Black Lagoon*. I loved that game. I never won any money on it, but it was darn fun to play, because if you hit the right combination, the machine played this little animated mini-movie with the creature and the girl, replete with cheesy music. It was pretty fantastic. At some point, they got rid of that slot machine, and penny slots with my sister just haven't been the same since. I decided though, that I'd write my anthology story on a sea creature, and suddenly the whole tale came. My story did not get picked to appear in the anthology, though. (*I finally saw the actual movie *Creature from the Black Lagoon* last year for my birthday and loved it).

"Zombie Survival"- I've never been very fond of this story, but a reader I know said she loved it, so…I threw it in here. It's supposed to be a double-entendre. While the three ladies are debating how to survive a zombie apocalypse, the point would be that they are pretty much your typical female zombie types. One could argue that the true survivor of the zombie outbreak is the woman at the end who schools those witless girls.

"Carnival of Thrills"- Damn, I write a lot of stories for anthologies. This one again, was a contest and the theme was 'Carnivals' or something to that effect. It was a horror anthology, however, so this is what I came up with. Not my best, by far, and it did not get picked.

"House Call"- This was originally published in Frightmares: A Fistful of Flash Fiction Horror, from Dark Moon Books, Copyright © DMB 2011. I really don't write a lot of flash fiction, and in all honesty, when I do, I don't enjoy it much at all. This piece made it into an anthology, however. Go figure.

"Lonely and Dead"- Not my best story, again, by far. I struggled with whether to even include it in this collection. In the end, I decided to allow the readers to be the judge. After all, out of ten people, nine might absolutely hate it, but that one random reader might laugh their ass off, or just really enjoy it. Reading is so subjective, I just didn't feel qualified to say what should or shouldn't go in here. I don't know how or why I wrote this one. No anthology contest here. The idea just occurred to me and I wrote it down. That's all.

"Six Degrees"- This short story first appeared in Surreal Grotesque Magazine, Issue #5, Aug. 30, 2012. You know, I say I don't write a lot of flash fiction (and I don't) and that I don't particularly enjoy it (and I don't), but looking over these notes, I've had fairly amazing results from a genre I hate writing in. I've literally only written five flash fiction pieces in my life, and three of those have been published. My success rate with flash fiction is much higher than my short stories (which are mostly long stories), maybe I should write more flash fiction and submit it around? I don't know where I got the idea for Six Degrees. Some ideas just appear, and I simply write them.

"Hungry"- This was originally published in the anthology Zombies Need Love, Too c/o Dark Moon Books, Copyright © 2013 DMB. Another zombie story, the theme for this anthology was simply anything to do with both zombies & sex, let your own imagination do the work for you. Probably the most fun I've ever had so far writing for an anthology contest. This one wasn't rejected and I'm pretty sure you can still easily find this on Amazon books, along with the other anthologies I've already listed.

"TELLCORD"- Okay, so I slightly stole this idea from an episode of Amazing Stories, where Andrew McCarthy plays this young guy whose grandfather dies, but he knows it will break his grandmother's heart if she loses her beloved husband, so McCarthy's character (in his very early 20's here) puts on make-up and prostheses to look just like his 80-year-old grandfather and hangs out in his grandmother's home, living there. The audience doesn't find this out until the very end, and now I've just ruined the surprise for anyone who hasn't already seen it. It was a fairly effective surprise plot twist (years before Shyamalan would ever even dream of being a filmmaker, perhaps), and people who saw it for the first time gasped and sucked in their breath (or even cried), it was so effectively done. Anyway, it gave me the idea to switcheroo it and play it up a bit, and have a grandfather pretend to be the dead grandmother through e-mail, in order to give some sort of resolution and peace to his troubled granddaughter. I highly recommend that Amazing Stories episode, along with the entire series. (Episode: *Grandpa's Ghost*, 1986).

"Twerp"- This was a fun little writing exercise. I challenged a group of writer friends to take part in a little contest amongst us to see who could write the WORST story in our little group. I'm not even sure, but I think we ended up deciding upon an even draw. My theory behind this exercise was that writers are always trying so hard to make their stories good, that the struggle gets in the way. I thought if the pressure to be good were removed, or even reversed, some interesting creative channels might open up. Whether it worked or not, all I know is, I had a blast writing this, and when it was done, I personally found it decently entertaining. Trying to write badly on purpose though? Just as difficult as trying to write well, believe it or not.

"Halloween"- This is not among my personal favorites, either. It's not horror, it's drama, I guess. I sort of just took a bunch of different Halloween's spanning from age 7 through (at the time) 28, and this is what I ended up with.

"Enjoy Your Stay"- Okay, I'll be honest with you. Putting this story into the collection was a real toss up. I actually had one reader tell me they hated this story with a passion, that it was awful, and I should burn it. A few other readers seemed so-so, but more so on the disliking it side. I never submitted this anywhere, partially due to the general hate of it, and also (this goes for a lot of the previously unpublished stories in here, in fact) because I couldn't find anywhere to send it. I write LONG, remember, and the simple fact is that

I've had a hard time even finding places to submit my work, due to the fact that a large majority of my stories are WAY over a lot of submissions guidelines word count limits. A large majority of my stories are horror (although my novels aren't, weird), and finding places that are accepting horror stories between 8,000-21,000 words? Very hard to find. Anyhow, the story is in the collection, love it or hate it. And it was loosely inspired by my love of Stephen King's *The Man in the Black Suit.*

"All Because of the Cat"- This story originally had a completely different ending. I sent it in to Dark Moon Books at one point, when the Publisher was considering releasing an anthology collection of my short stories and novellas. He sent ABOTC back to me and said it needed rewriting, because he felt the main character shouldn't be portrayed as such a helpless victim. The publisher wanted me to write a fight-back ending, and so I considered it and then did so. At first I didn't like it, but at some point it hit me that the story really was a lot better with the new ending. Strangely, after I sent the new ending in, the publisher never mentioned the story ever again. He opted to just release one novella of mine as a stand-alone e-book, called RAIN. You can find that one on Amazon as well. I think it sold all of four copies, I kid you not. That one is about a sea monster that terrorizes a woman trapped in a trailer park during a torrential downpour in Georgia.

*Incidentally, RAIN will be reprinted in a new collection which features five of my novellas in one book, *FIVE Tales of Fear.* There's a preview for that at the very end of this book, including some examples of the original artwork for the book, which I'm pretty excited about, but I digress.

ABOTC is, obviously, about a cat, and the first short story I wrote officially as an adult, the story that started my adult writing career. It's also the one (quite the opposite of

Enjoy Your Stay) that everyone says is not only his or her personal favorite, but also truly scary and good. Well, I had a beautiful little muse silently cheering me on for that one. I miss you, Shadow.

JENNIFER WORD
Oak Park, CA

-Shadow-

Acknowledgements

I would like to graciously and humbly thank the following people for their support and encouragement of this project. Without the following people, this book would not have been possible.

Thank you

Max Booth III; Tony Mello; Alex Irwin; Don, Beth & Meghan Ferris; Kristine; Theresa Catherine Huffman; Stan Swanson; Tommy B. Smith; Shenoa Carroll-Bradd; Richard Joseph; Brenda; Kristin Baldi; Søren Skøtt; Zach Van Stanley; Jenny Koenig; Arne Radtke; Scott McDaniel; Jennifer Thirlaway; Heather Pritchett; Todd Wilson; Anthony Mendoza; Pete Deutschman; Caleb Dennis; Michael Tomilowitz; Christa Backstrom; Jack Klauschie; Jaime Metoyer; Lewis Crown.

About The Author

Jennifer Word is an award winning poet, novelist and editor. She resides in Ventura County, CA with her two children, two cats, and a plecostomus. She holds a B.A. in Psychology from Pepperdine University, with minors in Education and English. She loves horror, both written and cinema. She has written multiple novels and dozens of short stories, half a dozen novellas, and award winning poetry. Follow her on Twitter @jenniferword, or visit her author page at www.jenniferwordauthor.com

JENNIFER WORD

FIVE

TALES OF FEAR

A Collaboration in Fiction and Art

FIVE Tales Of Fear: Five spine-tingling tales of the Supernatural that pit ordinary people against extraordinary circumstances.

You are trapped all alone with a beast that defies logic. You are a front-row listener of a song from Hell. You are invited to live through the terrifying final days of Edgar Allan Poe. You are brought face-to-face with the horrible consequences of playing a Supernatural game. You are forced to witness the most terrifying story ever written.

Rain- A young woman caught in a rainstorm becomes trapped with an unimaginable beast. This story is what would happen if you mated "Jaws" with the Lochness monster, in a trailer park.

Ancient Song- An eccentric art collector uncovers an ancient relic that holds a secret musical score. Some songs however, are better left unplayed.

The Poe Toaster- An aspiring reporter gets more than he bargains for, when he interviews a distant relation of Edgar Allan Poe. The mysterious final days of Poe's life are revealed in vivid and terrifying detail.

The Puzzle- A seemingly innocent past time of putting a jigsaw puzzle together plunges a married mother into a terrifying world of Supernatural wonder. The consequences of her obsession, however, may prove to be deadly.

The Lost Story- A Sociology student looking for a killer thesis may have found exactly what he's looking for. An urban legend of a story that kills its reader may prove to be more than a simple myth.

Excerpt From RAIN:

Shelby began to run, as best she could through the heavy water. It was slow going. It took another two minutes to reach the Wash, and with every step, her heart broke further, as the water rose higher and higher on her body. She could tell long before she reached the red Pinto that it was Mrs. Anscomb's car.

The headlights reflected off the water, the red taillights turning the Wash an eerie, glowing red as she approached the vehicle. Then she stopped dead in her tracks, and simply stared. At first, she thought she was seeing things. Mrs. Anscomb was on the roof of her own car, looking down into the water like a tiny child peering at minnows in a stream. By the time she reached the car, the water was up to her thighs. What broke Shelby's heart was seeing Mrs. Anscomb, her head shaking violently, her eyes wide and terrified. She didn't even seem to realize Shelby was there. She felt a twinge of guilt surge over her. How could she have let the old woman drive off alone like that?

"Mrs. Anscomb!"

More violent, uncontrollable head shaking. The old woman scanned the water intently, her eyes moving back and forth, seeming to see around Shelby's body. The driver's side door of the Pinto was ajar, the interior flooded. The poor woman had somehow managed to climb up onto the roof of her car, in order to escape a certain death by drowning.

"Mrs. Anscomb!"

The old woman's eyes did another frantic sweep, past Shelby's body, wavered, then darted back again, finally focusing on the younger woman with sudden awareness.

"Oh," the old woman's voice shook, and it broke Shelby's heart further.

"Mrs. Anscomb, I'm so sorry."

"You've got to get up here, dear. Hurry!"

"Mrs. Anscomb, I can help you down. I'll wade you through the Wash, and we'll find a ride together, okay?"

"No!" Mrs. Anscomb sounded crazed.

"Mrs. Anscomb, please. We have to get you out of this cold and rain."

"You have to get out of the water, dear," Mrs. Anscomb wailed. "It's going to get you!"

"What?"

"It's in the water!" she hissed. Shelby broke out in goosebumps.

She immediately shined her flashlight around, in a wild panic. Everything was a blur. Why would Mrs. Anscomb say that? *It's in the water*? With all this flooding run off from the surrounding creeks, her mind immediately went to dark places. Alligators, Water Moccasins, poisonous snakes. She imagined she would feel one brushing past her leg at any moment now, slithering around her in the dark waters only inches below her.

"You've got to get up here!" Mrs. Anscomb wailed again.

Shelby didn't waste any time in asking the old woman what was in the water. She freed her hands by quickly tucking in her t-shirt and dumping the flashlight down the front of her shirt. She was relatively young, at age twenty-eight, and in decent shape from standing all day long, waiting tables, yet, as she attempted to pull herself up onto the car's roof, she slipped several times, her footing only reasonably set against the wet metal and her large, clumsy rain boots.

Mrs. Anscomb was small, frail, and at seventy-two years old, not nearly as agile as Shelby. How had she managed to pull herself on top of the Pinto? It was a miracle, in this deepening water, that the old woman hadn't been swept downstream in the swiftly moving current here in the Wash. Then again, with a poisonous water snake swimming around, she supposed that would be ample motivation for anyone to get their ass in gear. Adrenaline gave false, temporary strength, or so she'd heard.

She briefly thought about how absurd it was to be thinking in words like 'swept' and 'downstream' in terms of roads she walked down every day, but this was not her everyday world. It was an alien landscape, transformed by what the meteorologist 'Dan' had called a 'monumental deluge.'

Shelby slipped again, and fell back into the water. Mrs. Anscomb reached for her, but her grip was too weak to pull her up.

"Please, dear, it's coming!"

"What?"

Shelby looked around briefly, and thought she saw a flicker several yards away, in the dim red glow of water from the car's taillights. She squinted, frowning. She thought she'd seen a green tail, with scales.

Five Tales Of Fear combines the chilling storytelling of five separate horror and suspense novellas with stunningly detailed and beautiful original artwork, to create a hybrid partnership of fiction and art. This full color, 250-page book will be the ultimate in horror fiction and art, tingling the senses and providing entertainment for hours, yet, leaving readers with a sense of dread and a fear of the dark. Enjoy this preview of some of the original artwork in FIVE Tales Of Fear, coming in November, 2015.

(And find the Kickstarter campaign under 'FIVE Tales of Fear' to pre-order your copy and receive other amazing merchandise! At www.kickstarter.com)